PEOPLE
OF MEANS

ALSO BY NANCY JOHNSON

The Kindest Lie

PEOPLE
OF MEANS

A NOVEL

NANCY JOHNSON

wm

WILLIAM MORROW
An Imprint of HarperCollins*Publishers*

HarperCollins books may be purchased for educational, business, or sales promotional use. For information, please email the Special Markets Department at SPsales@harpercollins.com.

FIRST EDITION

Library of Congress Cataloging-in-Publication Data

Names: Johnson, Nancy (Novelist), author.
Title: People of means: a novel / Nancy Johnson.
Description: First edition. | New York, NY: William Morrow, 2025.
Identifiers: LCCN 2024006609 | ISBN 9780063157514 (hardcover) | ISBN 9780063157545 (ebk)
Subjects: LCGFT: Novels.
Classification: LCC PS3610.O3668 P46 2025 | DDC 813/.6—dc23/eng/20240222
LC record available at https://lccn.loc.gov/2024006609

ISBN 978-0-06-315751-4

24 25 26 27 28 LBC 5 4 3 2 1

For my parents,
who met in a taxicab leaving a Chicago civil rights meeting

PEOPLE
OF MEANS

PART ONE

Nashville, 1959

Freda

On day one, Freda Gilroy stared up into the face of a woman more formidable than her own mother. Standing in a line of seventy-eight young ladies on the first floor of Jubilee Hall, Freda's legs quaked under the watchful gaze of their house mother. Even if dunked in a bucket of water, Mother Gaines probably weighed no more than ninety pounds, her silver curls standing in stark contrast to her midnight black skin. She had to be in her seventies, but women were not forthcoming with those details and Black women aged better than most, so one couldn't be certain. Either way, she cut as sharp as the blade of a chef's knife.

"If I get so much as a whiff of defiance or disobedience, you will be on a train back to whatever Godforsaken town dared send its worst to the best university in the world." Her voice reverberated from the high ceilings of this ornate dormitory for freshmen girls at Fisk University, and Freda found the words of Mother Gaines both chilling and inspiring.

The night before she left home for college, her father came into her bedroom while she was folding a wool sweater and packing it in her suitcase. He pulled a money clip from his pocket and peeled off a crisp twenty-dollar bill, and when he slid the money into her hand, he hugged her close, whispering, "You will be fine, baby girl. You are now part of a great tradition of excellence. A Negro aristocracy."

Papa's words and her history gave her wings. Fisk University was legend in their family, and she inherited that legacy from both her mother, Almeda Gilroy, and her father, the distinguished Dr. Booker Gilroy, named after Booker T. Washington, although his thinking lined up more with W.E.B. Du Bois. Papa didn't buy into the idea that the race would prosper if Negroes began their lives at the bottom. That's where their ancestors had started, and there was no sense going back there. No, he saw higher education as their people's true emancipation.

Freda only needed to follow the rules, beginning with the ones Mother Gaines outlined for the girls. "You are to dress as ladies and you must not wear jeans after two o'clock in the afternoon on Saturdays," she said. After a dramatic pause, she offered an ominous warning. "Look to your left and to your right. One of these ladies may not be with you at graduation. That all depends upon the choices you make."

Freda stood between her new roommates, Cora Hendricks from Murfreesboro, Tennessee, and Evaline Bates from Detroit, Michigan. Both girls beautiful in their own way.

Evaline cleared her throat. "Ma'am, if you don't mind my asking, what is so special about not wearing jeans after two o'clock and not one or three or four?"

Freda hailed from Chicago, up north like Evaline, but even she knew that disrespecting her elders fell under the category of things not to do at all and certainly not at Fisk. While feeling shocked at how crass this girl was, she secretly admired Evaline for being bolder than she ever could be. When a few of the other girls failed to contain their laughter, Mother Gaines said, "Miss Bates, you have forfeited your right to wear jeans at any hour of the day. And as for the rest of you, I don't want to hear loud laughing at inappropriate times. It's unbecoming."

In the demure voice of a baby kitten, Evaline said, "I apologize, ma'am. I will stick to dresses and skirts." Under her breath and only loud enough for Freda and Cora to hear, she said, "Besides, I look better in dresses."

That's when Freda confirmed this girl was fun and trouble all in one. Evaline was tall and dark with fine features, and in a more egalitarian time, she could have been a runway model gracing the covers of every lady's magazine in the country. A girl from Motor City, she bragged when they were first introduced about being from a town known for fast cars and fast music with the advent of Motown. "Fast girls, too!" Freda had teased, and Evaline threw her a smile and a wink, revealing nothing, which told Freda everything she needed to know.

Mother Gaines rattled off more rules, reminding them of the ones she'd already enumerated and warning them about regular room checks. Freda saw Cora nodding. They stood shoulder to shoulder, since Cora was short like her. She had skin the color of honey and wore her hair pulled back in a bun, her eyes shining like black pearls, wide in awe. "Yes ma'am, yes ma'am," she repeated softly, reverently, as if she were praying.

While Cora and Evaline couldn't have been more different, Freda could sense that she would grow to love them as if they shared a bloodline. The tight muscles in her shoulders loosened and she realized she would be okay, that she would be fine here so far from home. Vivacious, impetuous Evaline would push her to act on wild impulses she didn't even know she had, moving her beyond the limits her parents set for her as a girl. And Cora, sweet, sensible Cora, would be her conscience, the steady hand at the cliff, holding her in place before a precipitous fall.

The girls listened politely to more cautionary tales from Mother Gaines, who then said, "Do you know you're standing in the most famous residence hall in the entire world?"

Freda's gaze traveled past the old woman to a floor-to-ceiling portrait that she immediately recognized as a rendering of the Jubilee Singers, and she remembered her parents' stories of how Fisk began as a place to educate freed slaves, and that when the whites who ran the school heard the students singing slave songs, they were mesmerized. Eventually, the school's treasurer and music professor at the time took the young singers on tour to raise desperately needed money. The students began performing in local concerts, and one day President Ulysses S. Grant invited them to the White House to sing. A year later, they traveled across the pond for an audience with Queen Victoria of England. From there, they toured all over Europe until they raised enough money to build this dorm Freda would live in. Her legs began to feel heavy with the weight of all that history, the hopes of her entire family, generations of Negroes strapped to her back, all of them expecting her to do even better than they had.

"Miss Gilroy, are you listening to me, or have you found something more entertaining on the walls or the ceiling maybe to occupy your attention?" Mother Gaines stood two inches from Freda's face now, close enough to smell onions on the woman's breath.

"No, I heard you, ma'am. I was admiring the painting, that's all," Freda stuttered, her face hot, as she shuffled from one foot to the other in her stiff new pumps, the hard leather squeezing her toes.

Normally, she stayed focused and single-minded about serious matters. That's precisely why she had been overwhelmed with listening, watching, remembering, absorbing—the stimulation overtaking her. It was important not to start off on a bad note at Fisk or become known for the wrong things.

The truth was Freda had been training for this day as far back as she could remember. In third grade when she still wore pigtails and saddle shoes, she stood in another single file line with girls, their gloved right hands holding copies of *Goodnight Moon* on top of their heads. With each step, they maintained their balance, descending stairs and curtsying, careful not to curve their spines, stumble, and let the books fall to the floor. Their etiquette teacher, Miss Nicholson, intimidated them, as beautiful as she was in her floral dresses with pleated skirts that expanded and contracted like an accordion.

Their own starched taffeta dresses itched, but they didn't dare stoop to scratch. The space between the hems and the tops of their white knee socks exposed bare little-girl knees. In the mornings, their mothers greased their elbows, ankles, the spaces between their fingers, and of course, their knees. It was a requirement for girls like them to be presentable. They stayed away from the lotion-less, ashy children, as if their lack would rub off on them.

On Saturday mornings, Freda's mother brought her to these lessons in a three-story brownstone on Michigan Avenue called the South Side Community Art Center. Local Negro artists exhibited their paintings, and some had become quite famous. The building itself gained notoriety, too, with Eleanor Roosevelt dedicating it when Freda was a year old. Miss Nicholson reminded them often how privileged they were to practice becoming ladies in this space where the First Lady had led the dedication ceremony that was heard all over the world on CBS Radio.

Always one innately wired to follow the program, Freda considered that training common sense, vital like the teachings of Mother Gaines. She adhered to these precepts without question, for they seemed as sensible as her parents telling her to bundle up in the winter or she'd catch cold.

Mother Gaines continued with her list of admonitions. *You are not to leave this campus in anybody's car. Never look or act rough. You are now a Fisk lady. Carry yourself as a lady.* The girls grumbled quietly, each of them privately deciding which rules they would follow and which they would gladly break over the next four years.

***

In those early weeks on campus, Freda studied her course list—mathematics and biology, as well as a journey through American history from the country's inception through Reconstruction. And then the humanities obligation she dreaded—a philosophy class focused on a lot of dusty old ideas she would never use in the real world. Other than walking across campus to her classes, she stayed close to Jubilee Hall, sitting cross-legged on her bed either studying or laughing with Cora and Evaline. She was eager to find her place at Fisk and establish routines that made her feel safe in this brand-new world. She had meticulously reviewed the syllabus for each class, planting her thoughts and questions in the margins of notebooks with her careful cursive. She mapped out a schedule for herself, always fastidious about being on time. Every weekday morning at 8 o'clock before her first classes, she walked the stacks of the library. She ate lunch in the dining hall at 11:45 before the noon rush, giving her enough time to briefly study her class notes before her friends joined her. And on Sundays, she called her parents at 4 o'clock in the afternoon, when church service was over, and she knew they were still sitting at the dining table after an early supper.

Freda remembered her parents taking her to the 31st Street Beach as a girl, where she ran out to meet the incoming tide and they reminded her to only wade in water no higher than her ankles. Still, they were always there to pull her back if she ventured too far. And as much as Freda had appreciated that steady, guiding hand her entire life, she felt more like herself than ever now on her own as a freshman thousands of miles from home, for the first time, toying with the idea of wading in deeper waters.

One day, Freda was strolling by Fisk Memorial Chapel when she heard the raspy wail of music. She couldn't play any instruments, but she appreciated good music when she heard it. The wild, other-worldly sound drew her inside, and she followed it until she found a young man onstage playing a saxophone with a majestic pipe organ behind him. The chapel was empty except for this young man and his sax. He wore a black suit a few sizes too big, and his eyes were closed. She slid into the first pew, silently watching him riff as if he were communing with God himself. But when he hit his last note, it didn't seem like an ending. He must have sensed her presence and opened his eyes, looking sheepish to find her there.

"Oh, sorry, I didn't know anybody was here. I was . . ." He didn't finish his sentence or the song he'd been playing.

Standing and moving closer to the stage, Freda clapped. "That was the most beautiful music I think I've ever heard. Don't apologize. Why did you stop? Keep going. Play like I'm not here."

But he didn't. "It reminded me of mathematics," she said, grasping for a way to reclaim what had been lost when he stopped.

He smiled with questions in his deep brown eyes. "How so?" She liked that he didn't immediately dismiss her observation. A girl who excelled in math caught many people, even teachers, by surprise.

"I recognize the patterns in the music," she said, studying the face of this young man with dark skin and full, ripe lips. "The precision. Einstein and Coltrane have more in common than you think. The same geometric principles that governed Einstein's quantum theory can be found in Coltrane's music, and in yours."

He walked to the edge of the stage and dropped to the floor with his sax cradled in his lap like a baby. When he patted the space next to him, she hesitated for a moment but then gathered her skirt and lifted it enough to climb awkwardly onto the stage to sit beside him. When he reached for her hand to help her, she pulled it away instinctively, as if she'd touched a hot stove. If he took offense, she couldn't tell.

"A lady who knows math and music. I can appreciate that. Do you play any instruments?"

Now didn't seem like the appropriate time to mention the grand piano her parents had bought for her as a child that collected dust when she lost interest in lessons. Or the clarinet and flute donated to a local charity when she tired of them. Somehow she could tell that he didn't grow up with such extravagances that now seemed wasteful and embarrassing to her.

"I love music, but I don't play anything," she said.

"So, who's your favorite performer?"

"What if I said you?" Freda surprised herself flirting so shamelessly with a boy she just met. Didn't even know his name.

He laughed. "Well, I'm nobody. I mess around a little bit."

"Mess around pretty good from my ears."

Dropping his head, he shrugged off her praise. "But no, really, if you could see anybody in the world perform live, who would it be?"

She didn't have to think twice. "Nat King Cole. He's from my hometown, Chicago, but I've only seen him on TV. My mama and papa saw him in concert years ago and haven't stopped talking about it."

"Well, the King used to do shows at all kinds of joints on Jefferson Street, you know. Of course, he's big time now so we don't get to see him too much. But he's supposed to make a stop in Nashville right after his European tour."

"Really?"

"Yeah, I'm for real."

"Maybe I'll see you there," she said, trying to keep the thread of connection between them. She didn't have a lot of experience with boys, but this boy didn't seem like others she'd known back home. They usually led with their family names and prospects for future careers, one no different from the next. But not this boy, an artist who would take time to get to know her and that excited her. He had to be around her age and likely a Fisk student, but what if they didn't have classes together and she never saw him again on campus?

He looked up from his sax and met her eyes. "We don't have to wait until then to see each other. Nashville State Fair's going on. Come with me."

Throwing back her shoulders and lifting her chin, Freda didn't let on that the invitation thrilled and scared her at the same time. "I don't even know your name and my mother taught me to never go anywhere with strangers."

He leaned back lazily on his elbows and studied her with amusement. "I'm Darius. Darius Moore. A sophomore here at Fisk. Philosophy is my major." He extended his hand and she slid her palm into his, and their handshake lasted a beat too long before she broke contact. "So now you don't have any more excuses, Miss . . ."

"Freda. Freda Gilroy, mathematics major."

Freda

Freda sprawled across her bed poring over a problem set for her class on differential equations. It was early on a Saturday morning, and Evaline bounced on her mattress hard enough to make Freda's pencil slide across her note paper.

"Girl, look what you made me do *and* you broke my concentration." Freda was teasing but had to admit she was a bit peeved. Evaline spent more time in Freda and Cora's dorm room than her own, saying her roommate had an annoying habit of smacking her teeth when she talked.

On the opposite side of the small room, Cora perched on the edge of her bed painting her toenails. "All I know is you better not come over here, Evaline, and make me smear this polish all over my feet."

The girls had fallen into this easy rhythm, as if they'd always been in one another's lives. That's why Freda didn't flinch and smiled when Evaline slammed her textbook shut indicating it was quitting time. "Reading about math is dull and it's going to make you even duller. You can do that anytime. Let's go out and have some fun."

Solving differential equations was hardly drudgery for Freda, who gleefully unraveled its mysteries. Mathematics required more than reading because to master it, you had to practice and then practice some more. Evaline would be a lawyer someday and she didn't have to work as hard at her studies. She had enough confidence that everyone around her believed she'd do it because she said so.

Dawdling wasn't an option for Freda, though, and neither was whiling away her time on frivolity. She had come to Fisk for a single purpose—to study hard and walk across that stage with her degree in mathematics so she could make something of herself.

Usually, she could train her mind to focus for hours on a math problem, but if she was honest, even before Evaline interrupted, she couldn't stop thinking about Darius Moore and his lips wrapped around the mouthpiece of that saxophone.

"Did you hear me?" Evaline pretended to pout. "We're going into town to do some shopping. Come with us."

"I can't. I still have more work to do, and I'm meeting someone this afternoon." Freda knew she sounded cryptic and as soon as the words were out of her mouth she realized they would rouse the girls' suspicions.

Cora stopped painting her nail mid–brush stroke. "Wait a minute. You'd said there was someone your folks wanted you to meet in Nashville. It's him, isn't it?"

She was talking about Gerald Vance, a student at nearby Meharry Medical College. Last year, when things petered out with Charles Higginbotham, Freda's high school beau, the finagling began to find Freda an appropriate suitor. Her father in Chicago and Gerald's uncle in New York, both of them Meharry men, belonged to the same Negro medical society, and before Freda ever laid eyes on this boy, her mother began plotting a courtship and planning a wedding. An arranged courtship sounded so antiquated that it seemed too impossible for Freda to imagine.

"No, I haven't even met this mysterious medical student. His name is Gerald Vance. And he might have a wide forehead and bug eyes for all I know." They laughed picturing it.

"Then who pray tell are you meeting?" Evaline seemed more intrigued by Freda now than she had in the entire three weeks they'd known each other.

Freda shuffled her note papers of scribbled equations. "Nobody. Just some boy I met in the chapel. Nothing to talk about."

Cora squealed, spilling bright pink polish on her white bedspread. Evaline said, "We'll be the judge of that after your date."

Date. A spark of electricity shot up Freda's back.

And so began her dating life at Fisk, every man she met auditioning to be her husband without knowing it, possibly being *the one.*

***

Freda found herself surrounded by caged roosters crowing back and forth until she wanted to scream. When she put her hands over her ears, Darius laughed. "They can get pretty loud," he said. "I take it you don't see too many roosters in Chicago."

"I can't say I've ever seen one until now." What she didn't tell him was that she had never set foot on a farm, and this trip to the state fair was her first time seeing barn animals like hogs, goats, mules, and these loud, ornery chickens being coaxed to crow in fifteen minute intervals.

Freda chose to wear a simple plaid dress and matching cardigan with flat Mary Janes, which allowed her to still look up at Darius, who was only a few inches taller. Yet out here on the fairgrounds with these snorting pigs, mooing cows, and clucking hens, Darius was decked out in a dress shirt, jacket, and slacks, even dress shoes, and for the life of her she couldn't figure out why he was so overdressed. The dull, lifeless fabric and the frayed buttonholes told her his suit didn't come from the fine men's section of Marshall Field's, where Papa shopped because he could, paying no mind to salesclerks who glared as if to say how dare he.

Offering her a plate of okra, Darius said, "So when you were a kid, your folks never once took you to the fair?"

"Before you go judging me as some pampered princess from the big city, you should know that the state fair is all the way in Springfield, a long way from Chicago. At least three hours, maybe more. Besides, we had other things like art and music and literature." Now she sounded defensive and snooty without meaning to, yet he didn't blink an eye. He seemed to be enjoying himself at her expense.

"Well, I'm a country boy from North Carolina. Don't know much about all that high falutin' stuff," he said, and she could tell he was teasing. "Grew up on a farm getting my hands dirty. Now don't tell me you never had okra, girl."

She'd never even heard of it up north. "Well . . ."

He laughed. "My mama makes the best fried okra. That's how we eat it in North Carolina. She coats it in corn meal and then fries it up in a cast-iron skillet. Nobody makes it better than she does. People have tried and been put to shame."

"This one's a little slimy but it has a pretty good taste," she conceded, popping another one in her mouth and chasing it with a gulp of fresh-squeezed lemonade.

"They probably didn't soak that okra in vinegar first. That's the trick."

Out of the corner of her eye, she saw him wiping a grease stain off his pristine white shirt. "Why are you so dressed up around all these pigs and goats?" she asked.

Darius tilted his head up to the sky, quiet for a moment as if considering how honest to be with her. "Every day, I have to remind myself I'm a child of God even when some of these white folks are telling me I'm less than a man. I know they don't want me here in their city, at their fair. But I have every right to be here. My folks worked their fingers to the bone and never got what they deserved for it. Don't get me wrong now. When I put on my best clothes, I'm not doing it to prove anything to them. It's for me to remind myself of my own greatness, of who I really am."

His words chilled her. That was not what she had expected to hear. She assumed he'd make some wisecrack about how ladies liked a man who took the time to dress in his finest even to walk by stinky cattle stalls and step in manure. And then they'd laugh and flirt some more.

She hadn't been prepared for his somber eyes and serious voice. Freda didn't know what to say. They had passed several other Negroes out here at the fair and they seemed to be having a good time. She'd read the papers and watched the news enough to know that a lot of white people considered her a second-class citizen if they cared to think much of her at all. It seemed the Supreme Court ending racial segregation in schools in 1954 hadn't made it so everywhere. This year and last, students from all over the country had been marching to integrate schools. Carrying signs. Carrying on, if you wanted to know the truth.

Right now, she wished she could turn on the light in Darius's eyes. She had to whisper because they were in a small cluster of people now waiting for the tractor pull race to start.

"Don't let folks get you down on yourself. You're smart and talented. You're at Fisk, one of the greatest universities in the world. If that's not reason enough to hold your head high, I don't know what is." That sounded like something Papa would have said. And she would have rolled her eyes when he turned his back.

"That's not enough anymore," Darius said, throwing a cap end of okra in the trash can with such force, the projectile almost hit a lady walking past them. Freda hadn't seen him like this before, but she barely knew Darius. All afternoon, things had been light and easy between them. Yet she remembered Darius's face when they were waiting to drive the bumper cars long after a steady stream of whites took one, two, sometimes even three turns behind the wheel. It had been a flicker that she barely noticed at first but now recognized as indignation, even fury.

Being disregarded, ignored, set aside like that upset Freda, too, but neither of them could solve the race problem. This was precisely why she lost herself in mathematics, because as complex as the problems were, you could count on the answers to be definite, unambiguous. Besides, she came from a world where Negroes lived in their own beautiful communities yet still shared a friendly word with white folks from time to time. Back home in Chicago, the man who delivered milk to their front doorstep—Mr. Kirshner—was a white man. As a child, Freda would show off her math skills, rattling on to him about the difference in price between a gallon and a half-gallon of milk. She still remembered Mama standing in the doorway laughing at some joke Mr. Kirshner told or smiling when he complimented how healthy her house plants looked. Never a cross word uttered between them.

"Hey, I brought you out here to have some fun, not be all serious. I'd never forgive myself for ruining our first date." Darius bumped her shoulder with his and winked, the tightness in his face softening.

"Who said we were on a date?" she said, smiling.

"Don't tell me you got a boyfriend back home."

Freda couldn't help but be relieved to talk about something other than the discontent between the races. She told him she hadn't dated anyone seriously since Charles Higginbotham escorted her to the debutante ball her junior year in high school. He hailed from a well-connected Chicago family, a good social pairing everyone said, but the two of them talked very little at the dance. Her parents had presented her that night as a choice candidate for marriage someday, and in the pictures on the mantel in her family's living room, she and Charles resembled a bride and groom—him in a black tailcoat tuxedo and her in an elegant white ball gown with white satin gloves that stretched beyond her elbows.

"Wish I could've seen you in that getup," Darius said, laughing.

"Oh, it was a sight I tell you. But I must have been a terribly boring date because I never heard from Charles again after that night."

Darius kept his eyes on the grass. "Damn fool if he let you get away."

Her cheeks burned. He probably flirted shamelessly with all the freshman girls, but she played along, secretly hoping he found her uniquely appealing. "What about you?" she asked boldly, the knowledge that he liked her at least a little bit giving her confidence. She stood directly in front of him, hands on her hips. "Is there some girl back on the farm in North Carolina pining away for you?"

He met her eyes and that serious look of his reappeared. "No. No, there is no one." The intensity of his stare made her look away, stunned by the quiver in her chest. Darius was nothing like Charles Higginbotham or this Gerald Vance her folks kept talking about. He didn't come from a prominent family. Just the opposite. And Freda knew he wasn't the sort of boy her parents would approve of. But none of that mattered right now. They were two underclassmen having a good time.

The roar of a tractor pulling a dead-loaded sled drew them away from the moment. Spectators piled on the sled, screaming as their weight made the sled sink into the ground like quicksand, the poor drivers grinding it out to outdo another farmer. Freda had never seen anything like it.

The whole thing seemed dangerous, and she shuddered, covering her mouth as more people tried to climb aboard the sled. When she glanced at Darius, she saw that his playful side had returned, pumping his arms and cheering on the driver. Before long, she joined him in screaming at the turn of those heavy wheels. Thinking of the irony of growing up in high society with good manners and good grooming made her blush as if her parents and every prominent family in Chicago could see her making a fool of herself. She imagined the horror on their faces and somehow this tractor pull became outrageously funny to her and she laughed until her cheeks hurt.

"I NEED TO GO TO THE LADIES' ROOM," FREDA TOLD DARIUS SHORTLY after they sat in the stands to watch a pig race. "I'll be right back."

"I'll go with you," he said, standing and brushing dirt off the seat of his pants.

"No, you stay here." When he hesitated as if unsure how far to press things with this young lady he was just getting to know, she gently placed her hand on his chest. "I'll be fine."

Alone in her thoughts about Darius, she could smile as wide as she wanted, be giddy, and let the bubble of delight taking root inside her expand throughout her body. She liked how direct he was, the way he looked at her and surprised her in ways no other boy had. She skipped past a stand where a woman was selling boiled peanuts and then a row of tables filled with grown men, shirt sleeves rolled up to show bulging biceps, as they arm wrestled before a cheering crowd.

When she spotted the restrooms ahead near the entrance to the fairgrounds, she rushed toward them, the urge to pee stronger than ever. But two crude signs in bold, block letters stopped her.

WHITE and COLORED.

The air thickened. She had never seen signs like these before. At least not in person. Only in the news, and those little towns had seemed so backward and far from Chicago. Freda struggled to take a breath. White ladies and children bumped into her as if they didn't see her, as if she were invisible.

Chin up. Shoulders back. Perform confidence until you feel it. That had worked when she stood before the church congregation to recite poems as a little girl or when she was being presented to society at cotillions. But not now. She even turned to the one ritual that calmed her when she couldn't sleep, when the worries of the day encroached upon her nights. She counted in multiples of three . . . 3, 6, 9, 12, 15, 18, 21, 24, 27 . . .

Yet not even numbers could soothe the sting of the Jim Crow South indignities. It was one thing to intellectually understand this kind of cruelty to Negroes and another to experience it herself. Nothing she had read in the papers had prepared her for this. For the humiliation, the embarrassment of not being allowed to squat on the same toilet as a white woman.

If you asked her, she couldn't tell you how long she stood there, the sounds of happy white children outside the restrooms taunting her—their innocent laughter, Kool-Aid-stained fingers waving and ready to be washed, how oblivious they were—a reminder of freedoms they enjoyed that she couldn't. No matter what, she would not walk through the door to enter that colored restroom. Grabbing the skirt of her dress, she ran until she reached a cattle barn and hid behind it, a wet stream trickling down her legs.

Freda

The evening after Freda's date at the fair, she visited Drucilla Barn-ham's room in Livingstone Hall where sophomore students lived. She might as well have been a witness on the stand in some old Perry Mason film with Cora, Evaline, and Drucilla, all three in bright sweaters and corduroy pants, lying across the floor on their bellies, hands under chins, awaiting answers.

"Okay, so tell us about Darius. Do you like him? Are you in love, girl?" Cora said with that faraway look as if mistletoe was hanging over her head.

Evaline, already acting like a lawyer, dispensed with preamble. "Did you kiss him?"

"She must have," Drucilla said, tying her two long, thick braids under her chin like a beard. "Otherwise, she wouldn't be sitting here stone-faced like the cat snatched her tongue."

"Stop it, y'all," Freda said, her cheeks hot under their gazes. "We did not kiss. I like Darius just fine, but I don't know if I'll see him again."

Evaline sat up and leaned her back against Drucilla's bed. "That sounds fishy. There's more to it than that and I know it."

How could her new friends be so light and carefree when outside the perimeter of this campus there were people who believed they were less than human? And they had the law on their side. The night before, Freda changed quickly out of the dress she had worn to the fair, showered and avoided the girls, pretending the day had never happened. But that COLORED bathroom sign played like a movie scene in the back of her eyes, its imprint there in her sleeping and waking hours. How could anyone legislate and segregate something as intimate as a bathroom? When Darius finally found her, dazed and shaking, she had refused to look at him or tell him what was wrong.

"You're scaring me, Freda," he said. "Did I do something? Did somebody hurt you? Talk to me." He had pleaded with her as she woodenly climbed aboard the city bus that would take them back to campus. Growing up in the South, Darius had probably used more colored restrooms than he could count. May have grown numb to it even. Then again, if she had let him, he might have started preaching right then and there about the horrible plight of the Negro. Talking about it would make the indignity sting more, only reinforcing how powerless they were to change any of it.

"Darius didn't do anything wrong," Freda said to the girls. "He's nice enough. I'm just not sure he's right for me, so why waste time with him?"

Hopefully, she was convincing. Her quivering heart disobeyed the commands of her brain. But the memory of that restroom sign snapped her to her senses. How silly of her to have even gone to the fair with Darius in the first place. Nothing could ever come of a relationship with a boy from some little town in North Carolina no one had ever heard of. A boy who, Almeda Gilroy would be quick to point out, didn't have the right pedigree.

A skeptical look passed between Evaline and Cora, but they stayed quiet in front of Drucilla, knowing you don't tell your business in front of company, even though they were visitors in the sophomore's room.

"Shouldn't we get to work?" Freda pulled a notepad from her book bag and gave Drucilla a pointed glance. Knowledge of Freda's natural affinity for numbers spread quickly on campus and that's what led Drucilla to call on her for emergency tutoring on the eve of her geometry test the next day.

After an intense hour of Freda drilling Drucilla on solution sets to linear equations with three variables, a crescendo of banging erupted below them. The floor vibrated beneath their feet, and Freda thought it might have been the building's old steam radiator. But leave it to Evaline, always ready for excitement, to snap her fingers. "Is there a party going on over here?" she asked, looking for an excuse to take a study break.

Drucilla pressed her palm to her forehead. "Girls, I forgot they're training tonight."

The yelling downstairs had grown louder now, and a series of guttural noises accompanied the sound of bodies slamming against walls. "Training for what?" Freda said. "War?"

Drucilla belly flopped onto her mattress. "Yes, I guess you could say it's war. After Martin Luther King came here to Fisk to speak, he started sending his leg men to do training."

Martin Luther King. He was that Baptist preacher at the center of the Montgomery bus boycotts a few years ago. His name kept coming up in the news as some great messiah for colored folks. What in the world did he have to do with all the racket downstairs?

Drucilla must have seen the confusion on her face. "Nonviolent training, you know, teaching Negroes not to bash some racist's head in when he deserves it."

What surprised Freda more than anything was when Drucilla shut her math textbook and said, "Want to go watch?"

THEY FOLLOWED DRUCILLA DOWN THE DARK STAIRS, PAST A STUFFY storage room, and found the door to the lounge open wide enough for each of them to take turns peeping. What unfolded reminded Freda of a stage play or movie, the actors playing their parts with sincerity, honoring the gravity of the scene until the director yelled *cut* and the actors dissolved into laughter. A white student with sandy brown hair that fell over his eyes played the role of the racist, standing behind a young Negro student cracking an egg on top of his head and calling him a *nigger*. Freda had never been that close to hear anybody white say that word, and while she knew it was playacting, her muscles seized. Cora gasped, and Freda elbowed her to keep quiet.

"That's Gregory Wilcox from Oberlin," Drucilla whispered. He must have been one of the handful of white exchange students Freda had seen on campus.

"He can't be pretending. Listen to how he said that word. Like he meant it. I don't like it." Cora flinched as if a fist had connected with her cheekbone. "What's happening to us in this country isn't right," she said softly, and they all nodded.

No, none of it was right—not the segregated schools, buses, or that colored restroom sign at the fair—but this show they were witnessing now wasn't right either. Their classmates were taking things too far, getting involved in something that should have been left to others who didn't have professional careers waiting for them upon graduation.

Watching through the tiny crack in the doorway, Freda kept scanning for Darius, knowing how he burned inside over racial injustice, but she didn't spot him. Thank God he had enough sense not to be part of something like this. Chairs scraped against the cement floor and Freda noticed a few students—young men and even a few ladies—watching with rapt attention as the man in charge instructed them on why nonviolence worked and how to respond or not respond to provocation. Drucilla told them the man was a preacher and Freda had expected fire and brimstone, but Reverend James Lawson led the training in a calm, reasoned, measured tone. Definitely an intellectual.

His lieutenants riled up the students with a barrage of racial insults to prepare them for what they would face from real white mobs. At their direction, one guy hit one of Reverend Lawson's lead lieutenants squarely in the back and the young man demonstrated how to receive that blow without fighting back. When this lieutenant turned, Freda got a glimpse of his face and swooned. He was taller than any of the boys she had seen so far on campus, and he had beautiful brown skin, a solid build, and a head full of curly hair. Evaline noticed him, too, and was equally appreciative, finally showing more than passing interest in their little adventure. "Now that is a tree I would love to climb," she said, and they giggled.

Freda realized for the first time that she was a long way from home and her mother's watchful eye when she said, "What do they call this work? Civil disobedience, right? Well, if he's running the show, I see myself being uncivil and very disobedient."

"Ooh, listen to you with your fast tail self," Evaline whispered. She and Drucilla muffled their cackling as best they could.

Cora shot all of them a reprimanding look as if they had propositioned Jesus. "Shh. Show some respect. This is serious work."

Laughing, Drucilla said, "Yes, but you have to admit he is seriously good-looking. He's come a few times before to help Dr. Lawson, but too bad for us, he goes to North Carolina A&T, not Fisk. His name is Jesse. Jesse Jackson."

"Definitely cute, but girl, why are we whispering out here instead of going in there and introducing ourselves?" Evaline asked.

Drucilla had the exasperated look of someone trying to explain a complex idea to a small child. "Because they're not playing games and you don't want to get mixed up in this. It's dangerous work, not to be played with unless you know what you're doing. When these brothers and sisters put their plan in motion, whatever it is, no one will see it coming."

The training seemed no different than a performance with high drama and standout characters like Jesse playing scripted parts. One where Freda picked out the best-looking actors to fawn over from balcony seats. It didn't seem like a real possibility, like something that would actually happen to these fine young men. When she and her friends gently closed the door to the session and snuck back upstairs, it felt as if the curtain had closed at the end of a show.

LATER THAT WEEK, FREDA CALLED MAMA AND PAPA FOR HER regular Sunday check-in, when the long-distance rates were low. Her father picked up, and she could picture him sitting in the living room in his favorite rust orange chair that had worn over time and showed the imprint of his body. The same chair she would sit on the arm of as a young girl until he pulled her onto his lap for a hug. He had probably been reading the paper or poring over a challenging patient case, a glass of cognac on the side table.

Unsure of how her father might react, she casually mentioned the nonviolent training on campus, making it clear she had stumbled upon this activity and had not participated. At eighteen, almost nineteen, she could make her own decisions, and besides, she had no interest in the protest movement. Still, she became a toddler again, her palm hovering over the burner flame of the stove, well aware of the danger with no intention of touching the fire, but testing her boundaries, curious to find out how much she could get away with.

"We did not send you to Fisk to get involved in this nonsense," Papa said as if he hadn't comprehended her words. She pictured him rocking in his chair to gain enough momentum to stand to continue fussing. "Your head is hard, and you need to listen. We sent you there to get an education."

"Yes, Papa, but you are always talking about Negro pride and how we have to advance racial progress. How we need to uplift," she said, challenging him for once and barely breathing as she awaited his response. While she hailed from a younger generation and should have been more reckless, a renegade willing to take risks for higher ideals, she agreed with her father. She couldn't help it. Maybe it was his influence on her. But she didn't think so. She knew her own mind and no good could come from stirring up trouble.

"Our pride as a people is in what we accomplish, how we distinguish ourselves. I studied and worked hard for everything I got. I didn't agitate to try to force anybody's hand," he said.

"Yes, Papa, I know."

"Don't 'yes, Papa' me. We have a legacy to uphold." She could tell he was pacing the living room floor now, breathless, the long telephone cord wrapping around him. Then he did what he always did, reminding

Freda of his biography, his history and hers. He had been born to one of the first Negro postal clerks in Tennessee, a coveted position for anybody colored, and that made their family as close to royalty as you could get in the South. His mother was a hardworking washerwoman. Neither parent had much money or opportunity to advance but they saved every penny they made to send their only son to Fisk and then Meharry Medical College. As Papa put it, they poured into a future, a dream, they couldn't see.

When she was a little girl, Papa would tell her about her grandfather's work, and maybe that's why she would tear out of the house as soon as she heard the wheels of the mail truck on their street, eager for the mailman to drop off the bills, letters from long-distance family members, and of course, the always heavy Sears catalogue.

When she ran inside one time loaded with mail and delivered a letter to Papa in his office, he looked up from the papers on his desk. "Sanford Gilroy would get a kick out of seeing you right now."

"How come?" she asked.

"Because he was a mailman. Oh, he was big time in that spiffy uniform of his. Back then, if you worked for the post office, you were the cream of the crop."

"Like you, Papa?" she said, putting an envelope between her lips. "Like a doctor?"

He shook off her praise, smiling. "I don't know about all that. You didn't have a lot of Negro doctors in Tennessee in those days. Or Negro letter carriers. If you were smart and lucky enough to get the job, it came with a whole lot of prestige. Brought us up to be middle class Negroes. But it wasn't easy for your grandfather doing his job in those days."

"Why?" Freda asked, enjoying how that one word could frustrate grown-ups sometimes.

Papa didn't seem to mind the question, taking off his glasses and crossing one leg over the other. "Some terrible men came after him once. They wore masks and put a gun to his head one day while he was out delivering mail."

"Okay, Booker, she doesn't need to know all that now. She's just a child." Mama stood in the doorway, wiping soap suds from her hands with a dish towel.

Freda's eyes bulged, scared for a grandfather she never knew, a man who died before she was born. But she didn't let on in case Papa had more story to tell.

"She's eight years old. That's plenty old enough to hear it," he said, inhaling deeply, his nostrils flaring as he continued. "I was with my mother at the house she was cleaning, sitting on the floor playing with sticks, when a man we knew from the street we lived on burst in to tell us what had happened. My mother grabbed me off the floor, put me under her arm, and ran out the house to find my daddy. Sanford Gilroy lived to tell that story himself to anyone who would listen. Became a legend in our little town. And I have to say ole' Teddy Roosevelt stood by us. He said anybody who gave Negro postal clerks a hard time must not want any mail delivery. He threatened to shut it all down whenever some of the rough and tough men got out of line. But your grandfather was the real hero."

Freda would hear that story again many times over the years, certain details amplified for maximum effect.

Papa must have stopped walking and sat back down because his voice came through so loud and clear as if he were right next to her, and she could tell he was holding the receiver as close to his mouth as he could get it, his way of reaching through the phone line and across the miles to talk some sense into her. "Sanford and Delilah Gilroy didn't work hard, scrimp and save like they did, for their grandchild to sink into self-pity and blame other people for her circumstances. Life is hard, and no, it's not fair. But it is what it is. The kind of thinking you're flirting with right now will paralyze you and keep you stuck. You're only dealt one hand in life. May be a bad hand, but it's yours to play. You must play it well. Do you hear what I'm saying to you?"

Forcing a smile for the girls in her dorm who waved to her as they passed in the hallway, Freda lowered her voice and whispered, "Yes, Papa. I hear you."

Mama fussed in the background, telling Papa to hush with all that yelling, and Freda could almost see her bending over the back of her father's recliner trying to get a word in when he took a breath.

"What's she saying, Papa?"

Her mother must have wrested the phone from him. "What I said was that we don't need to get into all this business right now. We'll see you for the winter holidays and we can sort it all out then. I'm baking my famous sweet potato pie. You're welcome in advance, sweetheart. Oh, and we'll pick out a Christmas tree together. I told Booker we'd wait for you to get here first."

This was the part of the weekly call home Freda had been dreading and the rush of excitement in her mother's voice made it harder to tell her. "Mama, I know I said I would be coming home for Thanksgiving and Christmas, but Cora invited Evaline and me to Murfreesboro. It's so much closer, and you know I'll be back home all summer."

There was nothing but the sound of static on the line now and Freda wishfully thought they may have lost the phone connection. Then in a quiet, tight voice, her mother said, "Oh, I see. I assumed. I guess you are practically grown now."

"I love you, Mama," Freda said, holding the receiver tight against her cheek.

"And I love you. I'm glad you're making friends and making time for your social life. Now, listen to me, sweetheart. Your father and I want you to stay focused on your studies." Then she lowered her voice and Freda realized Papa must have gone in the other room. "But this part is from me. Don't focus so hard on school and friends that you miss out on finding your husband while you're there. And you know exactly who I mean. Get that Fisk degree and marry a Meharry man. Like I did."

PART TWO

Chicago, 1992

4

Tulip

The buildings dotting the skyline came to life long after the hum of the workday had gone silent. Chicago at dusk dazzled in its beauty, amid the downtown lights and the people dressed up, laughing too loudly, already a little tipsy. Tulip hadn't had a drink yet and maybe it was better this way—to take in the splendor of it all sober.

The mothers of Tulip's friends would have said *have fun* and maybe thrown in a *be careful* to their daughters heading out to a company party, but not Tulip's mother. She cautioned her not to embarrass the family that night.

"Really, Mom. I see these people at work every day. Heaven forbid, I drop my salad fork and it falls off the boat."

One of her mother's eyebrows lifted but her lips didn't even twitch. Serving one of those looks that only a Black mama can, she said, "Don't be flip. They're watching what you do. Everything you do matters."

The nebulous *they* indeed hovered over every single thing. As did Black excellence, always shelved out of reach. Like the good china they used when guests came over.

When Tulip was a child, her mother ironed her party dresses and smoothed her baby hair with gel, or as gauche as it was, with a quick lick of her fingertips when no one was watching. She reminded Tulip of table etiquette: Fork on the left, knife on the right, and chew with your mouth closed. Keep your elbows off the table. Offer a serving bowl to the person on your left and pass everything to the right. Don't spit tough meat gristle into your napkin. Never slurp soup from a spoon.

No matter how many times Tulip repeated to her mother that this wasn't Nashville or the 1960s anymore and Black folks didn't have to sit in, stand up, or do anything for that matter to get what was due them, Freda wasn't hearing any of it. She was from the old school and couldn't accept that this was a new day. "You're being hardheaded. You don't know the world the way I do. Whatever advantages you *think* you have must be protected, and if you're too naive to see that, God help you."

But Tulip was well primed. She'd matriculated from her parents' household with carefully orchestrated experiences to prepare her for the real world: Jack and Jill sweet sixteen parties, Links cotillions, and debutante balls. A world set apart with rules she grew to know well. Guest lists carefully curated and cross-matched with recognizable family names. A circle wound tight as a fist. Outside the perimeter of that circle, she would need to distinguish herself. Which she had tried her best to do when she'd joined Mattingly Public Relations five years ago, right out of college.

THERE WAS NOTHING LIKE SEEING THE PIER LIT UP AT DUSK, TINY sparkles dotting the water's edge. Waiting to meet the boat for the night cruise, she felt equal parts anticipation and trepidation, unsure of what to expect as Mattingly celebrated the agency's ten-year anniversary.

"Tulip, oh my God. You look amazing." Darby from accounting put an arm around Tulip's waist. The woman's eyes, the color of parsley, bulged in a perpetual look of surprise. Until that night, their conversations had been limited to tracking client invoices, but now Darby was pressing their hips together.

Tulip smiled, discreetly searching for her roommate, Sharita, a graphic designer. She was Hollywood beautiful with her chic, close cropped haircut that people said made her look like a dark-skinned

Halle Berry. Their buddy, Rudy, the in-house videographer, who was one of the few white people who had genuinely gotten to know Tulip, would also be there. Sharita and Rudy had joined Mattingly a year before Tulip and had given her the lay of the land, filling her in on who to trust, a small list indeed, and who to steer clear of. Darby had been on the avoid-at-all-costs list.

"You look amazing, too," Tulip responded, momentarily unable to conjure anything original or, for that matter, truthful. Especially since the public relations agency ordered the same uniform for everyone: crisp, button-down white shirts and black tuxedo vests to be worn with your favorite jeans. When she preened in front of her bedroom mirror earlier that evening in a sheer black blouse that surely would have been chic and unexpected under her vest, she could practically hear her parents' voices saying no, that five years didn't qualify as long enough tenure to buck the company dress code.

Tulip gazed all along the pier, where captains of industry and their minions blew curls of smoke into the night air. And then, lips and warm breath brushed her earlobe. "These white people trying to get crunk out here."

Key had snuck up from behind. The high-top fade was slowly fading from the fashion scene, but he managed to keep it looking current. His haircut reminded her of Kid's from Kid 'n Play or possibly Dwayne Wayne's from *A Different World* minus the shades on top. Her father said he looked like a black string bean plucked right out of the ground, and that was generous since it was the kindest assessment he'd made of any of her boyfriends. Key was a regular brother, but he had that special something you couldn't quite put your finger on that made people stop short and take notice. But right now it was his choice of words that she noticed, even though it was the kind of remark she might have made herself if it had been just the two of them. Luckily, he came over just as Darby had found someone else to fawn over. Maybe she hadn't heard what he whispered.

Tulip's eyes widened in reprimand, and on instinct her voice rose to a higher octave for anyone in listening range. "Alrighty then," she said.

"Now that you're here, we can board." A voice she reserved for business calls—brusque and authoritative—the way she needed to be in the world of media and PR.

"Okay, babe. I'm with you. Whatever you say." Key shrugged and a stabbing pain seized her chest, wondering as she always did if there was an air of superiority in her tone, anything that hinted at an unequal balance in their relationship.

They were not married and had been dating for only two years, but the truth was she could envision a lifetime with this man. Tulip appreciated Key's indifference about wealth and applauded his lack of interest in summering on Martha's Vineyard, even though she wondered if he was somehow stunting his ambition. She and Key had found their own groove, although it was not modeled off her own parents' relationship, which often appeared utilitarian. Yes her parents loved each other deeply—the way they loved her—because that's what good families did. But over the years she'd noticed one parent would miss cues from the other, their timing a bit off. Gerald with his hand outstretched to touch the small of Freda's back only to find she was out of reach as he pulled his hand back fast and stuffed it in his pocket. Or her mother waiting for affirmation about her cooking or a new dress when her father's face was buried in the pages of the *Tribune*.

Even without a solid blueprint for love, Tulip's heart found what she needed: a man who made her laugh until her belly ached and she screamed for mercy; a man who pulled her in to the crook of his arm and sheltered her from the storms around them. That had to be love.

Most weekends, they cuddled on the couch of his tiny apartment reciting hip-hop lyrics, her back against his chest, and all she could feel or wanted to feel was the electric current of his heartbeat. This was the first time he was joining her at a company function though. Something about it made her jumpy, and she began viewing Key through the lens of her coworkers even before they laid eyes on him. His rawhide rough hands and the traces of dirt under his fingernails made it apparent that he didn't work behind a desk all day. Then there was his height, which some found intimidating.

Key leaned close again and she smelled the sweet-and-sour scent of the Camay soap he bathed with and the sweat he must have worked up sprinting that couple blocks from some parking garage. She had teased about not wanting to show up at the company party on CP time and he knew she was only half-joking.

"You nervous," he said.

"What makes you say that?"

"Cause you tripping and you only tripping when you not feeling like yourself."

Her silence confirmed he had hit on the truth. He didn't understand how it was for her, dealing with tense work stuff. He drove a city bus for a living, which meant he never took his work home and he didn't have to put on the clown suit, as he called it, to impress anybody after his shift ended.

BRYCE MALLOY STOOD A FEW FEET AWAY ON THE PIER, CALLING TO them with his arms outstretched. Tulip's boss commanded a room with the way he stood, feet apart, his broad chest filling the space. A shock of dark blond hair streaked gray made a man his age consider himself more distinguished and important than he really was. Tulip hesitated, unsure of the rules of corporate America after-hours, certain that the employee handbook had not addressed hugging the CEO.

Bryce folded her in his arms, and she tried not to grimace at the shock or the mix of cigarettes and Scotch oozing from his clothing. He grabbed a martini from a serving tray and shoved the glass in her hand.

"What a gorgeous night and look at all this," she said. "You've outdone yourself." The words fell from Tulip's lips, pitch perfect. Ms. Tolbert would have been proud to see all her elocution training had paid off.

"And you must be—?" Bryce left the question hanging, glancing from her to Key.

"Oh, I'm sorry. Please meet my boyfriend, Key McCray." The men shook hands, so far so good.

They walked on the boat as if stepping aboard Noah's Ark, two by two. Every woman paired with a man, no other permutations. No one had told Tulip to expect this, yet somehow, she guessed right and so had invited Key.

Once on board, they all stood in that awkward silence of coworkers who knew one another, but only found common language within the confines of cubicle walls and under the harsh glare of fluorescent lights. Maybe they were all a little nervous, especially Tulip, who had her eye on a promotion. Key's solid hand gripped hers, and its roughness steadied her, the pressure of his hand forcing her to look up at him and see that crooked smile of his telling her everything would be all right on this night where she had something to prove.

She needed to show her boss she belonged at Mattingly. She needed to prove that she could stand on her own two feet in this world, not carried along on the shoulders of her parents' influence. She needed to prove that after five years with the company, she was worthy, she was enough.

Tulip ran one hand over her straight, smooth hairstyle, a fresh blow-out that made it move as effortlessly as any woman's there when the night wind whipped it. Those hours at the Van Cleef salon seemed a worthy investment.

A long blast of the boat's horn sounded, and the boat passengers cheered loudly when the vessel pushed off from the dock. Tonight would give her the chance to make an impression when her CEO's defenses were down, and his hard edges dulled by liquor and the lull of the lake. A handful of the team appeared at Bryce's side like Pavlov's dogs, making it impossible for him to forget on Monday morning who had played the role of the good soldier that night. That classical conditioning spared no one, not even Tulip.

Her father may have pulled the necessary strings to get her this public relations job, but nobody should be fooled into thinking she was un-deserving. In five years, she had built relationships with reporters around the country, gotten to know the ins and outs of her clients' products and services, and felt the rush of seeing stories she pitched appear on TV news and above the fold in the paper. *She* did that, nobody else.

Tulip had spent those years fighting for relevance, a bigger title, and more money at the agency with little to show for her efforts except for bruises she got from bumping her head against ceilings along the way. There was always a reason she hadn't advanced yet.

This client wants someone more experienced on their account.

You hardly ever join us after work for drinks. People don't know you.

Speak up more in meetings. You're much too quiet.

We like passion but try not to sound so aggressive, so angry.

On the drive downtown, Key had put a Public Enemy tape in the deck, and they rapped until their throats were raw about how their heroes didn't appear on no stamps and all that mattered was fighting the powers that be. Power that rested in powerful men like Bryce Malloy, whom Tulip so desperately wanted to impress. The hypocrisy made her queasy. The hypocrisy of resisting the powerful and cozying up to them at the same time.

Now, in front of an audience, Tulip angled herself toward Bryce, sweat pooling under her armpits. Half of success in corporate America involved inflating yourself, making the ordinary seem extraordinary. The other half—making up stuff and being bold enough to sell it. At least she had the truth on her side. In a voice louder than normal, she said, "I pitched Breakfast Bears to WGN, and we'll be on their morning show next week, bringing in some kids to eat their breakfast live on TV."

The chatter of other passengers kept up a steady hum but those in this inner circle said nothing. Many were likely contemplating their own careers and the promotions Bryce had hinted about making soon.

"That's what I like to hear. Morning TV is king right now. This is what tonight is all about. Rising stars in PR like you, Tulip." Bryce raised his glass, the liquid sloshing around and spilling over the sides like the waves crashing against the boat. His praise wrapped around Tulip as snug as a fleece blanket, all fuzzy and warm.

Mason from marketing, who always introduced himself that way because he appreciated alliteration, bumped Key's shoulder. Tulip figured changing topics was Mason's way of deflecting attention from her success. "How about those Bulls?" he said. "I say we might get a repeat. You think?"

"I don't think," Key said. "I know. No doubt. I can't believe you fixed your mouth to even ask that question. My prediction—we sweep it." He rotated his arms as if he were dusting the deck of the boat with a broom.

"You play ball?" Mason asked.

Here we go, Tulip thought. This night belonged in a comedy skit. *Saturday Night Live* could not have scripted it better, with David Spade as Mason and Chris Rock playing Key. Tulip would have laughed if it hadn't been her real life. Key was tall but he didn't bump his head every time he walked in a room. He made three-pointers all the time when he played with his boys on the block. And now that the Bulls were on the verge of handing Chicago back-to-back championships, almost every fan fantasized about being Jordan on the court. Still, any Black man would tire of such unimaginative inquiries, and that's why it surprised her when Key's smile widened, and he grinned.

"I mess around on the court a little bit," Key said, popping his collar. "But look at you. Bet you got good form on the jump shot. Bulls might trade Pippen for you, never know." That's when she realized he was clowning on Mason, and she hid her smile on the rim of her martini glass.

Mason came with his own jokes. He grinned then said, "Your name is Key, huh? Like a car key or a key to a safe? Or like the main idea, the *key* point?"

When it became clear that Mason obsessed over homonyms and could find endless ways to use her man's name in a sentence, Key interrupted. "Key is short for Keyshawn. My full name is Keyshawn McCray."

Tulip's cheeks warmed, realizing that for the second time that night she hadn't formally introduced her guest. "Key's my boyfriend and he's an entrepreneur," she said, adding that last part for good measure.

Mason jumped in before Key could say anything. "Ah, one of those tech start-ups. I'm sure you'll be going public in a few years." Mason made assumptions about everybody, tucking them into a neat category. Key stiffened beside her and that's when a gust of wind and a sharp turn of the boat sent a stack of napkins flying. They all grasped a few inches of the high-top table to steady themselves.

Wanting to avoid further discussion of her man's career plans, Tulip asked the group to excuse them. She and Key walked onto the deck for privacy, watching water splash onboard, spraying their legs and dousing white plastic chairs.

"Mason thinks he's so funny and clearly he's not," she said.

"Why did you say that?" Key asked, looking out onto the Chicago River.

"Say what?" The wind whipped her hair, and she pulled her vest tight around her chest.

"Don't play. You told that Max dude I was an entrepreneur." She shot him a look that said, *Well, you are. I wasn't lying.* She was right if one considered themselves a true extension of their parents.

Even on this crisp night, Tulip's whole body ran hot, her shirt clinging to her damp back. "Mason. It's Mason from marketing," she corrected him. "Your folks own a beauty supply store, and you help out all the time. You know they're grooming you to take it over someday when they retire. So, technically, you work there, and I was right."

Shaking his head, Key said, "I guess you had your reasons for not wanting him to know I drive a CTA bus for a living." He let that loose accusation hang between them.

Tulip grabbed two stuffed cucumber bites from a passing server and chewed slowly. She never meant to insult Key. Just the opposite. She had elevated him, hadn't she?

This is what she was good at, what they paid her for. To make other people's businesses and lives seem more successful, more appealing, more compelling than they were. At its core, that was public relations.

"I'm sorry," she said. "I got carried away. Babe, I was out of line." Her mea culpas escalated as she watched closely for a softening in the set of his jaw.

When he refused to look at her, she reached up and cupped his face in her hands. "I mean it. I'm proud of you. I'm proud to have you here tonight with all these crazy people I work with. You were right before. I am nervous. Or at least I was. I wanted them to really see me tonight."

Key finally met her eyes. "And I want you to see me."

"I know. And I do. Forgive me. Please."

The boat rocked and Tulip took the opportunity to press against him until he couldn't help but smile. The wind dwarfed the words he said back to her, and everything spoken between them now appeared to be pantomime. Where a lesser man might have held on to a grudge, Key opened his hand and set it free like a caged bird. Strands of her hair flew into his eyes and mouth, and she laughed and so did he, both of them breathing in big gulps of night air.

Tone Loc's "Wild Thing" blasted from the speakers and Tulip glanced over at a few of her coworkers dancing—she spotted Mason mouthing the words to the song. Two hours into the night and she barely recognized the people who nodded politely to her every day at the water cooler. Free alcohol flowed as deep as the river, lubricating these folks like a shot of WD-40. They gyrated wildly and called it dancing. On one of her trips to the bar, she ran into Sharita and Rudy. She and Sharita were the only Black people at the party—Rudy being a gay white man but honorary—and Tulip shared an unspoken language with them, all three making a pact not to succumb to any pressure to lead the Electric Slide.

"How you holding up, girl?" Sharita maintained a tight smile. "I don't know how you do it. At least in graphic design, I'm behind the scenes and don't have to be on like this 24–7."

Tulip laughed. "It's all performance art but it wears you out fast."

After a few quick laughs, they sprang apart to preempt any questions in the office the next day. Black people and their allies commiserating could be perceived as coincidence or a coup.

Tulip rescued Key from what was likely an uncomfortable conversation with her coworkers. A petite woman in ripped jeans and a crystal studded tiara tapped the top of her wine glass with her spoon to get their attention as if she were going to make a toast. It was Amanda, another account executive who played the part of the sun with everyone in the room a planet revolving around her. The petite, perky type that you just knew taxi drivers always stopped for when she waved her slender hand. "I have a client meeting out in LA next week and all they're talking about is that big verdict that's supposed to come soon. How do you all think it will go?"

Tulip consumed news voraciously as part of her job, but usually stuck to lifestyle trends and pop culture that could boost or kill her clients' bottom line. Yet anybody breathing and relatively conscious saw that video of those cops beating the crap out of Rodney King. Any verdict other than guilty wouldn't make sense—not with the whole thing caught on tape—and that's why Amanda's question seemed ridiculous.

In early March last year, Tulip had been sitting in the beauty shop chair getting a blowout when national news anchors broke into regular programming. After a routine traffic stop, police officers had kicked Rodney King and beaten him with their batons again and again. It was right there on the screen for the world to see, which was almost as startling as the beating itself. She couldn't look away, even as her stylist turned her back on the television, weeping softly and calling on the Lord for mercy.

Tulip would never have known, no one would have, if not for a man on the street with his camcorder who recorded the whole thing. With her eyes lingering on Key for some reason, Darby let her lips droop into a sad, mournful face. "That poor man, that poor, poor man. He didn't stand a chance against all those officers."

Key watched ESPN, not regular news, and Tulip doubted he even followed the case after the first day it made the news. Now, he seemed as perplexed as she by Darby's sympathetic tone directed at him. The only thing Tulip could think of was how when Darby mentioned mentoring children *in the inner city* one Saturday a month she usually gave Tulip a knowing look. Now Key lifted his glass of Jack and Coke. "Chances are hard to come by for some of us. That's life, what can you do."

And yet sometimes you had to make your own chances. For three straight months, Tulip's father had shown up at the racquetball court at the exact hour Bryce's next-door neighbor played. He lost games to that man long enough to move Tulip's resume to the top of the pile. Her father had come a long way from the slums of New York, and he would do anything to make sure his little girl never knew that kind of lack.

Mason spoke up next. "Poor man, nothing. King was driving errati-cally, and he was drunk. When you break the law, expect to get arrested. They're not gonna treat you like some grandma they're helping cross the street."

"A lot of people are divided down the middle—Black versus white—on how this thing should turn out. I must say I'm anxious to see how they come down on this one." Amanda's gaze locked on Tulip and Key.

Were people that divided? What happened to objective truth? PR was all about spin but there was nothing to spin in this case. The video didn't lie. Tulip cleared her throat. "I trust the jury to do the right thing. To look at the evidence and come to a proper conclusion. I think Black and white people should be able to agree on that much." She quietly praised herself for remaining logical and stripping any traces of emotion from her voice. Her parents would have been proud.

Being the only one in this boat party who could drink in excess and suffer no repercussions the next day, Bryce threw back two shots in quick succession. "Look, you got to call balls and strikes on these cases. These things are never black and white." He laughed at his own choice of words. "Rodney King broke the law and if he'd quietly gotten in the back of the police car, we wouldn't be talking about this right now. No harm, no foul. Forgive me for mixing my sports metaphors. But Rodney King got worked up. The cops got a little carried away. Adrenaline pumping. Now everybody's on edge. But I agree with Tulip that the jury will get it right."

Her CEO agreed with her, but she wasn't sure she agreed with him. It didn't matter though because what happened out in LA had little to do with her life. Sometimes you had to compartmentalize things or else go crazy trying to solve the world's problems. If that jury took the rest of the year to make its decision, that would be fine with Tulip. It didn't matter what her coworkers thought about a verdict in a city on the other side of the country. Relief, as short-lived as it might have been, passed over her when the night began to run out of steam, and the talk of that court case subsided, and they all sat in satisfied, tired silence waiting for the boat to take them back to the pier.

5

Tulip

Tulip watched her mother arrange evenly sliced potatoes, onions, and carrots in a roasting pan, making a tidy border around the meat like a picture frame. Freda swept tendrils of damp hair away from her face, revealing cheeks flushed from the heat of the oven and her own effort.

"Don't just stand there, sweetheart. Cut the Brussels sprouts and season them. Get that oil out of the pantry. We'll need it."

"Yes, ma'am."

Once the roast and the veggies were in the oven, Tulip joined her mother in the dining room where the table had been transformed into an auction house, every inch covered with items for the upcoming charity event she was hosting for women's heart health for the Links, an invitation-only organization of well-connected African American women committed to service and philanthropy. Her mother's appointment book stayed full with galas, meetings with philanthropists, church socials, school assemblies, university boards, and community foundations, all of it the engine that kept her going.

Freda rotated a porcelain bowl on the table to see how the natural light held it in its gaze. Front and center lay the items that would undoubtedly fetch the highest bids at the auction next month—a Bulls basketball from Jordan's rookie year and a pair of game-worn Air

Jordans, both signed by Michael himself. Tulip shook her head. Whoever won those would need armed security to prevent somebody from snatching that gear right off their bodies. So soon before the championship games, too?

Next to a one-of-a-kind oil painting by a brother fresh out of the Art Institute sat a card on which her mother had scribbled *dinner for two at a French restaurant*. Who would bid on a dining experience that sounded that uninspired? Without officially agreeing to play copywriter, Tulip regularly helped her mother wordsmith these descriptions.

"Mom, spice up the language on this one. Say, '*Step inside Les Nomades and take a culinary journey to France. It's more than dinner—it's art on a plate.*'"

The wrinkle of worry in Freda's brow smoothed and she smiled, satisfied with Tulip's suggestion. "I like that turn of phrase, dear. You have always been a gifted writer. That's why Mattingly hired you."

"Well, if you ask some people at work, they might say it was nepotism or that I was a diversity hire." Tulip spit the words out as if they'd tasted bitter.

Freda turned away from a handmade ceramic vase to look Tulip squarely in the eye. "Some people, huh? Your father merely opened the door for you at that company. That's what *they* do all the time. It's still up to you to excel there. But this doesn't surprise me one bit. This country was built on every group except us having somebody to look down on and lord over. They will try every trick in the book to get you to doubt yourself and your talent. Don't let them do that. Don't let them mess with your head. You can't control what those people on your job say, do, or think. You can only control you and how you outperform every last one of them. You hear me?"

That flicker of fire jumped to life in her mother's eyes every now and then, and Tulip had no idea where it came from. But whenever it appeared, she recognized the most real parts of her mother, raw and unvarnished.

"You have every right to be at Mattingly," Freda said. "Talk to me. What's going on over there?"

Her mother's love could be intense sometimes, burning bright as the sun. And that love came at you strong with the fierceness of a lioness protecting her cub.

Her parents praised her often, displayed her report cards on the refrigerator when she was a girl, bragged to friends about her top grades in English, but it often felt like a bribe to ensure she never slipped.

"It's been five years and I feel like I've proven myself. Only now, I'm starting to get noticed," Tulip began. "I want Bryce to trust me with new accounts."

What she didn't tell her mother, for fear she would worry, was that after an account executive at Mattingly hit five years without a promotion, they were on borrowed time, and everyone knew it. You either moved up or out.

"There's talk that he might be promoting someone to account director soon and I think people's claws are coming out now."

"Maybe we need to sharpen your claws," Freda said, and they laughed.

People often underestimated Freda Gilroy Vance, a daughter of Chicago's South Side—regal and proud, seemingly taller than her actual five feet, four inches, especially when she tilted her head upward as if breathing rarefied air. The part-time teacher of mathematics at the Montessori School, who could be on the faculty of any prestigious university in the world. It would be a foolish mistake to think that only trouble was found on the South Side, that the cream of the crop in this city only hailed from the North Side. Freda would be the first to tell you about all the hardworking people who lived there, including the doctors and schoolteachers and judges in the Gilroy family who earned their rightful place in this town, born and bred on the South Side like the Daley political dynasty.

Tulip ran her fingers idly over the smooth surface of a vase. "I'm finally getting coverage for the Breakfast Bears cereal. There have been a few good campaigns but nothing breakthrough, you know. Bryce didn't give this account to Amanda or any of his other prized, valuable people. It feels like he was trying me out to see if I could cut it."

"It doesn't matter how you got the assignment. What matters is what you do with it." Turning to the tea set on the buffet, Freda poured each of them a cup. She took a sip then said, "You have the talent, no question. Your father and I sent you to the best schools to prepare you for this moment. Even if you don't feel ready, you are."

The tea sliding down Tulip's throat warmed her insides almost as much as her mother's words. Sometimes you needed others to believe for you until you learned to do it for yourself. She would give everything to become a rising star at Mattingly.

Gerald arrived home from the hospital in time for dinner, and the three of them held hands at the kitchen table to recite a communal grace and met some unwritten age-old standard for what it meant to be a family.

Biting a huge chunk out of his corn muffin, Gerald glanced sideways at Tulip. "I hear that big-headed boy you've taken up with joined you out on that boat the other night. The boy with the malocclusion."

"The what?" Tulip said, patiently obliging her father.

"Forgive me," he said, his hands splayed across his chest in an act of mock contrition. "Let me put it to you like this. How's that boy with the buck teeth?"

It's true that Key's two front teeth protruded more than normal. When she suggested braces once, he told her this was his signature look and he didn't want to mess with perfection. Tulip said to her father, "I happen to think he has a beautiful smile."

Freda shrugged and spooned a heap of mashed potatoes onto her husband's plate. "All the same, maybe he should make an appointment to see Dr. Tanner or Dr. Rogers."

"C'mon, you guys. He already has a dentist, okay?" Tulip said, wishing for different dinner conversation.

"Dr. Tanner and Dr. Rogers keep busy schedules, but as a favor to your father, I'm sure they could get him in. If money is the issue or insurance . . ."

"Mom, really. Stop. Please."

After a full analysis of Key's dental challenges, her dear father quickly became cardiologist Dr. Gerald Vance and launched into war stories about how poor dental hygiene could damage the heart, with bacteria infecting the gums and poisoning the blood vessels.

"Not at the dinner table, Gerald," her mother scolded.

"Oh, come on now. That kind of talk used to get you all frisky during my Meharry days." He tickled the crook of her neck until her icy stare melted into a smile, but she still swatted his hand away as if it were an annoying gnat.

Unlike most adult children who cringed at their parents' public displays of affection, Tulip celebrated any playfulness between them. She had watched several of her friends' parents divorce, their families dissolving, and had nervously waited for it to happen to her folks. But it never did. Yet she sensed sometimes that Gerald desired something from Freda that she held back.

Tulip had pushed over the years. *What were you like in college?* She chose to attend Northwestern University in the Chicago suburbs because her parents never tried to convince her to continue the Fisk tradition. They rarely talked about their years there beyond the academics. Tulip had tried: *How did you know Dad was the one? What did you dream of being and doing with your life?* Instead of answering, Freda usually changed the subject to something more immediate, more practical, less nostalgic. But yet, Tulip never doubted her mother's love for their family. She had her own way of expressing it, like now with Freda resurfacing the story of how Gerald won her over by stepping on the yard one day.

Tulip plucked a carrot with her fork and winked at her father. "Yes, yes. So, I hear you were a regular Casanova back in the day. I heard how you wooed Mom. Go 'head then, player."

"Your mother likes to reminisce over how we met. I put the moves on her and swept her off her feet. Let all those knuckleheads know she was taken." Humility had never been one of her father's deficits.

Freda played along this time. "I don't know about all that now. Your dexterity needed some work. You kept dropping that cane trying to be all smooth."

"But it worked. I walked away with the prize in the end."

"Enough of that ancient history," Freda said, changing the subject. "I'm concerned that Keyshawn may be struggling more than we realize. Who are his people again?"

"Leave it alone," Gerald said.

"What? It was a simple question."

Tulip didn't know everything about her mother, but she understood that Freda Gilroy Vance saw the world divided into stacked boxes, each person she met fitting neatly into one of them: lower middle class, middle middle class, upper middle class, and then on top, the wealthy. Boxes and categories that defined how their family moved through the world.

After dinner they sat a spell before clearing the dishes from the table. According to Gerald, that extra time allowed for good digestion and prevented heartburn. Tulip loved having her own place, the Bronzeville apartment she shared with Sharita, but she came to her parents' house for dinner often. Neither she nor Sharita liked to cook and usually ordered carryout after a long day at the office. Getting out of her parents' house, which was suffocating at times, had been her goal for so long. But when it finally happened and she was on her own, she craved the family dinners she'd grown up with and showed up for meals now at least twice a week, sitting in the familiar kitchen chair between her parents.

"Let's see what's happening in the world." Her father licked his thumb to turn the pages of the *Chicago Tribune*, a paper much too large to be read at the kitchen table. The *Sun-Times* was more compact and widely read on the South Side; however, Gerald subscribed to the *Tribune*, insisting upon consuming the same news as those on the whiter North Side.

He rattled off the headlines. With a victory in the Pennsylvania primary, Bill Clinton moved one step closer to winning the Democratic nomination. The president of Italy abruptly resigned this week, leaving that country without any government at all. There was a story speculating on whether Mayor Daley would support a $2.5 million increase in local AIDS spending, something Rudy had to advocate for secretly, not wanting anyone at Mattingly to associate him with what some called the *gay plague*. Then her father got to what had everybody in the city hyped—game three of the playoffs where the Bulls would take on the Heat later that night.

"I'm warning you now," Gerald said. "Don't look at me, don't talk to me, don't ask me for anything tonight. I'll have my nachos, my beer, and my Bulls." They all laughed at the truth of that statement, learning the hard way over the years not to come between him and his beloved Bulls.

She had plans to go over to Key's place to watch. She got a kick out of seeing him make Nerf ball baskets in his bedroom like a little kid, and he dunked every time Jordan or Pippen did.

Before Gerald relayed the local news updates, Tulip flipped on the TV to see analysis of the Chicago-Miami playoff matchup that night. Her heart caught somewhere in her throat, strangling her breath, when she saw the breaking news banner and the text in the lower third of the screen. She had checked earlier in the day but heard no sign of the jury coming back anytime soon. Now they had reached a verdict in the trial of the officers who beat Rodney King.

She had been watching and waiting for more than a year, since last March, and Tulip had been convinced there was only one possible outcome after watching the videotape, that Rodney King would finally get the justice he so rightly deserved.

Tulip didn't personally know anybody who had even been arrested, let alone beaten by cops within an inch of their lives. Her parents shielded her as much as they could from all that. The closest she had come to witnessing any scuffle with the police had been earlier this year when she and a group of friends went dancing at De'Joie's in the River North neighborhood. Around 2 o'clock in the morning as they were leaving the club, two armed officers pulled their friend Nate from their group and without explanation threw him against the police cruiser. She could still see the fear in his wide brown eyes, begging for help but at the same time warning them not to get involved. They were all scared, huddling in the cold, refusing to leave his side until the cops released him. And they did let him go, no apologies, only a shrug, saying they thought he fit the profile of the mugger they'd been looking for.

Her agony over this verdict had been a private one. She couldn't explain to anyone that when Rodney King's bruised and battered face appeared on the news, her deepest fears overtook her, and sometimes her father's and Key's faces slid in its place. It wasn't until the boat party Friday night that Tulip began to have nagging doubts about the outcome of the trial. Her white coworkers made it sound like this thing could go either way, something she naively hadn't considered.

Now, on the small kitchen TV, grainy footage of the cops beating Rodney King filled the screen. The verdict was in, but Tulip would swear for years to come that she didn't hear the words, not right away. What would forever stick in her mind would be the video of the four officers hugging their lawyers in the courtroom after their acquittal. Sitting on her kitchen chair motionless and numb, she didn't scream or cry as she thought she might if things went this way.

A jury watched the same video Tulip had and decided nothing criminal had happened. How could that be?

"Oh, dear Lord." Freda let out a sigh, staring blankly, shaking her head. "Here we go again. It never ends for us."

"Turn it off," Gerald said. "I've seen enough."

"No, I'm watching." Tulip surprised herself at her own defiance of her father. She needed to see more. Some explanation. An answer to the woman in the do-rag being interviewed on some LA street corner, who asked the question for them all: "So, we not supposed to trust our lying eyes, huh?"

Her father shook his head, and Tulip willed him to stay quiet. She had a nagging feeling that whatever he was about to say would fuel her rage. "Now don't get me wrong," he said. "What those bastards did to him wasn't right, not by a long shot. I've been a Black man my whole life and I've bobbed and weaved trying to escape this very thing." Tulip nodded, grateful that he shared something so painful, but couldn't help imagining the fears and close calls he had carried alone all these years.

She touched his arm, but he pulled it gently from her grasp. He held up his hand to signal he had more to say on the matter. From the look on his face, something more that she wasn't going to like.

"As wrong as this all is, a true travesty of justice, I can look at this Rodney King fella and tell that nigga's got a hard head. Watch him wind up in some more trouble down the road."

Tulip cringed at her father's choice of that word, which he used liberally to make a point. He caught her frown, her disapproval. "Don't go judging me now. You bop your head to that word on the radio every day."

Freda spoke up then. "Gerald, you can't tell a thing by looking at him except that he may not have the same pedigree you do. But he's a human being and he didn't deserve it. End of story."

No one could argue with that, but the story did not end there. The continuous news coverage kept them at the table watching everything unfold. It didn't take long for people to spill into the streets of LA. Some throwing tire irons at store windows. Angry, violent swings at a justice system that withheld justice from them.

That's when Freda pushed back from the table and began taking dishes to the sink. "This isn't the way. Don't they know that? This is exactly what they expect us to do. To tear up our own neighborhoods. And then they'll say, *See, they're violent just like we always said.*"

Tulip didn't know what to think. Her parents came from the old school, a time when you had to be polite and agreeable to stay alive. Maybe being quiet and nice wasn't enough anymore. On the screen, young people her age wielded baseball bats and hurled chairs through store windows. Some climbed through jagged spikes of glass with shirts and pants and necklaces dangling from their arms.

"Your mother is right. These white folks are looking for any excuse to say I told you so. If it has to be this way, I'm glad it's happening out in LA and not here," Gerald said. "The bank down the street from my practice has a security camera. Everybody knows it, too, so that should keep the hoodlums away."

The news anchor pivoted then from the raw images of what was happening on the ground and did deeper analysis. The why. The inevitable comparisons to the protests for civil rights more than two decades ago.

Photos from LA of shirtless men with cornrowed hair played on the screen opposite ones of men in immaculate suits with close-cropped haircuts at the 1963 March on Washington. It took a minute to process and let things sink in, but when it did, Tulip recognized what was happening. Without making a verbal judgment, the news had done just that, the never-before-seen photos from the crowd at the famous march somehow elevating those men and women above the ones who had taken to the streets in LA. They were saying without saying that this new fight for justice was somehow less reasonable, less righteous, less respectable, and more violent.

The old video footage from the 1960s showed the dignitaries like Dr. King and Ralph Abernathy, celebrities like Josephine Baker, Sammy Davis Jr., Ossie Davis, and Ruby Dee, as well as ordinary men and women of all races looking determined and full of purpose. The camera zoomed in for close-ups of faces in the crowd, pausing on that of a young man in a suit with a round, boyish face—full lips and bright eyes. Gerald frowned and rose from his seat, moving a few steps closer to the TV, staring as if he'd seen a ghost. Tulip caught him stealing glances at her mother, who was cleaning the kitchen. Maybe sensing his eyes on her, she turned toward the TV.

Neither of them said anything, but a look passed between them that seemed to carry the heaviness of their history. The large dish in Freda's hands crashed to the floor, the china splintering, shards skidding across the tile. Brussels sprouts left over from dinner rolled like marbles under the table and stove. No one moved at first, their limbs wooden. Then Freda stepped over the shattered china and ran up the stairs to her bedroom, slamming the door. A moment later, Tulip's father walked to the front door, put on his coat and hat, and stepped silently into the night.

Tulip sat at the kitchen table alone, her mind cycling through what had just happened in the previous sixty seconds. She didn't know what to think. Her parents' marriage sometimes resembled an old washing machine banging and hiccupping as it wore out over time, but this seemed different. Not the usual barbs they traded or glowering glances after some misunderstanding. Not even tired silences after one had told the other more than once to complete some routine errand.

Tonight seemed different than other nights when they argued. What happened tonight ran deeper and seared them both. What had they seen on TV that spooked them? Who was that young man and how did they know him?

***

Rain soaked Tulip as she stood on Key's doorstep. She could hear the noise of the playoff game on the other side and leaned on the bell until, finally, he opened the door. He stood there shirtless and barefoot, only wearing his basketball shorts. "Girl, come on in out of that rain," he said, pulling her inside and peeling off her wet trench coat.

The frenzied sounds of the game filled the small shotgun house. His eyes kept darting to the TV. It was late in the first quarter and the Bulls were down fourteen points. Only after he wrapped her in a bath towel and pushed her drenched hair out of her face did he seem to notice her tears. "You crying," he said, looking alarmed. "What's going on?"

"Nothing makes sense," she said, hurling herself onto his threadbare couch, the wire from the springs poking her hip.

He pointed the remote at the TV and the voice of the announcer calling the plays went from hyped to barely audible. The quiet of the room calmed her, and once she found a comfortable position on the couch, she told him everything. First, the miscarriage of justice in the Rodney King case and then her parents' odd behavior over video footage of some young man at the March on Washington.

"All of a sudden, my mom freaked out and stormed off to bed and my dad left and went God knows where." She heard her voice rise as she retold it.

Key whistled softly. "Damn, that's pretty dramatic. Doesn't seem like their style. Of course, I don't know them like you do."

He didn't know her parents well at all because they chose not to get to know him. Now that she had her own apartment, Key and her folks rarely crossed paths. But back when she still lived at home a year ago and Gerald realized they were dating, he'd sit outside on the porch waiting for Key's car to pull up. He didn't say a word, but his glare and the set of his mouth delivered sufficient warning. Freda's first question for Tulip had been the same as what she asked at dinner earlier tonight. "Who are his people?" The McCray's were entrepreneurs, the George and Weezie Jefferson of the South Side. But that didn't amuse or impress her mother. And for the longest time, Tulip tried to convince Key that she wasn't as shallow as her parents.

Resting her head on his chest, she intertwined their fingers, kneading his palm with her thumb. "Before that strange guy's face came on TV, my dad kept saying things about Rodney King."

"Like what?"

A measure of guilt passed over Tulip for what she was about to reveal. "Well, he acted like the man was asking for a beatdown. Like he was a troublemaker, and it was his own fault."

Key removed his fingers from hers. "Wow. That's pretty cold-blooded."

Saying the words made her physically ill. "I'm sorry," she said, as if her father's words had been directed at Key. As much as she tried to shield Key from their judgment, she knew he felt it. He had to.

Key unfolded a blanket that had been draped over the back of the couch and pulled it over them. His eyes locked on the TV screen, but she could tell his mind had drifted, no longer focusing on the game. "I'm sitting here trying to put myself in your dad's shoes. Don't trip on your folks too much. They come from a different world than me and Rodney King. I drive a bus every day. Your dad saves lives and your mother shapes young minds as a teacher. They're doing big things and

I ain't mad at 'em. But they think their money, their position, is like armor. Like it's gon' protect them. Maybe it will. People do what they think they got to do to make it out here. It is what it is."

She extricated herself from the crook of his arm, sitting up straighter to look at him. Was he still nursing some hurt from the boat party when she didn't explain to her coworkers right away that he was a bus driver? "I'm proud of what you do for a living, baby. It's my parents. I don't want to think like them or be like them."

"Don't say that. They're good people."

Slapping his thigh, she said, "How do you know?"

"They made you, didn't they?" She couldn't help but smile at that.

"Can I ask you something?" he said. "Have you ever been scared for somebody you cared about?"

Where was he going with this? She said, "I worry about you, especially after what happened to Rodney King last year. You're not violent. You make an honest living. But if the wrong officer pulls you over when he's having a bad day, you could be hurt or worse. I know that all those folks out in LA busting windows are dead wrong, but I understand their need to protest. And there are legit protests going on. What's happening to our people is dead wrong." Her voice thickened with emotion, and she couldn't say more.

Key kept shaking his head. "Look, protesting won't do a damn thing. Do you think some cop would think twice about hauling my ass to jail or bashing my head in because some people were marching down the street chantin' and singin' 'We Shall Overcome'?"

That song had been the music of the Movement in her parent's day, yet she doubted her folks even knew the words. They would have steered clear of any protest or march. "We wouldn't be where we are today though without what they did. It was more than singing songs. They mobilized and changed laws," she said. "Like that March on Washington, that was something serious. I keep thinking about how my parents freaked out when they saw that video clip on the news. They got crazy worked up about it."

When Key spoke, he did so carefully, as if trying not to step on a landmine. "Maybe it's this whole Rodney King thing. People got their heads busted marching in the sixties. Some of them died. Don't forget your folks were around for all that. And then to see that march show up on TV? That's some PTSD shit right there."

Key was probably right. Maybe that's all it had been, a reflexive recoil. Sometimes you didn't have to fight in a war to feel its aftershocks. And her parents didn't owe her any explanations for how they reacted to something she had never lived through and had only read about in textbooks.

Key reached for his boom box and put in a new cassette tape. Marvin Gaye's voice surrounded them, singing about too many of their people crying and dying, and again and again he asked what's going on. A song that came out when they were toddlers, yet it still rang true all these years later.

The Bulls pulled off a win in the fourth quarter, but she and Key celebrated quietly with the volume down, still wrapped in each other's arms, the only sound the sweet anguish of Marvin's voice sweeping over them.

PART THREE

Nashville, 1960

6

Freda

A new year dawned, and the trees began to drop their leaves as fall receded in the face of the coming winter. From her dorm window, Freda spotted Evaline running up the hill from Meharry Medical College, her coat trailing her like a cape, clutching something close to her chest. She barely knocked on the door and practically tumbled into her room with Cora on her heels, her cheeks flushed from the cool air and the excitement of her news.

"You got to see this. Read it. Your man is at the top of the list," Evaline said, panting and shoving a wrinkled sheet of typing paper at her.

Tentatively, Freda took the paper, already anticipating she would need to match her friend's level of enthusiasm. A series of names appeared in a list with initials followed by surnames. They weren't alphabetical. Quickly, she recognized a ranking of students based upon recent academic performance. Growing impatient, Evaline jabbed her index finger at the initials near the top of the list.

G.V. 97th Percentile

"Let me see." Cora angled for a better view of the sheet. "Oh, I heard about this list."

"Well, I haven't heard a thing," said Freda, running her fingers over the letters.

Gerald Vance. She hadn't thought much of him with the whirlwind of starting college and then meeting Darius Moore, who had turned her head every which way. Now she wished she hadn't told Evaline and Cora about this Gerald, someone she had never met, but someone she already had history with if you asked her friends.

It made no sense, but Freda was strangely proud that this mysterious Gerald Vance had done so well in his studies, as if his success somehow intertwined with her own. It struck her as oddly intrusive though that everyone in this little Negro mecca knew the academic status of America's future physicians. Of course, it didn't surprise Freda at all that Evaline had become the town crier for such public pronouncements.

"So, did someone at Meharry just hand over this ranking sheet?" Freda asked, skeptical and unsure she wanted the details.

"Girl, please. No, Meharry posted it, and I tore it off the wall," Evaline said, waving her hand dismissively when she noticed how scandalized Freda and Cora looked. "This is what's called *research*, ladies. A primary source. Our future husbands could be on this list."

"Well, I told you both that my heart is with Percy Chesterton III." Cora's high school sweetheart back home in Murfreesboro came from a long line of preachers. The way she said *the third,* as if it were some honorific like *professor* or *your honor,* amused Freda.

"We know you are spoken for, sweetie," she said, wrapping an arm around her friend. Freda couldn't imagine being that certain of your future at nineteen when there was so much you didn't know about the world or yourself even.

All this time, Evaline hadn't torn her eyes away from the list, and while Cora seemed uninterested, filing a hangnail, Freda spotted her friend taking furtive glances at the paper.

"What? I'm curious," Cora said, though she knew they were on to her. And who could blame her for checking out the names of some of the most eligible bachelors in all of the South?

***

When Freda walked into her philosophy classroom, the only men she wanted to give the time of day to were Professor Redfield and, begrudgingly, Henry David Thoreau, whose quote scrawled in large cursive covered one-third of the blackboard.

"The mass of men lead lives of quiet desperation and go to the grave with the song still in them."

Her academic advisor had strongly suggested, insisted, that she round out her studies with something other than mathematics. And that's how she found herself in the classroom of Professor Redfield, a short, rotund man with a distended stomach that he proudly displayed with an unbuttoned suit jacket and white shirt that pulled as tight as a fitted sheet. Mama and Papa spoke of him often, as he was just a few years older than they when he joined the faculty and quickly made a name for himself as an intellectual giant. He had a habit of tossing verbal grenades at his students to spark lively discussion, baiting them with one-line missives that lacked context. The sly smile that hid behind his gray mustache told her he enjoyed watching them squirm before a debate.

On this more temperate winter day, Freda wore a powder blue cardigan set with low-heeled black pumps. How you dressed depended upon the professor more than the weather though. Professor Currier in the history department never wore ties and that signaled a more relaxed dress code in his class. Not so in Professor Hayden's English class, where he required skirts for the ladies. Monsieur Cottin, who taught French, would never allow a lady to cross the threshold of his classroom if she weren't wearing stockings.

The one student who walked into Professor Redfield's classroom dressed up in a full, waxy suit was Darius Moore. She hadn't seen him since that awkward end to their date at the fair. He had called Jubilee Hall several times looking for her, but she refused to take his calls. He reminded her of the ugliness of the world, the unfairness of it. And besides, why waste time talking to a boy she'd never end up with anyway. They were too different.

Once everyone settled in their seats and the chatter subsided, Professor Redfield pointed to the Thoreau quote and waited for the first bomb to drop. Some accused the famous philosopher of treating the world as a mirror, a way to gaze reverently at himself while opining about what the masses should and shouldn't do.

"What do you think about that, Miss Gilroy?" Professor Redfield leaned on her desk, head bowed, the light from the ceiling bouncing off his shiny brown head. He knew her name, which in and of itself wasn't unusual, but he said it with more familiarity than he might have with some other students in his class. This was the curse of walking the same hallowed halls her parents had.

The words on the board jumbled in her mind like gibberish, and she didn't know what Professor Redfield expected her to say. He had caught her off-guard, and she might as well have been dropped off in some foreign country where she didn't speak the language well enough to even ask for a translation. She would have preferred to listen silently. The first thought that came to one's mind was usually not the most prudent, but she couldn't help herself. "Respectfully, sir, if you ask me, Thoreau was all show and no go." She glanced quickly at Darius, who had been quietly waiting for his turn to speak, his face mostly unreadable with a hint of amusement, as if he were the one holding the big joker at the Bid Whist table.

Mr. Redfield blew a particle of lint off his jacket sleeve. "Ms. Gilroy, you dishonor your parents' legacy with that answer. I highly suggest that you dispense with colloquialisms and form a cogent analysis of the quote."

The heat of embarrassment sprang first to Freda's collarbone, and it rose along her neck to cover her cheeks. It occurred to her that as cultured as she was, she hadn't thought much about life's big questions before. Why had she been so flip and disrespectful to Mr. Redfield? Staring at scratch marks on her wooden desk, she waited for another student to pick up the discussion and it came as no surprise that Darius spoke next.

"Thoreau said the necessities of life for man are food, clothing, and shelter. Think about the Vietnamese or the Negro, trying to survive.

That's why so many haven't joined the cause of freedom yet. They're trying to stay alive, not right the wrongs of the world. I'm not like most men though. The pursuit of freedom is my food. It is my clothing. My shelter. It is what fuels me."

Who was this man delivering a soliloquy as if he were the next Thoreau? She fumed silently at his arrogance. Freda may have appreciated his cogent, inspired analysis if it hadn't followed her own bumbling attempt. She remembered the young man who had spoken so solemnly about declaring his manhood as a Negro and then laughed like a little boy at a pig race. She had never met anyone who had two intensely different ways of being, almost like two people in one, and as much as she resisted, she found herself drawn to both.

While it lacked the certainty of mathematics, Freda could appreciate this type of intellectual discourse, at least in theory. In a few months at Fisk, she had listened to guest speakers opine on the decline of European colonial empires and British policy in West Africa, topics that made her feel like a student of the world and not just a Negro girl in the Jim Crow South.

One student in the back row clapped. Then another. Soon, the entire class applauded, and Darius shrugged in that sheepish way of his as if to say God had struck him with this brilliance like lightning from the sky.

Freda cleared her throat, finding her voice again. "Well, I agree with Thoreau that a little misery visits all of us. We may not be perfectly happy, but we don't have to wallow in our struggles. Some of us have a beautiful song inside us and the world needs to hear it."

"Touché," Darius said, and she knew they were both remembering how he had played the sax the day they met.

Professor Redfield folded his arms and Freda thought she detected a smile hiding behind his mustache. Begrudging respect for her contribution to the class, and maybe she had redeemed herself. It was something, and she held on to it.

***

On one February day, blinding snow stung her face, pricking her skin like hundreds of toothpicks. In the campus courtyard, young men hurled snowballs at dorm windows as an invitation for the girls to come outside to play. Freda held back at first, the academic and social expectations of her parents back home in Chicago right on her heels everywhere she went. She envied whatever it was that freed her classmates enough to do this, their faces turned up to the sky, mouths open, letting the flakes dissolve on their tongues. But on a whim, she came outside and saw Cora and Evaline already on the lawn packing snow in their gloves. Some students who hailed from Mississippi and Alabama hadn't seen snow anywhere except on television. It was a delight to watch Tennessee-born-and-raised Cora running and skipping through the snow like a child on Christmas morning.

Soon, Evaline pulled her and Cora into a huddle to make rank assessments of each boy, as they were likely doing with the girls. Right away, they spotted older guys who had to be Fisk upperclassmen or possibly Meharry students, and a snow day suddenly took on new meaning and became an audition. They pummeled the young men with snowballs and ran slowly enough to be chased, caught, and tackled in retaliation. This reminded Freda of the playground games from her childhood, but none of them could claim innocence anymore, not with all those hormones thrumming through their limbs.

The fraternity boys in their sweaters and jeans kicked up clouds of snow, all of them cocky as ever. They reminded Freda of gazelles in a savanna, arching their backs and leaping high in tall grass.

Evaline had her eye on Ambrose Delacourt, a New Orleans boy and first-year medical student at Meharry. A smooth brother, fine as wine, near the top of his class but still below Gerald in the class ranking, which gave Freda an odd sense of superiority, even though she hadn't met the man and could lay no real claim to him. Without warning, Evaline marched right up to Ambrose and his fraternity brothers and said, "My friends and I have had a long day of classes and could use a little entertainment. Something other than a snowball fight. Surprise us. I promise we're an appreciative audience."

That was all these young men needed to hear, and a few pulled out their fashionable silver and blue canes, bent close to the ground, and rapped the snow-covered pavement. One stood out to Freda. She recognized Gerald from a grainy, sepia class photo Evaline had unearthed. In person, she could see he had a perfectly proportioned face with dancing, mischievous eyes. Light brown skin, a redbone to be sure, but not high yellow. Freda was not sure on a conscious level why that clarification mattered, but it did. A good-looking fellow, thank God. What a relief that her parents hadn't arranged for her to do a lifetime of charity work. Lord knew marriage to an ugly man was not her ministry.

It needled her that Gerald hadn't bothered to find her on campus before now. He knew her name and certainly could have asked around, yet she had to admit even as a dating novice that there was nothing more arresting sometimes than a boy's indifference, and the pursuit and evasion game could be more appealing than the victory or even the prize itself.

Cora caught her staring and whispered, "Now that I see him up close, he's skinnier than he looks in his picture."

"The point is he is a future doctor, but yeah, girl," Evaline said. "You'll have to feed him all sorts of mac 'n' cheese and neckbones and pigs' feet."

Ignoring them, her eyes stayed on Gerald, and he kept twirling that cane long after the others stepped aside. It seemed everyone realized he was performing for an audience of one. For Freda. He recognized her. She was certain of it. Even in the frigid cold, heat spread through her body, with her blouse underneath her coat sticking like Saran Wrap to her back.

On a particularly intricate maneuver, the cane slipped from his fingers and landed with a thud by her boot. He knelt in front of her in the snow and she thought he was either proposing or genuflecting at an altar. The crowd parted and their laughter dwindled to a hush just like in the movies. Looking down at Gerald, she saw snowflakes and freckles sprinkled across his cheeks like a dash of salt and pepper.

He picked up the cane and flipped it again and then put the handle under his chin with a flourish. His eyes sparkled like two shiny nickels. "My cane is smarter than I am. It knows how to find the prettiest girl on campus."

Evaline and Cora and maybe every other girl in earshot squealed and gestured wildly. Freda's tongue sat fat and dry in her mouth, and she struggled to form words. Finally, she said, "Now that your cane has found her, what's it going to do next?"

While the boys hooted and hollered at this and the girls shrieked in some combination of shock and delight, she wanted to disappear. Why had she said something so suggestive and wildly inappropriate? Her mother would have accused her of being common. Sensing her humiliation, Gerald leaped into the air as if he had well-oiled springs in his legs. When his feet landed firmly again in the snow, he ceremoniously asked her to be his date for Valentine's Day.

Right then and there, Freda decided that all the conniving women in his family and hers had been right all along, having been endowed with some divine intuition, because Gerald couldn't have been sent to her by anyone but God Himself.

7

Freda

Freda rarely visited the stores downtown, but a first date on Valentine's Day called for a new pair of stockings to match her new dress. She had chosen a swing dress in pale lavender—a subtle, muted color, definitely not the traditional red of the holiday—because Mama always said, "Negroes have no business wearing red."

Mama usually heaped that judgment on darker-skinned women. Under the light of the midday sun or even by the glow of candlelight, Freda could pass the brown paper bag test—her skin tone not quite as dark as the nutmeg her mother used in butternut squash. Yet, Mama still had the absurd notion that a proper Negro woman of any shade should avoid red lest she be mistaken for a lady of the night.

It was quaint and a bit pathetic how much she still followed her mother's old admonitions, even living this far away from her rules. And now, Freda was learning new rules in this part of the country, where things were segregated but civil. Take Nashville, a city that could have been a model for the whole country, an ideal for how the races could coexist. Aside from those dastardly restroom signs, whites and Negroes kept a polite peace, yet no one knew when that tacit agreement to stay out of each other's way might snap like a rubber band stretched too tight. By the time she reached McLellan's five-and-dime to buy stockings, she had no clue what she was walking into. No clue that the rubber band was about to snap.

Freda stepped into the store, where the warm air clouded her eyeglasses, and she immediately inhaled the smell of chocolates and the faux leather of the nearby purses. She found the hosiery near the shoes and selected shiny beige pantyhose, the same shade as the white woman who had perused them before her. There were no options to buy hose remotely close to her skin tone. A saleslady with a nametag that read "Barbara" appeared now behind the cash register, reminding Freda of someone's grandmother, with hands you could picture kneading pie dough and touching the foreheads of feverish children. When Freda handed her six one-dollar bills and the box of six pairs of nylons, Barbara frowned, her pale white face pinched red.

"Is there a problem, ma'am?" Freda asked. Each pair of stockings sold for ninety-one cents, and she was splurging for the entire box, so she'd have a few spares. Luckily, her parents had set up a bank account in her name for incidentals like this.

Having done the math in her head, she knew she should not owe much more than five dollars and forty-six cents, but Barbara continued to scowl. How dare this woman question her calculation? If Freda was certain about anything in life, it was numbers.

Cousin Leotha came to mind—her mother's first cousin who had moved north from Mississippi to live with her family when she was a little girl. He told her about the tests Negroes had to endure in the South just to vote, like guessing the number of jellybeans or soap bubbles in a jar. She had never faced such a test, but she half wished someone would present her with a counting challenge so she could show off her mastery of estimation and probability.

This Barbara woman remained silent, but her eyes constricted until they formed tiny slits and Freda followed her gaze. A small crowd had gathered at the lunch counter. Freda's legs buckled. How could she have not noticed before now? The scene appeared like the broken, chaotic, slow motion of a movie reel.

On every stool at the lunch counter sat young people in collared shirts, ties, dress slacks, dress coats, skirts, and heels, their Sunday best on a Saturday. Most of them Negroes. Some she recognized from Fisk. To her surprise, even a few women.

Young white men stood behind them, their faces contorted as they sneered and taunted. Seeing the ugly downturn of their mouths from a distance made her hear them better, their words clear and unambiguous.

"Get on out of here."

"We don't want your kind around here."

"Are you deaf and dumb?"

On the perimeter of the circle of men, white women watched as if they were spectators at a sporting event cheering on their favorite team and jeering at the opposing side. They carried babies in their arms and held the hands of children, all while shouting at her Negro classmates and the others.

Freda's body wouldn't move. She thought of the scene from the play-acting in the basement of Livingstone Hall. Except this seemed more real. Of course, it was. This must have been what they were training for. Peering at a rehearsal through a slit in a doorway was one thing, but this—this real-life protest of the law—made Freda nervous, and fear crawled up her back now. All she wanted right now was to pay for her purchase and get out of there as fast as she could.

The Negroes at the counter read from newspapers and Bibles and wrote in notebooks. None turned around on their stools to face the small crowd gathering to yell at them. Not a word. No reaction to the provocation. Just as they had practiced. Even when a waitress put up a hastily made, homemade sign that said CLOSED, the Negroes still didn't move from the lunch counter.

Barbara sounded like a child bloated with some fantastic tale as she called out, "We got trouble with the coloreds. Big trouble." Negroes could shop in the store, she acknowledged to no one in particular, their money as green as anyone else's, but sharing a meal together in public, sitting side-by-side close enough to touch—well that was taking things a step too far, and no lunch counter in Nashville would stand for it.

Freda had always been taught that laws existed for a reason, even when she didn't agree with them. A civil society depended on some degree of compliance, even acquiescence. But denying service to Negroes wasn't right. She had read about student activists doing something like this a few weeks ago at a Woolworth's in Greensboro, North Carolina. But why take the risk? Couldn't they go to a Negro restaurant or make a grilled cheese sandwich at home without all this fuss?

These Negroes should not be making spectacles of themselves. Future doctors, lawyers, and schoolteachers—the talented tenth that W.E.B. Du Bois spoke of—had so much more to offer the world. Mama and Papa had taught her not to take that responsibility lightly. The lot of all the other Negroes rested in their hands. One blunder like this one and soon they would all be flatfooted, shuffling through fields pulling cotton bolls.

Her great-grandfather was born into slavery. Freed at age two before he could talk well, yet before his death, he always spoke of it like he had fresh memories of that time. She barely remembered the man, yet Mama and Papa always tried to hush him because they didn't want her tainted by such ugliness so young. But Pa Gilroy talked when he wanted, not at the direction of his grandchildren. It was still hard to believe that her own grandfather's father had come into this world belonging to some white man, and that man set a price for him like a slab of meat you weighed and bartered over with the butcher.

They couldn't go back to that. She couldn't. She would not.

Freda recognized a few familiar faces from campus—some she had seen in classes or at the dining hall or around town. Louise Driscoll, a sociology major from Memphis, studied the menu like a textbook. On the stool next to her in a light tan suit sat John Lewis, a student activist leader from rural Alabama who attended American Baptist Theological Seminary. Next to him was Errol Hankins, who transferred from some tiny school in Mississippi. He kept his eyes on his shoes; they always sparkled, and she assumed he put an infinite amount of time into getting that shine the way some men waxed their cars. Only one white guy joined the students at the counter, Gregory Wilcox, the exchange student from Oberlin. Someone from the angry white crowd ran behind the counter and grabbed a pot of coffee and poured it in Gregory's lap. Unable to stifle his reaction, he screamed, and they told him he deserved it. In the minds of these folks, the only thing as bad as being colored had to be a white person who stood in solidarity with colored folks.

The other students remained still on their stools, but on the other side of Errol, a young man pivoted slightly, breaking with the obviously practiced routine to not make eye contact with anyone. He found Freda's eyes. She gasped. *Darius Moore.* She remembered their talk at the state fair, the outrage he barely contained, his righteous indignation rising, on the brink of overflowing his body. His frustration over the Negro condition. She had listened but admittedly didn't fully understand it.

She knew Darius cared deeply about the cause, but she didn't expect him to put his own body on the line for it. In their philosophy class every week, he opined about impractical, theoretical things like the difference between *existence* and *essence*, gibberish that made her yawn and would never earn him enough money to take on a wife and feed a family.

Why was he staring at her so intently now, as if he could read her mind like newsprint? Barbara at the cash register noticed the glances that passed between her and Darius. Freda stayed quiet, shaking her head as if to say *I'm not with him. I'm not with any of them. I don't even know them. I'm only here for the stockings.*

Betrayal, even the wordless kind, had a way of shrinking you, drowning you in shame.

A siren sounded in the distance, getting louder by the second. The drumbeat of fear thumped in her chest.

Barbara snatched up Freda's package of nylons and tossed it behind her on top of a ninety-seven-cent bed pillow someone must have decided against buying at the last minute. "These stockings are not for sale," she said.

"But—" Freda started when Barbara cut her off.

"Not for sale to you. Now go on."

Barbara put the money in the cash register, and Freda knew better than to ask for it back. Biting her lip, she tugged her coat belt that hung loose at her side. She didn't know what else to do with her hands. Feeling a set of eyes on her, Freda slowly lifted her head and spotted Darius still staring, his lips parted as if he wanted to shout or wordlessly mouth a message to her. Whenever she saw him in class, she noticed his lips, purplish and darkened from smoking. She imagined he polished off an entire pack to summon the nerve for something this dangerous. She had imagined those lips wrapped around his sax or her own lips. But now with the scream of the sirens growing louder, closer, all she wanted was to leap over the cash register and run to the lunch counter, grab Darius by the lapel of his cheap suit, and scream, *This is all your fault.*

Darius looked away first this time, his eyes returning to his philosophy textbook as if he were sitting in the quiet of the Fisk library and not perched under a banana split sign as white men waved their fists at him. The sharp edge of an elbow jabbed her back and the woman behind her shoved her out of the line.

That familiar hot feeling swept Freda's face as it always did before tears fell. Determined not to let these white folks breach the dam of her emotions, she walked slowly to the front door, chin up, back straight the way she had been trained. Outside, a police cruiser pulled up and two milky-faced officers, who didn't appear too many years beyond playing with tin toys, emerged. Freda knew that this whole ordeal, like the restroom signs at the fair, would haunt her dreams at night. Had she made a mistake coming to the South? What would happen to Darius inside that store? Deciding not to wait to see how zealous those officers would be in discharging their duties, Freda kept walking on the empty sidewalk, heavy snow still falling and covering her glasses like a white sheet. Only then did she allow herself to cry.

8

Darius

Darius sat up in bed that night unable to sleep, his back against the headboard, holding a cold compress to his neck. He waited for the three aspirin to kick in. For hours he lit one Lucky after another, going over in his mind how she wouldn't even look at him, and when she did, her face told him things he didn't want to accept. He watched Freda walk out of that store angry, frustrated, and—even worse—disappointed in him. Disappointment from a lady you were falling for, hard, could break a man. He saw it in her eyes, and for the first time in all the months of planning and organizing, in that split second at the lunch counter, he began to question whether he was doing the right thing.

She hadn't had much use for him since he took her to the state fair and she tried to run off. Made some excuse about needing to go to the bathroom and vanished. He searched practically every barn and cattle stall he stumbled upon. When he finally found her, she reminded him of a wounded, whipped cat. All hunched over, knees pressed together, and he could tell she'd been crying but didn't want him to see.

"What's the matter?" he had asked, scared. "Did somebody say something, try to do something to you?" They lived in the Jim Crow South, and anything could happen if you were colored. He should have insisted upon accompanying her to the restroom.

"Nothing," she answered, biting her bottom lip and pleading with him to take her home.

Every man learned early at his mother's hip that when a woman said nothing's wrong, something was always wrong. The way she looked that day reminded him of how she seemed earlier today at Mc-Lellan's, frightened and hurting. His overriding instinct had been to run to her, fold her in his arms, protect her, love on her.

He wanted to tell her things he couldn't, about the pride he had in what he was doing, and the impact they could have all over the South if they desegregated that lunch counter. Martin Luther King had been right when he said that by sitting down, they were standing up for the best in America.

For a long time, he asked himself *why me?* As studious as he was, he didn't have the intellect or the velvet tongue of Reverend King or the academic prowess of Reverend Lawson. He was just a country boy from Chatham County, North Carolina.

Ernie and Matilda Moore showed him and his sisters and brothers how to pull cotton off the bolls from the time they were knee-high to a grasshopper. He could still feel it in his hands, that cotton soft and downy, the bolls though, sharp as needles. Those burrs pricked every one of his fingers until they bled, and it hurt like hell.

For years, Mama and Pop worked white peoples' land as share-croppers, they and their children clad in clothes that grew dusty and soil-caked between sunup and sundown. Though everything was still separate and unequal, the white landlord finally allowed his folks to farm twenty acres of his land and keep one-third of the crop. They raised cotton and corn and tobacco, never earning what they deserved, and with fickle harvests and unfair contracts, they remained indebted to that landowner and tied to the land. If you wanted to know the God to honest truth, sharecropping was just slavery by another name.

Mama always said, "The good Lord allowed us to open our eyes and see the sunrise of a new day. If that ain't a blessing, I don't know what is." While a beautiful sentiment, that never seemed like enough, and one time when he was about nine or ten, hot and sweaty in the fields, his mother laid down the heavy sack she'd been pulling and pointed a bloody finger at him. "There's a whole lot we ain't got in this world, but you, you now, you gon' go out there and get it for us." She sucked her finger dry, started humming to herself, picked up that sack, and sashayed on down the row of cotton plants.

She had been right because that's not how the story ended. Not in those cotton fields. The greatest fruits of his folks' labor had been their six children, all of whom left that farm—Darius being the youngest and last to go—each of them making their way in the world. He never asked for anybody's pity for how his family earned a living because when the struggle bore fruit in the lives of the children, and they found their way to freedom, that's all that mattered, and by that definition, Ernie and Matilda Moore were indeed people of means.

His parents taught him what ordinary folks could do when they put their minds to it. But it had been his Fisk classmate, Maurice, who gave him the opportunity.

After English class one day, the upperclassman stopped him in the hallway and spoke casually as he shuffled textbooks in his bag. "Say man, what you think about everything they're doing to us?"

Seeing the confusion on Darius's face, Maurice clarified. "I'm talking about how they treat us Negroes out here, man."

Without hesitation, Darius said, "It's an abomination."

That's when Maurice bent at the waist and tried to strangle his laugh with a cupped hand to his mouth. "I knew it. I hear how you speak in class. You got a way with words, man."

Darius didn't consider himself a great orator by any stretch of the imagination, but he had listened on the radio to almost every speech and interview King had done. He tuned his ear to every intonation, the meaning and melody of the preacher's words reminding him of the music he made with his own saxophone. Maurice convinced him they could use someone like him to inspire other ordinary students to do the most ordinary thing of all—sit down at a public lunch counter and mind their business.

***

AS SOON AS THEY ENTERED MCLELLAN'S, DARIUS COULD SMELL THE baked ham and cheese sandwiches and hear the familiar purr of the soda fountain. Whenever he bought a hot lunch here, he'd have to get it to go and eat it outside sitting on a street curb like some alley dog sniffing around for scraps. But not this day. A few steps over the threshold, and someone bumped into the back of him. Turning, he saw Errol Hankins stumbling over his own feet, his face breaking out into a sweat in spite of the cold.

"Watch where you're going, man," Darius said in a heavy whisper. "Just act normal."

He didn't irritate easily, especially not with friends like Errol, but in spite of his own words, there was nothing normal about this trip to the five-and-dime. What they were about to do could get them arrested— or even killed.

They hadn't walked in all at once; instead, a few entered at one time, spacing their arrival at least five minutes apart to thwart suspicion. Darius attempted to browse casually, fingering the texture of a wool sweater longer than necessary. A salesclerk peered at him across the clothing rack, and he wondered if she suspected anything or if this was merely the routine disdain directed at Negroes.

Moving to another aisle, he passed Diane Nash, an English major with blue-green eyes who could pass for white if she wanted, but instead had become one of the fiercest fighters for Negro rights.

After what seemed an eternity, the seven of them stepped over that imaginary line separating the sundry items for sale and the lunch counter, the line separating white from colored. The moment he took his seat on that stool and perused the menu like any other man, his humanity rose and filled his entire body. That one simple act, nothing more. Briefly, he broke character and grinned at Errol next to him, whose face mirrored that same exhilaration.

There wasn't much to laugh about for long though when he ordered a grilled cheese sandwich, a cherry soda, and a slice of apple pie.

"The lunch counter is closed," the waitress said in a huff. She fell all over her words and her orthopedic shoes to get away from them.

It wasn't long before the white mob showed up. Men whose faces turned ugly with their anger. Their sons by their sides watching their fathers closely as if learning to shave for the first time. Their scorn and their taunts banged around in his head, but he decided to turn back to his textbook and meditate on the words of great philosophers.

Our greatest glory is not in never failing, but in rising every time we fall. —Confucius

Great deeds are usually wrought at great risks. —Herodotus

In the midst of chaos, there is also opportunity. —Sun Tzu

The first principle of non-violent action is that of non-cooperation with everything humiliating. —Mahatma Gandhi

We are hard pressed on every side, but not crushed; perplexed but not in despair; persecuted, but not abandoned; struck down, but not destroyed. —Jesus, 2 Corinthians 4

They sat at that lunch counter for more than an hour, with police watching them get harassed but doing nothing to stop it. At one point Darius sensed someone close behind him and then that burning sting he would never forget. One of the men in that vicious mob pressed a lit cigarette to the back of his neck below his hairline. Darius watched his own fingers curl into fists on that counter as if of their own volition, and for a millisecond he thought he might ignore the words of King and Lawson and Gandhi and act on his righteous anger, act on the deep, aching pain in his neck that went straight to the bone.

Freda had already left the store by then, but he focused on the imprint of her beautiful face in his mind, not the pain. A young lady he didn't know well yet but wanted to know everything about. His daddy always said that when he met the right girl, he would know. There wouldn't be a voice coming down from the heavens, but he'd feel it in his bones. And he did.

She carried herself like a woman who knew her own mind and was comfortable going left when everyone else was going right. And when she moved, you couldn't help but crane your neck and follow her with your eyes. He was a man and definitely noticed the sway of her hips and the way she walked upright, no conceit, all confidence. The slope of her back a winding road to parts unknown. That first day when he offered to help her onstage at the chapel, he observed her skin smooth like butter on a hot biscuit. Maybe that burn had fried his brain a little and made him hallucinate.

Now, lying in bed, still in pain, his doubts about his own future and that of his people gradually began to subside. Being a sophomore in college, still in the dress rehearsal for real life, he rarely thought of more than music or this Movement he was now part of. That's why Darius recognized he was getting ahead of himself, crazy out of his mind on pain pills, but he saw it all plain as his hand in front of his face—a life with Freda as his wife, the two of them and their children truly living free because of what he had done today. He would do it again. Sit in, stand up, again and again. His destiny solidified like stone. While he was sitting at the lunch counter, he wanted to tell Freda all about it, reassure her, and restore her faith in him—so badly—but the distance between them thwarted his best efforts. What he desperately wanted to say was that for the first time in his life he felt like a man.

PART FOUR

Chicago, 1992

Tulip

On the day after the verdict in the trial of those police officers, Tulip might as well have been invisible at Mattingly. No one uttered Rodney King's name, not to her at least. They didn't even speak to her on the elevator, but instead moved around her as if she weren't there, rubbing it in with their cheerfulness that their side had won. Newspapers from around the world appeared daily stacked in neat piles on a table near the reception desk, and on her way to a meeting, she spotted most of the national papers with photos of a night of chaos filling the space above the fold. She quickly tucked one of the papers under her arm to read later, in private.

The meeting had been called by Bryce, and the entire staff jammed into one windowless all-purpose room. They sat shoulder to shoulder in straight-back chairs—the hard ones where you had to lift one butt cheek to let it rest and then alternate to the other. Considering all the money they spent on liquor for the night cruise, you'd think they could invest in more comfortable seating.

On days like these, every account executive entered the room with something to prove. Amanda and Mason walked in with their game faces locked in place and sat side by side right in front of Tulip, who had to beat back her own paranoia and flagging confidence. From the other side of the room, she caught Sharita's eye and, reading her roommate's face as well as she did, she could almost hear her confirming: *Yeah, they're up to some mess.*

Rudy plopped down next to her and handed her a well-worn Dale Earnhardt 1990 Winston Cup NASCAR champion seat cushion then slid a matching one under his own backside. Her friend loved stock car racing because it rewarded loyalty and had no pretention. Leaning toward Tulip so that only she could hear, he said, "They're just worried we'll want to make a jailbreak if we can look out a window and see actual sunlight. And if the chairs are too cushy, they're afraid somebody will fall asleep."

"Stop," she said, trying not to snort. "If I get the itis up in here, it's over."

She could hear Mason speaking loudly to the others sitting in his row. "I'm taking Feldman to dinner this week. You better believe he's signing with us when I'm finished!"

Rudy turned to her and rolled his eyes so far up into his head you could only see the whites of them.

"The waffle maker guy?" Darby said, laughing. "You're still chasing that business?"

"He's not just any guy, he's their chief waffle maker guy, and soon, he'll be an official client." For an entire year Mason had been wooing Adam Feldman, who headed one of the largest consumer brands in the Midwest, yet mediocrity hadn't stopped anyone from calling Mason a marketing genius. Bryce would be handing out promotions soon and everyone knew that winning new business almost guaranteed a move up the ladder.

In two long strides, their CEO walked from his front row seat to the podium, and Tulip was grateful for a reprieve from Mason's self-aggrandizement. Bryce stood there for a few seconds with a dramatic pause before he folded his hands in front of him like he was either praying or begging. "We need to talk about the proverbial elephant in the room—what's happening out in LA and how it might impact our clients. I'm sure you're all following the news reports."

Tulip glanced down at the newspaper resting on her lap and began reading the article.

RIOTERS LIT UP Los Angeles Wednesday night, setting more than 150 fires throughout the city, torching and looting stores in a reign of terror that people watched unfold live on television. Authorities report that four people have died in the mayhem and more than 100 are in area hospitals suffering from gunshot wounds, including a firefighter who was shot in the face.

The racial violence began after a jury found four white police officers not guilty in the beating of Rodney G. King. Governor Pete Wilson called in the National Guard to support local law enforcement in quelling the deadly rebellion, the largest since the 1965 Watts riot.

The intersection of Florence Boulevard and Normandie Avenue in South Central LA became the epicenter of violence that quickly spilled over into other parts of the city.

A day-two story where public interest might have begun to wane, yet the heat of the conflict out west still seared Tulip's face. Even in a straight reported piece, journalism with a capital J without any editorializing, reporters knew how to arrange facts on a page, using words like *riot* and *terror* to define a community and to stoke the rage and the fear she saw in the faces of her coworkers.

Public relations work required an almost obsessive fixation on the news—what happened, when, why, and how it might affect their clients' business.

Here we go. Did this open the door to the conversation none of these people wanted to have about justice denied to Rodney King and everyone who looked like him?

Running his hands through his hair, Bryce said, "Things are so volatile in LA, I don't want staff going there any time soon. We can take care of our clients by phone for now."

What was happening out west deserved more of a conversation than just employee travel restrictions. But leave it to Amanda to make things worse.

"Our clients' offices may be totally fine," she said. "Some of them closed because one of the main highways was shut down. But I think so far it's just been the liquor stores and fast-food places that have gotten torched, in the parts of town that were already, you know, bad. Nowhere near our clients."

A small knot of fury picked up steam inside Tulip and churned like a hurricane. As if operating outside her own body, she rose to her feet. What exactly had Amanda meant about the parts of town that were already bad? Which communities? Which people? She was sure she already knew the answer, but she wanted to force Amanda to say it in front of everyone. As she was about to speak, Rudy tugged on the sleeve of her blazer.

"Tulip, did you have something to add?" Bryce asked.

The pull on her sleeve grew stronger and more persistent and Tulip snatched her arm away. "No, nothing to say. Just stretching," she stammered, sinking into her seat.

She glared at Rudy for interrupting what she was about to do. Probably sensing her irritation with him, he stared straight ahead, nodding as if to say she had done the right thing. She caught the relief in Sharita's eyes across the room, as if some unforeseen peril had been averted. But Tulip wasn't as certain. Of course, Rudy had been protecting her from embarrassment and possibly career suicide. This job meant everything to her, but so did standing up for what was right, speaking out against injustice. That last part was new for her, but maybe what happened to Rodney King unleashed a burning fire within her that she never knew existed. Racial profiling had been around for years, but people in her circle didn't talk about it—until now that there was a video making it hard to ignore. This was her generation's first real connection to a protest movement. Everything else had been hearsay—history from her parents' era that she benefited from but would never understand for herself. A time and a struggle that didn't belong to her.

***

SLIPPING AWAY TO HER OFFICE AFTER THE MEETING, TULIP WORKED through her lunch hour, the only way she could get ahead at this agency. Work harder. Work longer. Work smarter. One of her clients, New Breeze laundry detergent, needed to distinguish itself as tough on dirt but gentle on your fabric and skin. Opening a thick three-ring binder, she pored over media clips about their chief competitor with the obvious, too on-the-nose brand name, Scrubbed. A brand soaring in sales for all the wrong reasons and getting slammed in news coverage because teenagers were hiding out in their laundry rooms at home, sniffing the detergent to get high. Tulip jotted notes on typing paper with ideas about how to capitalize on the misfortune of Scrubbed and pitch New Breeze as a detergent that smells good but not that good. Chewing on her pencil eraser, she decided this approach might reinforce a negative for her client's brand.

Stymied after an hour of thinking, she took a walk to stretch her legs and made a pit stop in the ladies' room. Tulip locked herself in a stall. She hadn't been in the bathroom a minute when she heard a symphony of flushes, then the click-clack of heels, and soon after, women's voices, shouting to be heard over the sound of running water and hand dryers.

"She tries so hard, it's pathetic," Amanda said. "And she makes everything about race. Who knows what she was going to rant about earlier? Now I'm not saying she doesn't work hard, but makes you wonder if she would even be here if not for all these diversity quotas."

Then, Darby's high-pitched voice rang out clear as a bell. "Yeah, if you have to use your race plus get your daddy to convince the CEO you deserve the job . . ."

Someone else finished her sentence. "Then maybe you don't deserve it."

Every alarm inside Tulip sounded at once as if on the same circuit; she knew they were talking about her. She stood as still as she could, her back against the door of the stall.

Then she heard Amanda again. "Have you noticed her cozying up to Bryce lately? There's no way she's getting a promotion—she's wasting her time."

Tulip almost forgot to take a breath, realizing she'd been holding it in in case they could hear her. You'd think that women would support and lift other women, but not these at Mattingly.

Another voice said, "Did you see that guy she brought on the boat?"

"Oh, yeah," Darby said. "I even talked to him. Not a lot going on upstairs. Nothing intellectual about him."

Key. Her heart stopped.

Darby continued, "Now I will admit he was cute and muscular, so he really doesn't have to say anything. It is almost summer, and I could go for a chocolate popsicle right now." You would've thought this was the funniest thing these women had ever heard from the way they carried on.

In her five-year career, Tulip had never expected to hear anything so vile in the office. In spite of every ugly thing they said, it was their laughter that made her want to fight somebody. When she heard the outer bathroom door slam shut and the voices disappear, she flushed the toilet and stepped out of the stall. She stumbled to the sink and stood there in stunned silence. Wobbly, her legs threatened to buckle, and she gripped the sides to steady herself against a headwind of anger and a wave of nausea. Her reflection stared back at her silently asking, *What you gon' do now?*

She thought of her man, Key, out there on his bus route driving to the point of exhaustion some days. Broad shoulders, full lips, and strong arms. And that's all those women saw in him. It struck her that they could objectify Key, reduce him to biceps and a butt, yet want to snatch him from her because they found themselves supremely deserving of whatever caught their eye.

Shame shot through her though because before she grew to love him, she only admired his raw good looks, how he lived in a world apart from her own, one that her parents had warned her away from . . . which made him more attractive. He worked a job she had taken for granted her entire life, never pausing to notice who drove the buses that took her to and from her destinations. Key had merely been a spontaneous, reckless choice, like when some stranger offered you a drag on a cigarette at a party and you took it and enjoyed it because it seemed cool at the time even though you didn't smoke.

Walking out of that bathroom, Tulip understood the unwritten code that what happened in the ladies' room stayed there. But those co-workers didn't deserve a label as respectable as *ladies*. They had crossed a line, and if not for her pristine upbringing and the Vance name she carried, she would have carefully removed her jewelry and applied Vaseline to her face, rationalizing that sometimes being ladylike was not a universally understood language for every woman. But they were at work, not on some street corner outside a club; and besides, she had to convince agency leaders that she could bring in new business and also that she deserved a promotion. The stakes were too high to act a fool.

***

At Manny's Deli in the South Loop, Gino, known in the city as the sandwich man, built a skyscraper of corned beef with his own two hands. He wielded a knife with the precision of a surgeon and the flair of a flame thrower. For a moment, Tulip forgot why she was there, caught up like everyone else watching this culinary performance. The chopping and yelling and meat grinding blended into indistinguishable sounds that made Tulip buzz with almost as much anticipation as she had for what she was about to do. But what if her plan backfired?

Tulip had timed it right to join the cafeteria line behind Adam Feldman from CookCo's waffle maker division. It was common knowledge around the Mattingly office that state senators, mayor's staff, city council members, and Adam dined for lunch at Manny's several days a week. Tulip had spotted them there before.

Word spread that Adam was a no fuss kind of guy who couldn't be sold on anything and only did business with people he liked. People he was comfortable with. And that wasn't a long list because he usually ate alone at Manny's at a table by the window. Tulip had bowed out of her usual Tuesday lunch run for Italian beef sandwiches at Al's with Sharita and Rudy. It was impossible to get anything past them, so she told them about her plan to make a pitch to Adam before Mason got to him first.

"Girl, go in there with the confidence of an average white man," Sharita said.

Rudy laughed. "Our balls are smaller than you think."

"Oh, I'm sure, but in your minds, they are gigantic," Sharita said.

Tulip pulled her shoulders back and pretended to exude confidence until it became natural. It wasn't like Tulip to sabotage another colleague and that's not what this was. Most of the account executives, like Mason, could be considered mediocre. They set up new business pitches the way everyone else did—one secretary calling another to set up a meeting with detailed presentation notes typed out on high-quality laser paper. But this appeal called for creativity. Mason never would have agreed to a joint pitch, certainly not with her, so she had no choice but to resort to an element of subterfuge.

Winning this account would put Mattingly in position to be the PR and marketing agency of record for CookCo's other product lines—everything from food processors to cutlery, cookware, and coffee makers. She knew what this account would mean for Mattingly's standing in the agency world, propelling them to the ranks of major players like Edelman, Burson-Marsteller, and FleishmanHillard. And winning such coveted new business might get her promoted.

Gino piled the meat, Swiss cheese, and sauerkraut on rye and stuck a few Reubens in the presser. Adam hadn't noticed her yet.

"Where you from?" Gino asked the line of customers, no one in particular.

"Chicago. South Side," Tulip answered right away, louder than necessary. Her voice reverberated oddly in her ears.

"Where on the South Side?" Gino asked.

"Pill Hill."

That's when Gino laughed and pointed to Adam. "You're legit, un-like this one here from Lincolnwood."

She hadn't meant to start a turf war but then she recognized the trash talking she might have heard from her father or Key over basket-ball or a game of Spades, and the knot in her stomach loosened. "Hey, what are you trying to say? I'm legit," Adam said, trying to sound edgier than his starched white shirt and slouchy black slacks.

"Ah, don't give me that bull." Gino lifted the presser handle and the most delicious smoke bloomed around them. "If your zip code doesn't start with six-oh-six, you're not from Chicago."

Riding this wave of frivolity and summoning courage from God knows where, Tulip addressed Adam. "Well, I will vouch for your Chicago cred here under one condition, and that's if you'll join me for lunch." This man didn't know her from a hole in the wall and her suggestion set him back on his heels.

"Well, I uh—" Adam stammered.

"If you already have a lunch companion, never mind."

"Um, no," he said, caught off-guard and unsure of how to ditch her. "Let's find a table."

They found one in the back near a window. "So, I assume you work in the city. What do you do?"

Here was her chance.

"I'm in public relations with Mattingly, the agency."

Adam's eyes burned a hole into the side of her face. "What is this all about? I've met with your agency in the past and have another meeting this week with one of your colleagues. What exactly is the meaning of you approaching me here?"

All of a sudden, she lost her appetite. Self-doubt tore at her insides. She lacked the gift or curse of Mason's brazen salesmanship. Yet she wanted the CookCo business just as badly, maybe even more.

"You're right," she said. "I maneuvered things a bit so that we could have lunch together." When Adam bristled, his neck reddening, Tulip held up her potato pancake. "Manny's is almost as famous for these

latkes as they are for corned beef Reubens. People can't get enough of
how crispy and golden brown they are and it's an experience that reminds you of home and, for some, a religious tradition. That's the buzz
we need to create for your waffle maker. That it's about more than
breakfast. When a family has time to sit down together for a meal, it's a
bonding experience. It's history they're making."

Adam remained quiet and stopped chewing for the first time since
they sat down, and Tulip worried she may have taken it too far with the
comparison to latkes. Had she been culturally inappropriate, grasping
for any advantage she could in this classic old Jewish deli? Her father
always said the relationship between Blacks and Jews was complicated.
A tenuous bond had existed for decades, but things got dicey when they
began comparing atrocities—like which was worse, the transatlantic
slave trade or the Holocaust. Putting oppression on a scale netted no
winners.

Adam held up his potato pancake and Tulip could tell he was
locked in some memory. "Every Hanukkah, my mother used to fry
these in oil, and usually my job was to get the applesauce ready for
dipping. But one year when I was about seven, she let me flip a few of
the latkes fully realizing I might burn myself. And I did. A lot. Still
have the grease burns to show for it. It became our thing every year
though. A tradition."

Excited now, Tulip said, "That's it. Your experience growing up is
the kind of story we need to sell your waffle makers. Sure, we can ad-
vertise, but it's the credible, personal stories that will get the attention
of journalists."

"I'm intrigued," he said. "But your tactics to get to me are question-
able."

The game was changing now, the pieces on the board shuffling right
in front of Tulip, and she had to calculate her next move fast. While
the Mattingly handbook could be an enigma, it definitely emphasized
a united team approach, speaking in one voice to serve the client. She
didn't want Adam to think she was undercutting Mason.

"I realize my approach may be unorthodox, but I believe in your product, and I needed to share my vision with you face-to-face. Mason can run an amazing paid campaign that will guarantee your message gets out. But if you want people to trust your product and your brand, let me pitch consumer reporters I know. It won't cost you a thing and you'll earn credibility that can lead to awareness and sales over time."

Tulip was bluffing a bit about all her reporter relationships, but her rolodex had been steadily growing over the years.

Adam didn't speak at first and the din of deli noise filled the silence. Then he took another bite of his potato pancake. "This is the kind of passion and creativity I like from an agency. You make salient points. I'll think about it."

Adam hadn't agreed to hire Mattingly, but Tulip had gotten the agency closer to a deal than ever before. With fanfare, he ordered raspberry rugelach and chocolate-dipped macaroons. "Mazel tov," he said. Matching his mood, though with a degree of uncertainty, she repeated, "Mazel tov."

***

On the ride home from work, people shuffled on and off the bus with their shoulders sagging under the weight of debt, heartbreak, or the monotony of it all. Tulip would have stood in the aisle and announced her potential good news to everybody if she thought it would have made them smile even for a little while. But nobody on that bus cared about your joy or your pain but you. At least she was able to celebrate with Key, whom she'd called from her office to whisper-scream the news that she had gotten further with Adam than Mason, who had been trying for years to wear him down.

Like she did every workday, Tulip tried to sit near Key at the front of the bus where she could catch his eye and openly stare at his profile— strong and beautiful, always in control at the helm of the bus, his hand guiding the wheel while his torso arched and bent with each turn. The smile he flashed her from the driver's seat said *I'm proud of you. I knew you could do it. That's my baby.* It was impossible to have a private conversation on a crowded bus, but they managed to do it anyway through glances when he braked at intersections or pulled over for new passengers to board.

Those women at Mattingly got themselves all hot and bothered over the physical parts of Key, who objectively was fine as hell, but they didn't know the most real, genuine Key.

Pain shot through Tulip's head from front to back thinking about the awful things those women said about her in the bathroom. She had long suspected they didn't think she deserved her spot at Mattingly, but hearing them say the words rattled her. When would her performance and effort be enough to shut them up, to silence their chatter that kept up a racket in her head?

Tulip scooted from the aisle to the window and gazed outside, her breath fogging the glass. She relived the lunch with Adam Feldman to lift her mood. She imagined the kickoff meeting with the CookCo team after the contract got signed and began thinking about the project plan she would develop. The list of reporters she thought of to pitch kept growing. Before long, this one-of-a-kind waffle maker would grace the countertops of every kitchen in America. She knew she was getting ahead of herself, but she couldn't help it.

By the time the bus got as far south as Bronzeville, the white businesspeople had gotten off already. When the bus braked at a stop on King Drive, a wisp of a woman climbed aboard carrying an infant in one arm and pulling a reluctant toddler with her other hand. They took the only empty aisle seat, which happened to be next to Tulip. Following right behind them, another woman wearing long locs beneath a Kangol got on, too. The two women were in conversation about an organizing meeting, it seemed.

"We're trying to get justice for Latasha," said the locs lady. "LA is all fired up and so are we. It's gonna be a march in the middle of June and we need the community to come out. But there's a lot of planning to do.

Can we count on you for the meeting tomorrow night?" The woman's locs fell in front of her face, covering her eyes.

The mother blew air through her lips, clearly exhausted, and adjusted the baby in her arms, forcing a pacifier between his lips when he started fussing. "Yeah, I stay out there at the Ida B's, but I don't know about a meeting. I got a lot going on." She gestured to her children, including the little girl in the yellow jumper dress who was now wrapped around Tulip's left leg.

"Trust me, there will be plenty of moms with kids there. Everybody watches everybody's kids at these meetings so don't worry. We have to do this for Latasha. For all of us. That could've been me or you."

Confusion clouded the mother's face, and she said what Tulip had been thinking. "Okay, I don't even know who Latasha is."

The organizer swept her hair away from her face and brushed off a guy hawking Chicago Bulls T-shirts and ball caps. She spread her legs apart to keep her balance as the bus lurched around a corner. "Why do you think they're burning up LA right now? It's bigger than what happened to Rodney King, as fucked up as that was. This Korean lady who owned a store out there shot Latasha Harlins in the back of the head. Killed that girl over a bottle of orange juice that she didn't even steal. Latasha had the money right there in her hand. Fifteen years old and now she's dead. That lady won't hardly spend any time in jail."

Tulip logged this information in her head, the pieces slowly falling into place. She had forgotten Latasha's story. That teenage girl was killed a couple weeks after Rodney King got beaten up. No wonder LA erupted the way it did. Of course, people would link the two cases, both involving senseless violence against Black folks. Out of the corner of her eye, she snuck glances at Key, who was talking to a guy buying a transfer who wanted to know which bus he needed to take to get to a tailor shop on the west side. She couldn't tell if he was listening to this conversation about the protest they were planning in Ida B. Wells.

When the bus stopped, the little girl in yellow grinned at the sound of the air brakes squeaking and gripped Tulip's thigh as if she were high atop a ride on a rollercoaster at Six Flags. To her, the world wasn't a truly scary place yet, only in the make-believe ways that seemed designed for her entertainment. Tulip smiled back, wishing for a world that would preserve this child's innocence, but she knew better and scribbled a note to remind herself of the address for the organizing meeting.

Key

Key watched streaks of sunlight play across his bedroom ceiling. He thought of the different versions of Tulip—hurt and confused that night of the Rodney King verdict, yet proud and determined, reaching for the next promotion, desperately wanting her family, everybody she loved, and the world to be at peace. He nurtured ambitions of his own, but his desires were simpler. If he had basketball, wings from Harold's, hip-hop, money in his pocket, and Tulip by his side, he was good. Real good.

The night he accompanied Tulip to her company's boat party left a bad taste in his mouth, and Key had been turning that evening over and over in his mind like a steak on the grill. With her on his arm, he stood taller—a stray look or encouraging word from Tulip strengthened him as a man, molded him into everything he imagined he could become someday and more. But around other people, like on that fancy boat, Tulip changed into someone else, and Key shrunk so far into himself there was little left. He hadn't let too many women get close enough to make him feel that small. But every man could point to at least one.

One afternoon a couple years ago, Key had been an hour into his shift on the No. 3 King Drive bus, but already, his shoulders ached from leaning over the steering wheel. His eyes burned with exhaustion, and he struggled to keep them open. His body moved by muscle memory, turning and stopping the bus at all the right places. Calling out street names he recited sometimes in his sleep. *Van Buren. Harrison. Balbo.* Some little bean-pie-eating, bowtie wearing dude on the bus was the one who told him Balbo had been a strongman for Mussolini back in the day. He'd said, "A fascist. And you're calling his name out loud and proud like he's the Messiah." Who knew? He liked the way the syllables of *Bal-bo* vibrated deep in his throat. Key paid no mind to history or politics. Just making it minute-to-minute provided enough stress. He concentrated on the things he could feel, like the rubber of a basketball in his hands or that thump in his chest from the bass of some song he loved.

He'd stayed up late the night before watching the Bulls spank the Hornets by eleven. Then early that morning as he had all week, Key helped his parents unpack inventory at their beauty supply store.

Later that afternoon, a young woman in a lavender sweater dress and high-heeled black boots got on his bus. It was packed, but an empty seat opened up in the front next to the window. A hustler who rode all day selling hot goods sat beside her in the aisle seat. The man performed his usual routine, opening his dingy wool coat, the sunlight catching all the shine from the lining. "Want to buy a watch?" he asked. She drew up into a ball and pressed her body against the window and Key thought she might open it, stick her head out, and yell for help. Or worse, jump out the damn window. The whole thing cracked him up and he soon forgot how tired he was.

"Hey, knock it off. She's not interested," he finally said, but only after he'd been thoroughly entertained by her disgust.

Key had never seen her on his route before. He would've remembered. Watching her unwrap the winter scarf from her head reminded him of an apple being peeled. At last, her brown hair fell to her shoulders slick as a horse's mane. As the bus emptied the farther south they went, he asked her name, real casual, keeping his eyes on the road, showing enough interest in her answer, but not too much. She hesitated for a beat, likely trying to decide in that split second whether or not to give her real name, a fake one, or none at all. The way she separated each syllable of Tulip made it sound at least to his ears like she'd said *two lips*. Leaving an image like that in a brother's fertile mind could be trouble. So, when he came to the next stoplight, he made the effort to focus his eyes on hers.

A mini boom box he kept in the bus window played softly—only the clean versions of songs, so no riders could claim offense and report him to the city. Smelling the money and class on Tulip right away, he didn't expect her to know much about music, at least not his kind of music. He asked if she had any requests.

"I'm an old-school hip-hop head," she said.

He hid his surprise. "Okay, all right now. So you like Run-DMC, right?" He glanced over at her, expecting to see confusion on her pretty face.

"Sure, but I like to dig way back in the crate for Sugarhill Gang and Kurtis Blow. The real architects of hip-hop."

Key kept his eyes on the street in front of him, not wanting to let on he was impressed. Who was this woman and where had she come from? When the bus began to empty out, she stretched her long legs across the seat and rested her back against the window. Girls like her didn't ride the bus and he had promised to call out her stop when she admitted she was heading to someone's house for a book club meeting and didn't know where to get off. But he rolled right past it not saying a damn thing and she didn't know any better.

She forgave him for it eventually and, realizing her office was on his route, she started showing up on his bus. Through the long slog of winter and into the burst of spring, they treated those bus rides as dates. A few months into their relationship, she admitted her parents had bought her a new car to travel downtown to work so she wouldn't have to slum with the masses on public transportation. They even paid ridiculous monthly fees for her to park downtown. And crazy as it sounded, she would leave her folk's house in her Saab, park a few miles away, and catch the bus.

Key wondered why she chose to ride the bus, to breathe in that cocktail of urine and body funk and chicken nuggets. An act of defiance against her parents, maybe. But he liked to think it had something to do with him. When he wasn't collecting bus fares or belting out stops, they debated, whether it was the lyrical merits of KRS-One and Slick Rick or a choice for the best barbecue in town between Leon's and Lem's. Next to the grit and grime of his bus, Tulip bloomed before his eyes— beautiful, confident, and unexpected, a flower opening to him as her name promised.

He was a man—a visual creature—and he had plucked his share of flowers over the years. If nothing else, he was honest and he could admit it took time for his heart to catch up to his eyes. But when it happened, it struck him like the crack of a bat against a ball in the bottom of the ninth of the World Series. In months, it seemed they had traversed the whole country in that bumpy old bus.

The rhythm of them together came as natural to him as breathing. The first time they seemed out of sync had been one day last March when Tulip was riding his bus and he fumbled with the FM dial until he got to WGCI. They were in a news break, and he twisted the dial.

"No, go back there," Tulip said.

"They ain't playing nothing."

"I want to hear what they were saying."

Flipping back to that station, all he could make out were raised voices, people yelling. Sirens. Then the announcer repeated what Tulip must have heard a snatch of before. Cops had chased some Black dude out in LA. Rodney King. They beat him. Beat him bad. Yes, it was fucked up and likely racist, but it was too far away for Key to get caught up in that bullshit.

Tulip stared out the window as if she could see all the way to California. "It happened weeks ago but I can't stop thinking about that man. They could've killed him," she said.

The whole thing was wrong but not unusual. Once he'd seen one man shoot another's face off in a pool hall over a bad bet. Then there was the time a wino got to weaving in the aisle every time Key hit his brakes, and a cop who happened to be riding that day cracked a baton over the guy's head to teach him a lesson.

Maybe Tulip saw something outside that bus window that he didn't. The only thing Key could make out on the other side of the windshield was the Check Cashing store with its sign lit up except for the "g" that had burned out. And the asphalt running under the wheels of his bus. The asphalt that told stories of beauty and bloodshed in this city. He learned a long time ago to keep his eyes on the beauty or he'd go under.

Tulip

Back home at her apartment, Tulip couldn't stop thinking about the woman on the bus with the loc'd hair and the event she was planning. That community had nothing to do with her and she should have put it out of her mind, but she couldn't. She handed a chilled peach-flavored Bacardi Breezer to Sharita and kept a coconut one for herself.

"Lord, what a day. It feels so good to be home." Sharita's long legs dangled over the arm of the love seat. She cradled her sketch pad in her lap, drawing a nature scene, a far cry from the concrete of the city.

Normally Tulip kept her worlds separate, but rooming with Sharita made the overlap fun. They could talk about all the cornballs at work without having to explain who's who or the nuances of hierarchy in the agency or personality ticks. It also helped that Sharita worked in graphic design, so they never competed professionally. But sometimes she had to exercise patience, reminding herself how different the two women were.

Casually, Tulip said, "I met this woman on the bus coming home and she's planning a meeting in Ida B. Wells to talk about everything happening out in LA. That teen girl, Latasha Harlins, who was killed for something she didn't do, and the Rodney King verdict. It's too much."

The words sounded like rambling even to her own ears and she waited for a reaction from Sharita, but her roommate's eyes stayed on the paper as she shaded a lush forest with her graphite pencil.

Tulip waited, and after a minute, Sharita's pencil stilled, and she glanced up at her. "Hey, I pay my taxes and I vote now, thanks to you bugging me. But when I get done with all of Mattingly's bullshit, at the end of the day I just want to draw. Not for the agency, but for me. And I want to have my drink, that's it." She popped the cap on her bottle.

When Tulip stared at her roommate, Sharita said, "What do you want from me? I know you're all worked up and that's cool."

"Why aren't you?" Tulip said in a small voice.

Sharita swung her drink carelessly and took a swig. "Look, I know what we face every single day. That's just the way it is, one slap in the face after another. Just last week, I went all over the North Side trying to find a furniture store that sold the drafting table I wanted. I finally found one and the owner told me the table was very expensive and they don't do layaway." She swallowed and held Tulip's gaze.

"That's messed up." A new fire kindled in Tulip's belly. "What did you say?"

"What could I say and what good would it do? I walked right up out of there with my money in my purse. They sure as hell won't get my business. I know what we're up against, but I don't need to meet about it."

Sharita returned to her sketch pad and Tulip watched her, silently trying to understand what made some feel defeated or just resigned and others defiant in the face of horrible injustice.

It wasn't in everyone's constitution to fight back and not everybody saw their destiny linked to that of others, and that didn't make them selfish. Tulip reminded herself of this, but without support from Sharita, Key, or her parents, she felt alone and a little crazy inserting herself in other people's struggles.

The doorbell rang. Tulip got up and grabbed her Breezer before opening the door to greet Rudy. He brushed right by her to head to the kitchen to fix himself a bowl of cereal and pour from a jug of two percent milk. That man could consume cereal day or night, and he knew where

Tulip kept the case of Breakfast Bears the client sent to her as part of their promotions campaign.

"Now it's officially a party," Sharita said, clearly anxious for an excuse to change the subject and the mood in the room. She walked over to the stereo to play Chubb Rock's "Treat 'Em Right."

Putting the protest meeting out of her mind for now, Tulip danced and flung her hair, which still bounced after that last blowout. She had been waiting for Rudy to arrive to share her news. "You may be looking at Mattingly's newest account director after my little potential coup at lunch today."

Rudy seemed truly stunned. "So, your meeting with that CookCo guy went well! Did Bryce offer you account director? Bypassing account supervisor? That's unheard of. He must have big plans for you."

Maybe Tulip had exaggerated. "No, no. He didn't promise me anything," she said, explaining how she had finagled a lunch with Adam and how receptive he had been to her pitch.

"Whoa, that's what I'm talking about," Sharita said. "You know those chicks in the office will be hot about this. They're already playing dirty, acting like they can take your man and question your right to be at the agency."

"Wait a minute." Rudy's bowl made a loud clank hitting the glass of the coffee table. "Have you been holding out on me?" He legitimately looked offended, as if Tulip had sided against him in some death-defying duel.

Before Tulip could answer, Sharita blabbed everything she knew and half she didn't about what happened in the ladies' room. Tulip had only shared this with Sharita when they bumped into each other at the copy machine and her roomie noticed her tear-stained cheeks. Knowing her friend, she would have bugged her relentlessly until she gave up the goods. Tulip hadn't even told Key and didn't plan to. To those women, he had been a nameless body, someone to objectify and use as a weapon against her. The bile that had risen in her throat in that bathroom tasted fresh again. "Sharita!" she scolded her friend.

"And they had the nerve to insinuate you were an affirmative action hire?" Rudy looked appalled. "Why didn't you tell me?" He took a drink from his mango cooler.

The three of them stuck together like glue in the office and at the bars and clubs on weekends. But here's where things got tricky. Rudy was cool, very cool as a matter of fact, but he wasn't a Black woman and never would be.

"You know I didn't mean any harm, Rudy. I didn't think you'd understand. And besides, what they said hurt. It was humiliating and I didn't want to repeat it to anybody," she said, giving Sharita the stink eye. "And obviously, I shouldn't have told big-mouth over here either."

Liquor and milk together always made Rudy a bit weepy. "Well, I'm not just anybody. You didn't think I'd understand? I may be white but I'm gay and white," he said. "It isn't easy for me in that office either."

Tulip and Sharita sighed and gave each other the look they always did when Rudy tried to compare being Black and being gay. "Let's not go there," Tulip said. This turned out to be a knot for them to untangle again and again. A game that was fixed from the start. His longtime boyfriend had died of AIDS years ago, and Rudy hadn't been the same since with no real family to anchor him except for his friendship with them. The invisible fourth leg in their friendship stool was a man they'd never met but knew through Rudy's stories. Colton, a man corn-fed and bred in Iowa. A stalwart upbringing in 4H club with tractor pulls and pig races. It was Colton who had introduced Rudy to NASCAR. Nobody knew how Colton contracted the AIDS virus, and it didn't matter. Certainly not to Rudy, who took care of him until the end.

At work, everybody knew Rudy as the big strapping photog who carried fifty pounds of video equipment on his back without complaining. Whenever somebody in the office said something ignorant and heartless about the AIDS crisis or gay people, Rudy would laugh so he didn't stand out and call attention to himself or rouse any suspicion about his sexual identity. Then he'd curse them under his breath, only loud enough for Tulip or Sharita to hear.

They moved to sit on either side of him and each put a head on his shoulder, something they did when Rudy crawled into some hidden, unreachable place. The little bears in the milk had turned soggy.

"Boy, you know we can never keep milk in this house with you around," Tulip said.

"Milk, Twinkies, Hawaiian Punch, and I'm talking the two-liter bottle I just bought yesterday," Sharita said.

After waiting a beat, Rudy snorted. "You are lying. I only drank half that bottle. Oh, and did she actually have the nerve to say 'chocolate popsicle'?"

His reaction inspired Tulip to stand and dramatize what could have happened in that bathroom, hands on her hips with a theatrical walk from the couch to the TV and back. "I was pissed. I was ready to take off my earrings."

Sharita stared at her. "Girl, your ears aren't pierced, and you hardly ever wear clip-ons so stop."

"You know what I mean."

"What I know is we're spending way too much time on those corn-balls at work when we should be celebrating our girl." Sharita raised her bottle. "To Tulip, for getting the agency one step closer to new business and for handling her business like a champ. Yes, we're claiming this one. May you smash it when Bryce starts handing out those promotions."

"And may you smash all those hating heifers like ants," Rudy said, and they clinked their bottles for a toast.

"I'll drink to that," Tulip said. "Hear hear."

PART FIVE

Nashville, 1960

Freda

The week after the sit-ins, Freda joined Cora and Evaline in the dining hall where they pushed waxy gray meatloaf across their plates, doused the mixed vegetables with salt to flavor them, and pretended the powdered mashed potatoes tasted as creamy and buttery as what their mothers made.

"I might need to work in this kitchen to make some money," Cora confessed, dimpling her potatoes with two green peas to make the face of a snowman or a ghost.

Evaline said, "A few of the downtown stores are hiring counter girls. You could stretch out your arm and let those wealthy men sniff your wrist. If I weren't dating Ambrose, I might consider that myself."

She had started seeing Ambrose shortly after that day in the courtyard when Gerald took a liking to Freda. Snagging a future doctor—and a Meharry one at that—turned out to be quite the coup for both of them. And of course, Evaline was joking about the counter girls because department stores didn't hire Negroes.

Cora's eyes hadn't left her mashed potatoes.

"What is it, honey?" Freda gently rubbed her friend's back.

Cora's eyes glazed. "I got a letter from the Office of Student Accounts saying I'm behind on my tuition." After a pause, she quietly added, "Two months behind."

"Have you asked your parents about it?" Evaline said. "There could be a perfectly good explanation."

"That's right," Freda said. "Maybe their payment got lost in the mail. Sometimes my care packages come weeks after Mama sends them."

Cora shook her head. "No, it's not the mail. My folks aren't bringing home the money they used to."

She went on to explain they were teachers and had been using a pot-bellied stove to heat a frame school building with no windows, and the structure caught fire for the second time, leaving the students without a school and Cora's parents without jobs. They were using their own money to buy school supplies and educate the children themselves until the county found them a new space.

"I wonder if it's this hard for white teachers trying to educate white children," Freda said, unusual emotion raking her voice, sharpening the syllables. Hearing her friend's story broke something open inside her and she began tallying all the wrongs she'd either experienced or heard about during the six months she'd been in Tennessee. "They've segregated everything down here—bathrooms, lunch counters, even schools, and we always come out on the bottom."

"You right about that," Cora said. "The powers that be don't want to put all that money into Negro schools and my folks and the others from that school have to be so careful when they ask for help, polite you know, so they don't come across as offending or wanting too much. Well, I'm getting tired of being polite."

Truth be told, Freda was tiring of it, too. She had been naive about so much all these years. Of course, she understood that some less fortunate students and families struggled to pay tuition, but assumed benevolent associations and missionaries stepped in to cover the costs. If she were honest, she hadn't thought much about students who couldn't afford to be here because Mama and Papa told her not to worry about money.

A fine, proper education was her birthright, they always said from the time she started first grade.

"Maybe we can help with money for the school in Murfreesboro and for your tuition," Evaline said. Her mother worked as an attorney, one of the first Negro lawyers in Detroit, and certainly one of only a handful of female lawyers in the city. Her father was a college professor. Similar to Freda's parents, her folks regularly sent her care packages with pound cakes and spending money. Together, between both families, they would have more than enough to cover two months' tuition.

Pushing her plate aside, Freda leaned forward, her elbows on the table, and took Cora's hands into her own. "Evaline's right. Let us help. We can't lose you."

Those tears that threatened to spill earlier overflowed their banks now as Cora looked from one of her friends to the other, overwhelmed by their generosity.

"I love you both for this, but I couldn't accept—" she said, blowing air through her lips as if she were cooling a cup of coffee.

"Now hush," Freda said, unsure of how her parents would respond to this most unusual financial request, yet convinced she could persuade them. "You're a woman of God, right? So, receive your blessings instead of fighting them."

AS THEY WALKED OUT TOWARD THE EXIT OF THE DINING HALL with their arms linked, they noticed a crowd gathering. Mostly students, a few faculty members. A young woman's muffled voice said something about protest and momentum. "We did what we came to do Valentine's Day weekend, but we're not done yet," she said.

"Here we go again," Evaline said.

"What's this all about?" Cora whispered, squeezing her friends' arms.

"I don't know." Freda studied the crowd warily, feeling uneasy.

Her Valentine's date with Gerald never happened. What she had seen at McLellan's would forever remain etched in her mind. It was all over the news, a constant reminder of the hatred none of them could outrun with their money or fancy educations. When she had returned to Jubilee Hall, she collapsed on her bed in tears. She called Gerald, her voice shaky, telling him she didn't feel like celebrating. After seeing news reports, her parents called, concerned, warning her not to get mixed up in any disturbances.

There had been no riots or arrests, but that did little to quell Freda's terror. The sit-in had not been a spontaneous act of righteous indignation. She heard talk around campus that they had planned it for months and met up that morning at the Arcade on Fifth Avenue and then fanned out from there to Kress's, Woolworth's, and McLellan's. When the clock struck 12:40 that afternoon, they all bought items and sat down at the lunch counters of each store. Those businesses closed their dining services for the day, but none of them bowed to demands to desegregate. So what had her classmates accomplished?

As if in answer to that question, the young woman with short brown curls framing her face spoke directly into the microphone this time. "We will sit in again and again until they treat us as equals. We need as many of you as possible on Big Saturday. We're going back to Woolworth's, Walgreens, and McLellan's."

A few people called out *that's right* in a show of support and the crowd thickened in the dining room. Tables were pushed aside to accommodate more students who seemed especially emboldened when they stood, stomped their feet, and pumped their fists in the air. No one said the revolution would be a quiet one.

Evaline whispered, "My mother told me that Sammy Davis Jr. is going to hold a jazz benefit concert in New York late in the summer to raise money for this sort of thing, for civil rights causes."

"Really?" Freda said, finding it hard to believe that such a big star would be involved in something like this.

"That's exactly what she said, and you know my parents get tickets to all the major performances. My mother also told me that Aretha Franklin has been one of the biggest backers of the movement."

Freda wondered why Negro entertainers would attach their names to such activity when they already had the world at their feet clamoring for their voices.

"Thinking about joining us next time?" Darius had come up behind her. He had a fresh haircut but appeared to be wearing the same oversize suit he had on at McLellan's. She jabbed her finger at his chest. "You think this is funny, some game, don't you? You could've gotten me, all of us, killed that day. And for what? So you could make a point and be right?"

Her fury came hot and fast, and it dawned on her how scared she had been that day. His eyes didn't hold the same uncertainty she'd recognized when he looked at her from across the lunch counter Saturday. A steely resolve steadied him now and hardened his jaw.

Evaline and Cora stood beside her with their mouths open, unsure of what was happening. She had told them about her shopping trip to the five-and-dime when the sit-in happened. You had to be a recluse or dead not to have heard about the protests, so she couldn't very well keep it a secret. But she carefully omitted the parts about Darius because they knew nothing of how this boy both intrigued and agitated her.

Before Darius could address her accusation, the female student at the microphone called his name and asked him to come forward to speak. His eyes found Freda's for only a split second, and then he belonged to the crowd. He animated the room and spoke in the urgent, clipped tones of a young man too proper to be a preacher and not glib or devious enough to be a con man. The condition of the Negro right now couldn't have been worse, but if you asked Freda, he was selling freedom to anybody foolish enough to believe they'd get free this side of heaven.

Darius gripped the microphone with both hands. "We can sit in these classrooms in our finest clothing and fill our minds with the loftiest of ideas and ultimately graduate with letters behind our names.

But we can't sit at a lunch counter and drink a milkshake? There's something wrong with that." Students met his rhetoric with thunderous applause.

Then Darius transitioned smoothly from talking about segregation in public accommodations to voting rights. It reminded her of listening to him play the sax the day she met him as he moved effortlessly from cool, soft jazz to hot and loose bebop.

"We wouldn't accept a watered-down drink." Darius lifted his arms, the elbows of his threadbare suit shiny and showing its years. "So why would we accept a watered-down Civil Rights Act?"

Sanctified echoes of *well now* and *I know that's right* and *say it again* bounced off the tile floors, Negro students blooming with indignation the more Darius talked. President Eisenhower signed the Civil Rights Act into law this week and Freda had heard it would make it easier for Negroes to vote. The Fifteenth Amendment had said it was against the law to discriminate against Negroes who wanted to exercise their right to vote. But southern states seemed to always find a way to get around the law.

"Have you ever seen a man without teeth? His jaw sags. Limp. That's what this law is. Limp. No teeth to hold it up. Bloated in its early promises but emaciated in the end."

Darius was flanked by Professor Redfield and Dr. Stephen Wright himself, the president of Fisk, while the crowd roared its approval. Both men praising Negro students for their discipline and moral leadership. Freda was surprised school faculty and administrators went along with something this radical. Yet standing on the periphery of the circle, the more she listened, she surprised herself by nodding and slowly beginning to clap. Glancing to her left and right, she noticed Cora and Evaline clapping as well. Maybe this was a natural instinct, like getting swept up in the soaring oratory in church when the pastor worked the congregation into a frenzy at the climax of his sermon.

And none of this uproar would be over anytime soon. Supporters working with Darius moved through the crowd handing out yellow flyers with bold black lettering. It simply read *Don't Forget! Be there Feb. 27 for Big Saturday. We need YOU.*

Darius talked about plans for a larger sit-in covering more Nashville stores, and the passion in his voice needled its way under her skin like one of those wood splinters she used to get in her finger as a kid. The faces in this crowd proved that Darius had a way of casting a spell on people, and she, too, was falling under it.

13

Freda

The evening of her first date with Gerald, Freda barreled down the elegant staircase of Jubilee Hall two steps at a time until the voice of Mother Gaines at the top landing stopped her. "Now you know better than that. Make him wait. Make him work to earn your time and consideration. You'll thank me later," she said.

Freda slowed her descent. Gerald sat precariously perched on the edge of a classic Victorian chair with his hands folded, looking anxious. He'd been disappointed when she rescheduled their Valentine's Day date. All the uproar over the sit-ins had interrupted their plans and he resented the intrusion as much as she did. When she reached the bottom step with Mother Gaines behind her, he stood.

"Wow, you look amazing." Gerald's eyes roved over her like he was doing a quality inspection on an assembly line.

"Thank you. Ready to go?"

"Not so fast." Mother Gaines's voice grated like nails on a chalkboard.

Freda hoped the old woman hadn't noticed her rolled up pants legs hidden under her light spring coat. It was well past 2 o'clock on a Saturday, but dresses could be so primitive and fussy sometimes.

Mother Gaines said, "Now listen, young man. You need to have her back here by ten o'clock. That is curfew."

Freda waved to Mother Gaines, knowing full well she would miss curfew and that Evaline had agreed to prop open the side door of the dorm for her that night.

"Sorry about that." Freda squeezed Gerald's hand, knowing how intimidating her house mother could be.

"I think you offended her hustling us out of there so fast." Gerald laughed. "I would've won her over, you know."

Around the corner, down the street, and out of sight of Jubilee Hall and the prying eyes of Mother Gaines, Gerald led her to his 1952 Lincoln Capri coupe. She leaned against the hood while he looked for his keys.

"Ooh, ouch." The steel burned like an oven on her bare legs, even at dusk.

"Sorry," he said, opening the passenger door for her.

"I think something's wrong with your car. Why is it so hot?"

Frown lines creased his handsome face. "Yeah, maybe I need some coolant. I'll get to it." He explained that the car had been a hand-me-down gift from his family friend, Uncle Teddy, and some part was always going out faster than Gerald could afford to get it fixed. Without much discussion about money, Freda got the impression that part of Gerald's dream of becoming a doctor was tied up in his desire to make enough money that he never had to worry about it again.

Gerald's money obviously went into stylish clothes—the green ascot that matched his suit and the pomade that made his wavy hair behave itself and stay in place on a chilly drive with the windows down. They drove around the city, admiring its lights and each other, until they wound up close to campus again and parked along Jefferson Street to take a stroll.

When Freda first arrived in Nashville, she expected to see what Northerners pictured when they thought of the South: people in overalls speaking in a slow southern drawl, working hard, but having little to show for it. Not assumptions she took pride in by any means. She hadn't imagined this—Negroes on Jefferson Street, steps from campus, owning practically everything: bakeries and ice cream parlors, insurance companies and auto repair shops, dry cleaners and shoeshine stores, barbershops and beauty salons, churches and chicken shacks.

On this Friday night on the town, she walked down Jefferson with Gerald, his arm encircling her waist, and being with him this way felt right. Freda absorbed everything with the wide eyes of a child, mainly the entrepreneurs without storefronts claiming their piece of the pie. Supporting them made her feel a part of their dreams for themselves and this street. Miss Viola stood in her front yard calling out numbers like she was playing a Bingo card.

"Twenty-five cents, y'all. Fish sandwich for a quarter." Her high-pitched, sweet voice as distinct as that of a hummingbird. The stout woman with bare tree stump legs bent over a black caldron. Her hands—shriveled and speckled by age—dipped catfish in hot oil.

With the smell of fried fish and open beer cans in the air, Gerald and Freda looked down at the fine clothing they wore, laughed, and shrugged. A few fish grease stains wouldn't hurt anything. They watched Miss Viola place fat fillets between slices of white bread, and in no time at all, they were sitting on the curb sucking cornmeal from their fingertips.

"You know she is too old for this hustle." Freda shook her head at the line forming in front of Miss Viola.

Gerald bit into a crunchy piece of fish. "I hear she's behind on her rent and water bill. She doesn't have a choice."

"You know that's why these old heads are counting on us to do big things," she said. "Each generation expects the next to do better." They were quiet as they ate, and Freda worried about keeping up her end of the conversation. She said, "Tell me this. Can you see me at Meharry?"

He had the nerve to laugh. She stopped eating. "Why is that so funny? Are you saying I don't have what it takes to make it at Meharry? There are ladies in your class, you know."

Putting his hands together in contrition, he said, "No, that's not what I meant. I assumed you'd teach math someday since that's your major."

Gerald studied alongside plenty of smart, talented young ladies. Maybe he couldn't imagine the woman who could very well become his wife being a doctor. Not that she had ever entertained the idea either. Whatever she was meant to do with her life would make itself known at the right time.

Freda put a bottle of grape soda to her lips and sipped slowly. "When I was in second grade, my mother was complaining about having to make nine apple pies for a fundraising event. The recipe called for one-third cup of flour for each, and she was worried she didn't have enough. Right away I said, 'You'll need three cups of flour for nine pies.'"

Whistling, Gerald said, "You were a whiz at math even back then."

"Mama and Papa decided I'd make a fine schoolteacher. That was their vision though, not mine."

"Did you tell your folks you didn't want to be a teacher?"

"No. I guess it was easier to adopt their dream for me until I could discover one of my own. Maybe I'm a little jealous that you and Papa knew so early that you wanted to be doctors." She paused, and then casually said, "Do you ever think about the fact that you're at a top medical school and will be a doctor someday, but you can't sit at a lunch counter or ride the bus next to somebody white?" With a bit of paraphrasing, she asked the same question Darius had when he spoke to the student crowd. His words had made her think about how unfair it all was. But now, repeating them on this date with Gerald felt like a betrayal.

"I can't change their minds. So why bother?"

"A lot of students from colleges around here are planning to sit in again at the lunch counters. I can't say for sure I know it will do any good. But maybe it's worth it to try." As nonchalant as she tried to sound, his eyes probed her, likely wondering if she'd gone stark-raving mad.

"You can't be serious," he said, seeming amused more than anything. "People like you and me, we have the whole world in front of us and all we have to do is be excellent." He sounded exactly like her father, as if they had studied the same script.

"Do you ever get tired of being excellent? Let me change that. Not being excellent but pursuing excellence all the time."

"Where did that question come from?"

"I'm just wondering is all."

He hesitated before answering. "It's all I know. It's all we know," he said. "What else is there?"

Freda rested her head on his shoulder, watching the people walk by them, laughing and talking. "Oh, I don't know. Dreams maybe. Everybody deserves to go after one big dream in life."

"Not everybody can afford to dream. Sometimes you need a plan. And you need money to make that plan real."

Money could unravel dreams. She thought of Cora's financial predicament, but Freda never had to worry about money. Pushing gently, she whispered, "What was it like for you and your family growing up in New York?"

Gerald stayed quiet at first, carving lines into the ground with the base of his beer bottle. "I shared not just a room but a bed with my two sisters. Mama kept things clean, although some of the city rats liked to pay us a visit and cockroaches always came out at night. But you know what? Mama always said it was better than being strung up in a tree somewhere down south. I can't say white folks wanted us in New York either, though. Once Negroes started coming from down south, they got scared and put us in these little cages all on top of each other."

He described a life she had a hard time picturing. She wondered if her father would still consider him suitable for her if he heard that story. "What about your daddy?" she asked, desperate to know more about Gerald.

He flinched and pulled a flask from his jacket, taking a gulp of brown liquor. That's when she knew why Meharry Medical School mattered so much to him. It had to be as far away as he could get from whatever happened growing up in New York.

His hand trembled and the liquor threatened to spill over the sides. She put her hand on his arm to steady it and said, "It's okay. You don't have to talk about it."

At first, he didn't. "I don't have a father, not the way you do. I had a biological father. Leonard. He was the black sheep of the family. I think he acted out because everybody compared him to Uncle Curtis, the big-time doctor. The first to go to college, let alone medical school. I still smell the cigarettes on Leonard. Chain smoker. One right after the other. Smell the alcohol, too. He drank a whole hell of a lot." Gerald inspected the bottle in his hands and set it on the ground. "I was only a few years out of diapers the last time I saw him. But it's funny how you can remember some things that long ago. I don't know if he ever laid a hand on her, but I can still see the fear in Mama's eyes. I know he was a brute of a man. I could sense it."

"I'm sorry," she said.

"Why? Don't be sorry." Gerald rolled his shoulders and flexed his arms playfully. "I was the coolest kid in my neighborhood about the time I turned fourteen. Uncle Curtis stayed in Nashville after Meharry and when he came home to Harlem as this big-time doctor, he was like a father to me. All the cousins pointed to him and couldn't wait to tell people he was their kin. I looked up to him. Man, you should have seen the rolls of cash he carried." He mimicked peeling off dollar bill after dollar bill.

"I bet that impressed a lot of people," she said, laughing.

"You better believe it." He sobered, closed his eyes. "Nothing lasts forever, they say. He was making decent money, good money, at the hospital. But he wanted more. Started gambling, losing more than winning. The government took his house, took everything. That was too much for him and he drank himself to death."

That's when Freda understood what likely lured and terrified Gerald at the same time. He dreamed of becoming a successful doctor like his Uncle Curtis, the man he had revered for so long, while also fearing that he'd end up like him, like Icarus flying so close to the sun that his wings melted.

14

Gerald

Dr. Vance, what does it mean to you to be a Meharry man?" Dr. Stovall leaned back in his chair with his hands folded across his ample midsection. Gerald had no idea why the program chair for internal medicine had requested a meeting with him.

The question stumped him. "Sir, I'm proud to be a Meharry man." Gerald fidgeted in his chair, the wooden legs groaning every time he shifted in his seat.

"That's not what I asked you."

"I'm sorry, sir." The air in the office stagnated and Gerald tapped his hands on his thighs.

The spicy aroma of a pipe Dr. Stovall must have smoked recently filled the room. One of Meharry's most revered and feared professors stood and pointed to a gold-plated plaque that hung above his framed diplomas. "What does that say, young man?"

"Worship of God through service to mankind." The Meharry motto. Every student could recite this from day one. How foolish, Gerald thought, that he hadn't realized this was what Dr. Stovall was testing him on. It was such a simple question and he overanalyzed it to his detriment.

The window fan whirred and screeched, lifting the corners of papers on the wide desk. Dr. Stovall stood directly in front of Gerald. "You're a smart student. You come from good stock with your uncle being a Meharry graduate. I'm not asking you to identify the narrowing of the esophagus or how to treat a hiatal hernia. You know those things. That's the textbook definition of what it means to be a doctor. I want to know if you are pursuing this profession to be of service to your community or to make money. Which is it for you?"

Here was one of those situations where you had to decide if it was better to tell a lie or not. Gerald wanted to make money. Lots of it. Enough to guarantee he would never see another New York cockroach crawl from under a floorboard in his house ever again. When he was a kid, his mother gathered him and his sisters in the bathroom of their tiny apartment where she would rub garlic and a little peppermint oil on their arms and legs to keep the roaches away at night. She set out bowls of bay leaves and coffee grounds under their beds, too.

"We'll be out of here soon as I get the money together," his mother said too many times to be believed.

Gerald held Dr. Stovall's gaze. "I want to be a doctor to uplift my people, my community. They need me and their health matters to me."

And that was the truth. While money motivated him, he dreamed of helping people like those in his own family. Seeming satisfied with that answer, Dr. Stovall nodded. "There's a National Medical Association luncheon tomorrow. A regional meeting. They extended a most gracious invitation to the top medical students in the area. When they asked me for a recommendation, I thought of you. I think you'll represent me and Meharry well."

Gerald's throat narrowed as if he had swallowed a grape. "Me? You want me to go?"

Dr. Stovall smiled. "You're deserving to go. When you return, let me know which was better—the luncheon speaker or the rubber chicken they serve you."

***

Miles of curving country road stretched out in front of Gerald. He rolled down his window, listened to the whistle of the wind, and tuned his ears to the repetitive sound of his tires turning gravel.

Things were opening up for him now with this invitation to a prestigious medical gathering. An opportunity like this to rub shoulders with the most elite physicians in the South was practically unheard of for a second-year medical school student. And out of all the students in the class, Dr. Stovall had chosen him. The good marks Gerald made in his studies were merely the price of entry for an aspiring physician, but the people he met today would open doors for him. He could almost see his dreams rising to meet him.

Dressed in his gray pinstripe three-piece suit, he considered himself a new man, and if he weren't on this lonely country road, he would wave to passing cars, maybe even honk his horn to turn a few heads his way. With no one in the car to hear him and presume he had lost his mind, he practiced aloud how to greet the physicians he'd be meeting from all over Tennessee and surrounding states.

Good afternoon, why hello there. A pleasure to make your acquaintance. Yes, I'm a second-year student at Meharry. Top of my class. I hope to specialize in cardiology in my residency.

Maybe those Negro physicians might address him as "doctor," too, even if it were premature. Titles mattered.

His car rounded a bend and grew sluggish. Gerald mashed the gas pedal, and it picked up a little speed, but the car's get up and go had gotten up and gone. A clicking noise started, and it quickly turned into a thumping sound. He had driven this car many times between Tennessee and New York, but he figured it still had some good years left. Pulling over to the side of the road, he got out and touched the hood, and he swore when it burned his fingers.

"Damn." He had put off the maintenance work. Freda would never say she told him so, but she had.

Steam rose from the engine like it did from a tea kettle on the back of the stove. Gerald pulled on his overcoat to break the chill and paced in front of his car, glancing at his watch. The luncheon started in a half hour.

This was a desolate stretch of road and when he heard an approaching car, he waved it down. The white man who stepped out of the rusted station wagon had a big head and a wide neck, sitting on a compact body. His hair, the color of slush after a city snow, hung loose above his shoulders, long enough to braid.

"Having car trouble, I see." It was statement of fact. Judging from the streaks of gray in his hair and the lines on his face, likely for every decade of hard living, this man had to be at least in his mid-sixties. He walked around Gerald's car twice, inspecting it. "If I know my way around anything, it's women and cars."

"Yes, sir. Thank you for stopping. It started smoking on me. I might need coolant or the whole engine could be blown. I don't know what's wrong with it, but I'm in a hurry."

"We all in a hurry for one thing or another. The only something we can stand to be late for is death." He chuckled, amusing himself. "Oh, where are my manners? I'm Travis Lee."

"I'm Gerald. Gerald Vance."

Travis Lee sniffed around under the hood. "Speaking of death, what you think about our boys over in 'Nam? You can be honest with me."

Gerald had avoided the draft by being in college, but he doubted that information would sit well with this Good Samaritan. "I don't know what to think."

"Well, I'll tell you what to think. Our boys are over there saving those Orientals from the Commies. If that's not God's work, I don't know what is."

Travis Lee retrieved tools from his car and started tinkering under the hood. "You married? The way you dressed I figured it must be your wedding day. But I don't see no bride."

Gerald smiled at that. "No, sir. I do have a lady friend though." When Dr. Stovall extended the invitation, he had wanted to ask if he could bring a guest but didn't think that would be polite. The only thing better than going to the NMA luncheon would be to walk in there with Freda on his arm. He considered himself a traditional man and while he hadn't made their relationship official yet, he already considered Freda part of his carefully constructed life plan. As soon as his extended family told him that Uncle Curtis's best friend from Meharry wanted him to meet his only daughter, the rest became a fait accompli.

"Yeah, you look too young to be hitched. You not dry behind the ears yet." Travis Lee came out from under the hood long enough to study Gerald's face, and Gerald half expected him to pull an earlobe back to inspect it. They both laughed, and for a second—a millisecond, not a whole one—Gerald imagined them as two old friends shooting the breeze.

"You got time to get you a wife. I've got mine for forty years now. She's home sick," Travis Lee said. "I'm out now to get her some pepper-mint tea."

"Oh, what's wrong with her?"

"She got her a good case of the pneumonia. Not the old 'monia, but the pneumonia." He laughed at his own joke.

"Has she been to the doctor yet? I assume so since you already have a diagnosis. She needs to be on penicillin though."

Travis Lee shoved his hands in the pockets of his pants. "And what are you? A doctor?"

"As a matter of fact, I am," Gerald said, before correcting himself. "Or at least I'm studying to be one."

Travis Lee laughed harder this time, phlegm rattling in his throat. "Now that's a good one. You had me going there for a minute."

Gerald decided it would be best not to respond. The more Travis Lee poked around under the hood, saying nothing, the more Gerald's body tensed, every muscle firing its own warning. Either the man was bluffing about his knowledge of cars, or the damage was beyond repair.

Gerald hovered over the man's shoulder. "Do you think you can fix it?"

Ignoring the question, Travis Lee said, "So, tell me, boy, where did you get those fancy clothes and this car anyway?"

Anger and fear rose within Gerald with almost equal intensity, and he didn't know which one would govern his spirit that day. "I own this car and I bought my clothes at the department store where I'm sure you buy yours, sir."

"Are you sassing me, boy?"

"No, sir."

"The way I see it, you out in the middle of nowhere with a dead car. You don't want to be a dead nigger in a dead car, now do you?"

Gerald didn't live up north anymore, where folks wrapped their racism in civility. Why hadn't he seen this coming? Why had he assumed Travis Lee's intentions were good? His desperation had dulled his read on people. He had a good four inches in height on this man, but Travis Lee carried two steel barrels for arms and who knew if the old guy had a gun on him. "Look, I don't want any trouble, sir."

"They string y'all up on trees here in Tennessee and bring the whole family out to watch. That's not my idea of entertainment. It's not up to me to judge though 'cause I ain't got nothing to do with that. Only God can judge. I'm telling you how it is. So let me put it to you like this. Think of me as a friendly neighbor just being neighborly." Travis Lee slid one finger covered in black grease down the front of Gerald's freshly laundered white shirt.

Gerald balled his hands into fists, and then he contemplated the future clinical diagnosis if he busted Travis Lee's head: skull fracture with intracranial hematoma. His mother had kept him out of trouble in a rough neighborhood by reminding him that actions had consequences. He couldn't picture himself in a jail cell, but it wouldn't matter this time because he'd never end up in one. If he laid a hand on this white man, he'd be what Travis Lee said—dead.

Birds chirped, their songs as sunny as ever coming from high atop the trees. Gerald trained his mind on the beauty of the music they were making, surprised he heard anything as pure as that when his own rage clapped in his ears. Travis Lee walked slowly back to his car, and before he took off, he stuck his head out the window and yelled, "Nice meeting you, doctor."

The grinding of his wheels drowned out his laughter as he drove away. Gerald opened and closed his hands, inhaling deeply. He was still alive, but that man had sapped his spirit, making him feel low like some creature that crawled underneath your shoe. Gerald turned his anger inward. Why had he gotten ahead of himself, letting his hopes rise higher than his station in this world? Gerald stood next to his dead car, the exhaust from Travis Lee's station wagon covering him in a gray haze.

Freda

Something stirred in the air the morning of *Big Saturday*. So many students had the jitters, nervous energy bouncing from one to the other. Freda sat on the edge of her bed folding her laundry while watching Cora get dressed.

Her friend wore a white uniform with a V-neck and black stripes on the sleeves. She pressed her hands against the fabric of her dress.

"You make that ugly uniform look good," Freda said. "Where is Evaline with her crazy behind? Haven't seen her all morning."

"Girl, you know she's up under Ambrose somewhere. I don't think she came home last night. I peeked in her room, and her bed was still made from yesterday."

Freda had snuck in undetected an hour past curfew herself. "Mother Gaines is gon' have a fit," she said, knowing full well Evaline would find a way to cover her tracks as usual.

Cora leaned her back against the door to their room, as if she needed the sturdy structure to keep her upright. She kept wringing her hands. "What's wrong, sweetie?" Freda said.

But she suspected she knew what had her friend so apprehensive. The luncheonette manager at Woolworth's had hired Cora to work the sandwich board, cutting tomatoes and onions and operating the soda fountain. Desperate to make money, she took the job paying only $1.15 an hour. A piddly wage, but every penny counted toward tuition. She had been on the job less than a week and the whole city recognized this would be no ordinary day.

Cora sat down on the bed next to Freda. "I need the work, but I don't know what's going to happen today. I'm surprised they hired me in the first place, knowing I go to Fisk and that it's the college students from around here doing the protesting. We're the ones messing with their business."

Big Saturday was no longer a big secret now that the local businesses had gotten word of what was planned. When Freda saw her friend like this, the guilt threatened to consume her. What must it be like to have to study hard to stay in good academic standing and then have to work a job that put your life and dignity on the line to stay in school? Until she tried to get her parents to help Cora, she didn't even know the cost of tuition. They refused to help, saying they sympathized with her roommate's plight but weren't running a charity.

"It's not strange that they hired you," Freda said, comforting her. "I can't think of a harder worker or a sweeter person."

Cora went on. "The sit-ins are supposed to be bigger than before this time and that's what scares me."

Freda didn't need to be reminded. She had tossed and turned all night thinking about Darius, knowing he'd be at that Woolworth's lunch counter like he'd been at McLellan's. Would the white mob show as much restraint this time? She tried to convince herself that she cared because he was a classmate, a fellow human being. She was showing that agape love Dr. King had been preaching about from the pulpit of Ebenezer. But who was she fooling? It was more complicated than that. Yet she couldn't allow her mind or more importantly her heart to travel down that road.

Turning back to her friend, she said, "Girl, you're there to do your job. Keep your head about you and ignore all the fuss. I know it's easier said than done, but you have to stay strong."

Cora moved back and forth between Freda's bed and her own, her hands clasped under her chin. "I'm grateful to have the job but I know myself. And I know I'm going to feel like a traitor standing behind that counter serving white folks and refusing to serve my own people. How am I going to do that?"

Freda didn't have an answer, so she did the only thing she could and gathered her friend in her arms and held her tight. She would be glad when this day was over.

***

Police motorcycles lined Fifth Avenue in front of Woolworth's, an almost festive scene with people spilling into the street, and even children jumping on and off the curbs in exuberant expectancy. Some little ones, Negro and white, cast furtive glances, smiling playfully and inching closer to each other until their cautious parents pulled them back.

All morning, Freda had sat alone in her dorm reading about English literature and nineteenth-century poets until early afternoon when she couldn't stand it anymore. Holed up in her room, the wondering consumed her, and the isolation made her stir-crazy. After overhearing girls on the other side of her door in Jubilee Hall make plans to head over to the five-and-dimes, she couldn't stay away and decided to join them.

As much as she disagreed with these public airings of grievances, Freda was proud to see students from not just Fisk but Tennessee State and Baptist Theological Seminary marching with signs in front of Woolworth's. Dignified and resolute. All of them dressed like those on Valentine's Day weekend, sporting their finest as if it were Sunday morning.

A girl in a simple day dress with a fresh press and curl who mentioned being a student at Tennessee State reported back to everyone what she'd observed in the store. "It's so crowded you can't stir 'em with a stick. I sat down on that lunch counter stool though for two whole hours. Then I had to get up when some more of us came to rotate in, but let me tell you I didn't want to get up. It felt so good sitting there."

A small crowd swarmed her, hanging on to every detail that fell from her lips, and that girl became a hero in their eyes. Something akin to jealousy passed through Freda. She had never considered how noble and accomplished one might feel doing the simple act of sitting. That had to be the feeling that came over Darius and kept him doing this time after time.

"Did you see that Negro girl working behind the counter?" a young man wearing a brown wool fedora asked. "Somebody said she goes to Fisk. Can you believe she took a job at a place that won't even serve her?"

Another spoke up, raising his voice, obviously anxious to have an attentive audience when he made his point. "First of all, who would ever see the day a Fisk student is working at Woolworth's? Now ain't that something?" He laughed and others joined him.

Cora. They had to be talking about Cora. Freda considered telling them how much her friend needed the money from that job to stay at Fisk. She had tried all kinds of businesses and been turned away, none of them offering the flexible hours she would need to keep up with her studies. The ones that could work around her school schedule didn't pay enough.

The man in the fedora continued, "I haven't told y'all the whole story. It gets worse. I heard the only reason they hired her was for the newspaper cameras so they could say they have some young Negroes working there, that some of us don't have any problems with separate, unequal treatment. A damn shame."

"They just using her," someone said.

Unable to listen to more, Freda pushed through the crowd to move closer to the door of the store. A young woman ran out, her black coat swinging behind her. Darting into the street to meet her, Freda called, "Cora! Cora!"

Closing the distance between them, Freda grabbed her by the shoulders. "What happened in there? Are you okay?"

Cora seemed shaken. "They told me to go home, no explanation, but things were happening so fast. There's a mob in there, they knocked students off their chairs, kicked and punched them. Freda, it was horrible. They poured ketchup and mustard over their heads. I even saw one man stub out a cigarette on the side of somebody's face." Her breath came out in staccato beats.

Freda had to shout to be heard over the chanting and the hollow, much-too-late calls for law and order. "It's okay. Calm down. You're safe now. Why don't we go back home?" She rubbed her friend's shoulders that shook with cold or shock, or maybe both.

While Cora had been staring ahead wide-eyed, she finally looked at Freda as if recognizing her for the first time since she'd run out of the store. Her lips moved, but no sound emerged for a few seconds. "That boy from school, the one you were yelling at who spoke outside the dining hall . . ."

Panic squeezed Freda's throat. "Darius. Darius Moore. What about him? Is he all right?"

"Yes. I mean I think so. This officer was hassling him and roughing up some people before I ran out of there. I didn't want to stick around to see anything more, and my manager practically shoved me out the door."

Without another word to Cora, Freda pushed past people filling the sidewalk, Negroes and whites with signs asking the stores to desegregate. Some whites snarled and yelled racial obscenities and ginned up others to put Negroes in their place. She needed to reach Darius. "Excuse me. I have to get through," she yelled.

"Stay back," an officer commanded her, his hand tightening around his baton.

"I have to go inside," she said, and that's when she saw a line of Negroes and whites being walked out of Woolworth's in handcuffs, Darius in front. He remained stoic and silent on his march to the paddy wagon with close to a dozen students behind him and people shouting on all sides.

"No, you can't do that. He's a student at Fisk. Why are you arresting him? He didn't do anything. Darius!" she screamed and began running toward him when the officer who had told her to stay put grabbed her arm and flung her backward. She recalled seeing the bumper of a parked car and the approaching asphalt before everything went black.

Gerald

Gerald was catching some fresh air with Ambrose, who had stuck a rolled newspaper in the biochemistry building side door. Gerald had set the likelihood of his frat brother showing up to study with him in the lab late on a Saturday afternoon at zero percent. But he arrived close to midday, bleary-eyed and sated like a fat cat.

"So my man, you and Evaline are getting serious, huh? I saw her leaving your place before the sun came up."

"You spying on me now?" Ambrose pulled a cigarette from behind his ear and lit it. "She *is* a beauty to behold, and I'm serious about indulging in all she has to offer. You know I appreciate all the ladies who have been so generous to a brother." Ambrose had been doubly blessed with good looks and charm that often carried him places he had no business being. A man so much on the hunt that you could almost see the reflection of dead animals in his eyes.

Gerald dropped his head. "Man, I've had milk in my refrigerator longer than you've been with some of these girls. Do right by Evaline now. You know that's Freda's friend."

"Sounds to me like you the one who's whipped, my man." Ambrose took a long drag on his Pall Mall and tilted his head back to blow smoke.

Not knowing exactly what the future held with Freda, he had no interest in discussing his feelings with Ambrose, a man for whom everything had come easy—his legacy status at Meharry and in the fraternity, a security net to brace his fall when he made unforced errors.

Ambrose took another drag on his cigarette. "I've had enough studying for one day, and it is the weekend. I'm going cruisin' for a bit with some of the fellas if you want to come." He mimicked revving an engine.

"I'm cutting out of here, too. Save some liquor for me. I may catch y'all later tonight. Promised to put in a few hours over at Hubbard."

"Oh, you in for it now. You gon' get the winos and the men whose wives hit 'em over the head with frying pans."

Too tired to laugh this time, Gerald rubbed his eyes. "Man, I hope not. I need a slow night."

***

Patients slumped in chairs and a few even lay across the floor, many moaning and begging to be seen in the emergency room of Hubbard Hospital, named for the first president of Meharry. The teaching hospital for the medical school offered the only chance for Negro students to get clinical experience. Gerald shrugged out of his sweater and put on his lab coat, trying to shake off the doubts that that so-called Good Samaritan had put in his head when he left him stranded on the side of the road. He jogged over to Dr. Shaw, the resident physician and a Meharry graduate himself.

"Where do you need me?" Gerald said, looking around at the nurses frantically moving from one crisis to the next, realizing then that he wouldn't be joining Ambrose and his other frat brothers later.

Dr. Shaw had the look of a man who suffered no fools and kept his eyes on the patient chart in front of him. "What took you so long to get here? Go to exam room three. Burn patient." Gerald nodded and headed in that direction. Dr. Shaw called to him, meeting his eyes this time. "It's a child. Thought you'd want to know."

The exam room smelled of a combination of antiseptic and the strawberry drink that outlined the little boy's lips in a red circle.

A man in a plaid work shirt with wild brown eyes stood at the bedside next to a woman leaning over the bed to rock the child. "That's my son," he said. There was a raw pleading on his face that was hard to look at and it made Gerald want to turn away. This was only his second week working at Hubbard and the first time Dr. Shaw had sent him in alone to see a patient.

"What happened?" Gerald moved closer to the little boy, whose pants legs were rolled up to his thighs. The skin on his bare legs had turned purplish red and scaly.

The woman holding the boy spoke through tears. "I was boiling water for eggs and Isaiah was sitting on the floor. He's forever up under me and he pulled on my housecoat. I don't know how but when I turned around to see what he wanted . . ." She left her sentence unfinished, the words stuck in her throat.

Isaiah's father stepped in for his wife, picking up the story. "The pot of hot water fell on him. I saw it. I had just walked in from the store. He screamed something terrible."

The boy held the cup of red drink in his little hands, but he wasn't crying out in pain now, and Gerald got closer. "Hey, little man. Do your legs hurt?"

"He's in pain," the father said. "Do something."

Gerald kept his focus on Isaiah, who hadn't answered him but wasn't showing any signs of being in pain. He saw himself at that age, three or four years old, unable to articulate his feelings but terrified, not from the pain of a burn, but in fear of his own father who was known to dole out punishment whether it was an open hand or broken glass across the face.

Isaiah had nothing to fear under the watchful eyes of this couple that doted on him. "Look, I'm worried that the burn may have penetrated the layer of fat under his skin, what we call the hypodermis, and he may have suffered damage to his nerve endings. I suspect that's why he's no longer feeling pain."

"Can you treat him? Can you make him better?" The mother pressed her lips to the top of her son's head.

After washing his hands and putting on gloves, Gerald cleaned the burn, removing dead skin and tissue. Then he rubbed on ointment and gently wrapped Isaiah's leg in bandages. "You want to keep it covered and clean to prevent infection. I need you to be aware that he will likely start feeling pain in that leg. Be sure to mix some aspirin in his food." Bending down to rest his own forehead against Isaiah's he said, "Take care of yourself, little one."

WHEN GERALD STEPPED INTO THE HALLWAY, HE ALMOST GOT knocked over by a man darting past, carrying a woman in his arms. "We need help," he said.

Dr. Shaw and Nurse Rita ushered them into an open exam room. Standing in the doorway, Gerald watched them lower the woman's limp body onto the bed. Her head had been covered by the man's arm before but now he clearly saw her face. It was Freda.

Gerald ran to the bed and turned her head to face him. Her eyes were closed. "Freda! Freda, wake up. Do you hear me?"

"Hey," Dr. Shaw said, as imposing as ever, all five feet and three inches of him. "What the hell are you doing? Have you learned nothing in Dr. Nelson's neurology class? We don't know what kind of head trauma she may have. We need to keep her immobilized. In fact, you should leave the room."

Quickly Gerald pulled back bloody fingers from the gash in her head. "I can't leave her. She's my girlfriend."

Dr. Shaw raised his eyebrows and apparently thought better of whatever he had planned to say. His face softened. "I'm sorry, Gerald, but give us some time to check on her."

Outside the room, Gerald noticed the haggard man in the worn coat who had carried Freda into the emergency room. He was cupping his hands trying to light a pipe. The rage or maybe the fear overtook

Gerald and he lunged at him. "Who are you and what did you do to her?"

The man peeled Gerald's fingers off him. "Man, you got it all wrong. I ain't do nothing to her. The police tossed her like a little rag doll. She was outside by the protest at Woolworth's. Got too close to the action, I guess. Hell if I know. But I seen her hit her head on that car and then go down to the ground. I got my buddy to put her in the back of his truck and we brung her here. I don't want no trouble, so I best be going."

As the man shuffled toward the emergency room exit, Gerald said, "Thank you. I'm sorry. Thanks for bringing her in."

The man paused and walked back to Gerald. "You must be her husband the way you came after me like that. Look, I'm here to tell you man to man that she got knocked down when she went to hollerin' after one of those dudes who got hauled off to jail for protesting. Kept calling his name and trying to help him. She came to once in my buddy's truck and was still calling for him. Darryl or something like that. He's the one you need to worry about, not me."

Too rattled to continue on his shift, Gerald paced for an hour in the waiting room, walking so fast around the square perimeter of the room that he got winded like he had on the football field at Fisk. But nothing would quiet the deafening fear and the question he kept asking himself. Who was this other man that got Freda riled up enough for police to get involved? He swallowed his jealousy. After all, that bum off the street would make up any kind of story. He smelled the liquor on him.

All that mattered now was Freda's recovery. Helplessness stared back at him in the eyes of other people sitting in that room unsure whether they wanted an update on a loved one or not. Everybody jumped when Dr. Shaw emerged to call somebody back, and when it was Gerald's turn, Dr. Shaw said, "She suffered a minor concussion, but I believe she will be fine." Finally, Gerald released muscles he didn't know he'd been clenching.

"Oh, thank you, thank you," he said, looking up and offering gratitude to a God he hadn't been in touch with in a long time.

"Hear me now," Dr. Shaw said. "I told you I *believe* she will be fine. I still need to check her reflexes and coordination, look at her pupils. This was a head injury and she's fortunate we haven't seen any bleeding on the brain or brain swelling. I want to monitor her overnight."

Back at Freda's bedside, Gerald noticed the middle part in her hair and the soft curls matted by the blood now on one side. He realized he had never looked at her, not really. In their time together, he hadn't noticed the small mole next to her left eye or how her long lashes fanned out over her cheeks.

She lay there, still, too still, and he wanted to shake her but knew that would not be advisable medically. "You scared me," he whispered into her stiff hair.

Minutes or hours may have passed as he watched her until the flutter of her eyelids surprised him. "Freda," he said softly, thinking he may have imagined the movement he wanted to see.

Her eyes popped open wide, and she looked right at him, confused and alarmed. She bolted upright, fighting the bed covers. "Where am I? What happened?"

He grabbed her shoulders and gently pressed her back to the bed again, trying to forget what that bum had said about her crying out for another man. "You're at Hubbard, in the hospital. You hit your head, but you're going to be fine in no time."

Freda's eyes darted from side to side, frantic and glassy with tears. How much did she remember?

Just as suddenly as her eyes opened, they closed again. Now that he believed she would be okay, he wanted answers. What was she doing at that sit-in? She had spent last night at his place and never once mentioned going to that protest. Why? How could she put herself in danger like that? Was this Darryl, or whatever the hell his name was, the reason she had gone to the sit-in?

PART SIX

Chicago, 1992

17

Tulip

Tulip pranced around her parents' kitchen in dramatic fashion the way she had when she was a kid and got all As on her report card or had been named student of the month. Gerald kept his eyes on some sports story in the *Tribune* about the Bulls defense, but said, "I hope your news doesn't have anything to do with that buck-teethed boy you're spending time with."

"I must say I'm with your father on that one," Freda said, watching a pat of butter melt in the skillet.

Already, Tulip regretted opening her mouth, that huge ball of excitement inside her dwindling now to a pebble. "You know what? Never mind."

She walked toward the living room where a small radio played softly from the archway. Snatches of dialogue mentioned the LA riots—the damage to stores, the raging fires, the economic impact—but as far as Tulip could tell, no one on the news seemed interested in talking about why someone would feel devalued enough to lash out. These weren't spontaneous acts of aggression. The frustration had been building for a long time, and people could only take so much. Frustration weighed on Tulip, too, irked that her parents continued to put their noses in the air about her boyfriend.

Freda put one arm around her daughter's waist and squeezed. "Sweetie, I'm sorry. We always want to hear what's going on in your life. I could tell by the way you were about to burst a minute ago that you've been holding on to something good."

"Yeah, lay it on us," Gerald said, finally taking his eyes off the morning paper.

The hollow spot that had been growing inside her with their disinterest was starting to fill in again. She didn't expect her parents' admiration merely because they shared a bloodline. Now she had the validation she needed for it to be earned.

"Remember me telling you about that waffle maker account everybody's been trying to snag? Well, I may have helped win that business for Mattingly. I don't know whether we'll actually get the account but their lead guy was really listening to me and I could tell I won him over."

Gerald pounded the table. "That's what I'm talking about! My baby girl, making big money moves. Next step, a promotion."

"I don't know about that. We'll see if CookCo signs with us and we'll see what Bryce says. I think he considers me a rising star, though."

Freda wiggled her hips as she cracked eggs over the frying pan. "Of course he does."

"You'll be running that agency soon," Gerald said. "Mattingly Public Relations will be Vance Public Relations before you know it. Watch and see." The praise and predictions from her parents might have been over the top and embarrassing but they made her believe anything was possible, and sometimes you needed somebody else to see the vision when you were too blinded by your own doubts.

But Freda had to ruin it. "You said it yourself. Your star is on the rise. Don't let the company you keep bring you down."

"Why can't you give Key a chance?" Tulip poured herself another cup of coffee. "It's a pattern with you two, always about money and status. Like you, Dad. Look at where you practice medicine. You left the community hospital to go to the University of Chicago where the patients are richer and whiter. It feels like you're moving further and further away from who you are, who we are."

This was something she had never articulated before or known she even believed about her father until now.

"Tulip! You have no idea what you're talking about," Freda said.

Her father spoke slowly. "Yes, I have my own practice now with privileges at the U of C and that's how I paid your college tuition. Your mother did her part, of course, with her teaching position. But the reason you don't have any student loan debt to repay is because I kept pushing for more in my career. Hell, it wasn't until recent years that I started performing the more complex procedures. For years, because I'm Black, I got the most basic, unchallenging cases. You think that was easy for me?"

What could she say to that? Where did she assume the money had come from to fund her education? The truth was she never thought about it. That made her feel like the spoiled, ungrateful brat she long suspected she might have been. From expensive private schools to prep courses for college entrance exams, everything had been carefully crafted to almost assure her success. Had her position at Mattingly been truly earned when her father's racquetball club connection had gotten her the job in the first place? Had Amanda been right all along? "I'm sorry, Dad. I wasn't thinking."

"No, you weren't thinking at all." Freda slid Tulip's plate of eggs and toast in front of her while Gerald shoved a slice of bacon in his mouth before rising to head out the door to the hospital.

Tulip took her plate into the living room and stretched out on her favorite Eames lounge chair, sinking into the padded leather and luxuriating in the warm sunlight streaming through the picture window. She heard her mother's footsteps behind her. "Do you realize that early in your father's career he was only getting referred patients with Medicaid or no insurance? How well do you think that pays?"

Tulip stabbed her eggs with her fork, and they tasted metallic. "Everything is hard for me right now, Mommy." She hadn't called her mother by that name in years.

Freda tamed the flounce of her silk robe with a belt and squeezed into the chair with her daughter. "What's wrong, baby?"

"It's everything." Her throat began to close the way it did when she was about to cry. "These folks on my job are trying to undermine me. You should hear the vile things they say when they don't know I'm listening. I keep working my butt off without getting ahead. And then you remember when Nate from school got stopped and roughed up by the cops for no reason. And now Rodney King! When does it end?"

Freda gathered Tulip in her arms and rocked her. "I know, I know."

Lifting her head, Tulip said, "If you know, then why do you act like Key is something stuck to the bottom of your shoe?"

"I don't dislike Key," Freda said. "I barely know him. What I do know is that he drives a bus for a living and therefore his earning potential is limited. Your father and I want you to have the brightest future possible. Like it or not, the partner you choose plays a major role in that. You want someone by your side who can build with you in this rough world, not hold you back."

Tulip extricated herself from her mother's arms. "So what you're saying is you married Dad for his earning potential, not love." She threw that little grenade and waited for her mother to explode, not caring about sparing her delicate feelings, and besides, Tulip welcomed any reaction, anything to pull a real emotion from her. They could scream it out to heal the way one might sweat out a fever.

But Freda looked almost sympathetic and walked to the window to gaze out over the sculpted shrubbery that encircled their house like a moat surrounding a castle. "Love," she said. "You know nothing about love. The struggle is about survival. Love is a luxury."

***

Tulip got through the day without anyone at work mentioning the CookCo account, which meant neither Bryce nor Mason knew about her secret lunch meeting with Adam. No news was good news, she thought, but her mother's words haunted her, and she wondered what they meant. After work, Tulip headed straight to the Ida B. Wells housing project on the near south side of the city, bordered by Cottage Grove Avenue to the east and King Drive to the west. The Low End, folks called this part of town, and while she had lived in Chicago her entire life, she usually passed these projects without so much as a glance. She never even thought about them unless a drive-by made the news.

When people called Chicago the most segregated city in America, they had to be talking about the new Jim Crow where Blacks and whites still lived separate and unequal. They didn't bother to mention that some Black folks lived separate and unequal from one another, too. Maybe nobody cared about that.

A taxicab dropped her off at 559 E. Browning, the address on the flyer she saw on the bus the other day. As soon as she stepped out of the car, she turned to ask the driver to wait for her to confirm she was in the right place, but he had already claimed his fare and took off like he stole something.

Squat, reddish-brown, rectangular buildings seemed to go on for as far as she could see, each indistinguishable from the next except in height. Yet none as tall as those high-rise projects where they stacked Black folks on top of one another.

She stepped gingerly through broken bottles and weeds to get to the front entrance. Three men leaned casually against the building, cigarettes between their lips, a communal match setting them all aglow.

"Hey, pretty lady," one of them called out to her, and she picked up her pace trying to reach the door. "Where you running to so fast?"

"Nice tits," another male voice said, and she stumbled over an uneven patch of sidewalk.

Regaining her balance, she tried the nearest door, jerking on the handle, but it wouldn't budge. Wrong building, she realized. That's when she heard another set of voices a few feet away and whipped around to see three boys no more than nine years old shoving one another. One broke free from the others and leaped into the air, his empty hands high, grabbing a piece of the sky. "I'm Jordan," he said.

Another boy who circled him shot back, "You ain't Jordan with yo punk ass."

The first boy sidestepped him. "I bet I could dunk better than you."

Key would love this and probably join them. But Key wasn't with her because she hadn't even told him she was coming here. He would call this protest meeting a waste of time, and always protective, would worry about her safety. Something drew her to this place tonight, though, and she needed to find out what they were planning.

Even as a child, Tulip ran to the blaze when everybody else ran from it. She needed to be at the center of things. As a little girl, on the rare occasion when their door wasn't closed, she lay in bed between her parents to feel the warmth of their bodies surrounding her, the beat of their hearts close enough that they seemed indistinguishable from her own. Her parents would be livid if they knew she was here for this meeting, and her skin prickled at the thought.

Dusk chased the remaining daylight, and she found the door to a building clearly marked with the number 559. When she stepped indoors, shadows wrapped tight around her. A sour smell filled her nostrils.

"You here for the meeting?" a woman called from one of the first-floor units.

"Yes." Tulip's voice bounced off a ceiling that seemed too low. The light from the open apartment door also illuminated a man standing in the grimy stairwell facing the wall with his pants gathered at his knees. He jerked his head toward her and she tried to appear cooler than she felt and nodded, as if to say carry on.

The first-floor apartment belonged to Mrs. Bertrice Ward, as the woman introduced herself, the occupant of one of the largest units in the building and the only appropriate choice for community meetings during the week and church on Sundays. African masks lined the walls, standing guard above oversize furniture. A couple dozen people had already shown up and every seat was taken.

Tulip would have been on time, but she had worked extra hours at the office compiling a bound paper media list almost as thick as the Yellow Pages, a tedious task usually reserved for a junior staffer. But somehow this assignment ended up on her to-do list.

"I came along before Black was beautiful," Mrs. Ward said, catching Tulip admiring the artwork. The woman's face had a sharpness to it, and the lines appeared sculpted. She went on to say, "And then I saw Nina Simone come out with that afro in the sixties. Man, I tell you that was something. Rocked my world."

The woman Tulip recognized from the bus with the long locs stomped her foot to get everyone's attention. "Latasha Harlins will forever be a high school sophomore. She will never go to junior or senior prom. She won't walk across that stage at graduation or down the aisle at her wedding." A few murmurs of *that's right* and *she sure won't* echoed in the room. A tall man in a red Bulls jersey and black nylon MC Hammer pants stood in the kitchen and the low ceiling almost grazed the top of his head. The sign he held up spoke for him. It read *NO JUSTICE. NO PEACE.*

Tulip fidgeted and made squeaking noises on the plastic runner in the foyer until a young man in the back of the room offered her his folding chair. The organizer paced at the front of the room. "Latasha isn't here, and she no longer has a voice. *We* are her voice. *We* will speak for her." This meeting reminded Tulip of being in one of those Pentecostal churches where the spirit literally lifted you from your seat and you knew it was not of your own volition. That spirit overtook a woman in a utility worker uniform who rose to her feet first. "Yes, we mourn the loss of Latasha Harlins. Let's do this for her." People clapped and a few others stood also.

Carried by the rising tide of emotion, Tulip got up and without looking around to see who was watching, shouted, "Let's not forget Rodney King, whose head was beaten mercilessly." She clapped her hands once to make her point. Freda would accuse her of making a spectacle or showboating, but that's not what this was about. When everyone turned to look, something powerful surged within her and she kept going. "What will happen here in Chicago to you or your father or your husband or your brother or your son?"

"You not from around here," said a man with gnarled fingers at the card table in the corner of the room. He chuckled softly. Not like he was making fun of her. But one of those looks the old heads gave you when they believed they knew better than you about everything. Cousin Leotha on her mother's side of the family used to say, "I've forgotten more than you'll ever know, little girl."

The woman running the meeting paced in a small circle, obviously growing impatient at the interruption. "You're late to the party. Rodney King is why we're marching in the first place. But it's our sisters like Latasha Harlins who get left behind. Nobody marches for them."

A chorus of amens began, and Tulip looked like an idiot presuming to know anything about the history of this planned protest. "I'm sorry." Tulip took her seat again.

Another man at the dominoes table spoke up. "Who sent you here? 5-0?"

Tulip had chosen not to wear one of her Casual Corner suits to work that day, but she still looked conspicuous in her canary yellow capri set that she thought would make her appear put-together but not overly buttoned-up for this meeting.

"No, no way. I'm not with the police. I'm not with anybody." Her voice became a mere tattered thread that frayed the more she spoke.

A man with a pinched nose and a downturned mouth who had been in deep concentration over his dominoes game until now stood to face Tulip. "Who are you then? You look like Big Bird to me," he said, inspiring laughter that made her shrink in her chair. "You stay 'round here? I never seen you."

"Me neither," an elderly woman said.

That's when Tulip wished for once she had listened to her parents. She could have been home drinking wine coolers with Sharita and watching *In Living Color* as they did most Wednesday nights. Did everyone know one another here at this meeting? It appeared so but she wondered why they had passed out flyers on the city bus if they wanted only friends and neighbors to organize with them. It made no sense, but then it hit her. There may have been some strangers here but none who stood out the way Tulip did with her yellow getup and that overly eager, yet still a bit scared look of somebody who had never set foot in the projects before. She had all the makings of an interloper, a tourist minus a camera slung around her shoulders.

Looking around, Tulip realized she knew no one here. She scrambled to her feet again, this time to make her way to the door, when Mrs. Ward in her tan tunic and jeans waved her arms to restore order in her apartment. She said, "I know her and she's a guest in my home and you will treat her as such."

Tulip met the older woman's eyes and thanked her silently. After a bit of grumbling, several people said *yes ma'am* to Mrs. Ward and calmed down enough to continue the meeting. She must carry a lot of sway in this room and in this community, Tulip thought, but then they were all in her home and she had every right to decide who stayed and who went.

A man in a brown UPS uniform, who must have just gotten off work, raised his hand to speak. "I agree with that young lady. I can't get Rodney King's swollen, bloody face out of my head. I know he's not the first Black man to get beaten by the cops and he won't be the last. But something about him got ahold of me and won't let go."

Tulip understood. The misfortune of strangers rarely held her interest for longer than the time it took to say a silent prayer or fend off the guilt of promising to pray and not following through. She quickly forgot the people who lost their homes in floodwaters, or the children cut down by an errant bullet, or the ravaged bodies of those dying from cancer or some other dreadful disease. Not because she was callous or unfeeling. Those stories seemed distant.

Rodney King was different. The violence visited upon him was hard to shake. The way those cops pounded his face with their bare knuckles. And maybe it was different this time because of the video. Psychologists analyzed these types of up close and personal crimes and concluded they were often borne of passion. A personal grievance that drove out all ration and reason. In this case, the cops didn't know Rodney King personally, but they knew what he represented to them, and it wasn't anything of much value. At the same time, it was oddly personal. You had to truly hate someone to look into their eyes, feel their breath on your face, and then make their bone and cartilage crack in your own hands.

A young woman's voice, raw and raspy, drew Tulip out of her own thoughts. "They put us in these raggedy ass buildings and forget about us. Can we use what happened to Rodney King *and* Latasha Harlins to send a message to City Hall that they're giving us a beat-down every day with poverty, fucked up housing and education, and jobs that don't pay worth a damn?"

Forgetting herself, Tulip shouted, "That's right," and stood to clap, and to her surprise so did practically everybody in that apartment. It took a girl barely out of her teen years to make everything plain, to connect the atrocities in LA to those right here at home, right here in these projects.

Energized now, the organizer with the locs volunteered to write out a list of demands they would present to the Chicago Housing Authority and Mayor Daley. They agreed upon a date for a protest march. Some raised their hands to make placards with the faces of Rodney King and Latasha Harlins, and others offered to work out the logistics. The voice of the man with the downturned mouth rose again. "Okay, I'm down with writing out our demands, but I don't know about this protest. What good will it do for us to march around our neighborhood with signs? Who's gon' see us? Anybody downtown? Daley and his bunch? I don't think so."

As much as Tulip hated to side with such a sour man, he had a point. The world of PR had taught her that you could have a good story, but it didn't matter how good it was if no one saw or heard it. The energy in the room deflated like a popped balloon as people realized their efforts might be too small to matter and may not reach anyone beyond these projects. With their spirits low, one by one, people got up and headed for the door, mumbling that they'd be at the next organizing meeting. Mrs. Ward navigated the obstacle course of chairs until she reached Tulip and took her hand, leading her down a short narrow hallway to one of the bedrooms.

Closing the door behind them, Mrs. Ward gestured for Tulip to have a seat on the edge of the bed. The room smelled smoky and sweet like the sticky candy of Tulip's youth, and she noticed incense burning on the nightstand.

"Thank you for standing up for me back there," Tulip said. "That was very kind of you."

"You know how they say dogs can smell fear on you?"

Tulip nodded. "I've heard that, Mrs. Ward."

"Call me Bertrice," she said in a hoarse voice that usually came from a long relationship with cigarettes. "You didn't do anything to rile anybody up tonight. They could smell the fear on you, that fear of being singled out as not one of us, and I saw how scared you looked before you even walked in here."

"I wanted to blend in, not stand out. We're all Black, no matter what neighborhood we live in."

"Whether you admit it or not," said Bertrice, "you have some idea in your head about us. You know what you see on TV, but you don't know us. These projects haven't always been like this."

Tulip had first heard of Ida B. Wells a long time ago. This housing project was named for a woman who did not appear on the Black History Month bulletin board in school or in Tulip's textbooks, which time-traveled fast from slavery to George Washington Carver's peanut inventions, and on to Martin Luther King Jr., with the lesson ending there. A tall, sturdy woman named Mrs. Rhae Elizabeth Jenkins taught Tulip's fourth-grade class, and she made sure every student knew this housing project had been named after Ida B. Wells, a trailblazing journalist who exposed racists, shaming and holding them accountable with her pen. She almost told Bertrice that story but decided this was neither the time nor the place to show off her Black history bona fides.

"I've been here close to forty years," the older woman said. "Most of us do take pride in where we live. My daddy used to mop every floor in this building. He was no janitor either. But you know what he and my mother always said? You never let anybody else see your dirt. There's a lot of good people here, but a lot of neglect, too. I blame the city, not the residents, for the neglect."

Tulip wondered if she had been that transparent, that these residents pegged her as scared, entitled, and judgmental from the second she arrived. "I didn't mean to offend," she said.

Bertrice waved her hand, dismissing the apology. She leaned over to lift a picture frame from the ornate oak dresser. It was a black-and-white photo of young people walking down a street. "This had to be 1960 or maybe '61, I can't recall, but we picketed the Chicago Board of Education for not teaching Black history. When I say we, I'm talking about folks here at Ida B. Wells."

A young Black woman in a belted trench coat stood in the foreground of the photo. "Is that you?" Tulip said.

"It sure is," Bertrice said. "I was just out of high school. We made the placards in the church basement. I was rebellious back then, questioned everything. Haven't changed too much over time. Sometimes still strong and wrong." She laughed at that.

Tulip took the framed photo from Bertrice and stared at it. While she looked into the faces of these fierce freedom fighters from the '60s, she kept thinking of the black smoke of protest that still rose over Los Angeles—Tulip could almost smell the sour air and feel it billowing in her lungs. Shops boarded up. Courthouses torched. Streets unrecognizable. She could only imagine what it must be like to actively fight for your freedom in this world, not read and hear about it. Dr. Martin Luther King Jr. had been assassinated the year after she was born and people called her a civil rights baby, but that whole era seemed as foreign to her as the American Revolution and the two world wars.

Tulip glanced up from the photo to see Bertrice watching her, studying her face like she was trying to understand something. The woman hesitated until she found the right words.

"I don't know what your real motivations are. I don't know you at all, but you're here. You might have the means to do something about our plight. You walked in here scared, but you summoned the courage from somewhere to show up in the first place. I hope the same courage that brought you here to the projects will lead you to do your part to help us."

18

Key

Key sorted packs of human and synthetic hair in the backroom of McCray's Beauty Supply Store while A Tribe Called Quest's "Bonita Applebum" played softly from a boom box on the floor. The sound of Tulip laughing with his parents in the main part of the shop soothed him, the familiarity of it, as he rubbed his neck, the muscles contracting and releasing.

His long CTA bus shift that day left him tired, spent, wanting little more than a bed and a pillow, but everything he cared about was on the other side of that wall, and that's why he dragged himself to the store three days a week to help out his folks. The business carried his family's name, after all.

"Hey, you," Tulip said, tiptoeing into the stockroom like a kid who had eaten a pan of brownies before dinner and now sought absolution. With a bottle of SheaMoisture pressed against her cheek, she popped her gum with an innocence he had to admit seemed more manipulative right now than endearing. "I know I promised to do inventory with you, but your mother was suggesting some styles I might want to consider for the Links charity event on Tuesday night."

Throwing her head back and arching her back, she attempted a catwalk in the cramped space, and he couldn't help noticing her fitted jeans and white V-neck shirt, both of them clinging to her like a second skin. He could stare at her every day for the rest of his life and never blink once. Like any real man though, he understood that nice bodies came around as often as buses and could be more trouble than they were worth. But it was everything else about Tulip that held his interest.

"Come with me. And if I'm lucky, Bryce might have promoted me by then, and we'll have lots to celebrate."

On his job, all he had to do was control the vehicle, stay on schedule, and get people where they were going without killing them or wrecking the bus. But that company Tulip worked for made her jump through more hoops than a tiger at the circus.

"There's no *might* about it. I don't want to hear any negative talk. I tell you like I do the Bulls even though they can't hear me. Trust the process. Trust your training and shut out all the noise." He ripped the seal on a box and flattened it.

She stood with her back against the wall and slid down until she was on the floor with him. "I don't know. Bryce still has to meet with the guy from CookCo. Who knows how that'll go. And I don't know if Bryce thinks I'm ready for a promotion. I don't even know that myself."

To his way of thinking, Tulip had already won in all the ways that counted. They came from two different worlds. The invisible ink of their stories spelled out the truth—that she had gone to college and he hadn't. One time when she was feeling sentimental, she showed him one of those books where parents recorded their kid's development in the early years. Her mother had written down her first words: *Ma-Ma, Da-Da, bottle, baby*, and not long after, *college*. She even saved all those Barron's SAT and ACT test preparation books she used with a tutor who'd come to her big old house on Pill Hill. One Saturday morning when they drove past the fine arts building downtown on Michigan Avenue, she told him she'd taken a weekly course there on how to ace college entrance exams.

Key couldn't remember ever taking those tests. His parents never mentioned them or college. In his family, school was something you did because you had to, but when an aunt or uncle asked if you *finished school*, they meant high school, nothing more.

Like in basketball, not everybody could be Jordan. He saw himself as Tulip's Phil Jackson, the coach who kept her calm and tried to silence the voices that messed with her head. "I believe in you," he said, closing the distance between them.

"I know and I hear you. Thanks to your mother and these products, I will *look* fly even if I don't feel it. And you still haven't confirmed that you're coming to the benefit."

"You stay fly. And yeah, I'll be there." Key kissed her cheek. "Say, I tried to reach you last night. Don't tell me you closed down the mall buying a fancy dress for your mom's event."

Her face betrayed her, and while he had asked one of those rhetorical questions that didn't require anything but a laugh, now he wanted to hear what she had to say about where she had been. He waited, his smile slipping. After a pause, she said, "I went to Ida B. Wells."

"For what?" Nobody took an evening stroll through the projects.

"You remember that lady on your bus the other day, passing out those pluggers for a meeting?"

"Not about Rodney King, I hope."

"Yes, about Rodney King and Latasha Harlins. I went to listen, that's all."

He scooted away from her on the floor. Why couldn't she let this go? It was like the people who couldn't stop crying over starving children around the world when kids right on their own block were eating potato chips for lunch. Not that Key lost much sleep over either. It was almost impossible to recognize somebody else's hunger when the rumble in your own belly was so loud. He had enough troubles of his own—a past that stalked him like his own shadow, waking him up at night, his back slick with sweat. He didn't need to borrow trouble thousands of miles away.

"I don't have to explain my actions or my choices." Tulip sounded defensive. "This is important to me."

Her voice carried the rumble of a diesel engine and he had to be careful, or he'd say something to ignite it. As much as he found all that protest talk to be a waste of time, he couldn't fault Tulip for what he admired most about her. That passion for the people and positions she stood behind.

"I respect that," he said. "I don't have to agree, but I respect it."

"I love my job in PR, but that's not my entire life. I can't sit around and ignore injustice whether it's here at home or out in LA. I refuse to be quiet as much as my parents or you may want me to. I'm sick and tired of playing it safe."

"You sound low-key mad right now," he said, side-eyeing her.

"I'm never low-key anything. You know that," she said, and they both laughed, the glacier forming between them already melting.

Key pulled her to her feet and backed her up against a stack of pallets, leaning in for a kiss, his tongue loosening her lips and maybe her frustration, too. He tasted Juicy Fruit, sugary sweet, and being close to her like this, he wished he'd had time to shower after driving the bus all day.

KEY AND TULIP JOINED HIS PARENTS ON THE MAIN STORE FLOOR, and he watched them move around like they owned the place, because they did. His dreams lived inside those of his parents, who had worked for other people for so long—his dad doing construction for the city and his mother serving meals in a grammar school cafeteria. No matter how hard he tried, Key could never picture his beautiful, vibrant mother as a hair-netted lunch lady. Nothing made him prouder than the day they punched out for the last time and opened their beauty supply business.

While Tulip's folks walked one straight line all their lives, Joe and Wanda McCray zigzagged, trying to stay one step ahead of the system. A system that doled out food stamps for them when he was a kid so they could buy their baloney, Wonder Bread, and Miracle Whip. A system that put another hurdle in front of them just when they'd cleared the last one. His father had a few run-ins with the law back in the day and could only get small construction jobs, but he always worried his past would catch up to him. They saved and leaned on family and church donations to open their business six months ago. No background check needed. Seeing the McCray name on the outside of this building, having something of their own that nobody could take from them, was a mountaintop moment in a world full of valleys.

Wanda tightened the band on a wig that looked like something the Supremes might have worn onstage. Hairstyles made comebacks all the time, she said. After placing the wig on top of a mannequin head she fluffed the curls and stood back to admire her handiwork. "If Madam C.J. Walker could become a millionaire in the early 1900s, we have no excuse today." Those words came out of her mouth so often they should have been turned into a bumper sticker by now.

"That's right. Black folks built this hair thing. We got to step into our destiny," Pops said as he lined shelves with shampoos and conditioners.

Ma held up a long jet-black ponytail to the back of Tulip's head. "What do you think? We smooth those edges, and you will look fierce rocking this at your mother's benefit."

"Ooh, I like it, Mrs. McCray," Tulip said, stroking the silky hair.

Tulip spent a lot of time at the store volunteering, almost as much as he did, and his folks took to her like a bear to a honeycomb. Of course, he couldn't say the same about her parents, who had never once invited him into their home but lurked in the shadows when he picked her up or dropped her off at their house. That whole two different worlds thing, you know. That's why he wasn't so fast to accept the invitation to Mrs. Vance's fancy benefit auction.

Standing in front of a mirror at a display counter, Wanda flipped her hair, free from that net she used to wear.

Joe couldn't help teasing her. "Be careful. You gon' break your neck if you don't watch it."

Key couldn't get enough of seeing his folks like this, relaxed, having a good time, enjoying what they had built.

His mother flung her hair even harder to make a point. "The only thing I'm watching is our sales numbers and we are not going to let the Koreans take over our business."

The beauty supply game remained stacked against Blacks in Chicago, where Koreans controlled most of the manufacturing and distribution channels in the market and owned a lot of the stores not just here but around the country. Some Korean wholesalers refused to sell them products that would show up in a Korean store down the street.

It didn't take much to get Wanda started. "The worst is when they answer the phone in Korean and won't even switch to English when they know damn well I can't understand what they're saying."

Key said, "Okay, Ma, but it is their language, and they got every right to speak it."

Joe rolled up the sleeves of his shirt, revealing the prison tattoos that snaked around his arms, and continued shelving products. "They can have their language but stop trying to shut us out, 'cause we're not going anywhere."

The more Key's parents talked, the harder Tulip brushed the wig on that mannequin head. She almost pulled strands of hair out of the mesh cap. Her focus reminded him of somebody two pieces away from finishing a jigsaw puzzle.

"Koreans out in LA own everything in the hood," she said. "Grocery stores, hardware stores, convenience stores, liquor stores. Now they're taking over your industry here in Chicago. What do we have? Nothing. It's not right."

Here we go, Key thought. He wanted to call her out for acting like she had been in the hood in LA. She and her girls flew out there once to be in the audience of *The Arsenio Hall Show,* whirling their fists and yelling *woof, woof.* They hadn't ventured far from the Paramount Studios lot, and she never got close to any real smoke out there. He imagined her in Ida B. Wells last night. The streets in any city could swallow you whole, but if you walked in smelling brand new, you didn't stand a chance.

Tulip set the hairbrush down on the display case and addressed all of them. "There's going to be a march here on the South Side against those cops who beat Rodney King and the so-called justice system that refused to hold them accountable. It's also about how we never saw justice in the case against that woman who killed Latasha Harlins. There's a pattern here if you think about it. It's more than what they're doing to our bodies. They're trying to take dollars out of our community, too. Maybe you could tell your story at the march."

Nobody said a word at first. Key didn't put much stock in conspiracy theories that pitted one minority group against another. An old Korean man used to ride his bus route—Mr. Kim, a small, wiry dude with thick eyebrows who made fast, jerky motions. He ran a restaurant and rode the bus to work, hugging the window every time a Black person sat in the seat beside him as if they were about to pick his pockets. Reminded him of Tulip the first time she rode his route. Some kids would yell *boo* just to see Mr. Kim flinch, and at first Key laughed, thinking that racist old man deserved it. He mainly spoke Korean, not much English. Some days his daughter, Mary, rode with him, wearing bomber jackets and acid wash jeans with her black hair piled on top of her head with a scrunchie. Key figured she'd changed her name as a kid to sound less Korean, and he wondered if an American name earned her more friends in school and job interviews later on. Unlike her father, Mary talked even when no one was listening. Told Key her dad had come from a little one-horse farming town in Korea and had left behind everything he knew to make a new life in America, the beautiful country, and worked hard to become a business owner. She bragged on her dad and Key wanted to say that his family was trying to start a business too, but it hadn't been easy when banks refused to take the risk of loaning to a Black couple. Just getting to the starting line had been nearly impossible.

One day Mr. Kim's daughter helped her father onto the bus—a white bandage with crisscrossing tape covered the old man's left eye. When Key asked what happened, she said somebody had hit him in the head before clearing out the restaurant's cash register. The way she said *somebody* and broke eye contact, Key knew she meant somebody Black. Whatever happened to Mr. Kim confirmed everything he thought he knew about Black folks from watching the news.

Key had this crazy idea that if all the *have nots* squashed their beef and worked together, they could end up on the *haves* side of the equation. Since so many people came to this country looking for a better life and others were forced to be here and had to make the best of things, it only made sense to take advantage of their numbers and join forces. Marching about it didn't seem the right way, but Tulip's passion for it did. Her eyes all ablaze like that could set a room—and a man—on fire. Whatever she wanted to do, he'd support her, but he drew the line at getting his family mixed up in a protest.

Wanda pulled her hair back, twirled it around her fingers, and spoke with a bobby pin wedged in the corner of her mouth. "I hear what you're saying, sweetie, but I'm not trying to go to war with these folks or with the law. We can work with them or around them. But we don't need that kind of trouble, Tulip, not when we're getting established. I appreciate what you're trying to do but we can't be part of anything like that."

From where Key stood, he kept his eyes on everybody, and he watched Tulip's face cave like a half-baked cake in the oven. Joe's silence in these situations usually meant he agreed with his wife and would let her have the last word. He didn't need to rouse 5-0 and have them poking around in his business again, even if it was a clean, legit business this time. Key knew what was going through his father's head—the same narrative going through his. A past like his was something you could never shake.

In high school, one of Key's boys asked him to hold a 40 rock for him. "Just keep it for me a couple days. Things are getting a little hot for me," his friend said. Key had never messed around with drugs—using or dealing—but he did his boy that favor. Pops found the drugs under his bed and flushed it all down the toilet. "I'm only saying this once, so you hear me now and you hear me good," he said. "Don't be like me and mess up your life. Stay the hell away from that shit and the people who deal in that shit." Before Key could defend himself and say the crack wasn't his, Pops had walked back into the living room and sat next to Ma on the couch to watch reruns of *Good Times*.

Key caught Tulip looking at him now, waiting for him to say something, to take a side. Her side. But he stayed out of this one, knowing where his folks were coming from. When you lived on the margins your whole life, one error, one arrest, one missed paycheck, one lease termination notice from your landlord could lead you down into a hole so deep you may never climb out of it.

***

Stylz and Profiles Barbershop sat in the middle of a strip mall sandwiched between a chicken shack and a check cashing store off Stony Island. The sign at the top of the cinderblock building had dimmed over time. When Key needed to get his fade shaped up or trimmed, he came here. Tulip liked to clown on this business for bad branding and lack of a marketing plan. He tried to tell her this was more of a word-of-mouth business. You wouldn't see it on the news or in any magazine ads, but the shop kept free school supplies on hand year-round for customers to take home for their kids. None of it for publicity's sake. It was about lifting the community.

The place was jumping more than usual for a Monday night. "We ain't seen you in a good while," said Buddy, running a towel over his clippers. Buddy Ferguson opened this shop when Key was a kid, but he still looked the same as he did when he cut his hair for fifth grade picture day.

"I been busy, man. I try to shape it up myself, but I ain't got your skills." Key raked his hand over his hair from the nape of his neck to his forehead. He took in all the eyeballs tracking his movements through the shop. These brothers didn't miss a thing. He recognized many of them because they'd been regulars over the years—accountants, plumbers, lawyers, air conditioner repairmen, and the brothers who sold contraband—they all had to get their hair cut. He gave a general wave to the room.

The chair he sat in must have been there since the beginning of time. The armrests all chewed up and the ripped hard plastic grated his skin like a block of cheese.

"Damn, Buddy," Key said. "Get some new chairs. My arm's all scratched up." He held up his forearm to show the white marks on his dark skin.

Another barber Key didn't recognize jumped in. "We can't help it if you ashy. Get some lotion in your life, bruh."

This game had levels of play and Key had been out of practice. It took him a minute to formulate a proper comeback. He smiled slowly and said, "I used all my lotion on your mama last night."

The men hooted and hollered, letting Key know he had landed an effective shot. A customer with a long face who had the look of a man with nothing to lose turned to Key and said, "Be careful before somebody Rodney Kings your ass." The barbershop fell silent, no buzz from the clippers, no trash talking. Too soon, much too soon for that threat or joke or whatever the hell it was, Key thought. While he held no particular affection for Rodney King—didn't know the man—he understood what it meant to be a Black man in this country, and besides, the police response had been excessive, unnecessary, and wrong. Full stop.

The long-faced man pleaded, "C'mon y'all," trying to solicit allies.

Every man in that shop shook his head or turned away from that brother, one saying, "Go on somewhere with that. Not here."

But the man wouldn't let it go. "You mean to tell me you don't think Rodney King was driving drunk or hopped up on PCP?" When the silence lingered with no one saying a word, he said, "Y'all tripping," and walked out of the shop.

Before things got out of hand and turned ugly, Buddy held up one hand to signal *it's over* and there was nothing new to see here. Now, Key fixed his eyes on the Bulls posters, T-shirts, jerseys, and baseball caps tacked to the shop wall that faced the row of mirrors. Even when the barber swiveled your chair, you still had the opportunity to salute the home team.

The clippers buzzed near Key's ear as Buddy trimmed the hair on Key's neckline. He bent close and asked, "You going down to the stadium Tuesday?"

"Nah. Hate to miss it but my girl's mother is hosting a big shindig auction thing downtown and I'm the plus one. I guess they planned this thing way in advance of the Finals. They better have some big-screen TVs near that ballroom though."

In the reflection of the mirror, Key saw Buddy's face scrunch up with barely contained laughter. "Okay, now I see why you in a hurry to get this fade shaped up."

"Yeah, man. I'm officially meeting her folks there for the first time."

"Oh, so it's one of those 'Guess Who's Coming to Dinner' kind of nights."

"It's not like that, man." Key shifted in the barber's chair, and Buddy said, "Hey, hold still before I scalp you or slice your neck with this thing."

What was it like? For one, Tulip wasn't a white girl, but she might as well have been with her pedigree and privilege, the luxury to buck the system instead of being beholden to it. Until now, she hadn't let him spend any time alone with her parents. Not until some fancy banquet with hundreds of people around and high society enough that everybody would be on their best behavior. Still, he wouldn't put it past her parents to slip some poison in his food. This night would be their first chance to scrutinize him and itemize all the reasons he didn't measure up as suitable for their daughter.

Maybe Buddy sensed his nerves bouncing around in his chest like pinballs. He brushed loose hair from his smock and swiveled the chair so Key could see himself in the mirror. "Look at you. Sharp all day long. Show 'em what Keyshawn McCray is all about. Show 'em the Keyshawn McCray we know and love, and you'll be fine."

A man could use as many fathers as he could get, and he was grateful for Buddy. Key stared at his own reflection in the mirror, tilting his head to see every angle of his newly groomed hair. He felt fresh and clean, the way he needed to for a proper introduction to Dr. and Mrs. Vance.

19

Tulip

The Hotel Intercontinental glimmered in the urban sophistication of the '90s monied class, a nod to the grand cosmopolitan style of the roaring twenties. The indulgence of this night reminded Tulip of something out of the pages of *The Great Gatsby*, the only classic she read in high school instead of skimming the CliffsNotes version. Her mother surpassed her own standards this time with opulence that would have made Jay Gatsby blush.

Tulip sashayed into that banquet ballroom, ponytail swinging, with Key on her arm like it was the Grammy's and they were up for album of the year. Chandeliers sparkled and auction items lined the walls in an attractive display designed to inspire deep-pocket donors to open their wallets and bid high. But there was nothing pretentious about the music—a band was performing popular R&B music while couples and clusters of women danced hard to Mary J. Blige.

"Darling, you're here." Freda shined in a strapless emerald gown with an elaborate silver piece of jewelry adorning her neckline. She looked positively regal, representing the Links. It made perfect sense that they selected Freda to host the auction, an event steeped in a sense of control and precise calculations where everything had to add up, with partic4ipants deciding when to bid and how much to bid, whether to go low or high. One time her mother had broken down the probabilities, the mathematical theory behind optimizing one's chances at winning a bid.

Gerald walked up behind her, placing his hand at the small of her mother's back. In addition to heart research, the money raised that night would help fund a new cardiology wing at the hospital where he had privileges. This event could only be described as the perfect marriage of her parents' interests and sensibilities, somehow more logical to Tulip than their actual marriage.

She accepted a glass of Cabernet from a passing waiter and took a few sips. She needed this night to go well, for all the people she loved most to get along. Kissing her mother's cheek and then her father's, Tulip said, "You certainly know how to put on an event, Mom. I want you both to meet Key."

Tulip gripped his arm tightly and he smoothed the front of the black suit his father let him borrow for the night since they wore the same size. Not that Key couldn't afford a suit of his own. He didn't like to wear them, and since he wasn't a churchgoing man and no one in his family had died lately, he said he had no use for one. But she appreciated the effort he made for her sake.

"Ma'am, thank you for inviting me," he said.

Tulip stood awkwardly between Key and her parents. She stared at her fingers and twirled the chain strap of her handbag. Freda said, "Keyshawn, it's lovely to finally meet you. If you see anything tonight that tickles your fancy that you want to bid on, please do."

She knew good and well that Key couldn't afford the high-priced items up for auction. Key opened and closed his fists. "Well, I do see some Jordan gear I might want to own." Tulip smiled nervously, knowing that the one Jordan jersey even unsigned would go for a minimum of tens of thousands of dollars.

Gerald slapped Key on the back a bit harder than necessary. "I see we have something in common. A deep affection for the Bulls. Let's talk offense and defense and catch some of the game."

When her father started to lead Key to the lounge, her boyfriend glanced at her, unsure of his best play in the moment, and she couldn't decide how to interpret her father's invitation. Was he up to something? "Are you coming?" Gerald asked.

Maybe he wanted to get to know Key, man to man. "Go on," Freda said. "But you two better not spend the whole night watching basketball and miss filling out your bid sheets."

WHY HAD TULIP DARED HOPE HER PARENTS WOULD EMBRACE KEY? She had prepared for the worst but it was more awkward than she'd anticipated. Their words sounded cordial, but it seemed her mother was trying to embarrass him. Why couldn't she just give the man a chance? Tulip tried to shake it off and focus on the festive event that promised to be a fun evening. She joined her mother, who was admiring a one-of-a-kind oil painting, studying the balance and harmony on the canvas, when someone behind them whispered: "Now that might fetch a pretty penny, but you know it's ugly." They whipped around to see Auntie Ev, who claimed to be iconic enough to go by only one syllable these days. She stunned in a silver dress so silky it could have easily slid off her skin like rain. Bold, Black, and bougie as ever.

Freda wrapped her in a tight hug and screamed. "You made it, girl. Now we can get this thing started." Evaline Bates, Esq., was a formidable state's attorney in Detroit and definitely qualified as her mother's coolest friend. Sometimes, Tulip envied this woman who knew parts of her mother she never would.

"Yes, I escaped the courtroom. Cora sends her love but she's with Percy and the boys at revival this weekend." Admiring Tulip, she said, "Look at my beautiful niece all grown up and sophisticated." Breathless, she seemed distracted. "I just got here. See anything worth bidding on?" Auntie Ev's eyes roved the men in the room, not the auction items.

Freda looped her arm with her friend's and laughed. "Girl, you never change. When are you going to settle down?"

"Well, I guess you don't know me as well as you thought you did. I never settle." And with that, she took the hand of a philanthropist and shimmied her way to the dance floor.

***

"MORE WOMEN DIE OF HEART DISEASE EVERY YEAR THAN ANY other ailment," Freda said from the podium, encouraging bidding before dinner started. "Together, we have the power to save lives, and we can do it right here tonight. Keep bidding, the night is young." Her mother's voice and passion made guests halt their chatter mid-sentence, freeze on the dance floor, and snap to attention.

Tulip couldn't shake this idea of people power, and she kept thinking about Ida B. Wells. Some of those residents had never been as far north as downtown, and their voices never reverberated beyond their South Side community. They could be powerful if they reached more people with their message. But for now, she needed to reach Key and her father before dinner started and the wait staff brought out covered plates of surf and turf—filet mignon and garlic butter lobster tail.

Tulip left the ballroom and followed the sounds of a sports announcer's play-by-play for the Bulls game. As expected, in a small lounge clustered around a large screen television was where she found a group of basketball fans. Her father and Key stood apart from the crowd, glancing at the TV while speaking intensely. Key clutched a beer bottle while Gerald casually nursed a glass of fizzy sparkling water. Her father had teased over the years that he avoided alcohol, preferring to stay grounded, and Tulip prayed he would keep his cool with her boyfriend. She moved close enough to listen without them noticing her.

"Jordan's on fire with those threes," Key said.

"Yes, he is," Gerald said. "The Blazers are good and will be formidable competition, but they don't have the drive or athleticism of the Bulls. There are levels of play on court and in life, and you have to recognize your own level."

Still looking at the TV, he was steering the conversation in a direction Key surely hadn't been expecting. She could tell by the way her man's jaw tightened. "You're a good guy. You work hard, but you're on a different level, not the right man for my daughter. When I look at you, I see how I could have ended up if I hadn't made it out of the ghettoes of New York. Don't get me wrong. I had people lifting me up, but I also had drive and ambition to do more than was expected of me, to be more. That's what I want for Tulip."

With a swoop of his hand, Key smoothed his close-cut hair. Tulip had been a fool to think a fine suit and a fresh fade would impress her parents, who had already made up their minds about her boyfriend.

Key's fingers tightened around his beer bottle, and he looked like he wanted to crack it over the top of her father's head. "You know what? You keep judging me for not being good enough." And then he stabbed her father's chest with his index finger, causing Gerald to back up a few steps. "You're full of yourself and arrogant, and I don't want to be anything like you. But as long as Tulip wants me around, I plan to be right here. You got that?"

Other hotel guests in the lounge had turned to look and then smile sheepishly as if they hadn't been gawking. Where in the world had Key gotten the nerve to stand up to her father like that? She had never been prouder. Gerald smiled, something Tulip wasn't expecting. "Okay, all right, maybe I deserved that. But time will tell whether you're worthy of my daughter."

Key ground out his words. "Tulip's got a mind of her own."

Gerald dropped his head and let out a small laugh. "You're right about that. She always has, from her choice of music and clothes to what she chose to study in college. I couldn't bribe her enough to go the medical school route like her old man. Lately we can't seem to get her to drop all this protest foolishness over that Rodney King out in LA."

At this point, Tulip wanted to reveal her presence and set her father straight, but she needed to hear more. What would Key say? Would he defend her? After a long pause, he said, "She's got a strong will to change the world and I love that about her, but I do think it's dangerous business and won't do a damn bit of good, won't make this country any less racist."

Gerald looked at him steadily. "Now that's something we agree on. Not even Tulip or Freda knows this but earlier today I was in the hospital seeing patients, something I do once or twice a week. I was walking the halls of the cardiac ICU wearing my scrubs and a lab coat over that when a scheduling person I hadn't seen before stopped me. She asked me to get a patient dressed and transported down to X-ray." He shook his head at the memory, as if he could clear his mind enough to fully comprehend what had happened. "And get this? Then she asked me to take out the trash. I'm a physician, one of the top in my field. But she saw a Black face."

"I don't know what to say, sir. That's just wrong," Key said.

"Of course it's wrong, but it's real. It's the world we live in and all that burning down the city and marching through the streets of LA won't change it. I lived through it in the sixties. Things are better, yes, and we have more opportunity, but we still have to work ten times as hard to get half as far. Tulip's mother and I are where we are today because we kept our focus on being excellent, being the best."

Tulip stood rooted in place, shaking with anger over someone not acknowledging her father as a doctor, not showing him the respect he deserved. But he was wrong to think that protest didn't matter. Excellence had taken him only so far. She knew her history. He wouldn't be practicing at the University of Chicago without the activism in the '50s and '60s.

Gerald wasn't done. "Tell me, are you a connoisseur of fine jewelry?"

Key shifted from one foot to the other with his hands flailing like tiny fish in his pockets. "No, sir, no. I'm not."

"Well, there's a lot of fool's gold out there, counterfeits that can be deceiving to the untrained eye. Take my watch here." He rubbed his hand across the gold band. "There's a nitric acid test and a density test we can do, and they will prove without a doubt that this is real gold. I'm here to save you time and heartache. My daughter is pure gold."

"Dad, are you comparing me to a piece of metal?" Tulip interrupted, placing a hand on her father's shoulder.

Key spoke up first. "It's all right. Your father was reminding me how special and precious you are. I agree with him."

"Thank you," she said, snuggling close to Key and imploring her father with her eyes to stop this insidious takedown and give Key a chance. He held up his hands in surrender and returned to the ballroom.

Her presence had staunched the bleeding but the wounded relationship between her parents and Key lay open, raw and exposed. Was tonight divine prophecy, God's way of saying love—Black love—couldn't bear the weight of two people who came from different worlds?

IN THE BATHROOM AFTER DINNER, TULIP REAPPLIED LIPSTICK AND brushed away the shine of perspiration and exhaustion with powder. The door opened, and Auntie Ev walked in, grinning the moment she saw her. They refreshed their makeup together in the mirror. "What are you doing in here? Your face is perfect, so you must be hiding. Why?"

You could always count on Auntie Ev to skip pleasantries and get right to the heart of a matter. "It's everything with my mom and dad. They met my boyfriend tonight for the first time, and they don't think he's good enough. And I might be joining a protest on behalf of Rodney King. They're not happy about that either." Hearing the words pour out made her feel the weight of defeat.

Auntie Ev lined her eyes with a black pencil and added a lavender shimmer to her lids. "Oh, I have a lot of thoughts, but I'll say this: Your parents have been right where you are, we all have, making tough choices, having no idea how it would all turn out in the end. But living with the consequences." Her face hardened into an unreadable mask. "I've been young and scared and alone with parents in my ear telling me what to do. I say listen to your mom and dad and then do what feels right for you. Sometimes I wonder how my life might have turned out if I had trusted myself more."

Tulip had only seen her Auntie Ev sassy and joyful, but her eyes watered now. When Tulip reached out to touch her shoulder, she snapped her handbag shut and headed for the door. What in the world had gotten into her, and where had she gone in her memory to trigger such a response? Leaving the ladies room, she turned on the playfulness like a faucet. "If you tell your mother I said any of that, I'll deny it."

As she exited, Karama Turnbull from WGN entered. The popular news reporter and anchor was one of the most tenured Black journalists in town, and she had graciously agreed to emcee the benefit, turning heads all night in a fitted sequined gown that made her look like a mermaid rising from the ocean.

"Hello. I'm Tulip, Freda Vance's daughter. You made my mother's event a huge success, so thank you," Tulip said when Karama joined her at the mirror to spritz hairspray.

"I should be thanking your mother. I could've ended up at one of the bars near the stadium. All those drunks using the Bulls as an excuse to act a damn fool. I love my Bulls and I'm glad they won, don't get me wrong, but all that hollering gives me a headache. I'm happy to be here—it's for a good cause."

They hadn't met before but Tulip rarely fangirled over journalists when she met them in person the way the average viewer did. They always presented opportunities for her to promote her clients and their brands, and she had to sound like a confident PR pro, not a groupie at a Madonna concert. Maybe it was the wine or the permission Auntie Ev gave her to take a risk, but Tulip inhaled deeply and kept her eyes on her own reflection in the mirror, thickening her lashes with mascara. "I do PR for Mattingly and I may have a story for you. It's about Rodney King and Latasha Harlins in LA."

Karama waved her hand in front of her face to clear the fumes from the hairspray. She bore the exhausted, patronizing look of a television personality accustomed to strangers pitching her stories everywhere she went. "That's not a Chicago story. We would need a local angle."

"Ida B. Wells is planning a march in a couple weeks," Tulip said. "It's going to be huge. You'll want to cover it, trust me."

"A march?" Karama said. "Why? Just in solidarity?"

Tulip turned away from the mirror to face Karama. "Yes, but more than that. Everything happening in LA is what woke people up. You know Ida B. Wells has been suffering like all the other projects in this city for a long time. Run-down housing, poverty, no opportunity. People forget about them if they think of them at all. They're tired of it."

"Interesting. You know the station doesn't like to send us to the projects unless somebody got shot," Karama said.

"Ugh, I know, but there are plenty of angles to this story. I can get you interviews with the organizer and some of the residents who will be part of this. You can do a preview piece beforehand, maybe profiling a couple residents to humanize the story and drive attendance, and then hopefully cover the march itself."

"What day of the week is the march?" Karama asked.

"A Saturday."

"We always have a skeletal crew on weekends, but I'll be anchoring. It is the ghetto shift after all, so yeah, we can at least spray it," she said, meaning at minimum a thirty second voice-over with some video from the protest. They both knew that murder and mayhem elsewhere in the city could divert the crew.

"I'm familiar with your agency." Karama applied fresh gloss to her lips. "But are they branching out? Their clients are usually consumer products, more morning show feature type stories. Is this Ida B. Wells community group a client of yours? I can't see how they'd have the money to pay for a PR agency."

Her question caught Tulip off-guard. Karama was right, of course. Mattingly would never take on a local community group in the projects as a client. How could she wiggle her way out of this without digging a deeper hole? She remembered Bryce talking about corporate social responsibility and being good corporate citizens. "We reserve a small portion of our business for philanthropic work. We try to serve how and where we can."

Immediately, Tulip wished she could take back those words. What had she done? Why had she said that? She couldn't ask Karama to keep this to herself, not after she volunteered that pro bono work was now part of the Mattingly business model. But Karama had agreed to cover the Ida B. Wells story. If Bryce or someone from the agency found out that she'd misrepresented Mattingly and used her position to help her personal cause, she knew there'd be consequences. Her lie, as well-intentioned as it was, hung in the air, a dark ominous note on such a bright night.

PART SEVEN

Nashville, 1960

20

Freda

When the doctor told Freda she had suffered a mild traumatic brain injury, it sounded like an oxymoron, or perhaps the neurons in her brain were simply misfiring. Dr. Shaw had assured her she would fully recover. They only kept her in the hospital for two days in spite of Gerald's protests that she might need to be monitored longer. He had become her protector, and she knew she was as safe as she had been growing up in her parents' home. The morning she was discharged, he took her back to his place and picked up the phone to call her folks.

"No, please don't do that," she said, almost begging. "They'll just worry, and I don't want them to." Her normal day to call that week hadn't come around yet, so they wouldn't have been suspicious. But they must have followed the news about Big Saturday and would likely be anxious about her safety. They'd have had good reason. Unlike the first one on Valentine's Day weekend, this sit-in had turned violent with a white mob attacking Negro protesters.

"You have a concussion," Gerald said, raising his voice as if talking louder would penetrate the good sense sealed off somewhere in her brain. "They're your parents and they would want to know. I don't want them to think I'm not looking after you."

"I *had* a concussion, and it was mild, remember? It's not your job to take care of me, even though I appreciate that you are."

He shook his head, exasperated, but didn't reach for the phone again. He made her tomato soup and fluffed her pillows and asked her lots of questions she didn't have easy answers for. Like why had she been outside that sit-in, in the first place? What made her challenge that police officer and put herself in danger? She couldn't explain even to herself why seeing Darius hauled off in handcuffs made her desperate to do something.

When she had pressed Cora and Evaline for information about what ever happened to Darius, she must not have been subtle because they immediately accused her of having a crush on him. Did she? No, that was impossible. Her heart belonged to Gerald now. But one thing was certain. She would never admit to her friends how much Darius intrigued her because they wouldn't understand. Even she didn't.

It wasn't just that Darius was the wrong kind of guy, but he made her question everything she'd been taught, everything she believed to be true. He reminded her of a hangnail that irritated, yet you still favored it, rubbing your finger over its jagged edge because it refused to be ignored.

ALMOST TWO MONTHS LATER, FREDA WAS BACK TO HER REGULAR routine with a full class schedule, her headaches long gone, but she sometimes found herself more emotional than usual, bursting into tears over a carton of expired milk or a run in her silk stockings. On most nights, she had trouble falling asleep and would lie awake thinking. Dr. Shaw had advised her to slow down physically and mentally to let her brain heal. She tried but couldn't stop the furious onslaught of thoughts about that day at Woolworth's. Police arrested eighty-one protesters that Saturday, most of them Negroes, but nothing ever happened to their white attackers. No arrests. No fines. Not even a stern warning you'd give a child for misbehaving. Outrage snaked through her blood at the unfairness of it.

One afternoon, a week after Big Saturday, Freda snuck over to the county workhouse and tried to blend in with the gaggle of lawyers who had come to bail out some of the Negro students. The rumor on campus was that the protesters would be released into the care of their college deans, who still had to answer to anxious mothers and fathers. But close to one hundred were still being held at the workhouse. Showing up there, Freda was taking a chance on getting locked up herself.

The sound of old Negro spirituals filled her ears as student inmates sang while they worked, humming and harmonizing as they mopped floors and washed walls. It didn't take long before she spotted Darius, still wearing his wrinkled white dress shirt, in deep concentration meticulously rubbing a gray cloth over a jail bar like he was polishing silver.

"You gon' wipe the metal clear off that thing," she said, swinging her purse behind her back.

His head shot up fast. "Freda! What are you doing here?" He cleaned his hand on his pants before touching her arm. "I saw what happened to you. Are you okay? How bad were you hurt?"

"You're asking way too many questions at once. I'm fine, it was only a minor concussion. But why are you still here?" Freda was whispering now, digging into her purse. "I heard the bail went up to fifty dollars. I have enough. You don't have to stay here another minute."

He shook his head. "You don't understand. If we pay, they win. I'm not afraid, just determined. We'll never get them to meet our demands and desegregate if we take the easy way out. No bail."

She closed the clasp of her purse and cupped his chin in her hands until a guard snapped at him to get back to work. He hurried her out of there so fast she barely got another look at Darius. It was such a brief visit she sometimes wondered if it had happened at all, or if she had dreamed it.

Still, that glimpse of him was enough for her brain to simply defy doctor's orders to slow down. It sped up instead and she saw everything anew. The protests. The negotiations. Darius being hauled into that paddy wagon and his quiet determination in jail. Cora's humiliation at being used by Woolworth's. The faces and voices of the rabid mob outside the store. The officer who threw her to the ground. The contempt on that saleslady's face at McLellan's. The colored-only restroom sign at the fair. Every racial slight and indignity she had experienced since setting foot in Nashville played double-time in her head, magnified now. She looked at this town and her place in it for the first time with clear eyes.

***

Under the canopy entrance to Nashville's Club Del Morocco stood a tall man in a sharp, brown pinstripe suit with shoulders almost as wide as the front door he blocked. He extended his hand to Gerald. "Good to see you, man. He's in there." After some playful jabbing and backslapping, the bouncer stepped aside, and Gerald placed his hand on Freda's waist to usher her into the club. For months he'd accused her of being a recluse—going to classes and the library and the dining hall, but doing little else, certainly nothing fun. How could she enjoy college life surrounded by so much hate? "We're having a good time," he said, and it came close to a command.

Del Morocco was once a hotel for Pullman porters to get some shut-eye when they weren't working the rails. After the hotel was demolished and turned into a nightclub in the early '40s, soldiers from Fort Campbell flocked there to drink and dance away the wartime memories they couldn't shake any other way.

It took her eyes a few seconds to adjust to the darkness of the club with brightly colored lights and glass reflecting along the brick walls. Gerald had taken her to other lounges on Jefferson Street, but never here, to one of the classiest of them all. The spot where top chefs served Joe Louis, Jackie Robinson, and Count Basie. The club where this newcomer Jimi Hendrix was tearing up the local music scene.

She'd never had much use for philosophers, but she thought of what Aristotle said about the whole being greater than the sum of its parts.

Separately, she and Gerald had a shot at being something great, with her being born into money and him on his way to becoming a doctor. But together, they had a chance to be even more. More what? She had no idea, but taking in this swanky dinner club and all these beautiful Negroes, the picture was starting to form, and she might get used to this.

Gerald knew people here, and they knew him. And that meant they now knew her. When they walked up the narrow staircase to the piano bar known as the Blue Room, they ran into the owner, Teddy Acklen. The heavyset man wore a three-piece charcoal suit, a contrast against skin so light you might mistake him for a white man if you didn't know any different or hadn't seen him up close. His widow's peak stood out prominently and his hair made its own waves without a congolene pomade to burn his scalp.

Everybody called him Uncle Teddy, and she heard he ran a numbers racket in the secret, hidden rooms of Club Del Morocco. If he did, Freda didn't want or need to know, and she committed herself to not looking too hard at anything. She came here for the music and the good times, not the hearsay.

"Welcome. Glad to have you," Uncle Teddy greeted her warmly.

"I'm happy to be here. This club is extraordinary," she said, hoping she didn't sound overly enamored.

He nodded and turned his attention to Gerald. "I trust that school is going well."

"Very well, sir. I received an A in epidemiology and a B+ in biostatistics." Gerald made his studies a priority and kept this man informed of his progress since it was Uncle Teddy who paid his tuition.

"Glad to hear it," Uncle Teddy said, obviously impressed but not surprised, and he guided them to a small table for four with an unobstructed view of the stage. Evaline and Ambrose would be joining them soon for a double date. "You picked a good night to come. Nat's on later," he said, before disappearing into the smoky haze he emerged from.

She yanked Gerald's arm when they took their seats. "I knew Nat King Cole was coming. But he's here tonight?"

"I thought you didn't care who was playing." Gerald pulled her close, chuckling in her ear, lightly kissing the lobe. "He's fresh off his European tour. I mean he was everywhere—Paris, Zurich, and London. From what I hear, he flew home to the States to relax. Uncle Teddy's wife used to be one of Nat's dancers back in the day, and that's how he ended up becoming a friend to the club."

Nat King Cole had been a magnificent obsession of Freda's family for years. Mama and Papa saw him on tour in Chicago once, and Mama tucked that program booklet with Nat's autograph in the groove of her dresser mirror alongside her wedding announcement and the funeral cards of friends and relatives. Then she framed it and hung it in the living room for family and friends to admire when they visited.

"This was all part of my plan to take you out to see Nat perform," Gerald said with a self-satisfied smile. "Are you sufficiently surprised and delighted?"

"Negro, please," Freda said, slapping his shoulder.

Everyone sat close together in the club—suits, dresses, and hair pressed to perfection, drinking and laughing, the energy of their anticipation bouncing from table to table, all of them buzzing, trying to contain their excitement waiting for Nat to take the stage. That's when Evaline showed up, intertwined so closely with Ambrose they could have been one person.

Freda squeezed her friend. "You made it. I was getting worried."

With a slight wave of her slender hand and that dazzling smile that you knew got her whatever she wanted back in Detroit, Evaline summoned the waitress. "We would have been here much earlier," she said and winked at Ambrose. "But somebody wouldn't let me get dressed on time."

"I'm a red-blooded man. What can I say?" Ambrose pulled a flask from his suit jacket and threw his head back to drink.

Within seconds, a neatly dressed waiter arrived at their table with glasses, ice cubes, and a dish of peanuts. Nashville was a dry town, so establishments weren't allowed to serve any alcohol other than beer, at least not legally. Bootlegging happened in quite a few clubs, but typically the bar offered the setup and you provided your own booze. Luckily Gerald and Ambrose had struck up a friendship with a few Korean War vets, who were generous enough to share their brown liquor with medical students they looked upon as younger brothers. Gerald pulled his own flask from his suit coat and poured enough in each of their glasses to cover the ice.

THEY TAPPED THEIR FEET TO A WARM-UP BAND—DRUMMER, BASS player, no vocalist. And then Freda heard it—the deep, brassy, soulful sound of the sax. She almost snapped her neck whipping around to face the stage. She knew what—or rather who—she would find, and there he was. Darius Moore stood at the center of the small stage, his sound filling the club. He didn't build to a crescendo. Instead, he entered the music fast and frantic like a man running out of time.

If she wondered whether he noticed her, she had her answer soon. He played the same song he had when she first followed the sound of his sax to the chapel. When his eyes weren't closed in some dream state, they lingered on hers until she couldn't take it anymore and had to look away. The tumble of her heart took her by surprise because she didn't know when or how hard it would land. For now, she looked down at the ice in her glass.

"Isn't that Darius who spoke on campus, the one leading that sit-in at the five-and-tens?" Evaline said, knowing full well who Darius Moore was.

If it wouldn't have been too obvious, Freda would have kicked her friend under the table. "Yes, I think so. I believe it is." She hoped she sounded nonchalant. The last she had heard, Darius had done his time in the workhouse and was still demonstrating, making some gains with white business owners and the local government.

"That sit-in foolishness is what landed you in the hospital. You know him?" Gerald said, also trying to appear unbothered, but Freda heard the concern in his voice.

"I wouldn't say I know him," Freda defended herself. "He was in my philosophy class." Darius hadn't shown up for class in months, and she assumed his jail time set him back and that he would need to retake the class.

"Hmm," was all Gerald said.

Most conversations subsided and people fixated on Darius playing as if his life depended on it, the sound he made coming from some otherworldly place, too massive and ethereal to live inside one body. It held her, all of them, in its sway. Ambrose nodded his head and tapped his fingers on the table. "He's pretty good. He can blow on that sax."

Gerald shrugged. "I guess if you like that tinny sort of sound. Kind of thin and flat if you ask me."

When the warm-up band finished its set, Darius caught Freda's eye as he was leaving the stage, and that instant connection between them sparked. She tracked his movement from the stage to the bar where a bartender had a drink waiting for him. By now, Gerald and Ambrose were in a heated conversation about football, the attention thankfully no longer on Darius Moore. But she should have known Evaline would pick up on the slightest spark between them.

Her friend leaned close to her ear, covered her mouth with her hand, and whispered loud enough for only Freda to hear. "I saw that, you know. And people say *I'm* fast." Then she took an exaggerated sip of her drink and clapped enthusiastically for Nat King Cole, who was walking onto the stage.

Freda stuck her tongue out at Evaline, but her friend's eyes, like everyone's, were on Nat, a man with dark skin smooth as butter. And the way he moved effortlessly, the stage his natural habitat. You couldn't tell that a few years before, white men at a concert in Birmingham had rushed a stage a lot bigger than this one and knocked him off his piano bench. The way people told it, Nat never saw it coming.

When she'd arrived at school in the fall, she would've explained away what happened to Nat as a cruel but isolated occurrence, something that made news on the rare occasions it happened. But now, she knew better. After all, Freda still wore the scar on the back of her head from when that officer shoved her so hard she slammed into a parked car before hitting the ground.

Racism, she was learning, came for all of them, even an entertainer larger than life like Nat King Cole. A man beloved around the world, a performer they couldn't get enough of. Bigots had to knock a man like Nat to the floor because they didn't know what else to do with someone who hypnotized people with his talent. An excellent Negro. They couldn't handle that.

And still, they couldn't keep him down long. The man famous for pop music but rooted in jazz moved his fingers across the piano like a skillful lover, the audience rousing to every touch of the keys. He even crooned the romantic ballad "Little Girl," the song he never got to finish that night those hoodlums attacked him.

FREDA EXCUSED HERSELF TO USE THE RESTROOM, AND ON HER way back to the table she saw Nat King Cole emerge from a side door having changed out of his suit into a short-sleeve fitted white shirt and a checkerboard-patterned hat. He moved through the club quickly, greeting and thanking fans. A man like that had to smile and turn on the charm with friendly and unfriendly crowds, and she thought it must get tiresome. Seeing that he was headed in her direction by the bar, she glanced away, starstruck all of a sudden. What would Mama say when she told her she had been close enough to Nat King Cole to touch the man? She wouldn't believe it.

"I take it you enjoyed the performance." Nat stood in front of her now, enunciating each syllable carefully, his voice pure and clear as a bell, whether he was singing or speaking.

"It was magnificent. You were magnificent," she said, a bit breathless.

"I pride myself on giving the people what they like. You don't sound like you're from around here. Where are you from?"

While she had said only a few words, his trained ear picked up on the fact that she was not from the South. "Chicago is home."

A flash of kinship animated him. "I grew up in Chicago. Fortieth and Vincennes," he said, and she saw in his face the little boy who would become King. The way he announced his origins reminded her of folks back home, who took immense pride in their city block, street, and plot of land that belonged to them.

He had lived not far from where she grew up and he mentioned a few of his favorite spots—the clubs where he had performed and a few restaurants he frequented.

Words spilled from Freda now, and she knew she was probably talking too fast. "I'm going home for summer break. I can't wait to tell my folks I met you. They saw you in concert once in Chicago years ago, and they're still talking about it like it was yesterday."

Nat smiled. "Give them my regards."

Any minute now, he would move on to receive his due praise from any number of tables of fans, but she had an idea. Everything that had happened since she moved to Nashville played in Freda's head like an old record she had dusted off. She may not have liked the methods of some of the rabble-rousers, but she understood. Things had to change, and maybe there was something she could do after all. And with Gerald not by her side, this was her best chance.

Freda cleared her throat. "Mr. Cole?"

"Nat, please," he said. Bending his head, he put a Kool cigarette between his lips and lit it.

"Yes, Nat." Calling him by his first name seemed sacrilegious, like she had no home training, but she did as he instructed, more than a little flattered that he asked her to be so familiar. "I wanted to ask if you might consider doing a concert, a benefit to raise money."

Watching his face, she saw it turn from water to ice. "Raise money for what?" he asked. A man like Nat King Cole probably ran into con artists trying to shake him down in every concert city. She couldn't have him believing she was like all the rest.

"It would be for charity, a good cause. I'm talking about raising money for the fight for equal rights for Negroes."

A flash of Nat's brilliant smile reappeared as if in begrudging admiration of her gall at asking such a question of him. Then just as fast, that smile slid clean off his face, so she quickly rattled off the names of Darius Moore and Reverend James Lawson and Jesse Jackson, the only people she thought of on the spot, trying to show Nat she had ties to legitimate activists.

"I'm not a controversial person," he said, his expression unreadable. "I'm an entertainer. It's my job to perform, to give people my music."

She had said too much, maybe even offended him. Embarrassed, she looked down at her feet. That's when Gerald appeared behind her and casually cupped her shoulders, a subtle act of possession in a room full of possibilities. She smelled the alcohol on him and knew he was getting more tipsy than usual.

"What are you two looking so serious about over here? I can't lose my girl to the King. I'd never live that down, man."

Nat's long slender fingers tapped his cigarette on the ashtray at the corner of the bar. "You're a lucky man. She was admiring my piano skills, asking me if I'd do an encore and play longer, but I'm jet-lagged. I'm done for tonight. Now, if you'll excuse me."

Nat moved on, saying his final goodbyes to people a few tables away, and Freda, humiliated, escaped to the restroom to compose herself. When she emerged a few minutes later, she headed toward the table to rejoin Gerald, Evaline, and Ambrose, but a waitress in a fitted black cocktail dress sidled up to her with a glass of club soda Freda hadn't ordered and handed her a folded napkin. The way she slid it into her hand instead of placing it around the drink to absorb the condensation from the glass made Freda suspect there was something unusual happening. A hint of a smile crossed the woman's face, and you might have missed it if you weren't quick enough to notice.

When the waitress walked away, Freda gripped the folded napkin tightly. She sensed the hungry gazes of a few men at the bar. A phone number or a hello on a napkin struck her as a cheap, uninspired way to get a lady's attention. The last thing she wanted was for Gerald to think she was entertaining interest from any of them. But no one approached her.

She unfolded the white paper napkin. Words scrawled in black ink fanned across it, and whatever air circulated in the club right then bottled in her throat. The message was cryptic, but the flourish of the handwriting distinct. She remembered it from a blackboard in one of her classes.

Meet me out back.
D.M.

OUTSIDE THE CLUB, FREDA HEARD THE METALLIC BUZZ OF A TRUMPET somewhere on the stroll and it rivaled the sound of her own thundering heartbeat. The smell of the leftover scraps from dinner floated up to her from the trash bins. She wrapped her shawl around her shoulders to break the chill and that's when she heard his voice.

"You got my note." Turning, she saw him, and she had been right. Darius Moore stood in the middle of the small street behind the club, staring at her, mouth open like he had a million things to say but couldn't think of where to start. Bending close to the ground, he set down his hard shell saxophone case and closed the distance between them.

"I recognized the song you played tonight," she said. "And you finally did what I asked."

"What's that?"

"You shut out the world and played like all of us in the audience weren't even there. It was like you had come outside your own body with that sound. It was more beautiful than the first time I heard it, if that's even possible."

He blushed. "Thank you. I shut out everybody but you. Freda, I've been worried about you," he said, lightly pressing his palm against the back of her head.

When he reached behind her, he was standing close enough for her to smell the minty balm he rubbed on his lips after playing his instrument. "I told you before I'm fine. It was only a minor concussion."

"I know you did but that hasn't stopped me from worrying. I should have come by Jubilee Hall to check on you. I should have done a lot of things." His voice trailed off.

She shivered. "For what it's worth, I hated leaving you in that horrible jail where you shouldn't have been in the first place. When I saw the police drag you out of Woolworth's, I tried to stop them. I mean I don't know what I could have done. Instead, I got in the way, and then . . ."

Darius shrugged out of his suit jacket and put it around her shoulders. "I can't tell you how much I blame myself for that. I don't regret sitting in and trying to force those stores to do the right thing. And I don't regret those thirty-three and one-third days locked up." Then he took her hand in his. "But the last thing I wanted was for you to get hurt. I lied about not checking on you. When I left the workhouse, I tried once to see how you were doing. But people said someone—" He paused as if he were deciding whether or not to go on. "Well, they said someone was looking after you."

He must have heard about her relationship with Gerald. That meant he had to know his name, but he didn't say it and neither did she. Freda had no reason to feel guilty for having a boyfriend, but she did. There was nothing between her and Darius, not officially anyway. She hadn't betrayed anyone, had she? No one considered Freda the kind of girl to carry on with two men at the same time. No, not the classy daughter of Dr. and Mrs. Gilroy. Her mind went to Gerald inside the club, likely entertaining their friends with jokes, and she glanced quickly over her shoulder. What if he came looking for her?

She slid her hand out of Darius's grasp. She removed his jacket from her shoulders and rubbed her arms briskly, chilly again all of a sudden. "I should go back inside."

"Please don't. Not yet," he said. "I wanted to tell you I'm taking some time off. I didn't quit school. I plan to graduate, count on that. But I feel like now is the right time to make real change all over the South and it requires my full, undivided attention. The Movement is my classroom now."

She nodded because she did finally understand. Her own outrage apart from his had taken root inside her. But she couldn't imagine leaving school, not even for a little while, to gamble on something with no certain outcome. A life of taking chances, ruled by some higher purpose, baffled and attracted her at the same time. For a second, she considered telling him what she had asked of Nat King Cole, but anybody with good sense would laugh at such a silly proposition. And then it suddenly hit her that if Darius left Fisk even temporarily, she may never see him again. A physical ache surged through Freda at that thought, and she began mourning the loss of this man standing right in front of her.

"How will you survive and where will you go?"

"I'm still in Nashville for now. Took a job down at Union Station, doing a little of this and that at the train station in the mornings."

Darius must have read her mind. "I'll still see you. As a matter of fact, we're having an organizing meeting at First Baptist a little more than a week from now on Sunday right after service. It's right before some of us go out and march here on Jefferson. I'm speaking and I get a little nervous sometimes. I could sure use a friendly face in the congregation."

Having heard him speak before crowds, she knew the awesome power of his voice and how it mesmerized people. And his saxophone playing blew the roof off this club. He didn't need her presence, but he wanted it, and that distinction sent a thrill straight up her spine.

Before she had time to respond, he moved closer to her. She shut her eyes and his lips brushed against hers ever so lightly.

If she were asked to place her hand on a Bible and swear in a court of law as to whether or not they kissed that night, she might unknowingly perjure herself. She wasn't certain. What she knew for sure was that things were far from over with Darius Moore.

BACK IN THE CLUB, PEOPLE WERE DANCING AND TALKING LOUDLY, the haze of cigarette smoke covering the room like fog. The hour was late but the night still young. Freda slid into the booth beside Gerald and across from Evaline and Ambrose. "Where did you disappear to?" Gerald asked. "I was looking for you."

"I stepped outside to get some fresh air, that's all." She hoped her weak smile hadn't betrayed her.

"Girl, we were ready to come rescue you," Evaline said, cozying up to Ambrose. "I think we need more drinks." She signaled the waitress for fresh ice.

In all the commotion, Freda hadn't noticed Darius walking through the club shaking hands with people who had enjoyed his performance and passing out flyers. He said the same thing at each table. "Join us at First Baptist Church. We're fighting for the dignity and equality of Negroes. Learn the principles of nonviolent direct action. It works. We need you there."

Freda was surprised he came to their table but maybe skipping it would have raised questions. Ambrose winked at Evaline. "Direct action, huh? I specialize in direct action." Darius recoiled at how vulgar and flip he was being about something so serious. What infuriated her even more was the way Gerald and Evaline threw their heads back, laughing as if it were the funniest thing they'd ever heard. Of course, the alcohol was partly to blame but Freda couldn't reconcile or excuse her friends' immaturity.

When Darius held the paper out to Freda, she stared at it a second too long when she should have taken it and thanked him.

Gerald snatched the flyer from Darius's hand, balled it in his fist, and leaned back in his seat, an arm around Freda's shoulder. "We already paid you for your performance earlier. Nobody's interested in whatever else you're selling."

Uncle Teddy owned this club and hired the entertainment, not Gerald. He was out of line, and she realized he must have had a few more drinks while she was outside with Darius. Ever since she'd known Gerald, he had been cautious about his drinking, determined not to end up an alcoholic like his father and Uncle Curtis. Why was he acting this way?

"Leave him alone," she begged, noticing they had attracted the attention of other patrons.

Darius's gaze from those large, solemn eyes framed by thick-rimmed glasses never wavered. "I was inviting *the lady* to the meeting."

Gerald tugged at Darius's necktie. "You need to loosen up, my man. Get you a good woman and have some fun." He pulled Freda even closer to him. "Can you do that?"

Who was this man cuddled up with her in the booth, spewing hot, brown liquor venom and scorning someone for political speech? Gerald's jealousy made him look small and pathetic. Shrugging off his embrace, Freda said, "You're embarrassing yourself, acting like a damn fool. I've had more than enough for one night."

She grabbed her handbag, flung her shawl over her shoulders, and walked out of the club leaving Gerald, Darius, and everyone else staring at her back.

Freda

The night before the organizing meeting, Freda and Evaline sat on Cora's bed watching her douse pork chops with salt, pepper, and flour before setting them to sizzle on a hot plate. Sweet, innocent Cora never broke any rules except for this one. And if Mother Gaines caught her, she'd have her hide. Still, the truth was they all missed their mothers' home cooking enough to chance a dorm room fire.

"You know Mama and Daddy are back to teaching now," Cora said.

"What? They are? That's wonderful," Freda said. "So that means you don't have to worry about staying in school."

When Cora's job at Woolworth's lunch counter ended, she was back where she started with no money for tuition, so this was a huge relief. Freda's and Evaline's parents had flat out refused to pony up any money to help their friend. But Cora hadn't seemed bitter about it, turning the other cheek to life's blows, and now everything had worked out fine.

"I'm not running a restaurant here." Cora waved her flour-coated hands. "Can one of you cut up that onion for me?"

"All right, all right. You sound like somebody's big mama in the kitchen," Evaline said, chopping on the wood dresser until Cora told her the pieces were fine enough. Her knife pounded the surface harder than necessary, and Freda and Cora exchanged glances.

Freda tried to settle into the fun of a Saturday night dinner in the dorm with her friends, but she couldn't stop thinking about what happened at the nightclub the week before. Freda had walked back to campus alone late at night ignoring both Gerald and Darius, who had run outside calling to her. The last thing she needed to be was a ragdoll in a tug-of-war between two men. As expected, Gerald showed up at her dorm the next morning with fresh-cut flowers, sad eyes, and a hangover.

"I'm sorry," he said. "I lost my head. I don't like who I am when I'm drinking."

Her forgiveness needed to be earned and she would have told him so if she hadn't been overwhelmed by guilt over whatever was happening between her and Darius. Maybe she needed to ask his forgiveness, too.

"You're allowed to make a mistake but the Gerald I know doesn't treat people that way," she said.

"I was dead wrong, but I don't want you getting mixed up in that trouble," he said. "You landed in the hospital the last time you did. It isn't safe. Let somebody else fight those battles. Not you. I know your parents wouldn't want . . ."

"Stop. Please leave Mama and Papa out of this."

Gerald nodded silently and she sent him on his way, never committing one way or the other about the organizing meeting at First Baptist. When Darius invited her, she had every intention of declining. But then her thoughts turned to those hecklers outside Woolworth's, who cheered when Darius and the others were hauled off to jail for demanding basic rights and dignity.

Biting into a crisp apple now to tide her over until the pork chops were ready, Freda said, "I'm thinking of going to First Baptist in the morning."

Evaline stopped slicing mid-chop. "Since when do you go to church?"

"Hey, I'm no heathen."

"If she's found the Lord, who are we to discourage her?" As kind as she was, it was hard to tell sometimes if Cora was being sarcastic.

"Found the devil is more like it," Evaline muttered, keeping her eyes on the onions.

Freda tossed an apple wedge at her friend. "There's a meeting after service about civil rights and I want to hear what they have to say."

"Oh no, it's more than that," Evaline said. "She wants to hear what *Darius Moore* has to say. He's speaking."

Cora surprised her. "I may go with you." She poured onions over the pork chops. "That manager at Woolworth's used me to make it seem like mistreating Negroes was all fine and dandy to me. Well, it's not. I keep thinking about my parents. They're in a temporary building and working again. But they were out of jobs for almost three months. Even now they're still buying the students' school supplies out of the little money they get. They're so good at what they do, and they love those kids, but white folks back home treat them like something stuck to the bottom of their shoe. As much as I love my town and Percy, of course, I hate seeing my family going through that. Mistreating me is one thing but it hurts when I see it happening to them."

Freda put an arm around Cora. "I'd love to have the company. Now I don't plan to get involved in any protest activities—I'll be there to listen."

"You're mighty quiet all of a sudden," Cora said to Evaline, who was standing at the dresser holding the cutting knife without moving a muscle. "You should come, too, if you can get away from Ambrose long enough," she teased.

"That's a lost cause," Freda said. "She's stuck to that boy like clothes fresh out the dryer."

They laughed at how true it was. Evaline didn't even have a snappy comeback this time. The one always drawn to drama like a summer bug swarming a porch light never found herself at a loss for words.

Evaline set down the knife, wiped her hands on a dish towel, and sat on the edge of Cora's bed.

"What is it?" Freda asked, her brow folded with worry.

Flashing one of her notorious smiles as easily as flipping a light switch, Evaline said, "Stop it. Nobody died. Just the opposite. You girls are going to be aunties."

Once Freda processed the words and comprehended their meaning, she realized her best friend was going to have a baby.

Cora was wringing her hands now. Freda didn't know whether to congratulate Evaline or offer her sympathies. Her eyes went immediately to her friend's stomach, which was still flat as a tabletop. Tracking her gaze, Evaline said, "Don't worry about me. I can eat like a horse and not put on a pound. One little baby will not ruin my figure."

She said it with such a straight face that the tension dissolved and all three laughed harder than they had in months, rolling around on Cora's bed, tears streaming down their cheeks. Evaline kept going. "And if I must, you know I will walk on this campus with my belly all stuck out, struttin' like I'm on some Paris runway."

"I can see you now in the middle of Jefferson Street, all big as you want to be," Freda said.

All three laughed, and then everything grew quiet except for the crackle of the pork chops. The truth was Fisk would never allow a pregnant girl to stay on campus, but no one said it aloud.

Freda spoke first. "How are you feeling?"

Keeping her eyes on the ceiling, Evaline rubbed her belly. "I don't feel any different. I'm not nauseous or anything. You could set a clock to my cycle, it's always so regular. So, when I missed I got worried and went to the doctor. The nurse told me the test results this morning and that's when I thought I might faint."

Cora whispered, "But seriously, what are you going to do?"

"I don't know. I haven't told my parents, and don't try to convince me to call them either. They warned me years ago that a baby was the destroyer of good Negro dreams. Like it's a curse or something."

Freda understood exactly what Evaline meant, and one day they had compared notes and realized their families ran in some of the same circles—both putting unreasonable limits on the girls.

"They're saying that because you're not married," Cora said, getting up to check the pork chops. Seeing they were done, she unplugged the hot plate and returned to the bed. "Murfreesboro isn't that far away. I bet my Percy could marry you and Ambrose."

Evaline stayed on her back, unmoving. And then tears leaked from her eyes and streamed into her hairline. "Ambrose was the first person I told when I got off the phone with the nurse. But he didn't believe it."

"Didn't believe what?" Freda said, her voice rising.

"He doesn't think it's his baby. This baby and me, we're problems for him now. He didn't even ask how I was feeling. Can you believe that? Kept talking about Meharry and his plans to become a doctor someday. And then get married and have children. In that order. I guess my Negro behind messed up the order of things."

Freda's thoughts went to Gerald and their nights together. They had been careful, as careful as they could be. But anybody could slip up. They had never talked about what would happen if she got pregnant. It never seemed like a possibility until now. What would her parents say? She probably wouldn't have the nerve to even tell them. The bed shook now with Evaline's sobs. One on either side of her, they covered her body with their own and cried into her hair.

"I can't believe Ambrose," Freda said. "He was all over you at the club like a cheap suit and now has the nerve to deny his own baby. He doesn't even deserve you or this child."

"But it's his baby, too," Cora said. "They have to find a way to make it work."

Freda chose her words carefully, afraid to offend either of her friends. "There is another way," she said, propping herself up on one arm in the bed. "You don't have to keep it unless you want to."

Before Evaline could respond, Cora sat up straight. "Don't say that. Ambrose may still come around. He's probably in shock. I can see them being a real family."

They watched Evaline, who finally said, "Honestly, y'all, I don't know what I'm going to do, but it's my decision." Then she rolled onto her side to face Freda. "I do know this much though. Gerald isn't like Ambrose. He's a good man. You know I saw you the other night, pining away over that sax-playing civil rights boy. I can tell you feel a pull toward him. But Gerald can give you a real future. You can still be a doctor's wife. Don't mess that up."

***

Organ music played softly on Sunday afternoon at First Baptist Church. Sweet perfume and the sweat of the saints leaving service filled the sanctuary. A few ushers gathered cardboard fans and Bibles left behind on the pews. Freda stood in the back wearing a lilac suit and a silk scarf that obscured part of her face. Like some starlet vacationing on the French Riviera trying to avoid the scrutiny of the photographers. The whole getup seemed silly now because she wasn't avoiding anyone or anything except her own growing interest in this movement for change.

At the front of the church, her eyes landed on Darius in a brown suit, his pants legs a few inches too long. He hunched over a record player, and when he finally placed the needle on the vinyl, the deeply resonant voice of Dr. Martin Luther King Jr. thundered against the stained-glass windows. She would recognize that voice anywhere. Darius took a few steps in each direction, his hands forming a steeple at his lips as he spoke in tandem with King.

He echoed, "There comes a time when one must take a position that is neither safe nor politic nor popular. But he must do it because conscience tells him it is right."

His eyes were closed like a hypnotized man, so immersed in the words of the speech that he didn't notice her approach until she was standing right in front of him. "You came," Darius said, appearing undoubtedly pleased, but not totally surprised. Had he expected her to show up? The idea of him counting on her to be there made her skin tingle.

"I hadn't planned to come."

"But you did. I'm sorry about what happened at the club."

"It wasn't your fault."

"I know, but I hated to see you—"

Cutting him off, Freda said, "You memorized that speech?"

Darius removed the needle from the record. "Dr. King addressed the graduating class at Morehouse last year. The man is a revolutionary. He's talking about our inescapable mutuality not just as Negroes, but as citizens of this whole world. A man in Europe or Asia can't be his fully realized self until we are. You can't be free until I am, and I can't be free until you are."

His words began as usual with the macro, the philosophical gibberish that had made him sound pompous in class. But then his words became intimate, stormwaters ripping her out to sea, sweeping her away in their undertow.

Then she heard throat clearing behind her. "Where are my manners? This is my dear friend and roommate from Fisk."

"Yes, I'm Cora," she said, extending her hand.

Hesitating, Darius said, "I remember you. You worked behind the counter at Woolworth's?"

Looking embarrassed, Cora said, "Not something I want to be remembered for. I'm so very sorry for the way you were treated that day."

Darius took her hand and held it in both of his. "No, you have nothing to apologize for. The tentacles of an unjust system are far-reaching. They are designed to place us in opposition to each other, both of us Negro, you behind the counter with no power and me sitting on the other side of that same counter demanding service, equally powerless. But that's where the white man's thinking is stunted. He never counts on us rising up and resisting his false sense of moral authority and superiority. Our unwavering commitment to nonviolence is our power. Our resistance is our power."

He didn't need to mimic King or anyone else. He had the gift to stir people with his own rhetoric. Cora seemed spellbound, too. But before either of them could respond, Reverend Kelly Miller Smith called the meeting to order and Freda noticed the church pews had already filled with Negroes and a good showing of whites, too.

Reverend Smith talked about how protesters had been sitting in all over Nashville that winter and spring, trying to desegregate businesses, and then returning to First Baptist, their home base, for new marching orders. But marching wasn't enough. They needed to raise money to bail out dozens of jailed activists and plan for upcoming demonstrations.

The room stirred with electricity, everyone indignant over what had happened earlier in April to civil rights attorney Z. Alexander Looby. A bundle of dynamite shattered a window in his home early one morning while the man slept in his bed. Though he wasn't harmed, students and the whole community had seen enough. They marched and would march again right after this meeting. They mapped out the streets they would cover, the formation of each line of protesters, how they would respond if provoked by troublemakers.

Reverend Smith introduced Darius, who prepared the crowd for a protracted fight, encouraging them to keep on keeping on. "You know the battle we're facing," Darius started, "and we've come a long way, but there's more to do yet and you have to remain strong and committed to nonviolence. They'll throw eggs at you. Rocks. Bricks. And now we know dynamite, too. But you must resist the urge to fight back. The police may rough you up a little. Or a lot. Still, you must not fight back."

Some grumbled, but mostly they nodded and hung on to his every word, some even taking notes, and Freda found it hard to believe Darius was only twenty years old. A man ahead of his time, as they said. She imagined this was how Cora felt when she watched Reverend Percy Chesterton III in the pulpit. Darius had found what he was meant to do and be in this world.

Darius and Reverend Smith put out a call for volunteers: lawyers to get protesters out of jail, nurses to bandage anyone who got banged up, drivers to transport people to the sit-ins, caretakers to watch the children while their parents protested, a data collection expert to keep track of complaints, and a bookkeeper to organize their finances.

Peer pressure and praise could make folks agree to all sorts of things, and this organization had adopted both as recruitment tactics. Reverend Smith identified a few nurses in the crowd and asked a retiree to consider babysitting. A matronly woman in a floral house dress blushed when Reverend Smith described her rump roast as divine and said she made the best red velvet cake in all the South. Without having to be asked twice, she agreed to cook for the protesters and have a hot meal waiting for them at the church when they returned from the next sit-in. But she couldn't do it alone and needed help, and that's when, to Freda's surprise, Cora stood to volunteer. "Cooking is my ministry," she said to a chorus of amens.

Freda was still gazing at her friend in awe when she heard Darius say, "I think Freda would make a fine bookkeeper for us if she's interested."

The crowd followed his eyes and looked to her, and she shrunk under their gaze. She didn't even want anyone to know she was here, especially not Gerald. Luckily, she didn't recognize a soul except for Darius and Cora, who urged her to take on the assignment. "Oh no, I'm not interested," Freda said. "I mean I believe in what you're doing but I'm much too busy with my studies."

Darius left the pulpit to stand in front of her. "It would only be a few hours a week. You're a whiz at math. Everybody knows that."

At least he recognized her strength. It was flattering, she had to admit, that he considered her talented in mathematics, but she couldn't commit to anything like this.

Before she said no for the second time, he proposed a compromise. "How about you help me out with the bookkeeping for today and that'll get us over the hump until we find somebody permanent?" She didn't answer him.

When the meeting ended, Freda assumed Cora would head back to their dorm to study for an upcoming European history exam, but she stayed put, wringing her hands.

"What is it?" Freda asked.

"I'm going out there. Now."

"Out where?"

Cora's eyes misted. Her hands now balled into fists. "Today's march. I keep thinking about what they did to me at Woolworth's. The way they tried to divide us, use me as an example like I was some kind of sellout. Like I would ever betray my own community. I want to show them, show the world that we stand together and that we have a right to exist in this country like everybody else."

***

FREDA STAYED BEHIND, HER BUDDING INTEREST IN ACTIVISM shielded from the public, from prying eyes. Once the church cleared out, she removed the scarf from her head then sat across from Darius at a folding table to review expenses. Alternately, she chewed on her pencil and used it to draw a rudimentary accounting ledger. She caught Darius watching her, and her cheeks flushed. "Are you going to continue staring impolitely or fill me in on the expenses for the organization?"

"Okay, you asked for it. Here we go." He rattled off a long list of needs.

Who knew activists used so many resources? A fleet of eleven used, but well-maintained cars at $1,700 each, four used buses at $3,000 each. Documentation of the inhumane treatment of Negroes would prove to be essential, and audio-visual equipment would cost $2,400 for cameras, tape recorders, plus film and slide projectors. For more than an hour, she made calculation after calculation and wrote and wrote until the lead tip of her pencil broke.

Darius massaged his temples. "You need a break. We both do." He handed her a cold Coca-Cola.

She turned the bottle up to her mouth. "I'll be going home for summer break. I'm excited to see my parents and my cousin Leotha. But it feels like things are heating up here. I'll miss everything." What she didn't say was that she'd miss him. But it was more than a crush on some boy, or man, when you looked at everything Darius represented as an emerging leader in this community. No, it was the work itself for basic rights. Her eyes were opening now to see these folks were making a difference, more than empty rhetoric and troublemaking.

"Summer break is only a few months," he said. "This fight we're in for civil rights, for human rights, is a long one. It'll be here when you get back."

"Will you be here?" Her cheeks flamed.

Darius leaned across the desk to get closer to her, his eyes penetrating. "I'm around for as long as you want me to be."

Unsteady now, and unsure of what to say next without going too far, Freda glanced away and redirected the conversation. "You're making real change happen. I read about it in the papers."

He folded his arms behind his head and reclined in his seat. "You right about that. Like Diane Nash, who stood toe-to-toe with the mayor right there on the courthouse steps and put him on the spot, forcing him to desegregate downtown."

Freda remembered Diane from campus and the sit-ins, and now she suddenly had a new admiration for the young woman who was also from Chicago, one who had distinguished herself. "I like the way she thinks. I can't imagine having her courage to risk so much to change this city."

"Not just Nashville. The entire South. Ladies can lead this movement. You're stronger than you give yourself credit for," he said. "Diane's the one who came up with the idea of jail, no bail. It sends a message that we're serious when some of us take that stance, and it buys us more time to raise the money to bail out others. Brilliant strategy." He stood and raked his hands over his head and face.

"What is it? What's wrong?"

With his hands on his waist now, he dropped his head and shook it slightly. "I'm looking at your numbers here. The thing is we're making real progress, but we need more financial resources to sustain us for the rest of the year. Some of our people have been in jail long enough and more will go to jail, and while we believe in jail, no bail as a strategy, we got a lot of people still locked up and we need to get them out and back home. And we're working with civil rights activists all over the South now, so our need is more pressing and greater than ever."

The ledger Freda created lay open on the table and she scanned the numbers. Darius didn't have to be a math major like her to see the shortfall. They needed a major influx of cash to cover their expenses. She bit her lip and stared hard at every number as if she could multiply the amount in their account through the sheer force of concentration. She didn't know how, but she would help Darius raise money for the cause.

Freda

Nashville's Union Station reminded Freda of Chicago's with its huge, vaulted ceilings, stained-glass skylights, and marble floors. When she closed her eyes, she could still see Mama, Papa, and Cousin Leotha, who had moved in with their family when she was a little girl, all of them standing on that train platform back home where they sent her off to college, waving vigorously, smiling too brightly, all of them trying not to cry.

On this day, men traveling alone and with families brushed by her, most in suits or at least neatly pressed slacks and dress shirts. Everyone knew you had to be sharp when you traveled, especially Negroes. She wore a pale blue knit dress with low-heeled beige pumps even though she wouldn't be boarding a train.

Freda had an hour before her first class and came to surprise Darius with a biscuit and fried egg she'd taken from the dining hall and wrapped in tin foil. All she knew was that he worked at the train station but had no idea where or what he did. Truth was, she was curious and had been reliving their time doing bookkeeping at First Baptist the day before.

He spotted her first. "Freda." She turned when she heard her name, but the familiar voice didn't match the man in drab, gray work clothes cleaning the platform floor. He carried a large mop and a rag slung over one shoulder. None of this made sense. Why was Darius dressed like that? She'd never seen him wearing anything but a suit or a button-down collared shirt with dress slacks.

Anticipating her questions, he propped the mop handle under his chin and said, "Yeah, this is my job. Not glamorous, but pay's decent."

What kind of work had she expected him to do? They would never hire a Negro to work behind the counter selling tickets to passengers.

"I'm not sure what to say."

"Don't feel sorry for me," he said. "My folks told me a man can't live on civil rights alone. As much as it fills the soul, the belly is still empty. They were right. I was on scholarship at Fisk, had room and board then. But I lost my scholarship when I left school, so now I have to make my own way. Not a lot of jobs out here for Negroes."

Was he out of his mind? So different from Gerald, who had attended Fisk and Meharry thanks to the generosity of a benefactor and wouldn't dream of squandering such a gift. The choices Darius made seemed both shortsighted and ambitious.

Darius had matured significantly since the day they met at the chapel. She was looking at a full-grown man, chiseled out of hard work and hard-won wisdom about the world. She said, "A saxophone player. A student activist. A laborer. You're what Leon Battista Alberti called *a Renaissance man*, one who can do all things if he will."

Darius seemed to appreciate that assessment. "Yes, Alberti, the Italian humanist, art theorist, and philosopher." He winked at that last part. "The lady mathematician is full of surprises." Then gesturing to the wrapped food, he asked, "Is that for me or am I being presumptuous?"

Smiling, she handed him the breakfast, which he thanked her for then ate quickly, like he hadn't had a good meal in weeks. A train pulled into the station and Darius greeted the Negroes working the rails as if he'd known them for years, and they either nodded or playfully punched his arm. He had a way with people, she was convinced of that.

A white man with a side grin that curled one corner of his mouth stepped off the train. He folded his arms and watched a spiffy Negro porter lug his two suitcases, which must have contained bricks. "Thanks,

George," the man said. And then he repeated it to be sure his words of gratitude stuck their landing. "Appreciate that, George." The porter smiled and said *yes, suh,* which was about all he could do if he wanted to keep his job and his life, knowing good and well that the white man knew his name was Lionel because it was pinned to his lapel.

Lionel was a string bean of a man, with skin the color of firewood. His mustache moved funny when he spoke. Darius scrubbed smudges of dirty footprints while Freda stood nearby looking like a woman waiting to greet a passenger. When the porter finished with the rude man, Darius moved a bit closer, still mopping, and quietly said, "Hey, Lionel. You know that thing we talked about." A declaration, no question in there.

Lionel's smile stayed in place as he unloaded bags. "Yes, sir, I do. We need to get something to the boy over the next few months. Jonas will have a package for us soon, in early June. He'll be on the Atlanta route."

What kind of package and who was *the boy*? Lionel offered a nod and an exaggerated hat tip for every passenger, almost all of them white.

Darius cast his eyes downward on the ground as he swept. "Okay, but timing is the issue. I'll be in Mississippi for a few months. Maybe I could wait and get it from him when I'm back."

Lionel said, "Hate to have Jonas hold it that long on the train. Too many people passing through."

What were they discussing so intently? It dawned on her that this must have something to do with civil rights work, but she might as well have been invisible the way they talked in riddles, ignoring her.

"We'll figure it out," Darius said.

Lionel's smile stayed in place, but he inched away from her and Darius. "Yes, sir, thank you very much. Y'all enjoy Nashville now," he said to a white family of four.

Then without another word or even a sideways glance at them, Lionel acknowledged the white conductor who stood watch about twenty feet away and hopped aboard the train.

***

When his shift ended thirty minutes later, Darius changed out of his work clothes and walked Freda back to campus. She couldn't wait to ask him questions.

"What in the world was that all about back there?"

"There's no reason to get you involved," Darius said. "This is serious business, no room for error."

"Well, I'm a serious person and I don't make mistakes." She couldn't have been more insulted if he had questioned her computation skills. Louder than she intended, she said, "You're the one who dragged me into this Movement work and now you're shutting me out. Is it because I'm a woman? Either you trust me, or you don't."

"Of course I trust you."

"I'll be taking the train home for the summer. I can pick up whatever package this is," Freda declared, though she had no idea what she was volunteering to collect.

"I don't know, Freda. It could be dangerous. People's livelihoods and very lives could be on the line."

"If this is something I can do, let me help."

Darius nodded. "You know all the expenses we have right now. Well, there's a bunch of new challenges to *Brown v. Board of Education*. You got these school officials and towns doing everything they can to get around desegregation. A lot of it's being fought in the courts all over the South."

"But wait," Freda said. "I remember everybody talking about that case in high school. The Supreme Court decided that public schools weren't allowed to keep out Negroes. It's against the Constitution. That's been settled already." She heard her voice rising almost to the point of yelling.

Darius talked with his hands, the way he had Sunday in the pulpit. "You're right. That's how things are supposed to be. But some of these folks don't care about the law. Their hate matters more. You've heard of the civil rights lawyer Thurgood Marshall? He had that city mobilization meeting at the gymnasium a couple months ago, remember?"

Freda looked down, embarrassed that she had probably seen the flyers around campus but ignored them. "No, I can't say that I remember."

Darius went on, undeterred. "Well, I got to talk to Marshall when he was here, and he told us he could use our help. He's been in court almost every day since that ruling in 1954, trying to stop these people who refuse to follow the law and want to erase the progress we made. These court battles cost money."

Still confused, Freda asked, "Okay, so where does this mysterious package exchange fit into all of this?"

He took a deep breath. "Most people don't know it and they'd have no reason to, but some of the Pullman porters have been passing money along from big activists and entertainers who want to support the Movement. I don't know who, but somebody has something, a lot to contribute, and they'll be giving it to a porter named Jonas who will pass it on to us so we can help out Marshall."

Never in her life had she been consumed by this sense of urgency and purpose or taken part in anything this consequential. "I had no idea those porters did this. My God. They're heroes."

"They're like all of us. Ordinary people being called to do something during extraordinary times. You wouldn't have known. Only those of us who need to know actually do."

Darius stopped in the middle of the street to face Freda head-on.

"Are you in this with us?"

Freda had the chance to leave her fingerprints on this Movement she had known only through news reports but was just now seeing up close. She still couldn't imagine marching through the streets or sitting in at a lunch counter, but this was something she could do. The helplessness she had been feeling for months began to loosen its grip on her.

"Yes, of course, I'm in," she said.

Darius grabbed her hand and squeezed it, and she surprised herself by letting him. Then he jumped at least a foot in the air, scuffing his freshly polished dress shoes when they hit the ground. The late afternoon breeze lifted his voice as he said, "We're making a difference and we're doing it together." He put her hand to his lips and kissed it.

Then he grew quiet all of a sudden and they slowed their pace. "These Pullman porters are taking big risks. You know about Emmett Till, right?"

The name sounded familiar, but she couldn't be sure where she'd heard it. She read the newspapers on occasion, but she didn't commit every detail to memory the way Darius did. "Of course, I know who he is. What about him?"

Lying must not have come naturally to her because Darius proceeded to explain what happened in Money, Mississippi, five years before. White men maimed and murdered a fourteen-year-old boy named Emmett Till for supposedly whistling at some white woman. Freda was one year older than Emmett, and he had lived in a middle-class Chicago neighborhood a lot like the one where she grew up. He didn't live to make it to high school, and that one detail tore at her more than anything else. It all came back to her—she vaguely remembered Cousin Leotha walking through the house shaking his head talking about the boy who visited his home state and didn't leave alive.

She fought back tears and Darius pulled a handkerchief from his suit pocket and offered it to her. "I didn't mean to upset you. I want you to know what the Pullman porters did."

Her eyes stung and she dabbed at them with the cloth. "What do they have to do with what happened to that poor boy?"

"There were a lot of people in Mississippi who tried to deny the truth of what happened to Emmett. But his mother wanted the world to see how those beasts masquerading as men beat her son so bad you could barely recognize him. She insisted upon an open casket funeral. How do you think that boy's body came all the way from Mississippi to Chicago?" In spite of the ugliness of the whole ordeal, Darius smiled now with the satisfaction of a cat holding a mouse tail between its teeth. "The porters kept the body with them in the colored car of the train where white folks wouldn't dare lower themselves enough to go and nobody knew."

"My God, my God," she said. Imagining the discipline and subterfuge necessary for the porters to pull off something like that made her eyes moist. Her entire body expanded with pride. "I didn't know. I never heard of anything like that before," was all she managed to say before emotion strangled her voice.

"Not many people know about what the porters do to support our community. It's beautiful, but they could lose their jobs or be killed if people knew."

Darius had not let go of her hand, and she noticed how natural it felt, as if this was what they always did. "I'm glad you trusted me with the story of the porters and trusted me to carry this package."

"I do trust you." He stopped walking and turned to look directly at her. "You know we can't tell anybody about our little talk with Lionel or about that package you're planning to pick up from Jonas."

She was growing indignant now. "Who would I tell?"

"Not even Gerald can know."

Hearing Gerald's name broke the spell, and she gently slid her hand out of Darius's. Yet her commitment to the work remained. Maybe a girl needed secrets that stayed in her heart and never escaped her lips. A part of herself that was only for her and no one else. Maybe keeping this from Gerald wouldn't be a hardship after all, because when the talk between them turned to what was happening to Negroes in the South, he only reminded her that she would be a Fisk graduate someday and he'd be a Negro doctor, and somehow that would inoculate them. She didn't believe that any more than he did, but the illusion kept them going. For the time being, she would have to maintain separate lives, be two people, ensuring that her civil rights work with Darius and her life with Gerald ran parallel but never intersected.

She glanced up at Darius who seemed anxious, waiting for her promise. "Don't worry. I will take this to my grave."

***

Freda collapsed on her bed, grinning at the ceiling, still buzzing over how she, a simple college girl, had landed in the center of this strange time with all its importance and intrigue. A delightful shiver ran through her and curled her toes, to think of sharing this secret mission with Darius. She had closed her eyes to let these feelings wash over her when someone knocked at her door. Annoyed by the interruption, she reluctantly yelled, "Come in."

In the doorway stood Mother Gaines, hands on hips and in a huff already that morning. "You might want to get out of bed. There's an important phone call for you."

Who would be calling her on a Wednesday morning unless it was an emergency? She only talked to Mama and Papa once a week on Sundays, and they would never try to reach her any other day unless something was wrong. Her head pounded with every step down the hallway. The distance to the phone booth seemed to extend for miles instead of a few dozen feet, and there was no privacy with Mother Gaines right on her heels, obviously fully aware of who was on the other end.

"Hello," Freda said in a small voice, afraid to hear who might speak.

"This is Dr. Lillian Voorhees, professor of English, in case you've forgotten."

Panic shot through Freda's body when she realized her mistake. She had spent too much time with Darius at the train station and on their leisurely walk back to campus and lost track of time. Looking at her watch, she confirmed she was already thirty-seven minutes late for class. Freda had the utmost respect for Dr. Voorhees, a white professor, who had become active in civil rights work and even attended a predominantly Negro church. The professor would no doubt approve of Freda's Movement work, but none of that mattered now.

"I am so sorry, ma'am," Freda said.

"Miss Gilroy, why are you not in my class? We are waiting for you."

Then a dial tone sounded in Freda's ear, and she realized Dr. Voorhees had hung up the phone. Freda raced past the disapproving eyes of Mother Gaines and ran across the yard to her class building, fear and adrenaline pumping in her legs. Everything about this was so unlike Freda, who prided herself on being prepared and prompt. When she walked into the classroom, with all eyes on her, she tried to avoid the pity in their gazes and the disappointment in that of Dr. Voorhees.

Freda understood now what her parents feared—that she would get so caught up in activism and lose sight of her goal, the real reason she had come to Fisk. Now she questioned whether she could throw herself into the Movement without squandering her legacy, everything generations of Negroes and her own family had worked so hard to make possible.

PART EIGHT

Chicago, 1992

Tulip

A swishing sound pulled Tulip out of a sound sleep, and even before she opened her eyes, she knew it wasn't daybreak. Rolling over to Key's side of the bed, the sheets rubbed cool against her skin and she squinted. There he was at the foot of the bed, shooting a small basketball into the hoop mounted on his bedroom door.

"Did I wake you up?" In his baggy red basketball shorts with that sheepish grin spreading across his face, he reminded her of a little boy.

"Hey, what's going on? It's early," she said, her throat scratchy.

"How can you sleep when we getting closer to making history?" He pulled off a smooth layup and smacked the backboard for effect. It seemed childish for a grown man to still be doing this in the house. But she also realized that a Black man at play was surviving, creating joy in a world that didn't offer much of it.

The hope of an entire city rested with the NBA Finals, where the Bulls inched closer to destiny. Last year, Chicago caught the dream it had been chasing for more than a quarter of a century. Now, the Bulls had the chance to prove to the world they weren't one-time wonders, but true champions. It's all anyone talked about, whether they were squeezing melons in the produce section of the grocery, waiting in a pharmacy line, or sitting on the city bus. Race, color, nor creed mattered, nor did how much money you made. Following the Bulls had become its own religion. You didn't need to know the rules of the game for your chest to swell.

She pulled the covers up under her chin, her smile disappearing. It had been a week since her lunch meeting with Adam, and Mason's dinner with the man should have happened already. "I don't want to go in today. Bryce has been quiet, not a word about the CookCo account, and that's not like him. Nothing yet about promotions either."

Key threw himself beside her on the mattress. "Okay, so why don't you ask him what's up?"

"I guess I don't want to hear him say I'm not good enough." There, she said it, acknowledging that quiet doubt that nipped at the corners of her brain, making her believe deep down that her agency's inaction on advancing her career reflected some deficiency in her.

"Don't let him mess with your head." Key placed his hand under her chin and turned her face toward him, forcing her to look into his eyes. "He'd be a damn fool not to recognize you got skills."

Most of their conversations about work revolved around hers—client successes or some dip in a client's brand reputation or her anxiety about her position with the agency—but Key said little about his CTA job. He drove that same route every day without complaint. She imagined it grew monotonous. "Do you ever have bad days driving the bus?"

"All the time," he said, shaking his head. "People trying to ride with expired transfers, or you ask them nicely to get off the bus at the end of the line and they have the nerve to cop an attitude. As if that dollar fare entitles them to a night's stay like I'm running a motel."

"What do you do if they refuse to leave?" She rolled over on her side and propped herself up on her elbow.

"I try to handle it myself, but it's rough out there. Sometimes, two dudes or even ladies these days get to fighting on the street and then bring that mess onto the bus. The last thing I want to do is call the cops. Nobody needs that smoke."

He didn't say much about it, but she knew he was looking forward to the day he could leave the city bus behind and take over the beauty supply store. Even on days his exhaustion wore him down, the family business gave him something to be hopeful about.

Maybe their conversation had gotten too heavy because Key jumped from the bed again, leaping and bounding from one corner of his bedroom to another shooting that basketball, and she understood how he kept his private dreams tucked inside that of a basketball dynasty in the making.

***

On the nineteenth floor of Mattingly, where all the senior leaders had offices, a celebratory bell rang, but Tulip didn't hear it because she had been analyzing consumer research on a client product—a new deodorant made for career women on the move. For hours, she had been poring over slices of data on age, socioeconomic status, lifestyle choices, social interests, and worldview. It struck her that if all those things influenced how you chose to smell good every day, it only made sense that the world would be divided on the big issues like race and sexual orientation. She was contemplating this when a receptionist found her in the agency library and insisted she come upstairs in time to hear Bryce address the account teams.

"Winning the CookCo business is a huge victory for us, and we owe it all to our two shining stars partnering to make it happen."

Tulip found it difficult to breathe. They had done it. She had done it. The executive conference room erupted in applause, with Mason smiling uncomfortably like he would have preferred no public recognition at all to sharing the spotlight with her. Tulip licked off all her magenta lipstick trying to moisten her mouth, dry from the humiliation of knowing at least some of her colleagues were faking enthusiasm, believing she didn't deserve praise.

Popping the cork on a bottle of champagne, Bryce poured bubbly for every employee in the room, and toasted her and Mason. Grinning at them, he said, "Adam Feldman told me it was a one-two punch executed by the two of you. He couldn't say no to having us handle their PR and marketing business. This, everyone, is how you work as a team to deliver great results!"

Carrying her flute back to her small office, Tulip began to feel more confident, assured that Bryce, the only one whose opinion mattered, considered her a star.

She shut the door and let a deluge of emotions from gratitude to euphoria and fearlessness roll over her. If she could land Mattingly one of its largest accounts and put it in a new stratosphere in the culinary sector, she could do anything. She transformed into somebody she rarely saw in books or on the big screen—an honest to goodness Black woman superhero. On her desk were framed photos of herself at cotillions and charity events and graduations looking pleased but never victorious. Something always held her back from opening her cape and flying. When a high school guidance counselor steered her away from math and science in spite of her genetic predisposition to those subjects, Tulip accepted this as her own shortcoming. When she and her Jack and Jill friends swam in the gated pool of a white classmate, the neighborhood association security officer said they had no right to be there. For years, Tulip thought they must have violated some policy and couldn't bring herself to accept they had been kicked out for being Black. Maybe she hadn't wanted to see because seeing hurt too much. While she hadn't stood up for anything back then, she could do something now.

Tulip thumbed through her Rolodex until she found the card with WMAQ-TV Ch. 5, the NBC owned-and-operated station in Chicago, with the name Pete Caruso at the top. The youngest and most relentless assignment editor in the country, according to him. She dialed quickly and immediately sensed the intensity of the news grind he found himself swept up in every day.

"Hey, Pete. It's Tulip Vance. I have a story for you."

"What you got for me?" He sounded distracted and she heard the police and fire scanners squawking in the background—she imagined him at the desk with a phone receiver up to each ear.

She had to talk fast and communicate urgency. "Ida B. Wells is holding a protest march on Saturday and yes, I know that's the same day as the NBA Finals. But this is a big story, too. I wouldn't steer you wrong, you know that. They're protesting the lack of justice for Rodney King and Latasha Harlins out in LA. But there's a local angle with demands they're making of Mayor Daley and CHA. I've got residents lined up to talk Friday for a preview. You'll definitely want to send a crew to the march on Saturday."

A slight exaggeration. She would find the right stories when she visited Ida B. Wells the next night. A scratching sound and then Pete said, "A Rogers Park woman is missing. Police haven't said anything about foul play. Let's keep an eye on it. Yeah, Tulip, we'll get somebody over there. Send me the details. Got to go."

A dial tone rang in her ear before she said thank you to the dead air. The news cycle could be as fickle as the weather, but she had a verbal commitment.

"What was that all about?" came a voice behind her.

Tulip whipped around to see Amanda standing in the doorway with that self-satisfied look that said she had somehow one-upped you but would keep the details under wraps until they could inflict the greatest harm. How long had she been standing there?

"I didn't hear you knock," Tulip said, with a subtle reprimand and reminder of common courtesy.

"Because I didn't," Amanda said, her smile as chilled as an early winter frost on Lake Michigan.

Kill them with kindness is what Freda and Gerald always said. That killing part would surely satisfy Tulip's baser instincts, but the kindness would take a whole lot of prayer and practice. "How can I help you, Amanda?"

She sat down without an invitation being extended. "Well, I came by to personally congratulate you on the new business win."

"Thank you," Tulip said, playing along.

"I'm sure Bryce will be thrilled to hear that you're also advancing our agency's philanthropic efforts as well."

Tulip tried to appear calm, but the fear clapping her ears morphed into outrage. "Were you eavesdropping on my call?"

With a smirk, she said, "No, I just came by to bring you this. You left it on the fax machine."

After placing two sheets of paper on Tulip's desk, Amanda slipped out of the office as quietly as she'd entered.

Tulip's hands shook as she picked up the documents and panicked when she realized they were press releases for the protest that she'd tried to fax to the WLS-TV and WBBM-TV newsrooms. After five minutes of screeching and beeping, she'd left the fax machine to return to her office but had forgotten to go back to retrieve the releases.

A nauseous feeling gnawed at Tulip's insides. Amanda had proof that Tulip was pitching the upcoming march on company equipment and time. She may have even overheard her conversation with the channel five assignment editor. Amanda's guarded language was nothing but a veiled threat, revealing just enough to scare Tulip. Rummaging through her desk drawer, Tulip pulled out the employee handbook and skimmed it until she found the section on ethics. Had she violated the policy? It talked about keeping personal and political views separate from professional work, and it required that employees disclose any personal or business relationships with clients. It also mandated handling private business outside of work hours. Agency resources were limited to agency work.

Trying to calm her own breathing, Tulip knew she had violated company policy, but it had been for a good reason. How could she explain, defend herself if it came to that? She searched her heart and mind but only found her answer at the top of that employee handbook where the Mattingly mission made it plain: *We're creating a better world, one message and one story at a time.* Calling newsrooms and pitching journalists about a local march in the projects to get justice for an unarmed Black man and woman and a long-neglected community had to count as mission work, right?

***

Outside Ida B. Wells, dogs barked and cars backfired. Tulip had begged off on movie night with Key to come here. He couldn't understand her logic, and now she questioned it, too, and considered turning around and heading home. The Bulls had lost the night before, and a pall hung over the entire city, but it was her brief exchange with Amanda at work that she couldn't shake. Was being here a mistake? She had already pitched the story to journalists. Maybe returning here was taking things too far. She kept asking herself these questions while studying the tall, redbrick buildings to find the right address for this meeting: 3833 S. Langley. A fourteen-story structure that looked identical to the one from the last meeting and the other buildings—some abandoned, some not—all of which Bertrice now called *the fourteen-story cemetery*. So many unsolved murders here, people sleeping with one eye open, children seeing too much, growing up way too fast.

Tulip wore faded jeans and a nondescript gray hoodie this time, learning her lesson from her last visit. But someone still mockingly shouted, "5-0 in the house!" This apartment was more cramped than the last one and she climbed over outstretched legs and feet to find a seat. Client meetings had run long that day, making her late once again, and when she walked in, she held up one finger like she was in church asking for permission or maybe forgiveness for the interruption.

"I see you came back." It was the organizer, Christina Butler. She took in Tulip with what could be considered begrudging admiration or simply pity for a fool too dense to take the hint and stay away. "When you were here last time, you wanted to focus this rally on Rodney King. We have our focus nailed down, and we can't have any confusion this time. Our attention must be on Latasha Harlins first and foremost, getting justice for the Black female victims of racial violence who often languish in the shadows behind the men who make headlines. Just know that we cannot and will not have you come in here creating confusion."

A few women in the room clapped. "Sisters need to stick together," one said.

As much as that rebuke from Christina stung, Tulip accepted it.

"I agree with you." She stood and spoke, her voice shaky, trying to find its register. "The very first day I saw what happened to Rodney King, I was furious and outraged. I hadn't even paid attention to Latasha

Harlins, which is my fault and the media's fault for not covering that story enough. When the verdict came back saying those officers were not guilty, I couldn't believe what was happening. I know it unfortunately was not hard for many of you to believe. I've been wearing blinders, not seeing the racism right in my face." As she gained momentum, her voice grew stronger and people responded to it, some of them rising to their feet saying, *come on now.*

Then she turned to Christina in the front of the room. "You may be right about me creating confusion. But all I want to do is help. Those of you concerned about getting the word out to the masses are right to ask that question. If no one hears your message, what good is it? I should have said before that I know people in the media, and I've already reached out to the newspapers and TV stations, and they're interested in covering your story."

Two young women on either side of her jumped to their feet to hug her, but Christina didn't seem convinced. "So we're supposed to believe you *know people in the media.* I know a rapper from a party I went to once. I know a guy who unclogs toilets. We're smarter than we look. You have to give us more than that," she said.

She was right. Trust had to be earned. People with good sense and the scars from betrayal didn't give it freely. Tulip opened her arms, palms up, to show she came in good faith. "I contacted every news outlet in this city. The *Sun-Times* and the *Tribune.* Channels 2, 5, 7, 9, and 32. Plus news radio. There's never a guarantee of coverage but I'm telling you there's lots of interest. This is my job, it's what I do. Businesses pay my company to bring attention to their products and services. No one's paying me to promote this protest march. I'm doing it because I care about this community. I care about us."

She thought of everything she was risking, including her career, but she didn't tell them about that. It had been her choice. People without power and no megaphone suffered in silence—no one who could make a difference ever hearing them. They needed her to tell their stories. If only they would let her. With all eyes on her, Tulip stood there, awkward and gangly—all arms and legs—as she had in eighth grade walking onstage to receive her notable award for *most likely to succeed.* Her imploring words of compassion stunned them into silence, and when it almost became unbearable—before she sank back in her chair—people stood one-by-one and clapped.

Even Christina nodded. "Well, all right then."

Not wanting to lose the momentum, Tulip said, "Shall we put together a plan?"

Residents clustered around her and Christina as they mapped out the march route, made a list of community organizations to invite, identified a list of speakers and sign-makers, and made a note to check with the city again on permits.

Three hours later, Christina turned to Tulip and smiled at her like a real partner in this work, her entire face lit up like a blaze that could not be extinguished.

Tulip

A birthday party without the birthday boy could have been a downer but Rudy insisted he was up for it. Key stayed home to get some rest before his early bus shift in the morning. Tired after the Ida B. Wells meeting that evening, Tulip rallied, knowing she needed to be there for Rudy. She, Sharita, and more friends traveled to the Streeterville neighborhood's Second Story—a gay dive bar with low light except for the year-round Christmas ones. A place that welcomed the straight strays when they wandered in, no questions asked.

Rudy found family here at Second Story: There was Teddy, the investment banker in his Bermuda shorts and wing-tipped shoes. Marilyn, a bored straight housewife who drove across the state line from Indiana because she couldn't find any bars with good music in her town. Walker, the balding grandpa, who regaled them with Stonewall stories. Tulip loved seeing Rudy here where his limbs loosened and joy poured out of him. Dressed in baggy jeans and a NASCAR muscle shirt, he sipped an appletini. "Man, Colton would have loved this night," he said. His boyfriend would have turned forty-six that day.

"C'mon, you know he'd hate us celebrating without him," said Rafe, another friend of Rudy's and Colton's with a thick mustache that kept you guessing about his facial expressions. "Now if he's having a gin and tonic with lemon up there with the big guy, he might be too buzzed to care."

Tulip laughed, wrapping her arms around Rudy and nuzzling his neck.

Heavy bass pulsed through the room now when CeCe Peniston's "Finally" played. "That's our jam." Sharita grabbed Tulip and Rudy by their hands, pulling them through the dark, crowded bar until they stood under the light of a single disco ball, their appletinis spilling over their glasses.

"Rudy," Tulip said, shouting to be heard over the music, "you haven't mentioned the shoot for the sizzle reel. Am I scheduled to be in it or not?" She knew she sounded desperate. Every year, Mattingly shot a promotional video for prospective clients, featuring their senior account people. Who made the cut sometimes signaled who was in good favor with Bryce at the moment, and Tulip overheard watercooler talk about recent shoots. She caught Rudy looking at Sharita, who averted her eyes. She had her answer. "I didn't make the cut, did I?"

"We don't know that," Rudy said. "Let's not panic prematurely."

"That's right," Sharita said. "You never know."

They had been talking about her behind her back. "I expected you two of all people to support me."

Tulip stalked off the dance floor, finding a quiet corner of the bar to sulk, but of course her friends followed her. She shouldn't have brought drama to a night meant for Rudy, but she couldn't help feeling wounded.

"We do support you," Sharita said. "But you're one of five Black people in that whole agency and Valencia doesn't count because we know she only claims her Blackness when she tans in the summertime and can't exactly pass. Mattingly has never had a Black account director before. Now you trying to throw it all away to promote a protest in the hood? If Bryce finds out, it's over. And you know Amanda's mouth." Tulip had confided in her friends about pitching reporters for the Ida B. Wells event, and at the time, they seemed supportive. But now, Sharita said, "Don't mess this up for us."

Black folks always said they stood on the shoulders of Martin and

Harriet and Sojourner, all those who had come before them. But how could you ever be light and weightless enough to fly when you carried so many people on your back?

Rudy took a shot glass from the hand of a passing friend and leaned in close to Tulip. "Listen to me. Stop being sloppy, giving Amanda ammunition to use against you. Never let the right hand know what the left is doing."

Ever since she'd known him, Rudy had kept his private life private, even though dropping a few salacious details about your life—true or not—offered some cache at Mattingly, where facility with office gossip had become an unwritten corporate value. He said, "I know some of these queens in here call me a closet case. No, I'm not out at work but I produced videos behind the scenes that helped my community get Mayor Daley to stop dragging his feet and triple the money going to care for people living with AIDS. Nobody at the agency has a clue, and they don't need to know." His eyes turned glassy. "This is how I honor Colton's memory."

At that moment the bartender came from behind the bar with a lopsided birthday cake adorned with a fire-starter number of candles. Tulip pushed her troubles aside and focused on Rudy, who blew out each one then threw back a shot of fireball whiskey. Laughing roughly, he raised his glass. "Colton would tell us to live hard and love hard. Drink and dance while you can 'cause when you get up there"—and he pointed to a water stain on the ceiling—"the bartender's slow on refills and the DJ's stuck on repeat."

***

The next day, Freda must have been celebrating something, too, humming while she dusted the dining room table, freshening a fruit bowl, and arranging hydrangeas in the centerpiece. Then she pulled out a stack of exam papers from the junior high Montessori School where she taught math part-time. Tulip had stopped by the house simply because she needed her mother's wise counsel. Her mother would have a point of view, even though Freda's take on the world usually made her close her eyes and take deep breaths before she said something disrespectful.

"Somebody's in a good mood," Tulip said.

"Yes, it's such a relief every year when that damn auction is over. I'm pleased that we brought in twenty-three thousand dollars, exceeding our goal." Freda had chaired the event ever since Tulip could remember and it always took so much out of her.

"Why do you do it when you hate it, and it makes you tired and miserable?"

Her mother laughed, brushing dust off her calculator. "I wouldn't go that far now. You'll do all sorts of things you don't want to do but must before this life is over."

"I guess," Tulip said. "Is it because of Dad? Did he make you sign up for this when you got married?" She couldn't imagine being such an appendage to a man that his career interests became yours, too, because of a marriage license.

Smiling, Freda said, "It wasn't in the contract. Your father doesn't make me do anything, but when you choose to join your life with someone else's, there are certain obligations that come with that. You have to give yourself over to them. No looking back."

The morning sun peeked through the curtains and Freda stared into that sliver of light, serious now, like she was remembering something.

Tulip picked an orange from the fruit bowl and began peeling its skin—and the stories of her mother's past. "No looking back at what? You hardly talk about your life before Dad."

"My God, I was a freshman in college when I met your father, just a baby. There isn't much more history pre-dating that."

"Tell me about college then. Did you dance? Not like ballroom dancing where you have five feet of space between you, but I mean get your groove on kind of dancing? Did you ever miss curfew? Did you go to any of those civil rights marches?" Tulip surprised herself, her questions coming fast and seeming endless, like they had been piled up in an attic, and the door opened years later, everything tumbling out at once.

Her mother rolled her eyes. "No, I kept all my limbs perfectly still by my side and never strayed from my cloistered life." She pressed her hands together and bowed her head like a nun, and they both laughed.

"Yes, I had fun. With Evaline and Cora around, how could I not?" Sobering, Freda said, "Have fun with Keyshawn, but slow down. You have your whole life to meet the right man and a few wrong ones along the way. One hasty choice can change things and there's no undoing it."

Tulip bit into an orange slice. What did her mother mean? Had Gerald Vance been a hasty choice? Did she want to undo her marriage to her father, undo Tulip's birth? Tulip cleared her throat but couldn't bring herself to voice those questions because she wasn't sure she wanted to hear the answers. Instead, she said, "Do you know what else you might have done with your life if you hadn't married Dad?"

Tulip couldn't imagine her mother as anyone else, living any other life than this one. But had she wanted some other one that didn't include her own daughter? She wrung her hands, sweaty now, waiting for Freda to answer.

Her mother stared out the window as if she might find the answers there. "I honestly don't know what I would have done, but it would have been grand."

What did a grand life look like for her mother? A rocket scientist? Or maybe a diplomat? She knew so much was off limits for young Black women back then, but dreaming cost you nothing except the disappointment that came with wanting too much.

Tulip couldn't imagine Freda Vance being anyone other than a socialite wife, part-time math teacher, and mother. Consumed by her own grand plans, Tulip let a smile bloom on her face. "I have something to tell you."

Looking up from the student worksheets and removing her eyeglasses, Freda said, "What has gotten into you? First, all these questions, and now you're grinning like you won the lottery. Did Bryce promote you?"

Her mother was getting ahead of the story, and Tulip spoke before she lost her nerve. "Bryce is thrilled that I helped win new business, but

there's something else." How could she tell Freda that she had no promotion and might lose her job because of something equally important?
She had to choose her words carefully, and realized she needed to slow
down, to modulate her tone so she didn't come across as impetuous and
foolhardy, all the things her mother had tried to scold out of her over
the years.

The day she traded ballet lessons for modern dance, her mother's
eyes registered disappointment but she understood. The year Tulip
decided to study abroad in London after high school graduation instead
of beginning college with her friends, Freda conceded that this would
be a life-changing additive experience, nothing to derail the carefully
constructed plans for her future.

Now, she saw the apprehension in her mother's eyes, the way she
held herself together tightly as if ropes were tied around her torso.
What has this child gone and done now? was the look on her face.

"Stop worrying," Tulip said. "It's tremendous news. I got the *Times*
and the *Tribune* and channels five and nine for sure to cover a major
story I've been pitching for weeks. If there's no breaking news, that is."

"What kind of story?"

"A protest on Saturday at Ida B. Wells. We're marching for Rodney
King and Latasha Harlins. For all of us. Once we planned ours at Ida
B., that inspired other communities to organize marches—Stateway
Gardens and Altgeld Gardens. There may even be a march downtown.
Word spread fast. The whole South Side is marching now. I played a part
in making that happen. Don't you see?" Excitement and nerves made
her words come out in a jumble.

Freda spoke slowly. "What do you mean? How did you make it
happen?"

"Through public relations, just as I do with my clients. I believe in
what these organizers are doing, and I convinced a few journalists the
story was worth covering."

"Yes, your clients," her mother said, her voice much too calm. "These
community groups are not your clients."

"I know."

"These reporters you pitched. They're people you happen to know in networking circles, right? Not relationships you cultivated through your job. Tell me you didn't use your Mattingly connections to make this happen."

Tulip bowed her head. What could she say? The triumph from earlier drained from her body. Amanda had warned her in the office. Then Sharita made it seem like Tulip had pulled the career ladder out from under every current or future Black employee at Mattingly. And now this from her mother. "Well, I . . ." Tulip stammered. "I met these journalists through work, but . . ."

"Tulip, no . . ." Freda pinned her daughter with a hard stare. "Listen to me. This is what I want you to say at Mattingly if anyone asks. You happened to hear about this march and casually mentioned it to a few reporters in cocktail conversation. Discussing this with reporters was idle talk, not an official story pitch. You were not speaking on behalf of the agency."

"But—" Tulip began. Her mother had never encouraged her to stretch the truth before. Not Freda Vance, who believed in precision, calculating everything meticulously enough that she didn't make errors. For her to advise manipulation of facts, she must have feared the demise of her daughter's career.

Sensing Tulip's unease, Freda stood and walked to the other side of the table to cradle her daughter's head to her stomach. "You didn't do anything terrible. You're just trying to make the world fairer. It's going to be good, okay? You're going to be just fine." She repeated this, rocking Tulip the way she had when she was a baby.

PART NINE

Nashville, 1960

25

Freda

Darius refused to let her stand alone on the platform at Union Station. He carried her two leather suitcases and they waited together for her train home to Chicago. Exams were over and summer break was finally here, and she was ready for her hometown to wrap her in its arms again.

That morning, she lay next to Gerald, his stubble scratching her cheek. She had spent the last few nights at his place, now that school was out, soaking up as much time with him as she could before they were separated for three long months. She kissed him goodbye before he left for his shift at the hospital, promising him she'd be fine boarding the train alone.

"Are you nervous?" Darius pulled a handkerchief from his pocket and dabbed at the perspiration on the back of his neck. The morning sun beat down on them standing on the station platform.

"Maybe I should be asking you," she teased. "No. I'm a bit anxious, I guess, in a good way. It may seem silly if you've never been like me, standing on the outside watching other people do big things in the world. It's never been my turn until now."

He leaned against the light pole and met her gaze head-on. "That day at McLellan's was my first sit-in," he said. "I had practiced so many times that you'd think I'd be numb to it all and it would be routine.

But it was like I was carrying my ancestors and all the Negroes alive today and the ones not even born yet."

The warm morning air moved around them, filling her lungs, and she breathed deeply. "I was wrong for the way I treated you." He tried to stop her from speaking, but Freda shook her head. "I was raised to believe that Negroes fighting back stirred up more hate. That if we did what we're supposed to do, what they expected us to do, we'd be okay. I guess I've been afraid that if I acknowledged the hate and everything that's happening, I would have to do something about it. Well, here I am." She stood before him like a soldier reporting for duty before heading off to war.

Darius took her in for a moment. "You weren't wrong. You weren't ready." He stroked her jawline with the back of his hand. "You're something else, Freda Gilroy."

The ground shifted underneath her. She smiled, then looked down at her watch, struggling to regain her equilibrium. "I wonder if the train will be on time."

Darius dropped his hand from her face. "You can set your watch to that train, but we do have some things to go over before it gets here. When Jonas finds you on the train, just take the package and that's it. Don't ask him any questions he can't answer. It's safer that way." Freda understood: if anyone knew Negro porters were part of a secret network to finance the cause of civil rights, they were as good as dead.

A small crowd had gathered on the platform now. Freda lowered her voice. "Will you stop fretting? You're starting to make me nervous. Have a little faith in me."

Darius whispered, too. "I do have faith in you, but I also trust the discipline we all need in this kind of work. Speaking of discipline, don't open the package Jonas gives you. Hold on to it and bring it back to me after break, and I'll get it where it needs to go."

She bristled because she had been brought up with discipline her whole life. It guided every move she made, sometimes to a fault, and she intended to treat this package with the same care that her granddaddy would have if it came through the US Postal Service.

When Freda opened her mouth to set Darius straight about her sense of discipline and ethics, a gangly white man in a grungy T-shirt appeared over Darius's shoulder. He rolled his tongue around the circumference of his open mouth, exposing tiny, cracked teeth that one could mistake for roasted corn kernels. Darius followed her eyes and turned around, his body shielding hers, and he came eye-to-eye with this stranger. He had told her once about Negro women traveling alone in Nashville being attacked, and that's why he insisted on waiting with her even in broad daylight.

And she believed him. She knew even the North wasn't always safe for a Negro woman by herself. Once, when she was a girl, she was walking with her mother in a sketchy part of town back home in Chicago, being pulled along with the buckle of her Mary Jane's skidding across the pavement. They were looking for a fabric store and got turned around, the sun scooting behind the clouds, the sky glowing like a lantern. Time had gotten away from them. The street emptied. Almost. Freda still wasn't certain where he came from, but a man with a military-style blond buzz cut grabbed Mama from behind, clapping one hand over her mouth and putting the other in the cavernous place she had warned her daughter to never let anyone touch. When he was certain she wouldn't scream, he uncovered her mouth and, with her eyes bulging, Mama smiled down at Freda, saying everything would be fine, and that this nice man would let them be on their way very soon. Tulip was brought up to believe every word that came out of her mother's mouth, but Mama's eyes told her none of it was fine. When it was over, she made her promise not to mention it to Papa, and Freda didn't. In fact, they never spoke of it again.

Darius and this man eyeballed each other in a test of wills to see who would blink first. The white man spat a wad of tobacco that landed on the toe of Darius's shoe. There was only so much a reasonable person could take and she was about to unleash her venom on this man when Darius backed up a few steps, almost tripping over her, and raised his arms signaling he didn't want any trouble. "That's what I thought, boy." And then, the man walked off the platform.

When he was gone, Darius spun around to face her. "Are you okay?"

"I'm fine. Just mad he thought he could intimidate us. He spit on you. How could you let him get away with that?"

Darius pulled out his handkerchief and bent to wipe his shoe. "He didn't get away with anything. He has to carry that hatred inside him everywhere he goes. Meeting his hatred with more of the same won't do any good. I'm glad I came with you."

A horn blared and a bright light hurtled toward them, and there was no time to reconsider anything. There was more to say, and the gallop of Freda's heart hadn't slowed down yet, still hurtling forward in her chest almost as fast as the train. Darius had protected her from that awful man, but men like him were everywhere and she felt as exposed as if she were naked.

"Are you going to be okay?" Darius said, holding her suitcases out to her.

Freda grasped the handles, unsure she'd ever be okay again. Flashing him a quick smile so he wouldn't worry, she climbed aboard, and once seated, she peered out and found Darius searching for her face among the rows of windows. The train pulled away from the station, and she pressed her palm against the glass until he became a tiny dot and then faded into the landscape.

FREDA STAYED IN PRIVATE QUARTERS, HER PARENTS PAYING THE extra money for a Pullman sleeper car, sparing her the indignities of riding coach as they had on her train journey to Fisk last fall.

Nine months had passed since then, long enough to carry and birth a baby. If you looked closely at Evaline's bare stomach, you could see a slight rounding, barely recognizable under her clothes. She left for Detroit the previous week and Freda wondered what her friend's family would say if she told them face-to-face. Cora made it home to Murfreesboro this morning, and she was probably sitting on a porch swing right now with Percy Chesterton III. Freda wouldn't be surprised if the girl came back from break with a ring on her finger.

The first knock at her door startled her and she pressed the pleats of her dusty rose skirt suit and adjusted her sun hat. Jonas Hayes might be standing on the other side of that door and the great handoff would begin. She was even more nervous than she thought she'd be, and she blew air slowly through her lips to calm herself.

"Come in, please," she called out.

But it was only the white conductor there to collect her ticket. She tilted the brim of her hat to shield her face and turned to look out the window at tall prairie grass shuddering against the early afternoon breeze. Eventually, the stress of the day caught up to her and her eyelids grew heavy. She lay down, feeling the train rattle the bench beneath her and let the low rumble lull her to sleep.

A second knock at her door awakened her. The tall, dark-skinned man standing on the threshold carried an air of nobility, his long black jacket adorned with large gold buttons. Before she spotted the nametag on his jacket, she knew this had to be Jonas Hayes, the Pullman porter Darius arranged for her to meet.

"Ma'am," Jonas said, tipping his cap in deference to her, revealing closely cropped black hair with a sprinkling of gray. "We're mighty glad to have you with us." Underneath his officious veneer, she detected his delight at seeing her on the other side of the door. He smiled generously. "I'm here for whatever you need during your travels, Miss Gilroy."

This man was old enough to be her grandfather and stood about an inch or two taller than Papa, straighter than any man she had known, as if there was a string pulling him from the top of his head.

"It is almost lunchtime," he said, holding a menu out to her. "We have broiled sirloin steak, butter basted baked fish, and breaded pork chops. All delicious, ma'am."

"I'm sure it is, thank you. I think I'll take my meal in the dining car so I can stretch my legs and move around a bit."

Maybe she said something wrong because Jonas averted his gaze and paused. He gently pressed the door to her sleeper car until it shut quietly, an act of discretion she would soon learn. "Ma'am, I will be happy to bring your meal to you here in your private car."

"But—" she started to say, and she saw Jonas's earnest eyes pleading with her to understand, to not make him spell it out for her and embarrass them both. It was a kindness that likely came in handy to quell the irritability of the white, monied class, a way to manage their tantrums with delicacy and diplomacy. Suddenly it became clear. How could she have been so naive? This country had rules and so did the railways, and the one she conveniently forgot was that colored folks were not allowed in the dining car. Mama and Papa's money only went so far.

"In that case, I'll have the steak here in my room. Thank you, Mr. Hayes."

"Jonas. You can call me Jonas."

HER STEAK ARRIVED MEDIUM-WELL, AS SHE ASKED, AND IT LAY before her on fine china.

"Why thank you, Mr. Hayes," she said with a certain affectation, playacting as Mama would call it. Cora and Evaline would get a kick out of this story—her eating a fancy steak meal on the train, being waited on in a private car like some rich white lady.

He shook his head. "Like I said, you don't need to call me—"

"No, no, I won't hear of it. You are Mr. Hayes to me. Please, have a seat." Freda gestured to the bench across from her.

"Oh no, ma'am, I can't," he said.

"Please. I insist."

She had forgotten to ask Darius about the details—whether Mr. Hayes would simply hand her the package or if she should be so bold as to ask. All she knew was that he had been told to make contact with her on the train. Presumably, he had done this before, and she decided to follow his lead.

"I can only imagine all the people you've met," Freda said, sipping iced tea and trying not to appear too eager. Casually, he mentioned famous politicians, writers, and even entertainers like Ray Charles and Aretha Franklin, all of whom he had rubbed shoulders with on the train. With every reference of someone famous, Mr. Hayes slapped his thigh and laughed as if tickled by some old memory.

"I met every last one of them. All kinds of musicians and dancers ride the train. The bands practice their sets right in these cars and I get my own private concert. They're good tippers, too," he said with a wink.

"I bet they are."

"My, my, my," he said, watching her eat her baked potato. "Your mama and daddy must be so proud. I know I am seeing you here. The entertainers take the train more than you might think, but this is what I like to see. Going to Fisk University and riding home in your very own sleeper car? Ooh-wee. Now that's something else."

From the way he grinned at her like she was his own daughter, she knew he was sincere and not performing a compulsory act of flattery in the name of customer service. "Yes, sir, they are proud."

"What's your major, young lady?"

"Mathematics."

"Uh-oh now, you're one of them real smart ones." Mr. Hayes tapped his feet lightly and squeezed his eyes shut. Pure joy spread across his face.

"What about you?" she asked. "Where are you from? Do you have children?"

"My home is same as yours. I'm a Chicago boy, born and raised on the far South Side. Lot of us Pullman porters come from Chicago."

She couldn't help but notice his eyes, wide and alert, yet tinged red, and she imagined he didn't get much sleep due to long shifts on the rails. Darius told her about a porter he met who curled up on a couch in the smoking car for an hour or two each night, but that was all the sleep he got.

"I have three boys and a girl. My sons took their degrees from Alcorn and my daughter is down at Talladega right now. I couldn't have sent them to school without this job." She could imagine Papa bending some stranger's ear about her the same way.

After a respectable amount of time conversing, he excused himself to tend to other passengers and Freda sat there thinking he was no different from so many Negroes of that generation, working harder than they should have to, bowing before white folks, demeaning themselves to ensure their children and children's children had an easier life. Cora told her once that practically every Negro in her hometown gathered to see her off to Fisk. Each of them owned a little piece of that dream.

The train ambled north, and after the dinner hour, dusk slipped into the pocket of darkness. Mr. Hayes returned briefly, asking her to wait in coach while he let down her bed. There in coach, Negroes crammed their bodies into uncomfortable seats where they would sleep for the night, leaving them with leg and neck cramps in the morning. She remembered crossing the Mason-Dixon line on her train trip down to Nashville, when she and the other Negroes were forced to crowd up front where smoke from the coal car filled their lungs. She understood how fortunate she was to have her parents pay for an upgrade to save her the humiliation of riding second-class.

When she returned to her private quarters and slipped into bed, under the pillow her hand brushed against paper. A thick envelope. This had to be it. Jonas Hayes had left it for her to find. She sat up straight and turned on the light, her hands trembling as she turned the sealed envelope over in her hands. The words written in cursive said *For the boy.* She had heard several of the Movement leaders refer to Thurgood Marshall as *the boy* and Darius told her he would need an influx of cash to fight ongoing school desegregation cases.

Who had donated money to the cause? It could have been anyone. She was no handwriting expert, but the grand flourish of the words looked familiar. The letter O in *for* and *boy* contained unusual double loops. Had she seen this writing before? It didn't matter. Her heart expanded as she held the full weight of the envelope in her hands along with the responsibility it carried.

26

Freda

The house Freda grew up in was just as she'd remembered—the jasmine scent behind Mama's ear when she hugged her neck; the pot of beef stew simmering for hours on the back of the stove; her bedroom, tidied up, still pink and ornate; and the medicinal smells of alcohol and morphine on Papa as he had finished tending to some ailing patient.

It hadn't even been a year since she'd left for college, but she had almost forgotten the routines, like the rumble of the garbage truck at daybreak. Mama running the vacuum cleaner every afternoon at four o'clock before Papa got home. Cousin Leotha shrugging out of his slaughterhouse clothes after a shift and scrubbing the scent of animal death out of them.

Papa had picked her up at Union Station. As soon as they walked into the house, Mama wrapped her in a tight hug, then they all settled in the kitchen. Mama slipped on an oven mitt and took a pan of chocolate brownies out of the oven. "I know how much you love them. Tell me if it's moist and chewy the way you like them," she said, cutting the brownies into squares and placing one in front of Freda. "I melted the butter first, which is the trick to it, and put in an extra egg yolk. You still like them fudgy, don't you?"

"Of course, Mama," she said, taking a bite. "Mmm, they're delicious."

"Let me get a good look at you," Papa said, holding her hands and turning them over in his own as if he might read her fortune. "My daughter, the mathematician from Fisk University." He made the pronouncement as if he were introducing a foreign dignitary at a state dinner.

Why were they making such a fuss over her? Freda fidgeted on the kitchen chair, anxious to close herself off in her bedroom, stare at the envelope from Jonas, and relive her adventure on the train. She imagined the end of summer break when she could reunite with Darius and they could open it together.

"I haven't been gone *that* long," she said, smiling at her family's inspection, their eyes questioning as if something fundamental about her might have shifted over all these months. And maybe it had now that she was actively involved in the fight for Negro equality.

"You ain't seen nothin' yet," Cousin Leotha said, leaning against the doorway smoking a pipe. She noticed him favoring his left hand, one of his right fingers smaller, more like a nub.

"What happened to your hand?" she asked.

He quickly tucked his hand into his pants pocket. "Oh, it's nothing. A little accident at the plant. Nothing to worry about. Happens to the best of us."

Changing the subject, he said, "The whole town will be over here before you know it."

"What do you mean?" Freda had just gotten home and the exhaustion from the long train ride was settling in her bones. She wanted to rest.

Cousin Leotha blew a curl of smoke to the ceiling. "You don't think your mama's cooking and baking just for you, do you? Everybody knows you're home and they're coming to see you." He let out a great big belly laugh.

Freda instantly giggled, Leotha's laugh just as contagious as it always had been. Being home with him made her feel warm inside. She barely remembered a time when her mother's cousin wasn't a permanent fixture in their family. When she was eight years old, she, Mama, and Daddy sat on the wooden benches in Union Station's Great Hall one Friday afternoon awaiting his arrival all the way to Chicago from Mississippi, by way of Atlanta. She had never met him and was curious to meet this family member who was coming to live with them. Dozens of other Negro families waited, too, and she recognized the same nervous hope in their eyes that she saw in Mama's.

One by one, passengers stepped off the train carrying luggage mostly bound with rope and twine. Freda would later learn that these folks from down south had all bought one-way tickets, and she would wonder for years how somebody picked up a life one day and plopped it down someplace else without looking back.

She tried to guess which men might have been her cousin, who would leave Mississippi behind to take a job in Chicago's meat packing district. She failed to correctly identify Leotha, a square-back man in a brown suit that was too big for him. He had a kind face and a broad smile. In one hand, he carried a smelly paper sack and in the other, a pair of shiny brown shoes. Shrugging, he held up the shoes and said, "In case we go to church on Sundays."

On the way home, he opened that paper bag and pulled out boiled eggs while telling them all about his train ride. "Man, that train runs faster than a spooked horse." Cousin Leotha tapped her knee.

As a child, Cousin Leotha told Freda lots of stories about life down south, but she didn't understand the meaning behind them. Now that she knew firsthand the racism he'd experienced, she wanted to hear more from him. She planned to steal time with him this summer— plus, if anybody could understand how much she had changed, it would be him.

Mama took her hand and led her to the bedroom, where she sprayed a sheen over the top of the dresser and wiped it with a cloth. "Leotha's right. We don't have much time before the guests arrive." She paused her wiping and pecked her daughter's cheek. "I missed you, sweetie."

"I thought it would be only family my first day back home," Freda said, knowing she'd now have to perform and embellish stories about college life, enthralling their guests with the grandeur they would expect.

"It's a small gathering, just the Prescotts, the Hightowers, and maybe the McKinneys, if they haven't left yet for the Vineyard. They'll be here before you know it. I hope they stay outside in the yard. They don't have any business back here in the bedrooms, but I'm not taking chances. The last thing I need is for Lavenia Prescott to come snooping around in here and find a speck of dust I missed." Mama smiled now, only half-teasing, resuming her wipe-down of Freda's furniture.

Freda sat on her childhood bed where she had once polished her nails, written love notes to boys, and read under the covers late into the night. She loved this house and the memories it held but now it seemed stuffy, stifling, and small. Too small to hold the life of significance she was now moving toward.

NEIGHBORS AND FRIENDS SPREAD OUT ACROSS THEIR YARD, dressed in pastel and white short sets as if they were nineteenth-century European aristocrats as they made this gentle game of croquet their own. That afternoon, they celebrated summer, and more than anything, Freda—the hometown girl who had made good, the next in a line of Negro achievement. She scanned the backyard for Cousin Leotha but didn't see him and realized he was probably inside churning homemade ice cream, his specialty. He didn't find anything entertaining about croquet. Slow and boring was how he put it. "If you wanna put a ball in a hoop, you play basketball. Simple as that." That was Cousin Leotha for you, unlike Papa who loved the game of croquet. Freda wasn't sure if he loved it because it required delicacy and accuracy, much like that of a physician, more so than speed and quick reflexes. Or maybe he loved it because it attracted the elite, monied class.

She walked over to her father, close enough to hear him in deep conversation with Dr. Prescott, who said, "Well, I was talking with my friend in Detroit, and he heard that the youngest Bates daughter is in the family way if you know what I mean. They tried to keep it quiet, but you know how people talk. Such a shame for a smart girl to be so careless." They were discussing Evaline, whose parents must know her secret. If the tables were turned, Dr. Prescott would be bending someone else's ear at a backyard party about Freda's indiscretion and the humiliation she had heaped upon her family. This circle of great expectations spared no one.

"From what I hear, the father of the baby is a Meharry man," she said, glancing at Papa for a reaction.

"Well, that certainly bodes well for the child and Evaline," he said, finally noticing Freda standing nearby.

Pedigree meant very little, Freda wanted to say, considering Ambrose was denying the child was even his, let alone stepping up to his responsibility. Moving closer, she said, "Evaline will be fine no matter what."

"Of course, she will." Papa handed her a mallet. "Lavenia, I hope you'll get to meet Gerald Vance at some point. He's another good Meharry man who happens to be dating my daughter. That's my girl. Swing from your shoulders. Like a pendulum," Papa said as her mallet made contact with the ball. "Follow through." They watched her ball stop mere inches from making the hoop.

"So much talent in this family," Dr. Prescott said, standing with one hand in the pocket of her summer white shorts, her dark curls windswept as if she were a lady of leisure on some soap opera. "Your father was telling me about some protests down in Nashville that got out of hand. Such a shame and a distraction from your studies. I hope you've managed to steer clear of all that unpleasantness, dear."

Knowing Dr. Prescott, she wasn't making idle conversation. As a psychiatrist, she would want to know what made Freda anxious, depressed, angry even. You had to approach every conversation with this woman carefully as she peered beyond your eyes into your mind. "Thank you for your concern, Dr. Prescott. I am staying focused on what matters most," she said, careful not to reveal what exactly that was.

"Well, thank God. I see it on the news, how the masses are taking to the streets with no real plan or strategy. Unlike your father and I in the Urban League, taking a methodical, reasonable approach, these

Negroes don't have the intellectual rigor, and I fear that without proper direction for their outrage, they can handicap our cause."

Her father nodded his head. "We are making progress in the Urban League. Maybe not as fast as you young people would like, but it's still progress."

The old guard, stalwart organizations were always reminding students to be patient, to wait for change to come. Freda wanted to tell Papa and Dr. Prescott that assimilation and accommodation would keep all of them stuck in place, but they weren't ready to hear it. She herself hadn't been ready a few months ago, but she had started believing in something, even if she didn't fully understand it. She squeezed the mallet until her fingers cramped. "Fisk students helped organize many of those marches and they're as smart as they come. There is a strategy of nonviolent civil disobedience. I don't see the downside, or the handicap as you put it."

No one dared contradict Dr. Prescott, and Freda knew it would be seen as a sign of disrespect to her elder. She didn't make eye contact with Papa either to avoid any reprimand in them. But the woman was wrong and there was no tactful way to tell her so.

Her father dropped his head. "I apologize for my daughter's tone. Her mind is expanding with all the intellectual pursuits Fisk has to offer and I'm sure she's entertaining all sorts of philosophies these days. Just theory, that's all."

By now, Dr. Prescott had recovered and slowly swung her mallet, her eyes still on some distant destination across the yard when she spoke. "You know, Freda, I completely forgot to ask how you're feeling these days."

"I'm sorry," Freda said. "I'm not sure what you mean. I'm not sick."

Still studying the trajectory of her ball, Dr. Prescott said, "I meant that nasty fall you took months ago when you were protesting. That was at Woolworth's down in Nashville, right? Dr. Shaw from Hubbard Hospital is a dear friend of the family, and he mentioned it." Seeing the stricken look on Papa's face, she said, "I apologize for not saying anything to you, Booker. I assumed Freda would have told you she had been in the hospital, and especially something like this that was all over the news, with people going to jail and everything."

That protest had been many months ago. Had the pesky Dr. Prescott been holding on to this information to release it at the worst possible time? Mama walked up then with a tray of diagonally sliced chicken salad sandwiches and seemed unsteady on her feet all of a sudden.

"You were in the hospital? Because of a protest?"

An intense pounding began in the front of Freda's head at her temples, and she excused herself as graciously as she could without answering her mother, walking quickly back into the house.

MANAGING TO AVOID HER PARENTS THE REST OF THE NIGHT, FREDA found Cousin Leotha sitting on a folding chair in their garage, hemmed in by an Oldsmobile and a Cadillac. Tools and automobile parts lay strewn across shelves, projects Papa would never finish. Her father liked the idea of being a man who worked with his hands, but if he wasn't doctoring on somebody, he wasn't that sort of man. Cousin Leotha *was* that kind of man. Now, he bent over a metal bucket to churn vanilla ice cream, the veins in his forearms pulsing with each rotation. Their guests had eaten it faster than he could make it, leaving little for the family after everybody left. Of course, that meant he had to make more. He spooned out a helping for her and she realized he had been right all along about homemade ice cream tasting better than what you bought at the store.

"Eat some more," Cousin Leotha said. "You little as a banty rooster. What they feeding you at that school?"

Freda rolled the ice cream on her tongue. She had forgotten how creamy it was even with the lumps. "Well, I may be going to school in the South, but you still can't pay me enough to eat oxtails and pigs' feet."

He laughed. "Oh, you be eating everything after a while. Watch."

"My friend Darius from school introduced me to fried okra."

"Oh, yeah, mix you up some flour and corn meal. Fry it till it's nice and crispy. That's some good eating now."

"That's exactly the way Darius said his mother cooked it. And he said there's some soaking you can do to keep it from coming out too sticky." Rocking back and forth on an overturned pail as she ate her ice cream, she asked, "Do you think you could show me how to make it?"

"I never known you to be interested in cooking anything. From what I remember, you stay as far away from that kitchen as you can." Cousin Leotha stopped churning and looked at her, smiling as if over a shared secret. "Oh, I get it. So you sweet on Daytime, huh?"

"Who?"

"Daytime," Cousin Leotha repeated, laughing now.

Heat rushed to her face, and she flung her spoon of ice cream at him. "His name is Darius and I never said I was *sweet on him*."

"You didn't have to. I may be country, but I ain't stupid."

When they caught their breath from laughing, Freda paused before saying, "I've been wanting to tell you the South isn't what I thought it was. It's not how I imagined it."

"All right, watch yourself now." The cream thickened as Cousin Leotha churned faster.

The last thing she wanted to do was offend him. She said, "For a long time, I thought southerners were stuck in the past, always holding on to outdated traditions. And some are. But I've met people like Darius who are more forward-thinking than anybody I've ever known. I have this feeling that the South is going to make America look itself in the mirror and say *you sure can do better*."

Cousin Leotha stopped cranking the ice cream. "You might be right about that. I see what young folks are doing down there." He paused. "You part of it, ain't you?"

She didn't know how to answer him but realized he must have heard the commotion outside when everybody learned of her protest injury. She had one foot in and one foot out of the Movement. That package in her purse said she was now more in than out these days. "Mama and Papa will never understand or approve."

"I didn't ask about your mama and papa. I asked about you."

She lifted her eyes to meet his. "Yes. I'm part of it."

"I thought so. Good for you. Good for all of you young'uns doing what we couldn't do. Making us proud."

For the first time since she'd been home, Freda exhaled all the fear and doubt. "The South is growing on me, but I understand why you left it behind."

He shook his head. "That's where you got it wrong. I could never leave Mississippi and the South behind any more than I could step outside this body and leave it behind. The South is in me, Mississippi is in me wherever I go."

She held out her bowl for more ice cream. "Still, things have to be better here in Chicago. You got a good job and can go anywhere you want and not be treated like a second-class citizen."

After scooping another helping for her, Cousin Leotha laid his left hand on her arm, and careful not to flinch, she stared at his nub head-on.

"It was a dirty trick some white guys from the line played on me," he said quietly. "They acted like they were cutting meat and cut my finger. Trying to scare me. Said they didn't mean to slice it off like that."

"It wasn't an accident? Somebody at the plant did this to you *on purpose?*" Ice cream slid cold down Freda's throat and a chill spread through her chest.

Chicago and other northern cities were supposed to be different, tolerating Negroes if nothing more. How could anyone—decent or not—hurt Cousin Leotha, one of the kindest men she knew? A man with a smile as long and wide as the Mississippi River itself.

"That hate is everywhere, you can't escape it," he said, waving his hand in the direction her parents went from the dining room. "Their money can't fix this. But you. You young people are gon' change things. Don't stop." Cousin Leotha held his bum hand up to his face. "You gon' make this world better and when you do, I'll look at this old hand and every time, it'll remind me of how far we've come."

***

For weeks, Freda stayed away from the house as much as possible, lounging from sunup to sundown at 31st Street Beach with her high school friends, who were all on summer break from other colleges. She missed Gerald terribly and called him every Sunday night.

"I miss you, and I wish we could talk longer," he always said, but she could tell he was struggling to stay awake after long shifts at Hubbard.

"I miss you, too," she said, smiling into the phone before setting the receiver in its cradle.

When, on occasion, she shared a meal or spent time with her parents, they didn't mention the Woolworth's protest or her head injury. When darkness fell on the house at bedtime or when she walked into the kitchen some mornings before they had time to architect their smiles, she heard her parents whisper her name. She sensed the worry in their voices. One night, the family gathered around the TV in the living room to watch *Gunsmoke,* mostly to appease Papa and Cousin Leotha, who both romanticized the old Western.

Her eyes on the TV, Freda flinched when the marshal with the shiny badge came on screen and reminded her of the police officer who had shoved her to the ground in Nashville. Mama kept reading the latest edition of *Life* magazine while the men looked more like boys twirling imaginary guns in a shootout, yelling *pow pow.*

When the credits rolled, Cousin Leotha disappeared into the kitchen and came out with slices of pound cake and more homemade ice cream for each of them. Unlike most men she knew, he enjoyed baking. A little sweetness for a man whose days were soured by death in the Stockyards.

"Ooh, this is so light and moist, almost better than what I make," Mama teased, the rest of them mumbling in agreement, mouths full.

"I'm going to need cuz over here to bake another cake to take back to school with me. The only thing is, I'll need to hide it from my friend, Cora. She's got a sweet tooth like mine." Freda licked ice cream from her fingers while Mama pushed her spoon round and round in her small dish until her ice cream resembled soup. And Papa rocked faster in his recliner. Something was stirring. You could feel it, and it reminded

Freda of the handful of times she had disappointed her parents with a bad grade or a bad attitude.

"You didn't even have to say a word," Cousin Leotha said. "I was planning to bake two pound cakes, one for you to share with your friends at school and the other to keep somewhere just for you." This was the level of subterfuge they would have enjoyed plotting any other time. But Mama shook her head vigorously. "Your father and I have been talking a lot lately, Freda. And we don't think it's a good idea for you to return to Fisk in the fall."

Freda thought she may have misheard and looked at her father, the man who considered her to be his legacy, the embodiment of a dream, the new, updated version of himself. "Papa?" she said expectantly, waiting for him to clear up everything.

He stumbled initially and in a stuttering voice said, "There are plenty of other excellent schools here in the Midwest or of course on the East Coast."

"I don't want to go to other excellent schools. I want to stay at Fisk. Can you honestly give me one good reason why I should not be at your alma mater, the place you and Mama talked to me about so much growing up that I didn't even consider other schools?"

Her logic made sense and Papa couldn't say anything right away. It was Mama who said, "We're worried about your safety. We read the papers, you know. We're aware of all that's happening down there in Nashville. You already got mixed up in something and got hurt. You could have been killed, Freda."

All that's happening. Freda knew she was referring to the sit-ins and marches, to what some called a Negro revolution. Naming it carried some unspoken risk, as if talking about the fight for freedom might bring it to the Gilroy's doorstep. From the way Mama kept staring at the milky liquid in her cup, it was apparent she wanted to find out Freda's level of involvement without asking directly.

Papa stood and addressed all of them. "I'm sure Freda got injured being in the wrong place at the wrong time. Our daughter is too smart to get seduced by all of that. She's got her head on straight."

"Booker, you know what we discussed and decided." Mama's eyes bulged, insisting Papa fall in line.

"Yes, I know what we talked about," he said, and then pinned Freda with a gaze she couldn't turn away from. That was the look he used to discipline her growing up and it kept her in line. "The only way we'll let you go back there in the fall is if you promise us you'll steer completely clear of those demonstrations and the people involved in them."

There was no time to construct the perfect answer with both of her parents and Cousin Leotha waiting for her to speak. In a soft, feathery tone that Freda hoped communicated deference, she said, "I learned my lesson. You can trust me to stay on the straight and narrow, no more trouble."

Papa seemed convinced. "Hmph, we'll see, won't we?" was all Mama said before the two of them retired for the night.

FREDA SAT ALONE, ONE SINGLE TABLE LAMP CASTING A YELLOW glow around the living room.

"They don't mean no harm." How long had Cousin Leotha been standing in the shadows? He sat next to her on the sofa. "They scared for you, that's all. You should hear them talking about you when you're off at school. They brag on you all the time to anybody who'll listen."

She looked up at him. A pair of glassy yellowed eyes stared back at her. Infinitely wise even though he was still in the middle of his life, not an old man yet, but life as a Negro under a constant state of oppression aged a man beyond his years.

"I feel myself changing, finding my voice for the first time. Doing something important," she told him. "I'm not sorry about that."

"You shouldn't be. You not wrong," Cousin Leotha said. "But your mama and papa not wrong either. People get free however they get free."

After he said good night and went to bed, Freda sat there in the living room awhile longer, and her eyes landed on a wall hanging she passed every day without ever really thinking about it. Her mother's framed program book from the live Nat King Cole concert she and Papa attended years ago. It was hard to believe Freda had not only seen him perform but had talked to him.

Even when she looked away deep in thought about lying to her parents so she could return to Fisk, her gaze kept returning to that program book. She remembered Mama practically screaming in delight that the King himself had signed it for her. Something about that signature nagged at her and wouldn't let go. It was the double looped Os. She jumped up, ran to her bedroom to get her purse, and returned to the living room. Pulling out the envelope Jonas Hayes had left for her on the train, she held it up to the picture frame.

The handwriting matched. Both had the same slant with the distinctive double looped Os. They were identical. The envelope of money she had been carrying for the Movement had come from Nat King Cole.

PART TEN

Chicago, 1992

27

Tulip

It was Friday morning, the day before the protest marches, and Tulip was standing in Bryce's office, unsure of exactly why he had summoned her. Maybe he had finally decided to promote her after everything she had done to help Mattingly win the CookCo account. Or perhaps Amanda had gotten to him, a possibility she couldn't dismiss.

Seated behind his mahogany desk, Bryce leaned back in his swivel chair, laced his hands behind his head, and smiled disarmingly at her. How much did he know about her involvement with the protests and her pitches to local reporters? Angry words or even a snarl or frown would have eased her mind because then she could brace herself for what was coming. His pleasant demeanor made her more anxious.

Shifting from one foot to the other, her eyes darted from his gumball machine to the Elvis Presley guitar he told everyone he won in an auction. No one had a way to verify its authenticity, and you could never be sure if he was being straight with you because of his propensity for embellishing. He hadn't asked her to sit down so she remained standing.

"Tell me, Tulip, when did you stop believing in Santa Claus?"

What a seemingly innocent, unexpected question, and maybe that's why it unnerved her more than if he had accused her of something as preposterous as skimming profits from the company. "I don't know, I guess I was around nine or ten. Probably older than most kids."

"I'll never forget when my daughter was only eight. That Christmas she accused my wife and me of lying to her. She pointed out that our house doesn't have a chimney and it would be impossible for one old man to get to all those kids' houses around the world. And then she said, 'Why would he buy me all the same gifts I told you that I wanted?' She got us good, and we had to admit there was no Santa Claus."

Tulip smiled, unsure where this story was going. Couldn't he tell how uncomfortable she looked standing there while he went on about Santa Claus? Careful not to offend him, she said, "You have a bright, perceptive daughter."

"I do. Takes after her old man. We meant well creating that bit of magic for her those early years of her life. We knowingly lied to do a good thing."

The bottom of Tulip's foot itched like it always did when she was driving or doing anything where it was either inconvenient or inappropriate to scratch. It also happened sometimes when she was anxious. "I'm sure your daughter understands that your heart was in the right place."

"You're a lot like my wife and me. Heart in the right place trying to do something good. But you've crossed a line here with your sneaking around, misrepresenting yourself, and lying. We are not in the activism business." His face tightened, the anger spreading through him, turning his neck and even his fingers red. "You've exploited my business for your personal gain."

His words stopped her cold. Tulip was reminded of one of those horror flicks where the lone Black person in the room never made it out alive. She breathed deeply and remembered her mother's advice. "I think you may have misunderstood. I was talking to some reporters after hours and the protest marches happened to come up. No official business." Her voice squeaked the faster she talked.

The only other time she had seen Bryce angry was when one of their accountants had embezzled money from the agency, a crime the man paid for with prison time. Maybe that's how Bryce saw her now—someone on the inside gaining unfair advantage to hurt the company.

"Don't try to bullshit me," he said. "Your father has a flawless, storied reputation in this city. One of the top Black doctors in Chicago."

Top doctor, Tulip wanted to say. Being Black had nothing to do with it. Hearing her father's name associated with what she had done made her feel worse.

"In this case, the apple fell far from the tree. You've disgraced the Mattingly name and your family name with your deceit. And this isn't the first time. I publicly praised you for your part in getting the CookCo account. But I'm well aware of your unorthodox meeting with Adam Feldman. It worked so I let it slide. But I see now that it was an early indication of how underhanded you can be."

She almost collapsed in front of his desk. He hadn't appreciated her part in a successful business win after all. He hadn't admired her creative tenacity. Instead, he faulted her for it and was using it now as cudgel to make his point about her lack of character.

"I don't know what to say," Tulip started. "It's obvious I've disappointed you when my only goal has been to support this agency and serve our clients. But I also understand your position as CEO."

For a second, Bryce looked sympathetic, almost fatherly. Leaning forward across his desk, he said, "How deep are you in this protest business?"

Tulip recalled rushing from the office at ten o'clock in the morning earlier that week to head over to the City Transportation Department on LaSalle to fill out a form for "Notification of Public Assembly." She had written in Christina's name as the organizer but put down her own as onsite manager, a role for herself that she had never cleared with anyone. It had been a split-second decision as a disgruntled office worker stared at her impatiently. And since they would need a portion of King Drive closed for the march, Tulip applied for a parade permit. She had done it all on company time, but she often worked fifty and sixty hour weeks. It all evened out, didn't it? She told Bryce, "I'm trying to help my community, do my civic duty."

Bryce laughed but it was humorless. He clicked his pen on and off while she shifted her weight from one foot to the other. "You do your civic duty by voting. I won't tolerate deception or misuse of this agency. I'm running a business here, not a charity. Now, consider this your first and final warning. If I hear or see you handling personal projects on Mattingly time, you're fired."

***

Tulip took a big gulp of her Polynesian rum cocktail. The hostess at Tropical Hut sashayed by in her floor-length floral muumuu, smiling generously at Tulip and her mother, letting them know she was there if they needed anything while they waited. Tulip made an attempt to smile back, though her nerves were on edge. When she'd gotten home from work, she'd locked herself in her bedroom, away from Sharita, until it was time to meet her parents for dinner. She'd been humiliated and cornered, with few options and nowhere to turn. The ultimatum from Bryce weighed on Tulip, and now she tried to put it out of her mind long enough to enjoy a meal with her parents.

This Stony Island Avenue restaurant had been a favorite of theirs as a family since she was a little girl, the spot where they came to celebrate a good report card or simply the end of a harsh winter. Gerald invited them to dinner saying he had news to share, but he had been on-call at the hospital all day and would join them as soon as he could.

"What is it?" Freda had always been able to read her moods, whether it was sorrow over a broken toy or a broken heart. Before Tulip could answer, she said, "You talked to Bryce, and it didn't go well."

"He knows everything. I could lose my job. I mean he didn't fire me yet, but he made it clear I need to leave the protesting alone if I want to keep working there." Saying the words brought a tightening to the back of Tulip's throat. "I tried to say what you told me, but he didn't believe me."

"This march is important to you, isn't it?"

"Yes, Mom, it is." Tulip looked forward to her trips to Ida B. Wells, and in her client meetings at work anticipated what hilarious gems the men who played dominoes might drop, how they'd clown her speaking voice and professional attire the way well-meaning uncles might. The fire in Christina over this work ignited her own. And each time Tulip showed up to the projects, Bertrice stood in her open doorway and looked a little less surprised.

Freda reached across the table to squeeze her hand, something Tulip hadn't expected. "There's always a price to pay in activist work. The bill will come due. Only you know how much of yourself you want to give to the cause."

"I want to see this march through. But I don't want to lose my job or the possibility of getting promoted when I've come so far."

Freda took a deep breath. "Listen, you worked hard to make this happen, so put Bryce and the job out of your mind for now. We have a protest tomorrow, and I want to make sure you've thought of everything."

Had she worn her mother down? She said *we* as if they were in this together. A million questions swirled in Tulip's head, but she didn't ask anything that might break this spell or whatever it was that had come over her mother.

"Okay, like what?" Tulip asked, invigorated again.

Freda stopped the hostess to ask for a pen and began writing on the cocktail napkin. "I know it's a little late with the protest happening tomorrow, but you need to be clear about your objectives. I know one of them is to show solidarity with the community in LA over what happened to Rodney King and Latasha Harlins. You're also trying to change things for Blacks here in Chicago, especially those who are low income. You have to apply pressure on the city, hit them where it hurts, make them pay attention. You need legal observers, too."

Lawyers at the march had never occurred to Tulip. "Why lawyers?" she asked.

"Because you'll want them on the sidelines in case there are any clashes with opposing groups or the police. I'll call Judge Turner and a few of the attorneys in the Links to see if they know who might be able to go to different locations on your march route on short notice." Freda took a sip of her piña colada and scribbled furiously, filling one side of the napkin, turning it over to write on the other side.

Tulip hadn't considered these possibilities. "Do you think there could be confrontations?"

Her mother's eyes hardened, and she disappeared within herself. "There's always that possibility. You should have a volunteer ambulance crew there, too. Might have to pay them something, and I can help with that."

"Why not just call 911?"

Freda sighed. "Emergency calls to 911 go straight to the police. But if the violent confrontation is with the police, what good will that do?"

Since they were being so open, Tulip decided to tell her mother what else she was planning for the protest. "I've been thinking about speaking. I don't want to be the story. It's not about me, but I could say a few words."

Instead of the surprise or anger Tulip was expecting, she detected a hint of admiration on Freda's face. "These movements need more women like you at the forefront but you're right. It shouldn't be about you. Shine a light on the people in that community. Speak from your heart and find a way to tell their stories. Shame the city into doing better."

Who was this woman? Her mother now looked twenty years younger with bright, blazing eyes and barely contained energy. Something was going on with her, but Tulip didn't want to do anything that might stamp out the fire.

Tulip grabbed another napkin and continued writing. "Whenever our agency features puppies or children in a campaign, audiences go crazy."

Freda smacked the table. "What did Whitney say? *I believe the children are our future.* There you go. That's what you'll talk about onstage."

They clasped hands victoriously just as her father appeared at the table looking tired but happy. Freda quickly shoved the napkins with their notes into her purse.

"What are you two up to?" he said. "All I know is I'm the envy of every man in this restaurant dining with the two prettiest ladies in the place." Gerald pecked their cheeks before sitting down in their secluded booth. The Vance name usually got them prime seating in the dimly lit Tropical Hut, something she knew her father was proud of.

"We're ready now," he said, raising a finger to signal the attention of the server and making a show of ordering rotisserie ribs and prime rib for all of them.

"What has gotten into you, Gerald?" Freda said. "I haven't seen you this excited since I don't know when. Maybe the NBA Finals last year. Yeah, the Bulls are favored to win tomorrow but you need to prepare yourself because it could go either way."

Freda had a point, but Tulip knew those words were blasphemy to the ears of her father and Key and almost any die-hard Bulls fan in this city. He opened his mouth in mock horror.

"First of all, dear," Gerald said, "there is no outcome except for victory in the Finals tomorrow. What is it they say in church? The devil is a lie! And I'll have you both know that the Bulls are not the only game in town." He pulled on his suspenders and cocked his head to one side, very aware that he was building suspense.

Finally, he said, "You are looking at the recipient of the Meharry Medical College Distinguished Physician Award. They're presenting it to me at Convocation in October."

Forgetting to appear dignified, they jumped from the table to hug him, recognizing the magnitude of the honor. He had always just been Dad to Tulip, but for the first time she realized his significance to the medical community and his patients. This was what he meant all those times he preached to her about Black excellence. But he didn't just preach it—he embodied this as a way of life, overcoming so much to achieve it.

Her father had set the bar high, laying a path for her to follow. Instead of feeling inspired, she panicked, unsure if she could live up to his example, or even wanted to anymore.

Tulip

As the old joke went, the only folks stirring early on a Sunday morning were Catholics and criminals. But not on this day, when people packed supermarkets and restaurants buying sub sandwiches, chips and dip, meatballs, and wings. Strangers smiled at one another and even waved because today was different. Today they were celebrating their dream of a Bulls repeat that they didn't have to see yet to believe it would happen.

Inside the bakery, Key lifted her and spun her around while they waited for a basketball-themed cake with a number 23 topper in red. The plan was for Tulip to watch the game at home that night with Sharita and Rudy since Key would be out at a sports bar with his father and some of their friends. The cake would be theirs to enjoy for a private celebration the next morning. And with a frenzy like this, you couldn't wait too late to get your hands on anything stamped with the Bulls logo.

"This is it, baby," he said. "Birthday, Christmas, New Year's all in one."

Key gently lowered her to the floor, grinning at a little boy who had to be no more than three climbing on top of the store counter, inching toward the baked goods.

Not ready yet for her feet to touch the ground, Tulip tugged at Key's waistband, and she resembled a child herself begging for attention.

Remembering her, he looked down and said, "What is it? You look like you lost your best friend. I don't see how anybody can be down right now, not today of all days."

Key had said all along nothing good would come of protesting. He would say he had told her so. She almost lied and said nothing was wrong, but he knew nothing always meant something. "Bryce is mad about me getting mixed up with the protest," she said. "This is on my own time, not the company's, but I still worry that if I go through with the march today, I could lose my job."

Tears gathered behind her eyes. She had worked hard for her CEO to see her as more than Gerald Vance's daughter, a favor for a friend. She had put her all into her job for the past five years to earn her place in the agency, only to possibly lose it now.

"That's some BS," Key said, surprising her. "Taking away something you worked hard for because you did something he didn't like? Nah, that's foul."

"Now I don't know what to do," she said. "I'm not sure what's gotten into Mom these days, but she thinks I should go through with the protest. She even gave me some ideas, as if she knows how to pull this off when the only thing she ever sees as unfair is a hotel with no valet parking."

While Tulip talked, she followed Key's eyes and noticed he was distracted by that same little boy who was now dipping his fingers into a smooth, buttercream frosted Bulls cake, leaving a crater in it the size of a fist. The mother cursed and said it would be a cold day in hell before she took him anywhere again even as a smile curled her lips.

Tulip gave up, convinced that everyone had become consumed by Michael Jordan that day to the exclusion of everything else. An anxious feeling scraped her insides, waiting in line for a cake when the march was scheduled to start in a couple hours. Tugging on Key's arm, she said, "You stay here and get the cake, then take it back to your place. I'll call you later."

He looked relieved. "Are you sure? I know you wanted to talk."

"Of course, I'm sure."

"How 'bout them Bulls?" he said, flashing that smile that would normally buckle her knees.

"Go, Bulls." She stretched a smile so hard across her face she thought her jaw might break from the effort. And then she booked it out of there, breathing in the Sunday air. You had to pour gasoline on your own dreams sometimes because no one could fuel them for you. Everything became clear and she knew what she had to do.

***

Five blocks of Cottage Grove Avenue were blocked off when Tulip walked over with Christina, Bertrice, and a dozen of their neighbors. A pickup truck belonging to one of the residents carried the signs: JUSTICE FOR LATASHA HARLINS. JUSTICE FOR RODNEY KING. JUSTICE FOR IDA B. WELLS. NO JUSTICE, NO PEACE.

Christina's thick locs swung across her shoulders when she surveyed the street, directing a volunteer where to set up the makeshift podium. She noticed Tulip standing awkwardly on the curb, inspecting the same signs again and again. "Are you on something?" Christina asked her. "You're jumpy as hell."

The notion that Tulip, who had never even tried weed, might be high made her laugh. Her conversation with Bryce on Friday had spooked her, and as confident as she'd been this morning leaving the bakery, she couldn't help but worry again that she was jeopardizing her job. After checking with an attorney friend of her mother's, Tulip learned that Bryce couldn't legally stop her from participating in the protests since they were happening outside of company hours and were considered protected political activity. However, Mattingly could fire her for pitching this story to journalists on company time, using relationships she had developed through the agency. A more immediate worry gnawed at her. She had promised all the news stations and papers a story but still hadn't convinced any of the residents to talk to media.

A crowd gathered and families picked up signs, handing some to children, and they began marching. Several people hoisted placards with sketch drawings of Rodney King, his name emblazoned on T-shirts and ball caps. Others were in their Bulls paraphernalia still supporting the cause or lured by the excitement of any spectacle hours before the big game. Since this wasn't too far south of downtown, white people joined the protest, too.

One little Black girl, who had to be no more than five years old, with pigtails and barrettes on the ends, carried a sign almost as big as she was. It read: END RACISM SO I CAN GROW UP. TV and newspaper photographers crouched on the ground in front of her to capture what had made so many people stop and take notice. The girl posed, enjoying the attention.

"I think I remember you from one of the community meetings," Tulip said to the girl's mother. "What's your daughter's name?"

"Falana," the woman said slowly, as if considering whether she had made a mistake, and then she gripped the girl's hand tighter and tried to move her along quicker. "Why do you want to know?"

"I'm Tulip and I worked with the neighborhood to organize the march. Falana's sign is great but it's not enough. We need people who live in this community to tell their stories to the media, to the city. Nothing will change if they don't hear your voices." She wished she hadn't been forced to yell this to be heard over the chants of the growing crowd.

The woman shook her head vigorously. "No, I'm not telling anybody anything. And leave my child out of it."

"I understand your reluctance," Tulip began before the mother cut her off.

"You don't understand anything," she said. "You come into our neighborhood to do something that makes you feel better about yourself and then you bounce. Falana and I live here day in and day out. If we start making waves, it's going to be harder for us. And things are already hard enough as it is."

"Please hear me out." Tulip put her hands together the way she did before saying her nighttime prayers.

"Go back to the suburbs."

Tulip almost set her straight, telling her she was wrong, that she didn't come from the suburbs, that her family had lived in the city all their lives. But she knew what this mother meant. Tulip came from neighborhoods where people argued over property lines and privacy fences. Black privilege, but privilege, nonetheless.

"I can't imagine what it's like here for you and Falana."

Fire burned in this woman's eyes. "I'll tell you what it's like. I'm a single mother. It's just the two of us and Falana has nowhere to play, nowhere that's safe to run around and be a child. She climbs in bed with me when the gunshots go off. She takes cold showers at night because we don't have hot water. The city has never done anything about that."

Sorry would be inadequate and the woman was right for scolding Tulip for saying she understood when she didn't. But Tulip recognized that this one story could tell the larger story of the grievances of the residents at Ida B. Wells. Her PR work at Mattingly taught her that no one cared about issues, no matter how controversial or catastrophic, until you made them personal and human.

"I can't begin to know what life is like for you," she said to the mother. "We have a chance, though, with all these reporters here, to shine a light on the injustice. What if your story, Falana's story, breaks through? We won't know unless we try."

"Maybe another time," the mother said, shielding her daughter and turning away from Tulip.

What if this march failed after all this effort and planning? Some in the crowd hurled their anger at the cops, who stood in as proxy for the ones out in LA. A woman in a tight yellow tank top appeared next to Tulip and noticed her watching the police. She leaned over and whispered like they were neighbors sitting on the stoop trading juicy gossip. With a knowing look, she said, "They're as guilty as the rest of them. Just didn't catch these on camera yet." Tulip didn't blame everyone with a badge, yet there was no way to tell who to trust and who to fear, and so her shoulders hitched a bit around all of them.

The swell of the crowd pressed against her, and she realized that it would only take one small provocation for things to go bad quickly.

The medic vans her mother had hired were on standby, their yellow lights flashing in readiness.

Tulip carried a clipboard with the names of scheduled speakers and parted the crowd enough to allow a Black man with a megaphone through the tight knot of protesters. "Coming through," she yelled. "Please step aside." Grayson Evans pastored Christina's church and his baritone reverberated in her chest the way deep bass did at the club. There was something about the voice of a brother who had been cradled by Christianity, a man of God.

"Latasha Harlins was just a child in seventh grade going to the corner store because she was thirsty. That could have been your baby. She had her whole life in front of her and had it snatched away by a store owner with a gun in her hand and hate in her heart. Latasha Harlins deserved better," boomed Pastor Evans.

"The same can be said for Rodney King, an ordinary man behind the wheel of that car. He could have been you or me. All those police officers saw was a Black man. They swung at him with their batons. They hit his legs. His chest. His head. They didn't see Rodney King as a man. How could you see him as a man and do that to him?"

Echoes of *that's right* and *tell 'em* rose from the crowd. Spontaneous chants of Rodney King's name began, and in the call-and-response tradition of the Black church, Tulip heard her own voice answer with *Latasha Harlins*. She hadn't meant to say anything at all. But she started softly at first and then brought her full-throated voice. Before long, others joined in lifting the young woman's name, too.

AT A QUARTER TO SIX, CHRISTINA REAPPEARED, HER LOCS PULLED back in a ponytail, her face shiny with sweat. She had been negotiating with police to extend the time for reopening Cottage Grove to traffic. "Do you think we're gonna make it?" She frantically grabbed water bottles from her truck to hand to people in the crowd. "These people are gonna pass out, as hot as it is out here. We may not have time to do that thing you suggested."

They had planned a photo opportunity that would happen as TV stations went live at six. Tulip rummaged through Christina's truck until she found a box with photos, then grabbed two of the men she met at the organizing meeting the first night and enlisted their help to match the framed school picture photos with their parents in the crowd. When they had assembled the moms and dads, they lined them up in the front and asked them to silently hold up the pictures of their children all dressed up and smiling.

The mother Tulip had met earlier appeared at her side. "Okay. I'm Roberta. They can talk to me."

Tulip had gotten through to her after all. She brought over a reporter from the *Sun-Times* to interview Roberta, who began by saying, "This is Falana and she's my whole world. She's smart and helpful and funny. She's a kid. But we live in a building where things are always falling apart. Drug deals happen in the hall right outside our door and she has to step over needles to leave the house for school. Half the place is boarded up after somebody got shot in one of the apartments. That's how my baby has to grow up. When she gets older, if she gets older, I'm scared she could be the next Latasha Harlins or Rodney King. That's why we're out here."

When Roberta spoke, everyone nearby was still, even the children. The power of that mother's words touched Tulip so deeply she almost cried. The consumer products she promoted for her Mattingly clients never inspired such emotion. It was a paycheck, a good one, but she had to admit that's all it was. The only people who seemed unmoved right now were the police lining the streets, their eyes hidden behind the shade of their sunglasses.

TV STATION PHOTOGRAPHERS MOUNTED THEIR CAMERAS ON tripods and waited for the top of the evening news shows to go live. The news anchors would toss to them any second and if Tulip went through with what she had planned, her face would be broadcast all over the news. No more pretending. No more hiding. Everyone, in-cluding Bryce and her father, would know what she was up to.

Standing in front of the microphones and the bright lights of the cameras, Tulip froze until she felt a tap on her shoulder and turned to see Bertrice Ward from the 559 building giving her the thumbs-up sign and gesturing to the podium.

There was no time to think of the ramifications. Tulip stepped forward slowly as the stations went live and she tapped the mic lightly. "Is this on? Can you hear me?" As blinding as the camera lights were, she scanned the crowd and almost fainted when she saw her mother on the edge of the wide circle, nodding as if to say *go on, you can do this, your wings are fine, go ahead and fly.*

Everything was a blur to Tulip, now standing in front of dozens of parents holding picture day school portraits. She swallowed around the lump in her throat and began. "These are the faces of children in the Ida B. Wells community. They deserve a good education. They deserve housing where they can play freely and feel safe. They deserve a neigh-borhood where they aren't recruited by drug dealers. They deserve to walk these streets without fear. They deserve to graduate from eighth grade, from high school, to earn their certificates from a trade school, to graduate from college. They deserve to marry and have children of their own. They deserve to pursue their life's ambitions. They deserve a future."

The people shouted *amens* like they were in church, some with tears streaming down their faces. Those at home watching on TV would ex-perience this, too, and that's what Tulip knew she was good at, creating moments that touched people's hearts and moved them to act, to do something. Looking out over the audience again, she searched for her mother, but she had disappeared into the crowd. It was then that Tulip gained the clarity she had been seeking. This was the life she wanted, even if it cost her the career she was starting to build. For the first time, she felt free.

PART ELEVEN

Nashville, 1960

29

Darius

It had been a long summer. Back to Nashville after his organizing work in Mississippi, Darius immersed himself in the world of ideas, a state of being most young people his age would describe as lonely and dull. Stacks of library books formed a fortress around him, his face barely visible behind them in the basement of First Baptist Church. Philosophy. History of world conflicts. Theories of nonviolence.

As Darius pondered a particularly dense portion of text, he heard the click clack of heels, and before he glanced up and around the books, he knew who it was. Her lilac scent perfumed the room, and he heard her soft breathing. His heart did that thing it did when she was near. She hadn't told him what day or time her train would arrive in Nashville. Maybe Gerald Vance had been the one waiting for her at Union Station. That thought stung like a sharp sand burr sticking him in the chest.

"Did you rob a bookstore?" Freda asked. He absorbed the timbre of her voice, something he hadn't realized he had missed so much over the long summer. He peered out from behind the stack.

"Very funny," he said, grinning now.

People found it odd that he didn't believe in buying books, and only checked them out of the library because it seemed wrong to attempt to own ideas, since ideas were meant to be shared and expanded upon over time. That notion held little logic for most, but he told Freda this anyway to gauge her reaction. She shrugged and passed no judgment. He wanted to tell her that books were to be shared, but not beautiful women.

To be honest, he was stalling; they both were. Should he extend his arms for an embrace, slap her on the back like he would another fellow, or do nothing and stay rooted in place waiting to see what she would do? For better or worse, he chose the latter, and they both stared at each other, consumed with equal amounts of giddiness and awkwardness.

Freda finally ended this game of chicken. "Well, are you going to sit there or greet me as if you missed me all these months?" She planted her hands firmly on the small of her waist and he saw the playfulness in her eyes. His foot got caught in the leg of the chair and he almost fell over the desk trying to close the gap between them. Her lilac scent was stronger now, no good for a man already unsteady on his feet.

She pulled a white envelope out of her purse and laid it on the table. "This is it. I didn't open it and reseal it or anything, as curious as I was. I can't lie. I did hold it up to the sunlight and I could see dollar bills. Now I know Jonas Hayes is a good, honest man, but it's hard to believe none of the porters ever open the packages. Has any money ever come up missing?"

Darius shook his head. "As long as the Pullman porters have been transporting money for the Movement, we've never had reports of any of them stealing. It's hard to explain, but the ones who do it treat this as a sacred duty, an honor. Those men don't even tell their wives about this."

He began to ponder his own commitment to this work. There was a nobility and discipline you usually only saw from people in the armed forces, the way they saluted the flag, held on to military secrets, and marched in formation to stay on one accord knowing people were depending on them. He had to admit there was a spiritual aspect to it as well. Not like the worship of God or anything, but close. It was a higher calling that made you reverent and obedient in service to it.

Impatiently, she slid the envelope closer to him. "Well, open it already."

The envelope was bulky, and they realized they had something that would be useful in the struggle, something secret to bind them together. Darius appreciated sharing this with her and it held its own form of intimacy.

He used a letter opener to break the seal. A wad of one-hundred-dollar bills fell out with a note that repeated the message on the front of the envelope—*for the boy*. Freda quickly counted the bills and there were ten of them equaling $1,000. "Oooh," she said, releasing air between her closed lips as if she were blowing out birthday candles. "That's a lot of cash." She spoke faster now. "I think I know where it came from." Darius looked at her, intrigued. She kept going. "I knew the signature, the handwriting looked familiar, and for the longest I couldn't place it but then I finally figured it out."

Darius stayed silent, nodding but neither confirming nor denying any conclusion she came to, and that's what set her off.

"You knew all of this, didn't you?" she said. "You knew who gave the money, but you didn't say a word."

He hadn't intentionally tried to keep her one step behind in this thing, but these matters had to be handled with utmost discretion. Confidentiality, a must. The King had slipped him seventy-five dollars that night at Club Del Morocco to bail out Errol Hankins and two other protestors. But as Thurgood Marshall's court cases intensified in the following weeks, they needed a more sizable amount, and the porters came in handy when rich stars like Nat King Cole were on the road so much.

Freda was still waiting to hear what he had to say for himself. "Yes, I knew. He's good at making his fans think he has no interest in civil rights. You fell for it, most people do. These white folks tried to kill him onstage for being colored and famous. Imagine what they'd do to him if they knew he was taking their hard-earned show ticket money and using it to bail out some colored activists. I don't care how big of a star he is, he'd either be out of the business or a dead man."

Freda covered her face with her hands. "I didn't think about how dangerous it would be for him to tell me the truth. I feel so ashamed for thinking he had turned his back on Negroes and only cared about his own fame."

A man as well-regarded in white circles as Nat King Cole had to be careful. The beauty of it though was that as his star rose, so did the level of support he was able to provide for civil rights, even if it all had to be done under a cloak of secrecy.

***

Down the street from First Baptist, they found a bench to sit on in a secluded spot where they could linger and watch the golden leaves skitter along the curb.

Freda's head fell back, her face angled toward the sky. "I know I haven't always been supportive of this work, of you," she said. "It's the way I grew up, always hearing you don't get involved in these things. I was listening to my folks, and I even challenged them over it when I was home this summer."

Darius tried to picture stubborn Freda in some fancy house in Chicago, a city he had only seen in books, with her face enflamed, debating the finer points of civil disobedience. Standing up to her parents, an important family, her father being legacy at Fisk. "You don't need to apologize. You're a brave woman," he said. "My folks don't know everything I do, but there are things they know about that they don't like."

"Why? I would think they'd be proud of you," Freda said, glancing at him. "If they disapprove, I'm sure it's just because they're afraid you might get hurt."

That winter, weeks after his first sit-in, when police arrested him and many other Negro protesters, his folks in rural North Carolina got word. They knew he was involved in nonviolent work, and as devout Christians, they respected that. But to have their baby boy handcuffed and hauled off to jail in a paddy wagon like a common criminal brought more shame and disgrace to their family than they could bear. Freda's eyes watered, and she touched his arm.

No one saw Freda's affectionate gesture, and no one could report back to Gerald that something inappropriate was happening. He reminded himself that she was not a married woman. When she looked at him, Darius realized he had lost perspective on what was appropriate or not and he wasn't sure he cared.

"Someday, your mama and daddy will know that their son changed the world," Freda said, "and you better believe they'll let everybody in Chatham County know." She smiled, and he wasn't sure if it was her touch or her words, but a warm tingle snaked up his arms, moved through his chest, and nestled in his belly.

The irritation Freda once showed him could cut out a man's heart. And now here she was, close enough he felt every breath she exhaled. How long was it reasonable for them to go on like this, working together, falling for each other before the world intruded on them again?

"Do you think you'll ever tire of doing civil rights work?" she asked. "It can be so dangerous, and there's no guarantee sometimes that we will change anything."

He put a cigarette between his lips and lit it. "I'm an old country boy at heart. I know I may die young the way my grandparents and aunts and uncles did. It's the significance of what we're doing, the promise of a new day, that keeps me going. You keep me going."

Frowning, Freda said, "Some doctors, my father being one of them, say smoking may kill you now. It's new research. Did you know that?"

"Did you know a racist can kill you faster?"

He considered her warning though because he was growing to trust her as much as it scared him to do so. Removing the cigarette from his mouth, Darius rolled it between his thumb and index finger, studying it carefully, as if it might reveal to him its dangerous properties. "If this stick will do me in someday, I better change the world real fast then."

"What a shame it is that changing the world doesn't pay better." A sly smile turned up the corner of her mouth. "One time when I was a little girl, I asked my mama if we were rich."

"What did she tell you?"

"She told me that we were comfortable."

"I guess that's one way to put it."

All he knew about the Gilroys was that they were well-off, and that Dr. Gilroy matriculated at both Fisk and Meharry, carrying an elite dual pedigree that almost guaranteed a comfortable life for Freda, to use her mother's word. With her own mathematics degree from Fisk, Freda would be able to go anywhere and teach or maybe even attend medical school herself someday. As much as he hated to acknowledge it, a medical student like Gerald Vance, who had also attended Fisk and Meharry, would be the more acceptable husband choice for Freda in the eyes of her family.

"You don't know me very well, but I don't care that much about money." She dug the heel of her shoe into a crevice in the pavement.

He threw his head back and laughed. "Well, that's a sure sign you're rich."

"Oh, stop it." She punched his shoulder lightly. "But can you imagine yourself in twenty years or even forty or fifty years from now? Where are you and what are you doing? I used to play this game when I was little, and I could never see a clear picture of myself older. But I'll tell you right now that I will be traveling the world by train someday. All fifty states in America first, and then Africa and maybe Europe and Asia after that."

Maybe this explained his attraction to Freda beyond her obvious beauty. Both of them were dreamers. He pulled her onto his lap. Wrapping his arms around her, he said, "And after you've seen the whole world, where will you finally settle down?"

"I don't know," she said. "Settling down sounds a whole lot like settling to me. But when I've had my fill of travel, I think I'll grow old somewhere surrounded by a beautiful garden. I think I got that from my mother, who always keeps fresh flowers around."

Darius pressed his lips against her hair. "How about that? I like flowers, too."

Maybe Freda didn't believe him, a man admitting to admiring flowers. "Oh? What kind of flowers do you like?"

"Tulips," he answered. "You don't see 'em much in the South, only certain times of the year, but I've always been partial to tulips."

30

Freda

By the time the new school year had begun, Freda had joined the student movement that successfully desegregated lunch counters all over Nashville. The stores couldn't afford prolonged boycotts that would disrupt their businesses for weeks and months. While she came to the cause late, this victory had her fingerprints on it, doing bookkeeping, staying behind the scenes to ensure her parents didn't discover she'd broken her promise to them. She became even more rigorous with her school schedule, never wanting to be tardy for class again. Still, she remained committed to the Movement, convinced she could do both.

Dr. King challenged the student leaders to take their nonviolent direct action to every city in the South. Darius answered that call and left for Georgia to join King and thousands of students there for a sit-in at the Magnolia Room, the well-known restaurant in Rich's, the largest and finest department store in downtown Atlanta.

She missed Darius, but she trusted that their connection would always bring him back to her. Having him gone simplified her life, she had to admit, and when she was with Gerald, her devotion to him was complete. Love had a funny way of splitting a woman in two, dividing her heart and loyalty at the root. Gerald once told her that the human heart was the strongest muscle in the body, beating more than three billion times in one long lifetime. That must explain how one heart had the capacity to hold love for two men at the same time.

In Gerald's new off-campus apartment, Freda helped him decorate, furnishing the place to give it a sense of style and flair so that even when she wasn't there, he would be surrounded by her creativity and imagination. "How does this look? Is it even?" Freda stood on a chair, nailing to the wall a vibrant painting of Negroes dancing in a juke joint.

Observing from the cream-colored recliner, Gerald tilted his head as if a new angle might help his assessment. "I definitely like what I see, and it's not just the art."

"Stop it," she said, blushing and climbing down to go squeeze in beside him on the chair.

"I love you, Freda Gilroy," he said, kissing her hard on the lips, making her dizzy.

"And I love you, Gerald Vance," she reciprocated, her heart full. She had imagined the first time they would declare their love and assumed it would happen over a candlelit dinner downtown or at one of the swanky clubs on Jefferson Street. Not here in his partially furnished apartment, her sweaty in a plaid button-down shirt and blue jeans.

The new recliner held the weight of both of them, the piece of furniture every working man had to have according to the Bing Crosby ads. The chair reminded her of the one her mother had handpicked for Papa. The one where he did crossword puzzles, watched television, and fell asleep.

In her old-fashioned thinking, Mama said the gift of that old orange rust chair was her way of making things comfortable for her husband, making a home for them. Gerald and Freda weren't married and hadn't even discussed the possibility in any serious way, but they played house enough that the picture of them as a family didn't blur around the edges as much anymore.

***

That first week back on campus, she lay on her bed in Livingston Hall. She had a new roommate but lived down the hall from Cora and Evaline. She was alone in the room reading her syllabus for statistics when she heard a knock at the door before the handle turned. She jumped up to hug her friends, realizing how much she had missed them over break.

Her hands reached for Evaline's stomach, but her friend jumped backward, covering herself with her arms.

"I'm sorry," Freda said, letting her know she meant no harm.

Evaline sat on the edge of the bed with her arms still protectively curled around her midsection. Cora knelt in front of her, rubbing her legs.

"It's gone," Evaline said.

They wrapped her in a tight embrace, saying sorry again and again, even as the word sounded empty and hollow to their own ears.

When she found her voice again, Evaline said, "As soon as I got back to Detroit and told my parents, they dragged me to the car. I kept asking where we were going, and they wouldn't tell me at first. I lost my mind and threatened to jump out of the moving car until they told me. That's when they said they knew a doctor who could take care of things."

It took Freda a second to realize what that meant. *Take care of things.*

"No, they can't do that. You didn't even have a choice," Cora said.

Evaline shook her head. "*'This country is hard enough for a Negro girl. There's no sense in making it harder.'* That's what they said." She wiped her face with the backs of her hands and attempted a smile.

Freda remembered Mama and Papa admonishing her not to bring a baby home, but those were just words. A warning they started giving her the day she began menstruating. But they never explained why beyond the shame of it or the ridicule from the Dr. Prescotts of the world.

The three girls sat in that reality, looking at themselves and one another, seeing the color of their skin as if for the first time, something they couldn't change. Their Negro-ness. If they brought more of it into the world, their burden would be even heavier.

"How are you doing?" Freda finally said. "How are you feeling?"

Evaline waved her hand. "I'm okay. I want to forget it ever happened and go back to the way things were before you thought you were going to be aunties. Can we do that? Let's talk about becoming educated Negroes. Are we in any classes together this semester?"

Freda winced at the bitterness in her friend's voice. Instinctively, she knew it would take time—months, years maybe—for Evaline to heal emotionally. Would she ever be the same again? No one knew the answer to that. But if ignoring it was what Evaline needed to move forward, so be it. They would play along and try to be normal, whatever that meant. Freda searched her notebook for her list of classes.

Meanwhile, Evaline must have noticed how quiet and still Cora had become. "Don't tell me you got knocked up by Percy Chesterton III over break." A joke only Evaline could have made right then, and even Cora smiled, if a bit sadly.

Inhaling deeply, Cora said, "Something did happen over break." She looked directly at Freda, whose heart squeezed in terror, fearing that whatever her friend was about to say could break her. She wasn't sure she could handle more difficult news.

Cora rose to her feet and looked solemnly at both girls. "The school district where my parents teach found out that I protested in the spring. I guess I showed up in some news story. When the school year started, they told Mama and Daddy not to come back and so far, they haven't found work."

Cora had made news twice—the first time paraded by Woolworth's as a Negro poster child for segregated lunch counters and then marching against it. If *sorry* had been inadequate before, no words could express the unfairness for the Hendricks family to lose its source of income once again. They were prayed up people, too. How did the enemy keep coming for them like this? How could a school district punish this family for their daughter attending a march? Freda considered the full ramifications of this.

Evaline asked the question Freda was afraid to give voice to. "What about your tuition?"

It was obvious Cora had been preparing for this conversation all summer. She sounded rehearsed when she answered. With her head high as the day they met at freshman orientation, she said, "I came back to campus to speak with the Bursar's Office, but nothing can be done. I have no choice but to leave Fisk. I'll go home, find work, and help support my family."

This couldn't be. Freda refused to accept that the first week of sophomore year would be Cora's last. "No. There has to be a way," she said.

Evaline sunk into a chair, quiet, all the fight gone out of her. The girls stayed in their respective corners, together yet alone in their private anguish.

Freda remembered Mother Gaines's ominous warning that first day in Jubilee Hall. She predicted that one of the young ladies on either side of them might not make it all four years. That morning, she had warned them against bad choices. They never would have thought that standing up for their own humanity and dignity would become one of those choices.

PART TWELVE

Chicago, 1992

31

Tulip

Chicago held its breath in the fourth quarter of the NBA Finals. The Bulls trailed by double digits, and in her apartment, Tulip held hands with Sharita and Rudy, digging her nails into their palms at every play.

Even in the final minutes when Michael Jordan reentered the game, Sharita said, "I can't look. Tell me when it's over." Her eyes squeezed shut as if they had come to the gory part of a horror flick.

Rudy was no better. "My heart is weak. I swear if I die watching this game . . ."

"You two, stay with me now." Tulip pinched their skin harder. "You do not want to have to watch this for the first time in some replay or highlight reel."

Whenever the Bulls or Blazers called for a time-out, the station cut to a Chicago bar that to anyone outside this city would seem gaudy and overdone, with memorabilia lining the walls. More than a bar—a museum, a shrine, to the Bulls. But it didn't matter what anyone thought because this was how legends were made, how dynasties were built, with plot twists that kept you hanging on, believing. This series made so many forget their miserable lives and lay claim to a collective dream.

Behind by fifteen points in the fourth quarter, everyone was on edge—Tulip now on the floor clutching a throw rug to her chest, Sharita and Rudy crouching in front of the TV. Coach Jackson made a bold, risky move, putting in bench players who gave the Bulls new life and Jordan time to rest. In those final minutes, Jordan came back, found his rhythm, and scored ten of the Bulls' twelve points at the end, finishing off the Blazers.

Fairy tales rarely happened, until they did. Michael Jordan and the Bulls brought it home, sealing a historic repeat win for Chicago. Sharita ran laps around the living room in her basketball shorts shouting hallelujah, and Rudy fell to the floor, mimicking the heart attack he had predicted.

"We fucking did it," Tulip said, and she was talking about more than the Bulls victory. She meant finding her voice at the protest march, too, and finding her mother again, forging a new relationship between them.

She cranked open a window of their twelfth floor apartment, stuck her head out, and joined neighbors in a primal scream, because the victory didn't feel real until you shared it with strangers. She screamed until her throat was good and raw.

"Look at this," Rudy said, standing close to the television, pointing. People poured out of North Side bars onto Division Street, drinking and dancing. Two overturned taxicabs became trampolines for fans who jumped on them in their jubilation. The game issued folks a permission slip to be stupid, to lose their heads a little, to get swept up. There was a thin line between merriment and mayhem, though, and sometimes it was hard to know when you were drifting from one to the other.

"Can you believe they are acting a damn fool like that?" Sharita was still out of breath from her own race around the sofa. "Now if we did that, we'd be under the jail."

"I know that's right," Tulip said.

Stretching out on the floor again, Rudy said, "That's why I take my camera everywhere I go. My skills are in high demand. The Rodney King case taught us that, and if anything off the wall goes down, I will have the court evidence. Exhibit A, your honor."

They laughed, and Tulip knew they'd been lucky at the march that the protesters and police had stayed in their neutral corners, eyeing one another warily, but no confrontations.

"I'm just glad we didn't need cameras or lawyers at the protest to-day," Tulip said. "A few people had to see the medics for heat exhaustion and that was it."

"We saw you on the news," Sharita said. "I kept shouting at the TV saying, 'That's my girl right there.'"

Rudy nodded his head. "We flipped through the stations, and they all covered it. I never doubted you now, but I didn't think for a million years the march would be that big. But you never gave up."

Tulip was basking in the praise from her friends when the phone rang. She motioned for Rudy to turn down the volume on the TV. She didn't recognize the number that showed up on caller ID. Pressing one finger against her ear, she answered and heard loud street noise in the background. "Hello. I can't hear you," she yelled.

She was about to hang up when she heard a woman's voice. "It's Wanda, Key's mother."

"Wanda, we won!" Tulip screamed, her voice croaky, caught up in the infectious enthusiasm of the city, knowing that Key and his father were at some sports bar celebrating.

But something in Wanda's voice sounded serious and urgent, not celebratory. "They set the store on fire," she said. "We're all here. Every-thing's a mess. Key needs you. He didn't want to call you, though, so I am."

What had happened? And what did she mean? Wanda said Key didn't want to call, not that he couldn't. If he had been injured, she would have said so.

"I'm on my way." Tulip hung up then grabbed her keys and ran out of the apartment with Sharita and Rudy on her heels.

***

They maneuvered past impromptu celebrations, fans spilling into the streets, drenching themselves with beer and champagne. It was impossible to get near the South Side strip mall where the beauty supply store was because of the crowds and the heavy police presence, blue and red lights flashing against the dark sky. It looked like New Year's Eve with so many people out and about late at night. "Watch where you step," Rudy cautioned when they parked the car, got out, and saw broken glass glittering on the asphalt. When they got closer to the stores, Tulip gasped, gripping Sharita's arm. Busted windows. Jagged edges that people must have climbed through to enter the stores. It reminded her of what she had seen on the news out of LA. Empty clothing hangers and naked mannequins strewn across the parking lot.

In front of McCray's, she spotted Wanda and Joe walking around dazed like they had emerged from a tornado blast. Tulip hugged each of them, saying nothing because what was there to say? Wanda nodded toward a police vehicle, where an officer with a saggy butt was writing in a notepad and talking to Key. He was wearing his red Bulls tracksuit and a matching ball cap, and he looked like he was fighting to stay calm. "He won't admit it, but he needs you," Wanda said.

"What do you think that's all about?" Sharita said, already suspicious.

Right away, Tulip said, "I'm sure they're questioning him about damage to the store, if much merchandise was taken. Did he see the suspects? You know, normal procedure." All of this official protocol she referenced came from TV shows she'd watched with her father after school growing up.

"If you say so," Sharita said, still not convinced.

When they got closer, Tulip heard the officer asking Key where he had been that night and with whom, whether anybody could vouch for his whereabouts. He inquired about the insurance policy on the business. The officer was addressing Key like a crime suspect, not a victim of crime.

"Excuse me, may I ask what's going on here?" she yelled across the few feet separating them in that officious tone she had honed in elocution classes and perfected when pitching potential new clients.

Key shook his head at her, and before he looked away she tried to read what she saw on his face. Righteous anger, yes, but also embarrassment and humiliation. And something else she couldn't quite put her finger on yet.

"Stay here," the officer said to Key and then returned to his patrol car to make calls and click around on his dashboard. Before Tulip could rush to Key, a female officer extended her arms and told her, Rudy, and Sharita to stay back behind some yellow crime scene tape they must have overlooked.

"This is ridiculous," Rudy said. "I wish I had my video camera with me. I was in such a hurry I forgot it. This better not turn into another Rodney King case."

Tulip's head pounded and she wished she had come alone. "No, stay out of this. Please." She knew Rudy was only trying to help, but agitating the cops right now with threats about videotape could make things worse for Key.

A television crew she didn't recognize set up next to them and the reporter began his live shot. "Looters have ravaged a string of South Side businesses tonight, many of them Black-owned. But a handful of the stores torched and looted belong to Korean Americans. Many Koreans live in Albany Park, Edgewater, and Irving Park, but own clothing, wig, and grocery stores here on the South Side. Police believe this could be a confluence of events—the celebration of the Bulls repeat victory tonight and months of pent-up frustration over the recent not guilty verdict in the beating of Rodney King in LA. Community groups organized a series of protests all over the city today and it's only speculation, but some are wondering if that could have ginned up enough outrage to inspire copycat looters similar to the ones out west."

Tulip's head throbbed and she had a sense of things spinning out of control, as if some hidden hand manipulated the day's events, matching actions and reactions out of context, trying to wedge puzzle pieces that didn't fit. There was no confluence of events, despite what the reporter said. She wanted to grab his microphone and ask on live TV who he was talking about when he said some were wondering. When her eyes met Key's, she could tell he had been listening, too, and she saw a flash of something again in his gaze. He turned away quickly but she read it right this time. *Accusation.* That's why he hadn't wanted to talk to her. Key blamed her protest march for the torching of his family's store and the interrogation he was getting from that officer. Had her well-intentioned zeal for justice set something in motion that would hurt the man she loved?

The male officer opened his car door and approached Key again, and this time he casually placed handcuffs on Key's wrists and said he was taking him down to the station for questioning.

Panic ripped through Tulip, and she stood on that street corner, helpless. *Questioning about what?* she wanted to ask. What could they possibly think Key had done? Steal merchandise and set his own family business ablaze? He would never destroy his own inheritance, the fruits of everything he had labored over all those nights he worked there, bone-tired after his bus driving shifts. He helped build this business with his own two hands and would never tear it apart. Nothing about the justice system ever seemed just.

Key

He didn't sleep but still tried to shake it off like a bad dream—grown men and boys sitting and lying next to him, cussing and crying like babies, the holding cell reeking with the smell of their sweat, urine, and fear, or maybe it was his own. It was hard to tell. Key paced in this crowded, cramped space like a caged tiger. No windows, just heat, and every time he took a breath, it was like blowing through a plastic bag over his head.

This wasn't his first time behind bars. He tried to prepare himself mentally to go back to jail, to the scene of his nightmares, and when he closed his eyes for the first time the next morning, he heard the clank of the metal bars. Every man jumped when the officer opened the door and read off names, and finally, he heard his own.

"You're being released, let's go."

He had only been in lockup for a blink of an eye, but it had been enough to leave the marks on his mind, to tear at him like the re-opening of an old wound. In the lobby, sitting against a white wall with peeling paper listing government ordinances and protocols, were his parents and Tulip—the three he always thought of first and the last people he wanted to see him here like this.

His father rose first and gripped his shoulders with both hands, looking him over, knowing from experience what a place like this could do to a man. "We're getting you out of here now," he said.

Key laid a hand on his mother's back, which shook with sobs. "I'm fine, Ma," he said, thankful it was no longer Sunday and he could lie to her under these circumstances.

The last to rise to her feet was Tulip, who moved toward him like a toddler taking their first steps. "I've been so worried about you," she said, then she launched straight into logistics and details. "I talked to the people here and they realized they made a mistake. I called a few reporters I know to get information. The police arrested more than a thousand people last night for burglary, disorderly conduct, destruction of property, all of it. For some reason, they picked you up, too. I think they profiled you but thank God you're getting out of here."

Outside, Key closed his eyes and inhaled deeply, the fresh air filling his lungs. Tulip was still talking. "They just saw a Black face and arrested you. So random but not random at all."

He wanted her to be quiet. He wasn't a cause that she could rally around. This was his life, not a movement. His mother examined him in the daylight, her hands finding his cheeks and neck, and then his chest and arms, inspecting him the way he imagined she had done when he was first born, counting his fingers and toes.

Pops grabbed him by his shoulders again and stared hard into his eyes. "Keyshawn, look at me. This place is for animals. You're no animal. You're my son. Remember that." He heard the tears bottled up in his father's throat and beat back his own emotion.

"I know, Pops. It was only one night and I'm out now. Everything's gonna be all right." But it sounded more like a question from Key. Would he ever be all right again?

"The business will be fine, honey," Wanda said. "Come back better than ever. I'm not worried about the store. We want you to know that we love you."

He nodded, lowering his head, unable to face the deluge of feelings right now. It was too much all at once and he staggered under it. His folks patted his arms and told him they were headed back to the store to clean up. "Stop by the house for dinner tonight?" his mother said, and he nodded that he would.

IT WAS ASSUMED THAT HE'D GET A RIDE HOME FROM TULIP. WHEN he climbed into her car, she didn't start the engine right away. "We need to talk. Can we do that?" she said, the universal warning sign to a brother that a conversation was coming that he did not want to have. He sidestepped it by asking a question of his own. "How are things at the store? I didn't want to ask Ma and Pops too many questions. Didn't want to put them through that."

"There's smoke damage from the fire," she said. "Some broken glass. I don't think too much was taken. Some merchandise is salvageable. Police are guarding all the stores in the plaza so everything will be safe until your parents get back there. Some businesses were burned to the ground. You were the lucky ones."

There was nothing lucky about any of this. "That's where I should be, back at the store helping them clean up, assessing things."

She seemed surprised after a night in lockup that he was concerned with property damage. She didn't understand that sweeping up glass and counting boxes of wigs, edge control, and curling irons was something he could control. The rest of it, not so much.

Tulip sat there with her hands on the steering wheel, motor still off.

"Can we at least crack these windows?" he asked. "My accommodations overnight were a bit stuffy."

"I'm sorry, what was I thinking." She rolled them down all the way so he could stick his arm out and feel the breeze on his bare skin. Turning in her seat to face him, she said, "Are you angry with me? Do you blame me for being part of that protest? You didn't want me to get mixed up with the marches. And if that had anything to do with the smash and grab at your store and your arrest, I will never forgive myself."

Key was tired and needed to lie down in his own bed and sleep, but he knew sleep likely wouldn't come for a while. He wasn't too keen on sitting in the jail parking lot longer than necessary, but he couldn't let things go on like this. Her drawn face showed the toll it was taking on her.

"I was never against the protests." He took a deep breath. The truth didn't have a time stamp on it. So, he began.

"You could say I had my own selfish reasons for not wanting anything to do with protest work. Selfish or self-preservation, however you want to look at it. Whenever you get mixed up in protesting, you tangle with the cops. I didn't want any part of 5-0. I couldn't take that risk. You see, I have a record."

He paused and watched for changes in her face, a flicker in her eyes that she might have thought she could hide. All he noticed was her sharp intake of breath. "You never told me that," she said. "Why didn't you trust me with the truth? I wouldn't have judged you."

How could he make her understand that a man who had been in prison was branded like cattle and you wore that brand of felon, of criminal, everywhere you went for the rest of your life? How do you meet a young woman's parents, shake their hands, and tell them you're an ex-con? They already came from two different worlds. He wasn't ashamed of being a bus driver. In fact, he laughed at other drivers who introduced themselves to women at the club as transportation facilitators. No, driving a bus was good steady work if you could get it and he didn't try to hide how he made his living. But having a record was something different.

He reclined the seat and folded one arm behind his head. "I told you about my boy in high school who asked me to hold forty rocks for him. As I said, Pops flushed it all down the toilet with a lecture like something Cliff Huxtable would have done on *The Cosby Show* before going to commercial break. It's a great story but it's only half the story. Well, that wasn't the first time I'd been asked to do that, and it wouldn't be the last. I held drugs for one of my boys when I was nineteen. My folks had run into some hard times. I knew if I kept it for him, he'd pay me.

Well, the cops caught me with it. They got me on possession, and I was locked up for a whole year. First offense. Ain't that some shit?"

Her face registered shock but he could see her trying to hide it. Was she thinking *what the hell have I gotten myself mixed up in?* That suspicion turned his stomach more than anything. The last thing he wanted was her fear or pity. His hand jiggled the car door handle. "Why don't I call somebody to come pick me up? Or I can take the bus. I know the schedule." His laugh came out rough.

She reached across his body to pull his arm away from the door. "Stop. You're not going anywhere, and neither am I. Forgive me for not having the right words. This is all a lot to process. But none of this changes who you are or how I feel about you."

He took her hand and placed it against his cheek. "I was ashamed to tell you all this. You know that's why they arrested me last night. I didn't have anything to do with breaking into stores, but my name is in the system. I have a record, so when some shit goes down and they need to make sure somebody pays for it, a brother like me is the first one they look at. Even though they didn't have any evidence to charge me with a crime, they can say what you did earlier. There were a thousand arrests. I'm one of 'em. Did they catch the people who did the damage and tried to destroy what hardworking people built? Hell if I know. But arrests were made."

They stared out the window for a long time, Tulip's head resting on his chest. "You know I don't care about your past. You're my man, and I'm with you all the way."

He breathed in the sweet smell of her hair. "I can't guarantee that this is the last time this will happen. Because I have a record, I live my life looking over my shoulder, knowing they can come after me again and again and again."

Stroking the stubble that had grown on his chin overnight, Tulip said, "Then I'll be looking over mine, too, because we're in this together." With her voice muffled by his T-shirt, she asked, "You know what I want to do right now?"

His mind went where a man's mind usually went, but he didn't want to be presumptuous. "No, tell me."

"Let's go home and eat that basketball cake."

After only one night in lockup, the need to feel normal again overwhelmed Key. He moaned and could almost taste the spongy chocolate with the strawberry and vanilla flavored icing. All season he had imagined the Bulls victory and how he would savor it, but nothing tasted sweeter than having his freedom and the woman he loved right there beside him.

33

Tulip

Every time you turned on the news, analysts pontificated about the Bulls repeat and the destruction of the city in the same sentence. As if there was a cause and effect between the two. As if Black people couldn't celebrate a sports victory without tearing up their neighborhoods. When the TV pundits discussed the anarchy on the mostly white North Side, they described it as revelry, a good time that got out of hand. A week later, it was all anyone talked about, and the loose speculation about the role of the local protests persisted.

Anybody could make up a story about you and convince enough people to believe it. It went without saying that a true story left its mark on you and could define your entire life. Nothing prepared her to hear that Key had a prison record. If he had told her in the beginning when they first met on the bus, would she have still dated him? She had to admit probably not. But she had clarity now about her relationship— and her career.

"It's a shame, don't you think?" Darby said in the agency breakroom, eating her skirt steak and pepper fajitas. "They make all this progress and then undo it with violence."

She said it loud enough for Tulip to hear, and soon everyone in earshot had something to say about how the splendid joy of a city could go to hell so fast. This time, Tulip let it slide off her back like bathwater because she recognized Darby for who she was—someone angling for airtime, not the truth.

Mason walked by, arms loaded with boxes that he was moving into one of the corner offices, and he told anyone who would listen that Bryce had promoted him to account director.

"Congratulations," Tulip said, showing grace because she honestly didn't care anymore. Bryce had overlooked Amanda yet again, but she would undoubtedly grovel until he threw her some scraps.

TULIP KNOCKED ON BRYCE'S PARTIALLY OPEN OFFICE DOOR AND walked in. "You wanted to see me?" She braced herself for Bryce's wrath. He had summoned her to his office, and she knew he had to have seen the soundbites of her impassioned pleas on the news to preserve the futures of the children of Ida B. Wells.

She felt small standing before his massive desk, rocking on her heels, trying to decide what to do with her hands, the imbalance of power between them smacking her in the face once again. She could tell Bryce was drawing out the moment, his silence the string on a yo-yo.

At last, he spoke, his eyes on the papers he shuffled on his desk. "I saw your little stunt on television. Even after you swore you had the interests of this agency as your top priority, you still used our relationships with journalists in this city to promote your own personal agenda."

Tulip watched her professional dreams implode, every brick of trust and hard work she'd built over the years, collapsing on itself in seconds.

Bryce finally looked her in the eye. "Your father is a good, honorable man. But sometimes there's a breach in the bloodline. Can't be helped."

Bringing dishonor to her family was the last thing she wanted, and Bryce chose the weapon he knew would cut the deepest.

Folding his hands on his desk, he leaned forward and said, "You're fired."

Tulip had been expecting it and had come prepared for this conversation, but his actual words hit so hard they almost knocked the wind out of her. Then, she had a vision of Christina, Ms. Bertrice, the dominoes men, Roberta and her young daughter, Falana—the people she had risked it all for. If change happened at all in this city, it moved at the speed of a slug. But she heard from one of her reporter friends that the mayor and city council were paying attention now to Ida B. Wells. Nothing on the public hearing agenda, no promises of action, no guarantees, but people in power were listening. Ida B. Wells had come out of that protest more united and stronger. They were organized now and ready to fight the city and demand better living conditions. They were more committed than ever and so was she.

Bryce sat before her with an infuriating smugness spreading across his face. That's when she reached into her purse and pulled out a sheet of typing paper, folded in thirds. "It seems we're on the same page for once. I'm resigning," she said and handed it to him.

His eyes bulged but he tried to hide his surprise with a cough. He took the letter without reading it and set it aside. After five years of long hours, top-tier media hits, and a huge new business win, this was how it would end. He never had any intention of promoting her. He was already shuffling papers on his desk, effectively dismissing her. Without another word, Tulip walked out of his office and the doors of Mattingly for the last time.

On the bus ride home, Tulip rested her head against the window and assessed her life. There were no job offers waiting for her, not even interviews. Her resume wasn't on anybody's desk. She was *unemployed*. A status she had never had before. It scared her. Had she made the right decision, throwing away an entire career because she had helped lead one successful protest? That wasn't exactly something she could put on her resume. But Mattingly strangled her passion instead of growing it. And besides Sharita and Rudy, she couldn't count anyone else there as a friend.

They had reassured her that Edelman, Burson-Marsteller, or one of the other major PR firms would snap her up right away. She knew they were just trying to boost her at a low point, but she wasn't sure she wanted a position at one of those coveted agencies anyway.

She stayed on the bus long after her stop, until the end of Key's route that night, just another way they broke the rules to be together. She worried that he may have been unemployed, too, after that night of unrest and getting arrested. But his CTA supervisor valued honesty, and since Key had been upfront with him about what happened and no charges had been filed, it was like it never happened.

"I'm proud of you," Key said. "Not too many people would choose the community over a cushy job. You're a brave woman."

Rain battered the windows, and Tulip watched lightning rip the sky in two. The damp air curled the hair at the nape of her neck. "I don't feel brave, but I know I did the right thing. Who knows where I'll end up?"

Key made a wide turn into the bus garage at 77th and Vincennes. Letting the engine idle, he said gently, "You'll be okay. You can afford to help those folks even if they can't pay you what you're worth."

He was speaking the truth and they both knew it. Tulip had the means to walk away from a high-paying career, protected by the safety net of her savings and her parents to fall back on. "You're right," she said. "I'm going to find a way to bring PR and activism together to help our community."

"You're the real deal. Man, how did I get so lucky?" Key leaned over to kiss her.

"I don't know. You must be living right," she teased.

Key pulled his boom box from under the seat and played one of her favorites—"I Need Love" by LL Cool J. When she climbed onto his lap, straddling him, her hips accidentally hit the steering wheel and triggered the horn. They laughed and dipped their heads, feeling like two schoolkids without a care in the world, free.

PART THIRTEEN

Nashville & Fayette County, 1963–1964

34

Freda

The years passed quickly, while progress for equality came slow at times, with those in the struggle never ceding an inch. Like a war bride, Freda waited anxiously by the mailbox and phone for word from Darius, her soldier in the fight. He checked in when he could. In 1961, he joined more Negroes in the Freedom Rides to desegregate interstate buses. A year later, he worked to expand the campaign for racial justice in fair employment. He became so involved, he rarely talked about when he might return to Fisk. Knowing how much he loved and valued education, that made her sad sometimes, but he always said, "There's plenty of time for all that. What I've learned already in the books has disciplined my thinking. But the real education is out here on the streets of every city and town in the South. Our fight for equality is here and now."

Some progress Freda experienced for herself, when Nashville grocery stores, hotels, and movie theaters opened to Negroes. Even with Darius on the road, she didn't stay on the sidelines of the Movement. In fact, on Fisk graduation weekend in the summer of 1963, Freda was sitting in the basement of First Baptist working on a financial ledger when the church phone rang.

"I want you to come with me."

Darius only called on occasion when he had a free minute and access to a phone.

"Come with you where? Graduation is tomorrow and I'm busy trying to figure out how much money we'll need to get people on buses plus make all those signs."

Freda's fingers moved furiously over the adding machine, calculating last-minute costs for Negroes in Nashville to get to the March on Washington for Jobs and Freedom in a couple months. August would be here before they knew it and there wasn't much time left to get things done.

"That's what I'm talking about. I want you to come with me to Washington for the march. This thing is going to be big, and I want you there with me."

Dread seized Freda and ran up the length of her back. Doing the behind-the-scenes planning and bookkeeping was one thing, but boarding a bus to DC to join hundreds of thousands of people to face God knows what kind of trouble—that was another thing entirely.

And besides, she had already accepted a position she would begin after graduation. Since Gerald had finished at Meharry and was doing his residency at Hubbard Hospital, she wanted to stay in Nashville, at least for the time being.

"I can't," was all Freda said, her eyes on a stack of papers on the desk.

"Is this about Gerald Vance?" He spoke her boyfriend's name as if it left a bad taste in his mouth.

"No, this has nothing to do with him."

"I know what you're worried about," Darius said, "but you'll be safe. I'll make sure of it. This whole thing is based on nonviolence, you know that, and we have Congress and Kennedy listening to us now. You got A. Philip Randolph, Martin Luther King, Roy Wilkins, Whitney Young, James Farmer, Bayard Rustin. And John. All of those cats heading up this thing. Don't you see how incredible this is going to be?"

John. No last name needed. She smiled hearing their friend's name, John Lewis, among all those famous men. As young as he was, everybody knew he was destined for greatness.

Freda surveyed the list of expenses for the trip from Nashville to

Washington. "I hope we can get the money together to pay for whoever wants to go."

"We will. They're raising a lot of cash in Birmingham. They had that big shindig, the Salute to Freedom concert. I would've given anything to be there to hear Ray Charles. Nina Simone, the Shirelles, and James Baldwin were all there too, and Martin Luther King was in the front row."

All those celebrities in one place could bring in a lot of money to get Negroes to DC. Freda thought of Nat King Cole, whose name did not appear on the lineup of performers. Every time she heard someone say he had turned his back on the cause, she wanted to set them straight, but she would never betray his kindness or trust. Sometimes the ways one gave back were hidden from plain view, yet still important.

"I wish I could be as brave as you," she told Darius. "I'll never be that brave. I wish I could experience it with you, but I can't. You tell me all about it when you get back." She heard the disappointment in his long sigh. "Call me soon, will you?"

"You know I will," he said. "And congratulations, graduate. You did it. We'll celebrate the next time I see you."

***

The pipe organ bellowed in Fisk Memorial Chapel, and as she had many times over the last four years, Freda found herself standing next to Evaline Bates, this time at graduation, earning her bachelor's degree in mathematics. A cold draft fanned across Freda's arm from the absence of Cora flanking her on the other side. This milestone didn't feel complete without her.

"You know I got my jeans rolled up under this gown," Evaline whispered, still defying the ever-watchful Mother Gaines until the end.

"Shh. Hush, girl," Freda said, doing her best to bite back a laugh, not wanting anything to sully the dignity of the occasion.

It wasn't lost on her that this was the same pomp and circumstance that had surrounded her mother and father in this chapel when they graduated thirty years ago. She searched the audience and found her parents and Cousin Leotha seated next to Gerald.

After Commencement, Freda returned to her freshman year dorm Jubilee Hall one last time, the grand Victorian Gothic structure. She stood at the foot of the majestic staircase she had descended hundreds of times, her hand resting on the baluster, its wood sent from a former student in Sierra Leone. Would Mother Gaines be scaring the daylights out of some new class of wide-eyed freshman girls arriving in a few weeks? Probably so. Freda was the second generation to matriculate at Fisk, and while it occurred to her that she was romanticizing this place, how could she not?

To memorialize the moment, she took a family photo on the yard holding a bouquet of roses while Mama and Papa, Cousin Leotha, and Gerald gathered, smiling and congratulating her. She had fulfilled the dream of the Negro aristocracy her father had whispered about to her the night before she caught the train down to Nashville for the first time.

***

In November, Freda was living with a graduate student roommate and working in the mathematics department at Fisk assisting professors. It became a second home to her, a place where she continued to learn, surrounded by the comfort and certainty of numbers. The weekend before Thanksgiving, Freda thumbed through a *Reader's Digest* for tips on how to roast and baste a turkey. While they didn't live together because it would be improper, she spent most of her time at Gerald's place or he at hers.

"Don't forget the ham now. Add that to your list." Gerald circled her in the kitchen like a gnat. "I remember my mama's glaze. I think she used mustard, vinegar, and a whole lot of brown sugar. I can still taste it now."

When she looked up from her *Reader's Digest*, she found Gerald still standing there, waiting, perhaps expecting her to take note of his mother's recipe.

"Sweetheart, if you have a taste for your mama's glaze, I suggest you put your feet under her table this Thanksgiving. I am not some little happy housewife."

"We can always change that," he teased. Marriage sounded as far off as a trip to the moon. Evaline and Cora always called her foolish not to work toward it with the fervor she gave her academic goals. "You're too smart not to secure your future," they told her. Gerald dropped hints, but she suspected they might play house until one or both tired of the arrangement and broke things off. Right now, the only future Freda envisioned for herself involved being a faculty research assistant where she would explore modeling, simulations, and mathematical analysis while also reviewing student assignments. Numbers defied uncertainty, never nebulous, and it was their lack of abstraction that made her feel safe. It was a world she could count on.

***

A couple weeks later, Freda was grading papers in her kitchen early one morning when her phone rang. She recognized right away who it was from the sound of his breathing. "Darius?" she whispered into the phone, wrapping the cord around her wrist. Her roommate was out of town, and Gerald had spent the night. She peeped down the hall to be sure Gerald was still asleep in her bedroom with the door closed.

"It's been so long, too long, since I heard your voice," Darius said, and she blushed.

"So where are you?"

"West Tennessee, near Memphis. I'm out here organizing voter registration drives and trying to desegregate public accommodations. You'd think we never had a march in Washington a few months ago when you see how bad things are in some of these places here in the South."

Part of her wanted to hear all the details about the March on Washington, but guilt overwhelmed her. He'd begged her to go, and she hadn't. She watched on TV and saw the crowds, more than two hundred thousand peaceful people of every race and creed. She read in the papers that the march created necessary momentum for the Civil Rights Act President Kennedy was pushing to guarantee every American access to public accommodations, integrated schools, and the right to vote. She knew the facts, but she wanted the story, the color that only Darius could provide.

"What was it like? The March, I mean. I saw a little bit on TV, but I kept wondering how it was to be there." Gerald hadn't opened the bedroom door, so there was still time to talk.

"Oh, you should have seen all those people for miles everywhere you turn. Negro, white, and everything in between. It was a dignified day, all those important people there and regular folks too, and nobody made any difference between the two." He laughed. "And you know when we come together and have preachers, it's like an old tent revival. Some of 'em dressed like it was Easter Sunday. It was beautiful to see."

She tried to picture being there with Darius, by his side. She would have worn a dress that matched his suit and tie. On many nights leading up to the March, she had handled logistics from Nashville—calling on local churches to raise money for the trip to DC and then coordinating the trains and buses, making sure there were enough seats saved for the unemployed, since it was, after all, a march for jobs and freedom. It seemed foolish to have done all that behind-the-scenes work but not see it all come together. She regretted not going. "We did it," she said, trying not to feel sorry for herself.

"We sure did. Hey, can I ask you something?"

Freda pressed her mouth closer to the phone. "What is it? Ask me."

"I'll be in Fayette County in mid-December trying to help these sharecroppers. I want you to meet me. I've told you about my work, but I want you to see it with your own eyes. Remember when I said a group of us were registering these people to vote? You know this town retaliated and kicked them out of their houses and put them in this area called

Tent City. Some of these families were away from their homes for two years. They're back now and I'm helping them rebuild better than what they had. It's something to see. I don't expect you to get on a bus or anything but there's a group of folks I met at Otey's Restaurant who are coming then, too. Good people, and I already told them about you, and they said they have plenty of room in the car. One hundred ninety-one miles, just under a four-hour ride in the car. Say yes, please."

"Meet you? I'm not sure about that. You know my situation here." Another glance back at the closed bedroom door.

"Just for a weekend so we could talk, walk around, do nothing, whatever you want. Oh, you know what? I have my sax with me, and I can play some new music for you. Two days. That's all I'm asking for."

She was the girl who followed the straight line in life. No detouring. With her heart banging against the walls of her chest, she laughed softly at his crazy idea, giddier than she had been in a long time. "Yes. Yes, I'll be there."

Even over the phone, she swore she felt Darius's breath on her cheek. "Ah, Freda, Freda, that name of yours."

"What about my name?" she whispered, wanting him to say it again.

"Freda. It sounds a heck of a lot like *freedom* to me."

35

Darius

The Negro men sharecroppers of Fayette County who gathered on the corner hooted and hollered, teasing Darius about this woman who had his nose wide open.

She got you showing all your teeth.

She gon' empty this fool's pockets, you watch and see.

I bet you she drags him along the street by that necktie of his.

"That may be, that may be," Darius said, laughing. "I can't wait for you all to meet her."

It was only weeks before Christmas, and no matter how down on his luck a man got, the holidays seemed to lighten his load, give him something to smile about. Darius laughed with them, taking no offense, denying nothing. They were right. Freda Gilroy had his nose open wide enough to drive a combine through it. He was glad to give these men something to laugh about. They and their families had slept in army surplus tents for more than a year, through the long cold winter, after being evicted from their homes for trying to vote. Stores wouldn't sell any goods to them, and when these Negroes got sick, some doctors refused to treat them. Fortunately, the evictions lifted last year, and they would be back in their homes this Christmas.

Home. There was nothing like it, and he missed Chatham County,

North Carolina, where he could sit under the feet of Ernie and Matilda Moore. They gave him his roots and that would always be his first home. But the people in Fayette County, Tennessee, had become home to him, too, like his heart had found a new home in Freda. He had this crazy idea that introducing Freda to this place could be the start of something new and permanent for them, and Darius realized he might be ready to put away his traveling shoes and put down roots somewhere.

That afternoon, Darius wore the same green tie he had to the March on Washington—his best tie, the one that made him stand taller than his five feet, nine inches. He drove to the food market to buy chicken drumsticks, green beans, and baked potatoes. In the produce aisle, he found fresh okra, and he couldn't pass that up. Of course, he had to get the buttermilk, vinegar, and cornmeal to fry it for her. He might have to call his mama to remind him of the finer points. As he walked down the aisles, choosing ingredients, he whistled, and noticed the glares of a few white women in the store. He kept whistling until he left.

Trouble wasn't the only thing that could rob a man of his sleep. Replaying that last conversation with Freda kept him up at night. Doubt crept in. Had she really said yes to coming here to see him? He imagined her saying yes to another question he wanted to ask her but didn't feel he had a right to ask. Yet in his bed under the cover of darkness in a rooming house in some strange little town, he could dream, imagining how she might say yes if he ever asked for her hand in marriage.

Plato believed that love began with the contemplation of physical beauty and eventually went deeper to explore spiritual beauty. Maybe that was the best way to tell Freda he loved her. She would roll her eyes in that exasperated way of hers, always mocking him for quoting dead white philosophers. Then she would laugh, and he would laugh right along with her until they fell over from the force of it.

Checking his watch, Darius saw that he had a couple hours before Freda arrived. Enough time to spray on some cologne, tidy up the house, and lay out a feast fit for a queen. More likely enough time to walk a hole in the floors.

36

Freda

Freda had barely wiped the sleep out of her eyes when Gerald began bouncing around the house like a child on Christmas morning. It was almost that time, two weeks to be exact, and there was much to do. Gerald insisted they buy a tree for his home and decorate with tinsel and shiny glass balls. It was his favorite time of year, in spite of not having much of a Christmas growing up in that cramped New York apartment with his mother and sisters, whom he rarely saw anymore. When she asked him about his favorite gifts as a child, he always mentioned something homemade like a box he turned into a drum or a sweater one of his aunts knitted for him. He didn't even remember having a tree.

Thinking about his lack only served to stoke her guilt over what she was planning to do later that day, when, after Gerald had gone to work, she would leave him a note saying she was driving down to Murfreesboro to see Cora for the weekend and would be back before he knew it. She hated lying to him but had decided this visit with Darius was what she needed to make her decision once and for all. With which man did her heart and future lie?

She hadn't seen Darius in a long time. Naturally, he would look older, maybe wiser with national experience from the March and all the fieldwork he was doing in small towns. No longer was he the irritating boy who exasperated her in philosophy class. He was a man now. A man who was helping to change the world.

The perfume she wore was the lilac scent he always complimented her on, and she decided to buy a new bottle at Cain-Sloan. On her trip downtown the day before, she arranged to meet up with Evaline, who had some time off before starting at Howard Law in Washington, and Cora, who had recently moved back to Nashville to enroll at Tennessee State, another good but more financially feasible school. While Cora would graduate at least three years after her friends, she would get her degree, and Freda admired her friend's tenacity. And when forced to choose between her education and the ring Reverend Percy Chesterton III offered her, Cora gambled on the love of her life waiting until she graduated.

The ladies spotted Freda approaching them carrying packages— a new dress and a skirt and sweater set—because she couldn't decide which would be more flattering for her secret meeting. No one could miss the unbridled joy spreading across her face.

"This is the look of a woman in love," Evaline said.

Cora oohed and aahed, too. "Are you and Gerald going dancing this weekend?"

When she couldn't look her two best friends in the eye, they knew something was amiss. The three of them rarely kept secrets from one another, their lives as transparent as water and the air they breathed. Evaline practically tackled her. "There's another man, isn't there?"

"It's more complicated than that," Freda whispered, looking around as if shoppers strolling along Church Street cared about her indiscretions.

Tears welled up in Cora's eyes as if she were the one betrayed. "It's Darius, isn't it? I knew you were spending a lot of time with him on the direct action work. You know I like him so much and admire the work he's doing. But when he left Nashville to organize in different cities, I breathed a little easier knowing he wouldn't be a temptation for you anymore. But this isn't right. Poor Gerald."

"Okay, I was resisting this whole Darius thing at first, too. But poor

Gerald, nothing," Evaline said, wildly swinging her handbag as she talked. "My sister in Detroit has been reading all about women's liberation and she says sexual freedom is as important as financial freedom. Women have a right to be satisfied. And if Gerald isn't giving you what you need, then maybe Darius can. I'm all for it."

Turning Freda's personal dilemma into some campaign for women's revolution seemed absurd, and she knew Evaline was spiraling into a frenzy over the possibilities. Cora stared at them both in horror.

"Stop it," Freda said. "Evaline, whatever your sister is reading is about white women, not us. Not long ago, we couldn't even get served in restaurants or check into hotels. We're still sitting in the balcony of the movie theater. Talking about sexual liberation is ridiculous. I don't know what will happen with Darius, but I think I'll have my answer after this weekend with him. I need both of you to swear you won't speak a word of this to anyone, especially not Gerald. And Cora, I was sort of planning to use you as my alibi. He thinks you're still in Murfreesboro."

"Why, why would you put me in the middle of this thing?" Cora said. "Oh, Freda. I won't lie to Gerald, but I also won't volunteer any information. What I will be doing is praying for you."

The three of them wrapped their arms around one another in an embrace like the good old days. Freda may not have had their unanimous blessing, but she received understanding. This rendezvous with Darius would be an unorthodox way to decipher the desires of her heart, but as church folks said, the Lord worked in mysterious ways.

***

Freda stood in the kitchen in her bathrobe making pancakes, Gerald's favorite breakfast meal, unable to stop thinking about her plans for that afternoon. She was just about to pour batter into the skillet when there was a knock at the door.

"I'll get it." Gerald reached for the knob as if they were expecting company.

A flurry of familiar voices filled her ears. Her parents. What were they doing here? Still carrying the spatula and spilling batter on the floor, she moved closer to the front door. "What's wrong? I didn't know you were coming. It's not even Christmas yet."

"Oh, stop with all the questions," Mama said, removing her coat and tossing it on the back of the couch. "I love what you two have done with the place. It feels like Christmas."

Papa held both of her arms and studied her carefully. "You look good. Not too skinny. Your mother wanted to cook all sorts of food and bring it down here. But look at you making breakfast now. Your old man here is starving."

All this time, her parents hadn't said a word about visiting, which was unlike them, especially her mother, who refused to entertain dinner guests with less than seventy-two hours' notice. Freda ran a spoon through her batter, quickly doing the math. Did she have enough ingredients for all four of them to have pancakes? She cracked another egg into the bowl, stirred in more milk and flour, then set to frying four additional strips of bacon.

Mama shook her head. "Sweetheart, you don't have the fire up high enough. That's why those pancakes aren't cooking. And I saw you overmixing the batter. You want them fluffy, not chewy."

Freda pressed her lips together and willed herself to not respond to her mother's criticism. "She makes the best pancakes," Gerald said as he joined her father at the table.

As she set the stack of pancakes on the table, Freda glanced up at the clock on the wall. Only an hour until she was to meet Darius's friends for the caravan to Fayette County. But now her parents were here complicating things. What were they even doing here? They'd never done anything so impromptu.

"Freda, did you hear?" Mama was saying. "Your father asked you to pass the syrup."

She had forgotten the syrup and the butter and the orange juice. Turning to her parents, she said, "I don't understand. I love having you but why are you here?"

She went to the refrigerator, and when she returned to the table,

Gerald was smiling at her parents. "I'm the one who invited your mother and father. They're here because I asked them to come."

"You did what?" Freda said. "Why?"

As if he'd been waiting for her to press a button for him to spring into action, Gerald leapt from his seat, put his hand in his pants pocket, and pulled out a small box. He knelt on the linoleum and Freda noticed he had planted himself right on a yellow spot along the trail of pancake batter she had made earlier. The knees of his slacks would be caked with it.

"I'm not sure what's going on but maybe you and I should talk first. Alone." With her arms outstretched toward Gerald as if stopping him from running into traffic, she tried to intercept what he was about to do.

That's when Papa spoke up. "Don't worry, honey. He already talked to me and received my blessing. That's why we came today."

A fog lifted slowly from Freda's mind, and everything began to come into focus. Gerald on one knee. Her parents grinning expectantly. What was happening was already set in motion. The universe had already conspired against whatever was building between her and Darius.

"I love you, Freda Gilroy," Gerald began. "Our families did a little matchmaking, but we're the ones who fell in love. Our story is just beginning. I want you to be my wife. Will you marry me?" He opened the box and a beautiful ring sparkled atop a white cushion.

It all happened so fast. Her parents' blessing. The ring. The proposal. There was no time for consideration with three sets of eyes on her, waiting for an answer.

Maybe love wasn't the only raw material you needed to build a life, and she did love him. Gerald was a practicing physician like her father. A Meharry man. His work and his income would be steady. Her love for mathematics could be put to good use anywhere. They could lay down roots and raise children in the kind of house Freda grew up in, the kind of home Gerald longed for his entire childhood. They wouldn't have to worry about someone torching their house because they were trying to register Negroes to vote or desegregate a hotel or a five-and-dime.

Theirs would be a quiet, good life that followed a straight line, and there was nothing wrong with that. That was how you resisted, Papa would tell her if she asked him right now.

"Freda? You haven't answered me." Gerald teetered precariously on one knee, his forehead damp with perspiration. "Will you marry me?"

37

Darius

At three o'clock in the afternoon, their appointed meeting time, Darius stood in the gravel driveway of the house that a local Baptist church loaned to him when he was in town organizing. He scanned the road for the green Oldsmobile that would drop off Freda. When white folks drove by, he smiled, nodded, and tipped his hat in the customary show of respect. As a native son of the South, he knew not to invite trouble. Normally he didn't parade around outside like this calling attention to himself, but he was keen on spotting her the moment she arrived.

Darius had been in and out of Fayette County for more than a year, trying to register Negroes to vote and sticking with them, going so far as to spend nights sleeping alongside them in Tent City. So many of these tenant farmers had never stepped across the county line and couldn't even picture the dream Dr. King painted for the world at the March on Washington. Darius had come to bring the dream to them. When Freda agreed to come see him, he decided right then that he would cut back on his travel and give up some of the more dangerous aspects of the Movement work. His Fisk University diploma was still waiting for him.

His watch now said it was twenty minutes after three. Of course, she wasn't the one driving, but it wasn't like Freda to be late. He could picture her in that car fuming. Like clockwork, she had always been one of the first to arrive to philosophy class, sometimes even beating the professor there, sitting pretty with her legs crossed, tapping on the desk as others filed in.

An hour and thirty minutes later, he paced in a small circle, making tracks in the dirt. He stuffed his hands in his jacket pockets where no one could see him clutch his stomach, which was churning now. The best cure for that anxious anticipation was to lower your expectations or not want anything or anyone so badly that their absence could wound you.

No time now for Darius to guard his emotions. It was too late. He loved her. He wouldn't allow himself to believe she deceived him or misled him and had no intention of showing up. The sky was as blue as he'd seen it though, no bad weather to delay them. What if they had car trouble and were stranded on the side of the road with no way to get help? What if they had gotten lost? One little town could be indistinguishable from the next if you didn't know the area. There was no working phone in the house so if they had wanted to reach him, they couldn't.

When it had been two hours, Darius walked back into the house. Two plates of drumsticks, green beans, baked potatoes, and fried okra were warming on the back of the stove. He reached for his car keys so he could drive around looking for the car that was supposed to bring Freda.

DARIUS DROVE UP AND DOWN EVERY COUNTRY ROAD FOR MILES around and stumbled upon one of the sharecroppers he'd helped, leaning against a woodshed smoking a pipe.

Slowing the car almost to a full stop, he yelled out, "Codell! You see a green Oldsmobile go by? They would've been coming in from Nashville."

"Not since I been out here." Codell drew on the pipe like he was sucking a straw. "Who you expecting anyway, all jazzed up like that?"

Self-consciously, Darius became acutely aware of his gray dress pants, crisp white shirt, and clean coat. "My girl. I've been looking everywhere."

Codell grinned. "Your girl, huh? I like the sound of that." Then he shrugged. "I'll stop by your place and let you know if I see anybody."

Darius inquired in convenience stores, food markets, and hardware stores. After that, he stopped at a gas station to fill up before going inside to ask the white man working there if he had seen a green Oldsmobile that may have run out of gas or had car trouble. The attendant shrugged, but said nothing, continuing to chew on the toothpick hanging from the corner of his mouth.

The sound of tires kicking up dirt got the attention of both of them. Darius spun around, his desire to see the car carrying Freda and the others so great that any vehicle gave him reason to hope. He ran to the door of the station and came face-to-face with two white men in flannel shirts. A truck had pulled in behind Darius's car and another man popped up from the bed, where it appeared they'd been hauling supplies.

The tall one with a lazy eye spoke first. "I think I know you."

Darius didn't recognize any of them, but he recognized trouble when he saw it. Backing up a few inches, he held the man's gaze. "No, I don't think so. I'm passing through town." The pastor who had loaned the house to Darius had left a twelve-gauge shotgun for him in the pantry. "Just in case," Reverend Buford said. "I'm a God-fearing man but I'm no fool." Nonviolence had its place, but Darius wished he'd thought to bring that gun with him.

"Ya hear that?" said the spry one who had hopped out of the back of the truck. "He's passing through like he's got important business to tend to. A traveling man."

None of them were dressed for the weather. No coats. Maybe they didn't need them, all three hot with hate. You could see it in their eyes that didn't match their laughter. The other one said, "He's the one been getting these colored folks all riled up thinking they have the right to do anything they please."

Darius knew the KKK and other white supremacist groups had terrorized Negroes here for trying to exercise their right to vote and serve on juries to ensure Negro defendants got fair trials. Folks all over this county knew he and a handful of other young people had been helping sharecropper families. Now he was grateful Freda hadn't shown up and prayed she didn't. He kept his hands hidden in his coat pockets, his fists clenched so tight his fingers ached.

Without speaking to each other, the men grabbed him by his arms in an ambush, knocked him to the floor, and dragged him to the back of the gas station. The attendant held up his hands as if to say he didn't want any part of this and ran outside. The floorboards creaked and one small, dull bulb in the ceiling provided the only light. The heavyset man who was the last to join his buddies carried Darius's saxophone, which he had left laying on the backseat of his car. He had bought a new mouthpiece and was planning to play music for Freda that night.

While two men held him down, the other one lifted his saxophone over his head. "This yours? Why don't you play us something real sweet?" Then he slammed the instrument against Darius's head.

In a second of lucidity, he heard the distinctive strike of a match and tried to move but his limbs refused to follow the commands of his brain.

The last thing he saw before he was out cold was orange flames leaping high in the gas station. His mind screamed at him to get the hell out of there, but his body still wouldn't obey. The fire inched closer, and he closed his eyes, remembering Freda telling him once that she counted in multiples of three to find peace in times of anguish. And so, he began: 3, 6, 9, 12, 15 . . .

38

Freda

Seven days after the surprise proposal, Mama's hands trembled as she pinned Freda's curls and then helped her slip into a white dress with delicate lace that had been her own wedding gown when she married Papa. "You want me to wear this?" Freda asked incredulously, knowing how well her mother had preserved it in a special box, not letting anyone touch it. "Are you sure?"

"Of course, I'm sure. It's tradition. Gerald reminds me so much of your father. Decent and honorable. A good provider. You'll never want for anything a day in your life." With that, Mama stepped out of the small dressing room and went to get Evaline and Cora to apply her makeup.

Alone, Freda stared at her freshly washed face and ruminated on what Mama said about her not wanting for anything. How could anyone be so sure? Gerald had hastily arranged their wedding, assembling their closest friends—Evaline and Cora, Uncle Teddy, and a few of his Meharry classmates—to witness their vows. Gerald's mother and sisters came by bus, and they showed all their teeth, probably more in awe that he'd become a doctor than a husband. There was something romantic and reassuring about Gerald handling everything and she knew he would take care of her for the rest of their lives.

Her mind went to Darius and what he must have thought of her when she didn't show up. His friends she was supposed to ride with decided to make a detour to another town once they were free of their obligation to her. She hadn't wanted to let anyone down, but she had. Most of all, herself. Robbing herself of the choice she needed to make.

There was a light tap at the door, and Cora and Evaline came in. Gerald had told the girls himself after he proposed, and both, even the newly liberated Evaline, found his spontaneity something to swoon over. Evaline immediately began applying the bride's powder in heavy brushstrokes. "Don't overdo it," Freda said. "I want to look natural, like myself."

Painting her friend's lips a deep plum, Cora said, "You're doing the right thing."

"Do not cry," Evaline said, noticing the pools of tears forming in Freda's eyes. "If you do, you'll ruin your makeup. If you can't be truly happy today, you will at least be beautiful."

Evaline was wrong. She would be happy because she would work hard at it as she had everything else in her life. It occurred to Freda that this would be the last time the three of them would be together like this as single women, irreverent and free in a way she hadn't fully appreciated. Her life would be different as someone's wife, a new set of expectations on her shoulders. Her eyes misted and Evaline hovered with the mascara brush. "Don't you dare." Evaline's voice cracked. "We will always have us, I don't care how many husbands we have between us by the time it's all said and done."

Their laughter caused such a ruckus, Freda's parents and the minister poked their heads in to see if the bride was about ready.

Standing alone at the back of the chapel, Papa walked toward her, held her hands out from her sides, and said, "My, my, my. You look as beautiful as your mother did in that dress when she walked down the aisle to become my wife."

"Oh, Papa," she said.

"I still remember you as a little girl sneaking in my car to go with me on house calls to see patients. You always wanted to be where things were happening. You had such big dreams for yourself. Hold on to those dreams. Marrying Gerald doesn't make you less of who you are. Just the opposite. I wouldn't be half the man I am today without your mother." He admired her in her dress again, and she could tell he was still reminiscing about his own wedding day and then unfurling the scroll of memories of his little girl over the years.

Standing at the altar on a day when everything happened so fast, Freda forced herself to slow down, to take it all in—her best friends holding hands and wiping tears; Mama and Papa, her first loves who were beaming proudly, satisfied with this long-awaited outcome. And then she stopped looking back and faced Gerald, who seemed like a man reborn, baptized by love and destiny. Freda placed her hands in his and pledged her love and fidelity to him. And she meant it. But of course she couldn't help but think of Darius and wonder if she had made the right decision. Life had a way of sorting things out, removing ambivalence and replacing it with the blessed assurance the small choir sang about.

***

Before the ink was good and dry on their marriage license, Freda and Gerald moved into a small house for rent off Jefferson Street. She browsed the Sears catalogue as her mother advised and ordered a new washing machine and refrigerator.

Never a natural at cooking, she exhausted recipes she remembered from watching her mother, and turned to *Better Homes and Gardens* for instructions on how to make pot roast and stews and candied yams. That turned out to be a mistake. Now Gerald entertained wild expectations as a husband. When she had made pancakes or French toast for breakfast while they were still dating, it was because she thought it was a romantic gesture or she was hungry. Now, Gerald looked at her oddly when she didn't immediately head to the kitchen in the morning. Mama was no help, for she only said, "He's your husband," as if that explained everything.

By that summer, she had convinced Gerald this was 1964, not the

1950s anymore, and he needed to do his part around the house because she worked long demanding days at the university—just like he did at the hospital. "I love and appreciate you. I don't know what I'd do without you," he said as he washed dishes after she cooked, and on many nights he would rub her feet after an especially stressful day.

FREDA HADN'T HEARD FROM DARIUS SINCE THE DAY SHE LAST spoke with him six months before. There was no way to reach him since he always called her unexpectedly from a different location. Part of her hoped he didn't call because she wouldn't know how to face him after standing him up and then marrying another man. But right now, she couldn't help but think of him with President Johnson signing the Civil Rights Act of 1964 into law. President Kennedy had pushed for this before his assassination and now it had finally happened. The law guaranteed equal treatment of every American regardless of race. Every sit-in. Every march. Every arrest. Every indignity. They had all been worth it.

Nostalgia led her to First Baptist Church on her lunch break one day. At first, she didn't see anyone and found her way to the last pew in the sanctuary and took a seat. She had spent so many long days and nights there doing bookkeeping for the Movement, but eventually gave it up to focus on her university job. Her adding machine lay in her nightstand now.

As she was about to leave, a young man walked into the church. Her presence must have startled him because he jumped. She recognized him right away. Darius's friend from Fisk, Errol Hankins. She remembered that he had been arrested multiple times at lunch counter sit-ins. When he moved closer, she noticed his shoes still had that spit shine she remembered. Excitement shot through her to connect with him again, knowing how close he and Darius were.

"Well, I'll be," she said. "If it isn't the pride of Mississippi. You used to cut up something terrible, always making the Nashville papers. But everything you did paid off. We finally got that Civil Rights Act passed." She touched his arm lightly, thrilled to have someone to share this milestone with. "What are you up to these days?"

He didn't return her smile and seemed put off by her good mood, and the only reason she could think of was he knew she had stood up his friend. Maybe Errol had been in touch with Darius and learned she hadn't honored her commitment to meet him in Fayette County. Looking down at her hands, she caught the blindingly bright glare of her wedding ring in the sunlight from the windows. Errol looked, too, and seemed surprised.

Clasping her hands behind her back, Freda cleared her throat. "How is Darius doing? Have you spoken with him?"

He dropped his head and wouldn't even look at her.

"Errol Hankins, what in the world has gotten into you?"

Finally, he met her eyes. "You didn't hear?"

"Hear what?"

"I don't know how else to say it, but they got him."

"They got who, Errol? And who is they?"

Silence.

"They got who?" She was shouting now, her voice reverberating against the church walls. It's odd how you could know something to be true in your spirit before anyone confirmed it for you. She knew what he was about to tell her before he said the words.

"He had been staying in Tent City," Errol said. "We thought everything was getting better there once the eviction notices were rescinded and Negroes were allowed to vote and move back into their homes. But some people couldn't stand the change or the changemakers. From what I heard, it happened back in December. One of the sharecroppers said Darius was expecting a carload of friends from Nashville that day. When they didn't show up, he drove all over town looking for them. He stopped at the gas station, and somebody burned the place to the ground. Sounds crazy, right, white folks burning up their own business, but that's how irrational hate can be."

Freda stood still, unable to process Errol's words. "But maybe Darius walked away from the fire."

"They found his body in there."

"No," she shouted.

Balling her hands into fists, she beat Errol's chest until her strength gave out and her body sank into his.

"I know. I can't believe it myself," he said, easing her gently onto a pew.

"We were supposed to—" she said. Freda left her sentence unfinished. She was supposed to meet Darius two weeks before Christmas on a Saturday, but instead she got engaged and married another man. Darius had been out looking for her. If she hadn't broken her promise to him . . .

The church sanctuary became claustrophobic, and Freda struggled to regulate her breathing. "No, you must have gotten it wrong. He would have found his way out of the fire. Maybe he did. You can't be certain that he's gone."

The front of Errol's shirt was damp now with her tears. Holding her shoulders gently, he spoke to her as if she were a small child. "It was him. They found his sax. He loved playing that thing almost as much as he loved the fight for freedom."

Freda shook violently, the wooden pew groaning beneath her. She remembered how his music had drawn her to him in the chapel freshman year. She ground out her words. "But it doesn't make sense. You said somebody did this. On purpose?"

Errol leaned forward with his elbows on his knees and made a steeple with his hands. "You know how it is. The police are pretending it was an unfortunate accident. They won't investigate, but people knew what Darius was doing for that community." He put his arms around her again and, holding her tight, said, "As much as I hate to say it, this was no accident, Freda. They killed him."

So many times, Darius had talked about the dangers of this work, the risks he knew he was taking, but he kept going anyway. Everything he had done to make people's lives better had cost him his own. All the fight, the denial, drained from Freda's body, her tear ducts dry, too, and right then a part of her died with Darius. She freed herself from Errol's arms and ran from the church.

***

THE ONLY PERSON SHE HAD LOST IN HER LIFE BEFORE NOW WAS Grandma Gilroy, a woman full of joy who lifted her flouncy skirts and danced even when there was no music. Freda was only seven when she looked down on her in that box, wearing one of her fancy dresses with a full skirt, her face as waxy and rubbery as one of her baby dolls. While she was too young to understand her grandmother's death, she at least saw the funeral men shut the box, bolt it, and heap mounds of soil until it disappeared in the earth. But this was different. All of Darius's suits were too baggy and men didn't get buried in untailored suits. A man always on the move wouldn't sit still long enough to be stuffed in anybody's pine box. So, if the evidence of her loss didn't exist, maybe it had never happened.

The next morning, Freda stood in the kitchen washing dishes when the room flooded with sunlight. Gerald had opened the drapes. "Close them, dammit," she said, remembering walks with Darius under the mid-day sun, laughing. Good times that were never to be again. Now the light mocked her. Even God had moved on. How dare He? When she told Cora and Evaline the news, they expressed the appropriate surprise and sadness at the loss of a classmate, but their response was muted. Freda was a married woman now, and for that reason, her friends' condolences couldn't begin to match her grief.

Gerald came closer and watched her scrub the same grease stain in the frying pan again and again. Stilling her hands in the soapy water by covering them with his own, he said, "What's wrong?"

Not bothering to choose her words carefully or sugarcoat them, she said, "I lost someone, and I can't say I'll ever be the same."

"Oh no. Is it someone I know, or someone at work?"

She looked up at her husband, her face exposed to the light, swollen with grief. "Darius Moore. He was murdered back in December, and I just found out."

Shock tore at Gerald's face and then, she couldn't be certain, but there might have been a flicker of relief in his eyes. He wrapped her in his arms while she stood woodenly in front of the sink. "I am so sorry," he said.

"I know you didn't have much use for him but if you'd really known him . . ."

Gerald tilted her chin, forcing her to look at him. "He was a friend of yours, sweetheart, and that's what matters."

Gerald was saying all the right words but the sound of his voice ripped at her insides, her guilt. She had made her choice, and she couldn't take it back. Her choice may have cost Darius his life. How could she live with that?

Freda didn't just grieve the loss of Darius, but the loss of who they might have been together. What she might have done with her life and given to the world because of him.

***

People said grief lessened over time and time healed everything, but that was only partially true. The truth was you got accustomed to carrying that grief with you like another arm or leg. When Gerald decided there would be better opportunities for him at hospitals up north, they packed up and left Nashville for her hometown. Sometimes Freda wondered if Gerald wanted to leave behind the place where she had known and loved Darius. If maybe he thought her nightmares that sometimes awakened her in a cold sweat might dissipate hundreds of miles away. That the memories would fade with distance.

Every part of Freda's life had changed since she learned about Darius's death. During the day, she merely went through the motions, and when she was home with Gerald in the evenings, she barely found the energy to talk before heading to bed. The best way to describe their lovemaking in those days would be to say it was efficient. It reminded Freda of how they drove to the grocery store or the bank without putting any thought into how to get there. Their hands on that steering wheel knew without help from their brains because they had done this so many times before.

That's the way they moved in bed, as if you could wind up their bodies and let them go.

A few months after they moved into their new home in Chicago's South Shore, they found out she was pregnant. Freda was determined to get on with her life, to live out this legacy of Negro excellence she had prepared for her entire life. She put off looking for work and focused on becoming a mother. Her parents and Cousin Leotha were close enough now to check on her. Mama came over during the day when Gerald was at work to rub her belly and jump excitedly every time she felt the baby kick.

Being home all day, Freda sat in front of her picture window and watched Negro couples stroll by hand-in-hand and children play hopscotch. Otis Redding and Nina Simone played on the hi-fi. Most afternoons, she watched television news, paying close attention to the Chicago Freedom Movement to end de facto segregation in schools, jobs, and housing. Dr. King and other civil rights leaders came to Chicago that summer and accused northern cities of colonizing Negroes in their slums.

Growing up, she had thought things were so much better and more equal up north, that everyone got along peacefully. But it took a long time for Gerald to find work in his specialty of cardiology. Large white hospitals in Chicago turned him away with an excuse about his credentials or lack of experience or no openings for physicians. That demoralized him as they were starting over, starting a family. She encouraged him as much as she could, understanding his urgency to provide now that they were expecting their first child.

When their daughter entered the world on a warm day in 1965, she needed a name, and Freda admitted only to herself that she desperately had to keep some part of Darius alive. Memories appeared less crisp and clear with each passing year. Details of his eyes and nose and mouth had grown fuzzy now. Surprisingly, the more Freda forgot, the heavier her grief became. So, when Gerald looked into their daughter's face and asked what they should name her, Freda answered right away. "Tulip," she said. "We'll call her Tulip."

PART FOURTEEN

Nashville, 1963 & 1992

39

Tulip

In the fall of 1992, Tulip did what she thought she'd never have a chance to, and walked in her parents' actual footsteps, peeking into their lives as students in Nashville. She sat next to her mother in the Meharry amphitheater, the two of them beaming with pride as Dr. Gerald Vance walked onstage to accept the Distinguished Physician Award bestowed upon him by his alma mater, Meharry Medical College.

She pictured her father back in the day, long and lean, a fine frat boy and medical student spitting game, turning her mother's head. Wooing her with some old Sam Cooke songs until she surrendered. Their love story reminded her of her own for the first time. She thought of all the ways she and Key would evolve over the years, the way her parents had, while the love and happiness they shared remained unchanged.

In the awards presentation, Meharry's president praised Gerald's long cardiology career in Chicago, the color barriers he broke, and his groundbreaking work in peripheral artery disease and aortic repair. Many of those stories were not new to Tulip, but she paid particular attention to what they said about him serving poor, marginalized people dating back to his days at Hubbard Hospital in Nashville. A young man who had been a burn victim as a child spoke about how Gerald may have saved his life. She listened to story after story about her father's treatment of poor Black people in Nashville who would have been turned away by white hospitals.

"It has always been and continues to be my honor, my privilege, to serve mankind through medicine," Gerald said from the podium, looking sharp in his Brooks Brothers suit, holding his award.

It dawned on her for the first time that her father had played a pivotal role as a physician in the Jim Crow South. Listening to all the tributes, it seemed as if they were talking about some other man, a stranger from history. No one would call Dr. Gerald Vance humble, but he had kept many of these Nashville stories to himself. How embarrassing that she had thought her father cared only about the almighty dollar.

People resisted and saved the world in their own ways. It had been four months since she quit Mattingly, and she still didn't have full-time work. But she had joined with a handful of community groups on Chicago's south and west sides, helping them advocate for themselves and get their stories covered in the media. They paid her what they could when they could, but it was never much. Maybe these were her Hubbard Hospital days, the lean years when she would plant seeds for her life's purpose.

AFTER CONVOCATION, TULIP AND HER PARENTS VISITED THE RE-modeled Hubbard Hospital and walked over to the Fisk campus.

"That's Jubilee Hall where I lived freshman year," Freda said, looking like a college girl again, practically skipping in her long argyle skirt and matching sweater, her arm linked with Tulip's. "So many good memories there." Tulip wanted to hear every single one of them in all their excruciating detail but didn't push. Her mother resembled a flower, opening fully in its own time.

In the library of Fisk, the musty smell of history surrounded them as they poured over the archives, the spines of old books cracking. Tulip found yearbook photos of her mother and her two best friends, Cora and Evaline. Images of them in snowball fights alongside ones of intense discussions in classroom lectures.

"Your mother was a beauty back then and still is," her father said, an OG now, trying to prove he still had it, tickling the back of Freda's neck.

Her mother blushed, something Tulip hadn't seen her do often, but this place and these memories were bringing her back to her roots, softening her somehow. Thumbing through the book, Freda said, "It was a strange, bittersweet time."

Tulip had opened a different volume of photos from 1960 and stumbled upon one of a young man perusing a spreadsheet or ledger of some sort. His face looked familiar, but she couldn't place him. He was seated next to a woman with a scarf covering her hair. When Tulip brought the book closer to her face, she recognized the woman's cheekbones and wide eyes. "Mom, here's another one of you," she said. The caption confirmed it: *Fisk students Freda Gilroy and Darius Moore at First Baptist Church organize behind the scenes for upcoming nonviolent direct action campaign.* Those words stopped Tulip cold. They didn't make sense.

"Let me see that," Freda said, her hands shaking as she lifted the yearbook.

"I don't understand," Tulip said, looking around to ensure they were alone in the archive room, still trained to keep up appearances. "You were active in the Movement? How come you never told me about this? Especially now that you know activism work means so much to me."

Gerald rose to his feet, pressing his nicely tailored suit with his palms. "This is neither the time nor the place."

One of the librarians entered the room to reshelve a few volumes, and seeing Gerald standing, asked if she could be of assistance. With a tight smile, Freda shook her head. "No, we're fine."

"We're not fine," Tulip said, raising her voice now, forgetting decorum, and the librarian slipped from the room quietly to give them privacy.

"I want to know why you never told me you demonstrated in the sixties. I kept asking you what it was like in those days, and you acted like you hadn't been involved at all. But you had, and that's how you knew what I should do for the Ida B. Wells march. I'm right, aren't I?"

"Leave it alone, Tulip," her father said.

"No, Gerald. We've been dancing around this for years. It's time she knows." Freda's head hung low, defeated, tired. "Sweetheart, from watching the news and reading the history books you would think that everybody Black was involved in the Movement. Many were on the Fisk campus, both students and faculty. But it was such a dangerous time and some families like mine didn't want me to get involved."

"So you protested secretly?" Tulip asked.

"Yes," her mother said. "I did. I tried to keep it from my parents and your father. They didn't want me to get hurt. I did what I could to help but I never told them about it." She lightly touched Gerald's jacket sleeve. "Then your father offered me this wonderful new life, and we had you, and I never looked back."

Tulip's eyes widened. "You're saying that you gave up a life in the Civil Rights Movement to marry Dad and be my mother?" She didn't know whether to be grateful or sad for what Freda had sacrificed.

As she processed that, her gaze settled on the photo again. "Where do I recognize this man from?" Her parents exchanged a look.

"Go ahead and tell her," Gerald said.

"Tell me what?"

"Darius and I were in classes together and we became friends," Freda said. "He was a passionate advocate and led a lot of the student demonstrations at that time, helping get laws changed in Nashville and all over the South. You don't hear his name today because some racists killed him in 1963." Her voice broke and she dug in her purse for a tissue.

"Oh no, that's awful," Tulip said.

"Darius is the young man you saw in the footage on TV from the March on Washington. He's the one who introduced me to activism, as much as I tried to stay away from it. We got close and had feelings for each other, but it never went anywhere because I chose to marry your father," Freda said, now looking at Gerald.

Her father's lips twitched, and he grabbed the side of the table to steady himself before sitting down. "You chose to marry me only because I didn't let you run off to go be with him." He might as well have sucked on the yellow rind of a grapefruit, his face and words were that sour.

Freda's face cycled through disbelief and horror. She put a hand to her mouth. "What do you mean?"

Gerald may have surprised himself blurting that out, but he dropped his head and began a story nearly thirty years past due.

40

NASHVILLE, 1963

Gerald

Gerald had been up late the night before handling several difficult cases in Hubbard's emergency room. A heart attack. A badly injured man who was walking under scaffolding downtown when it fell on him. A little girl with a small toy stuck in her airway.

The phone rang that morning at Freda's place, where he had spent the night, and it startled him. He had overslept and reached across the bed to feel for Freda, his hand only coming in contact with the rumpled sheets. He fumbled to find the telephone on the nightstand before whoever was calling hung up.

When he picked up the receiver, he heard two people talking. Right away, he recognized Freda, who must have picked up the line in the kitchen. She was speaking in hushed tones. The other voice belonged to a man. Gerald hadn't planned to eavesdrop, and he would have gently returned the receiver to its cradle, but he was curious. They discussed the assassination of President Kennedy, a tragedy that even strangers in a supermarket or on a street corner might stop to ponder and lament. But this conversation grew more intimate. For the second time, Gerald was about to hang up when he heard the man ask Freda to meet him in

Fayette County in a few weeks. Who was this proposing a rendezvous with his girl? The haze of sleep had muddled his brain, and he shook his head to clear it. That was when the voice and the name came to him. He should have known. *Darius Moore.*

This cat was a want-to-be hero, a sycophant of Martin Luther King Jr., a counterfeit revolutionary. Gerald was no fool. As much as Freda tried to hide it, he knew she had been sneaking off to First Baptist, helping Darius and the other activists collect money and supplies for the Movement. That man's hold on Freda, he suspected, had been more about the soul than the body, and that sent Gerald spiraling down into a pit of hell where a man found no relief.

He couldn't allow this secret meeting to happen. A man's pride could only withstand so much. Did she not appreciate the long hours he spent at Meharry studying to become a doctor, preparing himself for a future worthy of her investment? Did she not understand he was a Negro building a respectable life that could change the trajectory of Negroes for generations to come? The most simple, basic question was the one he feared the most: Did she not love him?

He had to stay on the line long enough to hear Freda's answer to Darius Moore, which mattered more than the proposition itself. There was a long, excruciating silence while she considered the offer, and Gerald held the receiver close to his ear, waiting. Hearing Freda say yes to another man should have been enough for him to walk away, to not risk a future with someone whose loyalties were compromised. Maybe it was his pride or his precious manhood or plain old love, but he couldn't lose her.

Freda gently turned the knob to the bedroom door and peeped inside. "You finally woke up," she said. She straddled his torso and kissed him lightly. He bristled at her touch and at the forced cheer in her voice. And at the same time, his body moved toward hers as if some magnetic force superseded the warning sirens in his head.

"Who was that on the phone?" he mumbled under the pressure of her lips on his.

"It was just somebody calling to raise money for a charity," Freda said, disentangling from him and moving to her side of the bed. "I politely declined. They can be so persistent, especially when they used to come to your door selling stuff. It's a lot easier to say no over the phone." She shifted toward him and rested her head on his bare stomach.

How did a lie surface so quickly and roll off her tongue with such ease? Even after a lifetime of living in a house full of women—his mother and his sisters—and then dating his fair share, Gerald would never understand them. How could they wound you with one hand and then bandage you up and soothe your pain with the other? In spite of what he heard on that call, Freda was still the salve that healed his broken places.

GERALD HAD WATCHED THE NEWS THAT FALL ABOUT THE MARCH on Washington and all anyone could talk about was the Reverend Dr. Martin Luther King Jr. having a dream that he said was deeply rooted in the American dream. Nobody cared much about a Negro's dreams, but Gerald could relate to the good reverend. He had a dream of his own to wear the white coat of a medical doctor, to become a renowned cardiologist, and to lift his community that way. In every iteration of that dream, Freda Gilroy was by his side.

If Gerald wanted to hold on to his girl, he had to act fast. He had less than two weeks or face the possibility of losing her to another man. Marriage was an expected rite of passage for most men, and he had known for a long time that he wanted to marry Freda. He just needed to move more quickly than he'd originally planned.

While she was at work the next day, he called her parents in Chicago, both of whom already held a favorable opinion of him. Still, every father expected a suitor who was serious about his daughter to formally ask for her hand in marriage. That is exactly what Gerald did and the blessing from Dr. Gilroy came faster than he expected.

There wasn't enough time to plan a formal wedding before that date in December when Freda planned to see Darius Moore. He convinced her parents to come down to Nashville so that he could surprise their daughter with a marriage proposal. The secrecy and intrigue and romance of it won them over. Of course, Freda wasn't expecting it, and that was the point. He blindsided her, and with her parents traveling all that way for this elaborate proposal, she couldn't say no. And after getting engaged, there was no way she could in good conscience drive to Fayette County to meet up with some other man.

It would be months later, after they were already married, that he'd learn of Darius Moore's untimely demise. He couldn't lie. That news hit him like a two by four between the eyes. He couldn't stand the ground Darius walked on but he never wished him dead. It was all circumstances—wrong place, wrong time—but Gerald's had been the invisible hand steering fate.

He carried the guilt with him every day of his marriage. If he could turn back time and undo what he had done, would that man still be alive? Would Freda have chosen him?

41

Freda

She heard her husband speaking and it was 1963 again. He was pacing among volumes of books in the archives room, baring his soul, telling them things she didn't want to believe. Relieving his conscience had been a selfish act, one that might break her. "How could you have done this?" she asked, her voice ragged and raw, knowing that no answer would satisfy her. How could it? "You played God with my life and with Darius's life. For what?"

Gerald awkwardly slid along the wall and landed on the floor, still clutching his distinguished physician statue, and he had never looked so small and insignificant. "I was wrong. All I can say is I did it because I was afraid of losing you. I did it because I love you."

"You call that love? I call it manipulation. I'm too old for this, Gerald. Where do we go from here?" Her chest tightened and she struggled to breathe.

"I don't know," he said. "My whole life, I've been chasing this fucking dream I could never run fast enough to catch. The game was rigged." Gerald wasn't looking at either of them but staring blankly at the volumes of books lining the wall.

A sniffling sound got Freda's attention. In the corner of the room, Tulip had curled up into a ball on the floor.

Freda had almost forgotten Tulip was there. Through her fury, and as much as her heart broke for what could have been with Darius, she looked at her beautiful daughter and she couldn't help but believe everything turned out the way it was meant to.

Gerald went to Tulip first, crouching close to her. "I'm sorry we let you down, baby girl."

"I don't even know you," she said to him, and Freda understood she meant both of them.

Tulip scooted back to put space between them. "You were so against Key, gave him such a hard time when he hadn't done anything wrong. And here you've been keeping secrets my entire life, and a man is dead because you always have to get what you want."

Gerald inched closer to her. "I thought I knew best."

"You didn't," Tulip said.

"I know that now. I'm trying." Gerald appeared pitiful and desperate. "You have a good man in Key. I won't stand in the way of you two, not anymore."

"What about you, Mom? You've kept so much from me my whole life. All I ever wanted was to know you, to really know you."

How had they gotten here? The walls of the archives room got closer, little air moving around the musty books, so many of the ghosts from the past rising around them. "I can only say I'm sorry." Freda hoped those few words conveyed what she was unable to voice.

Gerald dropped his head, and he had never looked older or more broken than he did now. "I was chasing success, this thing called Black excellence." His laugh—dry and ironic. "I thought I was being a real man, making big moves. But that's not what manhood is about." Then he turned to Freda. "It's about telling the truth, doing the right thing, letting go, not holding on so tight you suffocate the people you love."

Freda realized her husband was setting her free—nearly three decades too late. Too late to make it right. Her crime had not been loving two men, but not loving herself enough to take her time, let her heart or maybe that small voice that whispered to her in her quiet moments be the one to guide her. To drown out expectations of the world for a Black girl's future.

"I'm done living for you, for other people, for what someone else expects of me," she told Gerald's bowed head. "I have to live for me."

What if Darius had lived? Would they have continued to pursue civil rights work? Would they have married and had children of their own or would nurturing the Movement have been enough? Impossible questions you would never know the answers to, which might drive you mad. This game of rewriting history and playing out all the scenarios never came to a neat, clean end.

***

A yellow taxi waited on the edge of campus to take them to the airport for their flight home to Chicago. Gerald had already climbed inside, his eyes and outstretched hand begging her to follow. But Freda had refused, remaining on the curb.

They had all been silent for hours after they left the library, as if the truth had wrung the words out of them. That night, she'd curled up in the bed next to her daughter while her husband slept in the other bed, alone. How had they gotten here? It was time to go home, whatever that meant, and she felt Tulip by her side, pulling her close for a hug, but Freda's arms hung limp, lifeless.

"We'll get through this," Tulip said, the roles reversed, her daughter now comforting her.

How had she made so many mistakes when she knew better? Pedigree meant nothing when it was encased in Black skin. Pedigree meant nothing when it cost you everything in service to it. She had raised Tulip the same way she came up, and she wanted to tell her daughter she was sorry, again and again.

The cab's horn honked, and it jolted Freda to move again, to say something meaningful to her daughter. She knew that the words of a parent, no matter the intent, could save or ruin you. Brushing Tulip's hair from her face, she stared directly into her eyes and said, "You are the best thing to ever happen to me, and I'm so proud of the woman you've become. You're doing everything I didn't have the courage to all these years."

"But you did, Mom. You were fierce." Freda smiled through her tears and began to believe she had done something right. Tulip continued, "Are you sure you don't want to fly home with Dad and me?"

Freda shook her head. "Not now. I have something I need to do." She watched her carefully constructed life pull away in that taxi.

An hour later, navigating a rental car onto the highway, she tried to process everything that had happened that day—Gerald's confession and her own guilt—and she wished she could untangle it all and lay it out in a linear, logical way that made sense. But the only map she had to follow was the road map that guided her from one mile marker to the next.

***

In Chatham County, North Carolina, Freda stepped gingerly around overgrown weeds to find the cemetery plot with his name. Lush green sod covered the ground and she knelt there, placing her hand on the stone.

DARIUS MOORE
Son. Brother. Child of God.

Her fingers traced every letter, and from all the fresh flowers surrounding his tombstone, she could tell his family and friends visited often. Like her, they hadn't forgotten him.

When she spoke, her voice came out croaky. "It's me, Darius. You promised to show me your hometown, where you grew up. Well, I'm here now. I don't know where to begin. I live in Chicago, back home, I guess. I teach math to grade school kids. Some of them think it's hard and confusing but when they finally get it and light up, it's a wonderful feeling. Let's see, what else? I have a little girl, well she's twenty-seven now. I named her Tulip, how about that? She's an activist, can you believe it? I wish you could meet her because you'd love her. She'd love you, too. Oh, and I almost forgot to tell you, I learned how to make fried okra and it tastes pretty good. And hush, yes, I soak it in vinegar first the way you taught me. Look at me going on and on like you can hear me. One more thing. Everything we did for *the boy* turned out better than we'd imagined. He went on to become our very first Black Supreme Court Justice. Can you believe that?"

When tears sprang to her eyes, she stood and brushed the dirt that had caked on the knees of her pants. Before she walked away, she said, "I guess what I want you to know most is that I love you, Darius. Always have, always will."

***

After paying her respects to Darius in North Carolina, Freda boarded a train bound for Washington, DC, and when the conductor appeared by her side in the aisle, she almost did a double take, looking at this sharp Black man in a position unheard of when she rode the rails as a student in the late '50s and early '60s. Times had changed, of course, but she thought of that old porter Jonas Hayes and wondered what he would have made of this, certain he'd get a kick out of it.

"You look as beautiful as the day ahead of us," the conductor said, and she looked down at her emerald-green dress with the string of pearls she'd changed into after her visit to the cemetery.

"Thank you."

"Will you be touring the White House?" he asked, with a bright smile and kind eyes only shaded by his conductor's cap.

"I don't know. I might visit the Lincoln Memorial to stand on the grounds where the great March on Washington was held."

"Good choice. Lots of history there. Where else will you go?"

She hesitated because for once she had not mapped out anything, had no itinerary in mind, no plan to follow. "I haven't decided," she said, smiling and turning her head to face the window, watching a whole new world open up to her.

The summer of 2020 ignited a firestorm around the world. George Floyd died with his neck underneath the foot of a white police officer for close to nine minutes. Protests erupted immediately, with people from every race, gender, and class lifting their voices to say this is wrong and we won't stand for it. Almost two months later, the legendary crusader for justice, Representative John Lewis, died. As I contemplated this so-called racial reckoning in America and watched a documentary about the life of Lewis, I imagined him as a young college student of only nineteen years of age. How did he find the courage to lead those sit-ins for racial justice at segregated lunch counters in Nashville and stare down rabid racists while also studying, dating, and going through the typical rites of passage as a young man?

These monumental moments in time triggered questions about my own place in the world, what I believe to be true, and the choices I might make in similar circumstances. And thus, the seed for *People of Means* was planted.

To better understand my late 1950s and 1960s characters—Freda, Darius, and Gerald—I spoke with Fisk University students who were on campus at that time and found themselves at the epicenter of a Movement. They told me that everyone recognized those days as a watershed moment in the country, whether they participated in activism or not. Many joined the fight for equality while others had family back home telling them the risk was too high, the sacrifice too great, and that their focus should instead be on studying hard and making something of themselves.

One of the Fisk alumnae I interviewed was the iconic poet and author Nikki Giovanni. Her intellect, quick wit, and *tell it like it is* spirit captivated me from the start. It was Ms. Giovanni who told me about the role of Nat King Cole and the Pullman porters in the fight for freedom. "You won't find this in the history books," she said, and that's when I knew I had untold stories of heroism and quiet resistance that needed to be shared.

I grew up surrounded by activism. Every Saturday morning as a young girl, I accompanied my parents to Operation PUSH civil rights meetings on Chicago's South Side, and at night, we gathered around a record player to listen to the soaring oratory of Dr. Martin Luther King Jr. However, the first time I chose activism for myself was my junior year at Northwestern University in response to the acquittal of the four officers who beat Rodney King. I remember marching through the streets of Evanston, Illinois, with my classmates, my fist in the air chanting, "No justice. No peace." I was curious and naive, yet righteously enraged and hungry for change, very much like the character of Tulip in 1992 who had to calculate the risk and reward of answering the call to fight injustice.

I keep thinking about what stops us from standing up for what we believe in and fighting for the change we want to see in the world. What holds us back from living life fully on our own terms? Most parents want their children to do better in life and surpass them in every metric of success. That's only natural and a sign of evolution and protection and love. But for those in my community, this specter of Black excellence can hold us hostage to the expectations of others, whether it's our families, workplaces, or communities. I grew up in a home with Black parents who tried to prepare me for an unjust world by insisting I work ten times harder than others to stay afloat academically and professionally. I continue to hold myself to that standard, but at what cost? That burden can be an incredible one to carry, and I often wonder why we can't just *be*?

I recognized that titling a book about Black folks as *People of Means* may have seemed to some a bold choice. But it's natural for me and is the way I think of my own family. My great grandfather was born enslaved, and he was freed at the age of ten. His descendants went on to found Prentiss Normal Institute in Mississippi and make their mark at Fisk, and their descendants are now neurosurgeons and ophthalmologists, attorneys and architects, educators and engineers. But you don't need to have a fancy degree, title, or money to have means—just the grit and gumption to live and love and leave your imprint on the world. By that definition, we all have the capacity to be people of means. The question is what we do with those means.

My greatest hope is that this novel will prompt you to reflect on your own means and that you will have the courage to live your life boldly and on purpose. A profound thank you for reading.

Nancy Johnson
February 2024

ACKNOWLEDGMENTS

It truly takes a village to make a book, and I'm immensely grateful for mine. It is only fitting that I begin with my brilliant editor, Liz Stein, who believed in me and *People of Means* from day one. Her indelible fingerprint and insights live on every page. Huge thanks to my wonderful literary agent, Danielle Bukowski, the one who takes my random, frantic phone calls, translates publishing, and talks me down when I need it. The entire William Morrow/HarperCollins family has embraced me, starting at the top with Liate Stehlik, president and publisher. I'm indebted to my rock star dream team, led by the incomparable Eliza Rosenberry, my publicist, and the incredible Tavia Kowalchuk, who leads marketing. Thanks to both of them for their creativity, passion, and tenacity in getting *People of Means* in front of booksellers, librarians, media, tastemakers, and, ultimately, into the hands of readers. Thank you to my astute copyeditor, Kate Lapin, for asking those questions in the margins to see if I really meant what I thought I did. Thanks also to my superb production editor, Jessica Rozler. My beautiful cover exists because of the genius creativity of Ploy Siripant.

To understand what it was like to be a Black student on the campus of Fisk University in the late '50s and early '60s, I turned first to the iconic poet, author, and activist Nikki Giovanni, who filled me in on the hidden history about the roles of Nat King Cole and the Pullman porters. Other alumnae I spoke with about being on campus during racial unrest included my cousin Barbara Carson, and her friend Virginia Bland, and Natalie Whitlow and Diana Ashurst, both of whom I was introduced to by Jennifer Turner. Music defined Nashville in those days, and to get a feel for the vibe and club scene, I spoke extensively with Lorenzo Washington, founder and curator of the Jefferson Street Sound Museum.

As a native Chicagoan, I often passed by the Ida B. Wells homes on my way someplace else without spending time in that community. Leslie E. Harris described his experience growing up there and the immense pride his family had in that housing development and the legendary journalist it was named after. Thank you to Sylvester Harris, a retired Chicago Transit Authority driver, who answered my questions about the particulars of driving a city bus. Also, thank you to Michelle Park Hines for her insight about the Korean American immigrant experience.

I owe much gratitude to my writing village. Thanks to Sadeqa Johnson and Jean Kwok for reading fast and early, and providing beautiful words of praise that gave this book legs in its infancy. My tribe of authors is large, but these are the ones who provided consistent pep talks, accountability, late-night brainstorms, video editing, book promo ideas, impromptu bookish trips, and more: Julie Carrick Dalton, Michele Montgomery, Denny S. Bryce, Sarah Penner, Vanessa Riley, Alison Hammer, Heather Webb, Desmond Hall, and Christie Tate. So much love for all of you!

I'm indebted to these communities for nurturing and sustaining me: Black Authors in Residence, Writer Unboxed, Tall Poppy Writers, Women's Fiction Writers Association, Friends & Fiction, Friends & Fiction Official Book Club, Reading with Robin, A Mighty Blaze, GrubStreet's The Muse & the Marketplace, The Wonder Writers, and Zibby Books Author Advisory Board.

A special shout-out to Ron Block, Robin Kall, Tammy Smithers, and Caroline Leavitt (my literary fairy godmother), who are always whispering in someone's ear or shouting from their platforms about the next great read! I appreciate your sincere love for books and how contagious that is in every community you touch.

As authors, we can't survive without our beloved readers. It's dangerous to start naming them because they are legion, but a few comment regularly on social media to support my work and I swear that keeps me going on tough writing days. Thank you to Annissa Armstrong, Francene McDermott Katzen, Michelle Marcus, Julie Naji, Gisele Hennings, Shelby Lake Riley, Mindy Ehrlich, Monte Norwood, Gerri Rivers, Bubba Wilson, and Robin Klein.

Finally, I must thank my family, friends, and colleagues who asked all the time how the second book was coming along. You never wavered in your steadfast belief in me, and please know your faith sustained me. My dear mother, Doris Johnson, watched me quietly for many hours as I wrote from her home on weekends. Thank you, Mommy, for every precious memory we have made and for still being the wind beneath my wings.